HEIRS

Part I

By
Celia Gabor

Order this book online at www.trafford.com
or email orders@trafford.com

Most Trafford titles are also available at major online book retailers.

Printed in the United States of America.

ISBN: 978-1-4669-6412-9 (sc)
ISBN: 978-1-4669-6414-3 (hc)
ISBN: 978-1-4669-6413-6 (e)

Library of Congress Control Number: 2012919739

Trafford rev. 12/17/2012

www.trafford.com

North America & international
toll-free: 1 888 232 4444 (USA & Canada)
phone: 250 383 6864 ♦ fax: 812 355 4082

CONTENTS

PART I

PART I

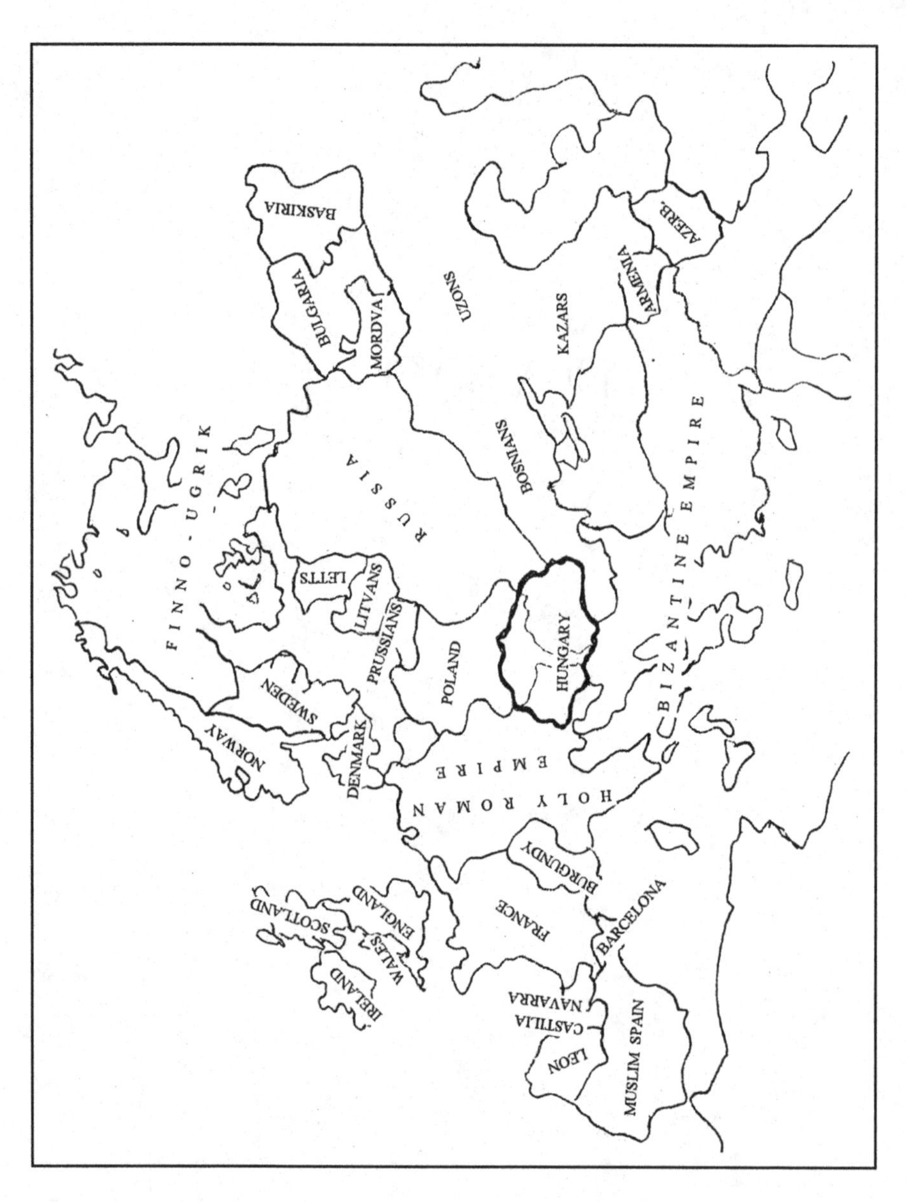

The map of Europe in the year of 1000 A.D.

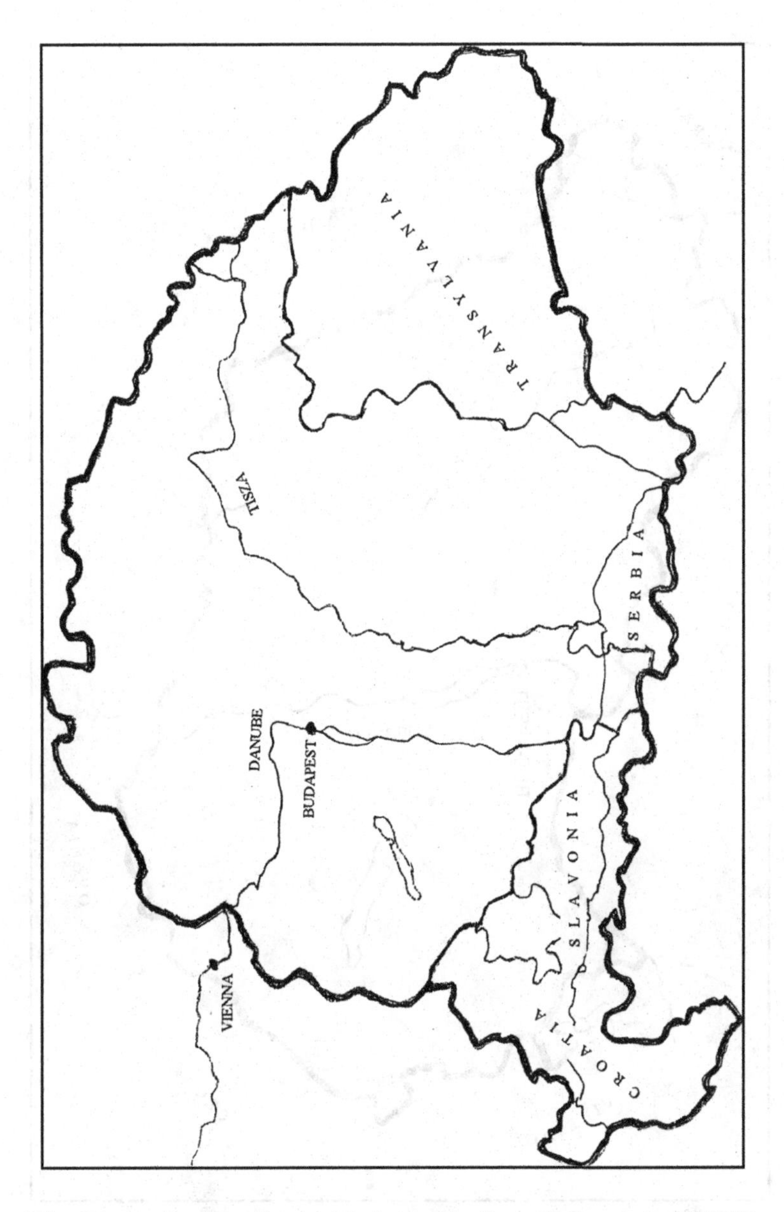

The Hungarian Kingdom with the territories, till the end of W.W.I.
With little changes in size from the lOth and 12th centuries.
Area: 325.411 sq km, 125.641 sq mi

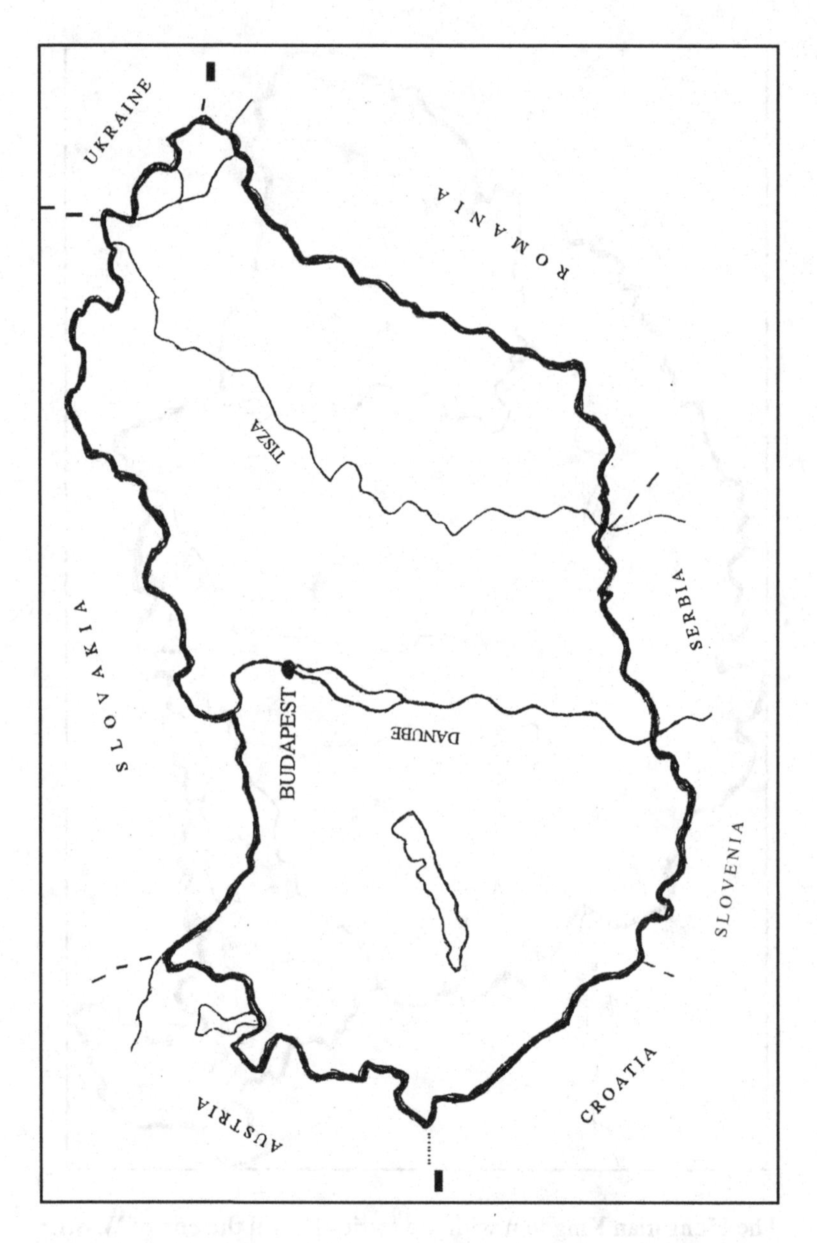

The map of present day Hungary, after the annexations of 1918.
Area: 93.030 sq km, 35.919 sq mi

List of Main Characters

The Garays

First generation:
Arpad Garay, and his wife Erzsebet

Second generation:
Their son: Istvan Garay, and his wife Julianna

Third generation:
Their twin sons: Tass and Huba Garay,
and their wives: Miriam and Franciska

Fourth generation:
Tass and Miriam's son: Zoli
Huba and Franciska's daughters: Helen, Kati, Julia

Their adopted son: Geza

Fifth generation:
Helen and Zoltan's children: Hunor and Eneh
And a son, out of wedlock: Tohotom

The Devenys

First generation:
Zombor Deveny

Second generation:
Zombor Deveny junior

Third generation:
"Old" Zoltan Deveny, and his wife Anna

Fourth generation:
Zoltan Deveny, and his wife Helen

Fifth generation:
Hunor and Eneh Deveny

PREFACE

If any time in the last sixty years Franciska opened the door to the storage, an inscription caught her eye. "1838". By staring at it, she would ask then: "Why do we keep it here? It's magnificent! Besides. It can be used for another hundred years. Why not?"

But when she closed the door she forgot all about it. While the inner layer was made of brass, the exterior had the finest woodwork. The style itself came closest to Baroque by being busy with finely carved flowers and fruits and leaves, for expressing the final, lamenting period of an era that might have slipped into decadence, but perhaps not to the point of deviating the user from the original plan, or idea of usage. Well, let's just hope not in this furniture, since it was a bathtub! It had been a tub for a hundred and thirty years and could still serve that purpose in 1975, when Franciska had her last chance to look at it.

CHAPTER 1

The Garays

SEVEN PLUM TREE NOBILITY

Well before the time of the Great Revolution of 1848, the Garays belonged to an illustrious lot, whose birthright secured the title "Seven Plum Tree Nobility", and the hazy notion of being privileged, without showing substantial land for it.

An imbecile must have given the name, implying: "The size of their land is sufficient for holding seven plum trees."

Exaggeration or not, it's true they worked hard along their fieldhands at reaping on most Summers, rather than paying a worker's wage in barrels of wheat, which meant yellow gold here in the South, by the Triple Koros region of the Great Magyar* Plains.

In simple terms, the Garays' title far exceeded their inheritance. Unless of course there was someone among them in future generations who for reasons of his own was striking out to make them rich.

In any case it would have been-and still is-foolish to ignore the social significance of the title. Even if the "Seven Plum Tree" had at times a mere symbolic connotation to it.

This was real. A lower rank nobility, good enough to secure the right to one's place among the "better" families, and to retain it as far as the Garays showed interest.

Indeed, even then failing to provide more than status, one was proud to be enmeshed in the scheme of a social hierarchy which came about ten centuries ago, and was still holding.

---

* Magyar is Hungarian.

If a country is as old as Hungary, people's roots do twine deeper into the soil with each generation, adding substance to the nation's unified soul throughout history, and to its soil in all eventuality. But those of us above ground still have the chance to elevate this lot, possibly with the same substance, what must be mind and bones, that outlast the rest.

These people (among them the Garays) were gratified to hold the proof to the title, a parchment made out of dogskin with a scribble on it in Latin, having been signed two or three centuries ago by a king. One assumes, with no exception such families had a conviction to be compensated for their lack of funds with that faint-smelling old scroll in the drawer. Maybe so. But it was known, such nobility worked hard for a living by doing peasant work if he inherited the land before his brothers. Small as it was, their estate could not be divided equally among the children, for it was the youngest to inherit all (having this legacy by ancient law), unless his father made provisions otherwise. The rest of his sisters and brothers had options to marry well, practice law, or start an army career.

This has changed in later centuries when the oldest would get hold of their estate to take over land and farming, whether he wished it or not. But he had no choice. He was the privileged.

ERZSEBET AND ARPAD

Considering they lived in the same house two generations ago, Franciska often thought of them. Back then in the 1850s, people said they were the perfect couple. If Arpad was regarded the measure of Southern handsomeness with his reserved and dignified manner, then Erzsebet superseded him in popularity, for being playful and just a bit flirtatious, perhaps for her own amusement. She was not only beautiful to look at. She was bright too, if made it a success to diverge from the defense-line of her generation of women, which was trenched in a world of smelling salts, occasional fits and fainting spells.

The family could not learn about the early years of Erzsebet, and even less how she met her husband Arpad, because the couple had no desire to tell. True, they managed to keep a lid on it, but their secrecy worked like a red flag, by giving ground for countless speculations down the line of a hundred years, when their offspring still wondered who she was and what she was. If indeed she had been a stage actress who gave up a career for the sake of a handsome hussar, then it was not a small matter. Well the two had met in Pozsony in those years when the city was the seat of Magyar Parliament-the Diet*-whereas in a few short months they fell in love. It would not stop there. Erzsebet did not like things half done. She left the world of make-believe on the stage where it belonged. Something told her to follow this man to another world, this time to a real one which turned out to be vastly different from anything she had thought, heard or played before.

Not to lose her man, a decision was born.

"Did she aspire getting into the category of brave women so early?" wondered Franciska. "Hard to tell. And again she might have been convinced, Arpad Garay wasn't just any man, but somebody worth pursuing."

It all happened in 1847, in the same year our young man's father died. In this kind of emergency, Arpad could do one thing, to resign his commission at the cavalry. Bound by a promise to his father, at the moment he had but one option, and that was taking care of the family and the land, for reasons of having no brothers, only a sister next to his mother, and aunts on both sides; subsequently he returned home.

An army man at heart, Arpad forced upon himself a new identity by assuming a role, the one sooner or later he expected to play, which only God knew would come so soon. But things happened fast, and Arpad had to act on them. One presumes this was the time he planned to have sons by the dozen, even going as far as thinking out their future, saying: "I would encourage them to take professions they choose, and under no circumstance would I hinder them in it"-which seemed provocative, considering he was still a bachelor.

"At first, there wasn't much known about great grandmother Erzsebet beside the fact that she was a lady who travelled with a portable bathtub, like she would on the day when great-grandfather Arpad brought her home to this province . . ." would describe Julia, one of the great-granddaughters, in her journal, some hundred years later.

Here on the Plains a new way of life was introduced to the lady of the stage. A life which held no respect for luxury or pleasures unless it was about food and drink, or the revival of heroic centuries, conveying not only bloodshed and wars but glory and a sense of greatness too, what would surface now and then, enhanced with-if not entirely dependent on-a bottle of good wine.

These sentiments weren't taken lightly by those who lived here! Anybody who claimed to be a good Magyar was proud to have ancestors

* Legislative assembly. Derived from "Dieta" (medieval Latin).

fighting for this country which helped to maintain her identity alongside with their own.

COMING HOME

Their story, a love story, has been told over many times. And of course the favorite-their arrival-was told more often, something I only have to repeat.

In 1847, just months after they have met, one April afternoon Arpad did return to the South with a lady in his carriage. Those who saw the homecoming were captivated. "That beautiful woman! Look at her!"

Erzsebet, who had a keen sense of appearance, was wearing a well-tailored cloak and matching hat for the journey. By stepping to the ground she removed hat and coat, so everyone present could see a perfect and flexible figure and lovely face, which seemed to reflect her eagerness to the new life.

"The master is home! With a lady!" Most people from Arpad's household ran out for the news, but at first all they could do was to gawk a bit stupefied at the sight of such lady who smiled at them quite naturally, as if she was coming home.

There was another woman in the coach. She made herself busy with the luggage and did not smile. Instead, she would start shouting to the people who looked at them from the courtyard. "Hey you! Stop staring! Get going! The ladyship's luggage has to get in somehow! Or did you think she was sleeping outside? In the barn? Or in the stable?"

The sneer in her voice made Erzsebet nervous. She stepped closer, to instruct her maid: "Kati! Don't intimidate them! You end up being hated." Apprehensive as they were, the servants carried in a huge trunk, and returned to pick up her suitcases. With each piece inside, it looked more like a move than just a visit.

Erzsebet did not rush into the house. At first she walked around the garden, leisurely ran her eyes over the bushes and old trees, the built brick fence, or those other buildings at the distance, where they had the stables.

Everything seemed to be old here. Old, and quite natural. Very different to what she was used to. If it looked backward at first, it was familiar too in a way, though was difficult to put in words how. Well, not only the richness or the value attached to it. No. It was something else. She knew it by instinct what she couldn't yet formulate by saying. This place with the house was going to be the scene of great deeds somewhere in her future, which evidently she came to meet! Yes. Now she knew. That's why she came. It was all clear. Discovering as much, for a second Erzsebet felt dizzy.

"It must be the country air!" she thought, just when Arpad who went to see his horses, came back and joined her.

"My mother and sister are expecting us for this evening. I am sure they will love you." He talked like any man who loves a woman, and believes everyone feels the same for her. "You know, their house has more comfort. More charm. This house is quite rigid. It is my inheritance. My love, you do whatever you please with it."

Erzsebet was still looking at the garden. Suddenly, almost absentmindedly, she asked him: "Tell me. Was this garden always so flat?" "Yes. Why do you ask?" "I don't know," she said, "I have no idea."

She shook her head and a minute later proposed the following: "Show me the house. I am really very curious."

Erzsebet occupied the sunniest room of the building. Within an hour of their arrival word went around. "The lady wishes to take a bath!"

To the genuine surprise of Arpad's household, the guest was travelling with her own portable bathtub, which appeared to be as ornate and finely carved as the lady herself. Mari, the old woman would evaluate her so, who brought in the fresh bed sheets and clean towels to her room. Well, it's true. The craftsmanship was exquisite. While Mari stood there staring for a long minute, she gave away her ignorance in matters of the sophisticated world to the lady's maid, who ordered the basin to be filled. "At once!" she said.

"Soap too?" asked Mari, to which the maid retorted: "I can't imagine you having fragrant soap in this house! Or, have you?"

Mari, who would not dignify this with an answer, has grumbled on the whole length of the hallway: "What did you think? We ain't no sitting in fancy bathtubs for half a day. Hmm. Here, we work and work. And eat and sleep and wash and work and work . . . hmm. Fragrant soap! My foot!"

Arpad, who happened to see the tub earlier, was greatly impressed by its dexterity. His interest in fine woodwork would take an upswing by then, meaning he made inquiries on any notable cabinetmaker of the region. "It's fair. She has the tub, I have the carriage. It tells me how much we have in common."

Soon, buckets of hot water were sent up to the visitor's room, as fast as Mari could warm it in a huge outside cauldron. From then on, that's how the picture is best described: The bathtub stood at the middle of the room. The maid stood guard at the door, whose job included the taking of hot water buckets from the manservants, who truly enjoyed the job and became more and more vivified. Later that afternoon it occurred to Arpad: "This scene . . . with the buckets. It looked, the house was on fire!"

Everything was different here! Everything. Here, men would take a bath at the well in the yard. Yes, they washed outside even in Winter, and women washed themselves in secrecy after the whole house with everyone in it have retired. There was a chamber with a washbasin for that purpose, a pot of warmed water and a bar of homemade soap. Only the essentials. The bath itself would be taken as one of the duties of the day in which one was not supposed to find joy more than one does in cleaning up rooms, dusting rugs or washing windows. Here, women couldn't imagine sitting in a tub like that in broad daylight. And certainly not in the middle of the room! It was quite unheard of what Erzsebet was doing, combining hygiene with pleasure and cologne bottles and mirrors and talcum powders and silk gowns.

So, on the very first day the servants had this hunch:

"The master is in love, and the lady guest will stay. Stay for good. Then it's going to be a different world here, I tell you!"

In any case, they were right. She stayed and the house did turn upside down. For a while it wasn't even clear who was going to give orders. Him, or her? Or if it should be obeyed as if the master gave them?

But then the two were married, and Erzsebet thought best channeling her talents to the new household. She tried to inject a new energy into their life, though the house, her family, and the people she met could not react to it only very slowly, as if changing the patterns of this slow dutiful world would take more than just a woman.

And it seems nobody as yet suspected that other change; an imminent change on a larger scale.

Well, who could tell then-since few ever thought of it-that the winds of Revolution will gain strength . . . just in a year?

CHAPTER 2

The Great Revolution

The exhilaration of 1848 renewed hopes all over Europe for a chance to write a glorious page in History, when nations would search for national identities and political freedom. From Paris to Vienna and Budapest, the air was filled with the spirit of freedom and independence. For a very brief moment the classes abandoned their differences or seemingly forgot them, so they could think of unity.

Oh yes, the thought of independent Hungary brought everyone together from aristocracy, nobility, bourgeoisie, intellectuals, lawyers, civil servants, artisans, farmers, workers and the serfs.

The nation became one, and Arpad could witness this unity! Statesmen, politicians, thinkers, writers and poets took on an active role formulating their needs, in behalf of a nation. People were informed and inspired. There was hope. Something very important has begun.

Most everyone agrees, 1848 could be termed "the year of revolutions" for Europe, in light of the sweeping fires from country to country. The French this time fought for social justice and declared France a Republic. German speaking countries and principalities wanted a united Germany. Italians sought national unity and central government. The many countries of the Habsburg Monarchy fought for hundreds of reasons and various forms of independence, for self-autonomy, within or without the Empire. The Viennese wanted reforms. The Hungarians also wanted reforms, but above all, hoped to get an Independent Hungarian Ministry.

The Revolution broke out in Hungary on March 15th, 1848. It was a joyful day in Pest-Buda! The great poet, Sandor Petofi-also a revolutionary-was leading it. The crowd joined in. They printed the

"Twelve Points" and recited his new poem,: the "National Song", of which he wrote the previous night. Students, artisans, administrators, workers, merchants, radicals and everybody else was together rejoicing with the growing crowd. Those of the Parliamentarians, still in Pozsony at the Diet, were too seizing the moment, by trying to reinforce the "Twelve Points" or "April Laws" to be sanctioned, if not by the aristocratic Upper Table (House) of the Diet, who would not endorse a people's revolution, than by Vienna! Such boldness! Or, should we call it bravado, as the Emperor felt of it? In any event the Magyar delegation took to Vienna, where an enthusiastic crowd welcomed them on the streets.

The undisputed leader of the Hungarian Revolution was Kossuth, a brilliant man, who was determined, hardworking and persevering. However, Count Szechenyi the great reformer, was cautious. He didn't believe it was going to succeed, and felt it was premature going to Vienna with the "Twelve Points"-as Kossuth and the radicals insisted on doing so. Yet this was what happened.

The Habsburg court has been terrified by the revolts of Vienna and that of Pest-Buda. When the Hungarian emissary arrived at Vienna, they could gain access to the Palatine of Hungary, who at the time happened to be Archduke Stephen (representing the Hungarians at the Habsburg court, and also chairing the Diet at Pozsony), was sympathetic to the Hungarians. He was, like every other Palatine of the Habsburg era, a close relative of the Emperor.

Because of the emergency, he persuaded the Emperor to sign what was proposed as reforms, named here as "Twelve Points" or "April Laws". In a previous drafting, via the Diet, its content was already known to the court, and was not entirely unknown to the Emperor himself.

He signed it, and the Magyar Emissary has returned to Pest-Buda. It was total victory! Within days the Hungarian Ministry has been formed, which was headed by Count Batthany. The cabinet included Kossuth, Deak, Baron Eotvos, Count Szechenyi and others, also of remarkable talent.

THE GAIN

"So it happened! Unbelievable! At long last, the emancipation of the serfs! Everyone at his right mind welcomes it. Even some of the big landowners, I am told," proclaimed the county clerk, during the slow hours of after—lunch to the young page, who just came back with the papers.

True, everyone seemed to welcome it, regardless of the fact, this new social setup has created a new under-class, and a very populous one at that. These people still supposed to work, only now for wages, which went obviously far too low.

Nonetheless the liberals promulgated it was a giant step (which it was!). "High time the serfs were free. It's a shame, not earlier," they said, but beyond that could not be bothered with details.

And those, observing this ideal world from a different balcony (like our county clerk with the papers) would riposte gleefully: "Yes. They are free to do what they've always been doing!" And of course they weren't either far from the truth. Because the poor devils who took a drink from the cup of freedom for the very first time, were about to face an existential dilemma, or a so-called uneasiness. "Are we going to be as poor as we used to be?" they had to ask. Well, as it turned out, the new law has not been short on deliverance. It just had its share of inconsistencies, in regard to the nation's economy. And that, couldn't sweeten anybody's drink. Playing a major role in grain production, now these people weren't forced to work by law. Only by necessity. In response to this kind of reasoning, the radicals still maintained: "Necessity is beside the point. The whole thing is about that ideological war between the classes that's brewing on underneath for centuries."

Well, maybe they too were right.

THE DEVENYS, AND A GREAT REFORMER

The debate on who served the nation best, Kossuth or Deak, had been on the mat between the two families-the Garays and the Devenys-ever since the Revolution of 1848, and long after that. In the first generation, Arpad's opponent in the matter was Zombor Deveny, a logical and clearminded Southerner, who would reason out the Revolution and its aftermath unlike others, who preferred to throw themselves in it. Ah, yes. They were the full-hearted supporters, a concurring breed of the times.

Yet this man stood apart for being distinct and peculiar. Not only in his expressions though. He was also tall and lean with blond hair and moustache, that is markedly incongruous from the dark-haired people of this region, whose pale skin and high cheekbones referred to bits of either Hunnish or Cuman ancestry.* The people here talked with passion, by letting their likes and dislikes come out in plain view, which again could change their fluctuating moods in the most unpredictable fashion. Such behavior didn't apply for Zombor Deveny! He kept to himself all he could, and had no moods. Instead, he took comfort in his analytical mind, for he had a "mind of his own", as his wife would loosely but passionately characterize him at each turn. Others would say he looked like a man from a different country with different substance in his veins from the rest of his compatriots, whose blood was most likely red and white and green, running in unison with the national flag, which perhaps explained why they felt and acted the way they had.

Zombor Deveny, who elected himself in a group of liberal intellectuals, believed reforms were supposed to come gradually and peacefully. He stood for turning Hungary from a sleepy feudal state into a strong modern nation. Back in the 1830s, as a young man, he agreed with Count Szechenyi's proposal, that progress should be the first step on the road to the future. Political independence held not much promise, if it didn't bring economical independence along. He believed in the Reform Age, and saw opportunity in it for everyone.

"No wonder the Count was called 'The Greatest Magyar', realized Zombor Deveny. "Why? He set in motion the Reform Age for Hungary." As an aristocrat, he challenged the nobility to take action and pay taxes if they hoped for any progress at all. "If you are high-born and privileged, it has to bring heightened responsibility towards your country," he said, and by giving an example, he established and founded the Hungarian Academy of Sciences in 1825, and donated a year's income for the cause. He would also initiate the political clubs, hoping the nobility might take an active role in affairs of state, in view of improving the conditions of economy and politics, something he judged backwards if he compared them to the leading countries of Europe, such as England.

Count Szechenyi worked on the regulation of waterways, thus controlling floods on valuable farmlands. He built out also a road network, organized better and safer transporting conditions and secured the navigation on major rivers. Long before the operation of the first steamshipping began, he almost died in a rare tropical fever, which

* Before the Magyars, the Hunnish lived on the land in the 4th and 5th century. The Cumans came later as settlers to 14th century Hungary.

he contracted on his vanguard journey taken with a handful of men to explore the lower reaches of the Danube, where at certain regions they found undrained marshlands, which prevented them from both embarking and returning.

His next project has not been easier. The Count conceived the idea of building a suspension bridge over the Danube, by connecting Buda and Pest which at the time wasn't yet one city. He followed through all the stages of raising funds, to giving the commission for design and construction. The bridge came to be called the Chain Bridge, the symbol and pride of Budapest. Also he worked for Industry and modern Agriculture. He was involved in horse-breeding, and built the first horse-race tracks. He initiated Bank and Credit organizations for the country.

In the growing tensions of the 1840's Europe, Count Szechenyi still believed that essential reforms for Hungary's future could be achieved through parliamentary legislation and the bills being ratified by the Habsburg Emperor, as it was practiced. But events speeded up-partly because of Kossuth—and were taking quite another route, which evidently brought on agonizing results to patriots, as well as to those who preferred to remain active in politics.

What followed the Summer months was hard to take for Count Szechenyi. Pressures and mounting conflicts with the Imperial Court was one of them. The question of his loyalty was another one (a double loyalty, to be precise) what supposed to go to both, country and Emperor, if only they wouldn't stand on opposite sides now. All of these made him ill by wearing his nerves down, which within a year made him lose his reason. From that time a pattern was to follow in his health. He could enjoy periods of well-being and sanity, which could reverse into extreme anxiety and torment. By taking up residence in a private institution, he retired from politics, but could still work and write his pamphlets and memoirs, or could receive guests. But eventually after long years of instability, the Count took his own life. (There is a speculation up to this day that perhaps he was killed by the Secret Police).

THE POLITICS OF 1848 AND 1849

At the time of the Revolutions, Austria had financial problems and a busy agenda of battling their own-three Vienna revolts, keeping at bay a long struggle with Prussia, and again going to war to northern Italy, when they hardly finished the previous one. Vienna was in constant need of soldiers. Consequently, each country of the Monarchy has had an obligation for sending an army to fight the wars of the Empire. Therefore, Vienna could not afford losing Hungary from the Monarchy, for she was a strong country with the territories and nationalities incorporated to the Hungarian crown.*

The Imperial Court maintained it was better if they hadn't had too much freedom! And knew that soon, very soon, a solution ought to be found on how to get it from them. Otherwise those rebel Magyars were too damn quick to solve their own problems. This so-called "Responsible Independent Government" of theirs didn't sound good at all . . . The Hungarians shouldn't have gone that far . . . and would be a disaster, if they would go further! The Habsburgs wanted to change things back to how they were just weeks or months ago, before the Revolution. They wanted to restore the old arrangement. Yes. But how? Legally, they couldn't do it. Not anymore. It all looked really bad, considering Emperor Ferdinand has already sanctioned the new Hungarian Government! Even was taking oath to the Hungarian Crown.

Yet something had to be done, something drastic, which might teach the Magyars a lesson in obedience. But who was going to teach them and fight them? "Oh well. If there is a will . . ." And so, a frenzied Imperial Court would resort to seek out little alliances . . . within the Monarchy. This time Vienna set an eye on those nationalities, or minority groups who were having their own grievances, or at least an antipathy, in regard to a strong Hungary, and the idea of "Magyarization", which has meant a proposal of Hungarian for official language (instead of the German and Latin, as it was practiced) throughout greater Hungary, which included the territories with various ethnic groups. Possibly, these nationalities had their own ambitions! Perhaps to achieve something similar for themselves? They were the Serbs, Romanians, and the Croats. Other nationalities or foreign settlers either didn't mind fitting in, or had less pronounced grievances.

So, the days were right for the Habsburgs to search actively for Hungary's potential adversaries! A situation had to be created which said: "My enemy is your enemy, and you fight my war! Especially, if you and they are both subjects in my Monarchy."

* The territories included the Highlands (Slovakia), Croatia, Bosnia-Hercegovina, Slovenia, Transylvania, and parts of Romania and Serbia.

Through this effort, an alliance was born. A Croatian freshly made "ban" Jellacic-also a soldier of rank-would be commissioned secretly to fight the Hungarians. Still, before he invaded Hungary from the South (in September 1848), he would be approached by Count Batthany, the Hungarian Prime Minister, in order to conduct secret negotiations about the fate of Croatia. By this, Croatia was to gain similar political independence within Hungary, as Hungary gained one from Austria, just months earlier. However, the final recognition of it was refused by Vienna, considering it wasn't in the Emperor's interest.

Eventually, the armed invasion took place as planned, but for Kossuth's call a hurriedly armed regiment would beat them out of the country.

At the end of the same year the Habsburgs decided that Emperor Ferdinand should abdicate, so they can put instead the young Franz Joseph on the throne. Conveniently the new emperor would have no obligations carrying out his predecessor's promises, or would he be bound by his signatures, they maintained.

As a follow-up to this kind of maneuvering, Vienna had abolished the "April Laws". It was a step to discredit the Hungarian Government. And then by abandoning even the sign of diplomacy, the Habsburgs would reinstate the "Age of Absolutism" once more. In this turn of events, several members of the Hungarian cabinet, like Prime Minister Count Batthany, Count Szechenyi, Baron Eotvos, and Deak, the Minister of Justice had resigned, for being unable to work under those hostile conditions.

Kossuth did not give in, it seemed his time was yet to come. Concerned about the threat of a coming war, he declared himself a dictator. Indeed, he had a lot to do. Because from this time on until the end of the war he coordinated the matters of defense, and altogether the survival of Hungary.

Chapter 3

The First Generation

Motto:

> "My generation looked for ways to give. For us, country came first. For the call of war we dropped everything and were ready. Then, for a long while, family or personal interests had to wait . . . They came second."
>
> —Arpad Garay

PEACE AND WAR

Ever since 1847 when Arpad brought her to town and the two walked down the aisle, people were fond of her, and seemingly she hadn't had to do a thing for it. Have they discovered the ideal bride?

One can never tell what they've seen in the young woman but Erzsebet stabilized her role as a centerpiece of this flat and dusty old town, where everybody would know everybody perhaps inside and out, if for generations the majority of locals were born here, raised here, lived here, and died here. And if the extent of their affinity wouldn't have been served so far, they also married here, among themselves. One assumes (perhaps wrongly), these marriages couldn't cater too much new to the newlyweds, if five times out of ten one has married his second or third cousin.

No wonder, when at last Arpad presented a bride who was of outside stock, it turned their wedding into the great event of the year. With every eye on her (lucky for Erzsebet) she stood the limelight, was cheerful, appreciative and pleasant, and had a nice word to each well-wisher. "What a woman!" they said, when learned she was also considerate, a quality that made her an admired woman overnight.

At first, 1848 was a joyous time for the Garays . . . When the Revolution came, they were so happy. If only things could progress the way they were designed! But things never stay the way they are, and seldom progress the way they should found out the young Mrs. Garay. Things happened fast, and politics became confusing for everyone. It seemed, there was going to be a war.

Arpad who planned to join the army couldn't quite go before October, until the harvest was done . . . but prepared his wife and family, in good time. "Look. I must go. I am a soldier! I must fight. It . . . it won't be long. You will see. Only a couple of months? . . ."

So on the first days of October he did volunteer to join the Hussar Regiment again, as a captain. Considering the Revolutionary Army had financial problems, soon after leaving, Arpad would return home, to provide the horses, uniforms, and weaponry for himself, as well as for his orderly. Also he made provisions to pay for various extra equipment.

In those days, Erzsebet thought he was more handsome than ever, and they were more in love than ever before . . . The separation was not easy, but they agreed in principle, country came first. So in the third week of October 1848, Arpad Garay the Hussar Captain left the town of K. the second time, to save the Revolution, if it was still possible.

Life was quiet back home, with Erzsebet expecting. In 1849, with the Revolutionary War raging, she would pray to have a healthy child. Her prayers would soon be answered, she had a son who came to this world on the Day of Surrender, when Hungary lost the war. The news was terrible, but Erzsebet had hopes, her husband now would come home.

Well, the whole town showed up on the Christening, from where only the father was missing. And within the week young Mrs. Garay had to learn, her husband won't be returning from the fights after all.

Arpad Garay would be sent from battlefield to prison.

A DIARY AND A NEWBORN

After the surrender of the Hungarian Army, Arpad sent home his sword, his war diary, and a long letter to his wife, knowing it might take some time till he would return. "My dearest, an inquest of some sort is unavoidable," he wrote. "In wars like this, it happens. I am an army man, so I won't mend in politics, but I know from the bottom of my heart, I fought on the right side and for the right cause. How can anyone repudiate it? I thought of you every hour of the day and night. You must know this! I think of you and me and our future child . . . together soon . . . Well, two or three weeks the most? For your big day, my love, I'll be home."

Just a week after the date on it, the package was delivered. It would have been a small miracle in those days of getting here so fast, if it wasn't for Pali, his orderly, who upon arrival brought Arpad's things to the house. The man, himself from this town, said it with empathy: "Ma'am! I know only this. Emperors and Czars always figure out something . . . so they can win. We are nothing to them. Just cattle. Go! fight! die! caput . . . That's about it. We are good for only this." He looked pitiful and tired and so genuinely at the end of his patience, that Erzsebet began to cry, just listening to his words. She didn't think of it this way until now, how these people must have felt . . . "Oh God! Everyone, really everyone is taking advantage of them. They are harnessed in all their life, even as children." Erzsebet looked for a solution. "Do you hope for army pension? It is due to you I believe . . ." she asked, for which Pali replied, "Ma am, we lost the war. And it was a bad war. If Kossuth could stay, he would fight it out for us. But, there is a prize on his head. They want him dead. Nobody is going to speak up for us now!"

When this visit did take place, Erzsebet had already had her son Istvan, who was born on the 13th of August, 1849. The excitement of war made that day extra difficult for the young Mrs. Garay who had to send for the doctor. In the house, there were only servants and women, with Arpad's mother at the helm. After the doctor arrived, he predicted complications which became true only in an arduously long labor. Erzsebet's in-laws with childbearing experience spent the day at the young woman's side, and some even moved in for one or two weeks. Istvan, the first son of the young Garays proved to be a healthy boy, who had regular features and blue eyes.

Since for a while the new mother was advised to stay in bed, Erzsebet spent the good part of the day reading through her absent husband's diary. She also sent a letter to Arpad's orderly: "Pali, I want you to come and see me in two weeks time. Bring your wife too. We will discuss what can we do for you. At the same time I hope you tell more about my husband . . ."

Well, Arpad's diary was quite a reading. He put on the first page: "God bless Hungary!" On the second page: "I write just the essence of the campaign." (I'll improve it when I get home). Then, he gives the title: "The Revolutionary War." "It is a good sign, the first invasion against Hungary ended in victory. Jellacic was beaten out of the country."

1848 September

"For Kossuth's call I volunteer, to get a commission from the National Army." "I get home, and come back in late October."

Erzsebet put down the book and sighed. She remembered so clearly everything. At first, 1848, the days of Revolution and the new cabinet! It was a wonderful time. "Oh, I hope we still be that happy!" she said, and went to see the child who needed nursing. Reading it further on the same afternoon, Erzsebet realized, in last October her husband was already writing the diary.

1848 October

"The reorganization of the army will be an enormous task for Kossuth." "The third attack (in October) against Austria is not successful. We have losses. Gen. Moga is badly injured." "Gorgey is the new Commander-in-Chief."

Throughout the book Arpad wrote either a sentence or just a word on something, while at other places he would elaborate on different subjects from dates and troop movements to battles and army morale. Yet during their campaign, he inscribed the general following of war quite conscientiously.

1848 Nov.

"Gorgey dislikes the make-up of the new army. Kossuth's proposition of employing recruits and various other units (all good fighting men) does not meet his idea of the good army. Gorgey trusts only well-trained professional soldiers." "The news from Romania is more than disarming. Puchner fights on the side of the Habsburgs. Worst, his incitements lead to a Romanian peasant-rebellion against their lords. They take arms, killing thousands of Hungarian nobles (civilians), including women and children. The Szekely Guards moved against them, apparently late."

"Transylvania is lost. It is now in Habsburg hands."

1848 Dec.

"The Polish general, Bem-who fought his way from Revolution to Revolution through Europe-is appointed by Kossuth to win back Transylvania (from the Romanians). He gives him an army. General Bem wins back-most of it!!"

"Windischgratz's army invades Hungary, pushing downwards from the North. The major war began."

1848 End of Dec.

"The capital is evacuating. The Magyar Government moves to Debrecen." "Shortages in arm supply . . . we need more swords, bayonets . . . and everything else."

Erzsebet who read it with great interest (sometimes just one inscription) imagined him there, under the conditions of war. She attempted seeing things through his eyes.

1849 January

"Gorgey doesn't see eye to eye with Kossuth. It is bad for the war! Delays everywhere . . . Officers are deserting Gorgey's army." "Attack from the North (Galicia), Kassa falls. Strategic disadvantage (opens up the country)." "We regained our advantage by Perczel's move."

1849, February

"A winning battle on the Northeast. Great victory!" "Kossuth reorganizing the whole army into eight army corps."

1849, March-Apr.

"Maneuvers on the Great Plains. At last the decisive battles. We push Windischgratz to the North. Major victories." (Vac, Komarom, Pest)." "I lose five of my men. Writing letters to their families."

1849, Apr. 23

"Austrians evacuate Pest. Fights around Buda. General withdrawal of Imperial forces. We take back Castle Hill." "I get minor injury. Rest for a few days."

1849, May

"We won back the Capital! I was promoted for the rank of Colonel." "Change in Austrian high-command. Windischgratz is replaced by Haynau." "The Emperor asks military help from the Czar!"

1849, June-July

"The Russian army invades Hungary at three major points through the Carpathians. (At two points on the East.) Heavy fights. Also invasion from the North with overpowering force. They divide their Northern army, one division turns to Pest, other to Debrecen. The heaviest fights which we experienced. Great losses." "Austrian army approaching from the Northwest. Pest is conquered."

Aug.

"We are pushed to the South. Major battles."

After this, Arpad writes only one sentence: "Aug. 13, 1849. Gorgey surrenders the Hungarian Army to the Russian high command."

As her husband put down the final sentence, Erzsebet remembered how it was with her. "I had this prayer. The very same night: Dear Lord, I thank thee for the child. In our loss, you gave hope. And on the next day, I wrote a letter to my husband: Arpad, my dearest, I begin with a good news. The Dear Lord gave us a gift. Our son was born. Just as you wish, his name shall be Istvan, like our first king. I am waiting you home, thinking of you day and night.

Sends all her love, your Erzsebet."

"But now," she said, "what am I going to do now? With you away."

She stood by the window, looking outside to that old pine tree that she liked so much, for it was corpulent and shapely like those trees on the Highland, where she spent her childhood. Pine trees! There was no answer there, she realized, or it wasn't immediate. one had to wait for it. "After all it must be true, we pay for everything," she thought briefly, before left her room to find work in the house.

THE FUGITIVES

"Madame! Madame, wake up! Someone is here . . . outside." Erzsebet was asleep when about one o'clock after midnight the maid ran in her room. She was quite alarmed.

"A man is here! At the streetfront. His knock on the window awakened me. I can't make out though who he is."

"Wait!" said Erzsebet. She leapt out of bed and put on a robe. "Give me that candle. Get the gun. Bring it here.

Tell Jozsi to get the dogs, but put on a leash. When I tell him, he can let them go." Erzsebet opened the curtains and then the window. With gun in hand she leaned forward and looked outside. She saw a dark figure standing at the corner of the house, but couldn't see the face. "Who is it there?" she called out. The man turned around and came to the window, running. He stopped for an instant. "Don't shoot Madame . . . I am friend. Colonel Revicz sent me. He said I can trust you, and you will help me." She asked, "Help you? How?" The man replied, "I am a convict . . . I fought for the Revolution." Erzsebet put down her gun. "I see. You can come in. The colonel is a good friend of my husband. Now, careful . . . don't go to the main gate . . . someone may see you. Here you can climb the fence . . . my dogs are on leash. But can you get this height, to my room? All right . . . Psst! here is a chair. Step on it . . . there."

The light was put out until the stranger climbed to the room, then the window and curtains were closed again. Erzsebet went outside to let Jozsi know the dogs could be released, and instructed her maid: "Why don't you put some cold meat and bread and wine on a tray. This man must eat. Bring it to the dining room. Oh! Another thing. Draw the curtains in the whole house, will you? Draw them tightly! He is a fugitive." The stranger was led out from the lady's dressing room into the dining, where by taking a good look at him, she discovered he had a limp. "New wound?" she asked.

"No. Not new. It just had no chance to heal." In the next minute, the newcomer proceeded to introduce himself in the proper manner of a Southern gentleman. "Mrs. Garay, please forgive my intrusion. My name is Laszlo Veroczy. I live in S county. I served in the Southern division of the army, under Gen. Erno Kiss." "Pleased to meet you. Sir, are you being pursued? Escaped? Can you tell me how?" "Yes . . . let me sit down for a . . . second," said the man who looked very pale as his strength momentarily left him. At this hour he was unable to tell even a short story of his life. He must be exhausted, Erzsebet realized. "A glass of cognac will help," she said and was running to get it. True, the man regained some of his energy. "I am an absentee convict . . . they couldn't find me. So, I wasn't imprisoned. But, all the same . . . or almost . . . because I am on the run ever since."

The food was brought in on a tray and he ate most of it. "Drink that wine," offered him Erzsebet, "it will soothe your nerves. We put you up . . . literally up! for tonight. Our best place is in the attic. Far the safest in the whole house!"

Half an hour later the three of them carrying warm blankets, a cushion, some provision of food and water, were on the way to the attic. They went across the kitchen and passed two storage rooms where the staircase was located. The guest helped to keep the upper door for the two women while Erzsebet carefully shielded the candlelight. When all three walked up he saw an oblong shaped spacious attic, and at the corner yet another part that seemed to be equally large. The mistress of the house went ahead, the other two followed. She seemingly disappeared to a small room at the middle attic, where mostly old books were kept. The floor of this place stood on a lower level, so they had to take three steps to get inside. Here was the center of the building. Two oblong units joined in an L-shaped structure, meeting in this room. It also suggested, one wing has been built earlier from the rest. Keeping down her voice, Erzsebet broke the silence. "This is a good hiding place. When we leave you here, we will place this plank over your entrance. It's temporary, but . . . I am thinking. We have to find a more permanent solution to cover it. And now, Mr. Veroczy, you must sleep."

Erzsebet herself could not go to sleep for the rest of the night. Getting into such thing was quite an excitement, and getting out promised the same. Yet wasn't sure, she was in a hurry to get out. "Would I do it for this man, were my husband not in prison?" she asked, and knew she would. "I mustn't think of the danger this man could bring on my head. For God's sake! In the last year, thousands risked their lives. Men, who fought and died, or were prosecuted, or imprisoned, or went in hiding. If they could do it . . . I can do it. I will put up my own fight. I just have to learn how."

There is no way to go around it. With the first fugitive in the attic, the house converted into a hiding place. But then Laszlo Veroczy proved to be a gentleman, who looked for ways to be helpful. He had to repay the risk this woman was taking. Obviously Erzsebet let him stay longer, while he would make a covert entrance to the secret room by blocking it completely from view. The concealment was ready in a week. He built a bookshelf and installed it as a revolving door. At the same time, the room was put in order, cleaned and furnished, and the books moved to the shelf-door. After this makeover, the attic didn't look more than what it was, or if it had to hide anything. It looked just an attic! But still it was not easy! Weary of the situation, Erzsebet used common sense. She could not let anybody go up, only her inner servants. She decided, four people should know only about the scheme, the three who worked inside, and Jozsi, the stable boy. After the first night, the lady made them take an oath not to mention the stranger in the house, but eventually with the operation shifting into larger scale, she had to yet confide in the gardener who proved to be essential in furthering and executing Erzsebet's plan.

The next phase of her plan was carried out in a month, by which time she realized this was the most difficult task she had to do in her entire life.

From then on, if a revolutionary was sent to her, she took him in. Often it wasn't only one who would hide there.

Why did she do it? She thought of Arpad. Accommodating others for a day or two was not difficult. The house was big and there was food, and to help these hunted people made sense. And the fact that she could send news to her husband, or get news of him, was worth it, even if the news was not that good. But it wasn't the worst, as far as he was alive.

Erzsebet did not give up hope that the Austrians will let him out, but if it wouldn't be soon, she wanted to find the key to his release. She thought about it day and night. She wanted to make it happen. As of her own situation, Erzsebet did not delude herself. It was crystal clear from the day she opened her house for helping the fugitives, she became part of the underground. "So be it!" she said, while was truly amazed of her progress. For years she was not political in the least, and now she was a revolutionary! Just like Arpad. She pledged to do it, and at the same time she had no choice.

Chapter 4

The House of Renegades

A SECRET LIFE

"I don't envy young Mrs. Garay," one often heard in the village, because by 1850 people regarded her as someone who carries a heavy load. They found it disconcerting also, that Arpad's firstborn should come to the world at the time of "Armistice". "Why on that unfortunate day when we lost the battle of Vilagos* where Arpad himself fought? And now a year nearly passed, and still he cannot come to see the child! Don't tell me, it's not a long time!" would townspeople ponder, who took upon themselves a heartfelt duty, that Erzsebet should be visited at least a couple of days of the week by someone from the community. "The least we can do for her!" they said, and by affirming it kept coming, considering "The young Mrs. Garay" wasn't only nice and beautiful, but also a cultured woman.

The visits went seemingly well until about a week ago. After that whoever came found the gate locked, which wasn't very pleasant! One had to wait and yelp and wait some more, often as long as half an hour standing there speculating: "What made her close it?" On top of it, as if everyone was deaf inside, came no response, until an old servant would get out and slouch his way to the gate where he had the nerve to sort out the right key from his collection of keys, as slowly as humanly possible. "I don't understand why does she keep a senile old manservant? It's not very inviting to the visitor, you know!" they would say in protest, but to the lucky ones who earned their way inside, Erzsebet readily

* The decisive battle of the Revolution

explained how things "really" were. Sitting next to her in the Garay parlor, they certainly believed everything she had to say (we mustn't forget her talent for the stage) whereas everything would fall in place. "You see my dear, I was taken ill by a strange melancholy," so would start young Mrs. Garay, "I wish . . . oh how I wish, it was going away! Well, sometimes it does . . . for hours? But comes back. And . . . and I can't tell apart days from the nights. Haaah! . . ." uttered Erzsebet her story, finishing it, with a sigh.

It was bad news for the village, very bad. "The poor creature! And so young . . ." they would all say in sympathy. "How she must suffer. Oh my! She must be frightened to death, of being so . . . so alone. I reckon she must be crying a lot. Yes. I must come, and see her more often!" And still having no clue on how things really were, people came to see her. But considering the traffic, visitors had to notice a change in the Garay garden. "It's peculiar. She hasn't done much gardening before! Why the sudden interest? Unless we think of the benefits, like for instance, she won't be so depressed. Oh yes. Now I understand!

The gardening of Erzsebet Garay took surprising turns. It appeared she was building a garden, where above all, the ground had to change. Just in a month little mounds of soil were put down everywhere, as if to form earth-dike corridors, geometrical patterns and serpent lines, thus providing a basis for evergreen shrubbery, which of course came next, by being planted in a dense and controlled manner, so they could face a life of perpetual adjusting and trimming. That's how with all that work Erzsebet built a sculptured landscape reminiscent of the French garden, and some of the fashionable designs of the Romantic period.

"A topiary, garden? What a display of eccentricity! How did she get this idea?" shouted her critics. "Building a labyrinth garden on the Great Plains just months after we lost the Revolution? That's what I call lunacy! Could you tell she will lose contact with reality?" Well, who could answer these? Nobody understood her. Nobody. And nobody could predict it either (not in the first year anyway) that Erzsebet's design will be that perfect setup for a game of seek and hide for rambunctious future children, who might wish to be lost one day in their grandmother's maze of high class gardening.

People in town knew nothing. They didn't know, while the country mourned the Revolution, the young Mrs. Garay led a double life. One was a play, for the public. The other one was private, where she fought her battles against a regime, that would keep her husband in that Austrian prison for almost a year now.

A STRANGER IN TOWN

The only reputable boarding house in town was run by Magda Gal, the widow. She had only six guest rooms and a room for herself and her fourteen year-old daughter, who helped with the service. The girl would set the table three times a day in the dining, since most guests ate three meals at the house. There was a woman who cleaned, and another who cooked. Magda liked to check all rooms once a day. She had three permanent boarders employed at various town's offices, and an agent of some mechanical factory who was there often, even though just passing through, and now a man who came to town almost four weeks ago. Of him, Magda knew nothing. When she asked why was he here, and for how long, he quipped: "Who knows? It could be weeks." There was no mention of the reason for his stay. He paid well and in advance each week, and even tried to be friendly. No landlady could ask for more. Today, his room was checked at noon. By stepping in, she noted there was no fresh water. So she went to fetch the jug. Only, a letter on the table had caught her eye. It wasn't yet enveloped, just folded in two, which for a second looked tempting. "What if I read it?" she asked, before would decide, "Oh well. Why should I resist?" Magda left the door ajar to hear if someone was in the hall, until she read it through. From the tone of the letter it could have been some report to a superior, but it wasn't addressed to anybody. It went like this:

> "I am in my third week in this dreary hole, where people know each other by name and sniff at strangers. The job is not easy. I've put the house under surveillance. One of our agents is posted at the street and watching it all day. I used to go there myself when it's not too obvious. According to my man, within the last two weeks two strangers approached the house and were let in. But we didn't see them to leave. From the Southern fort-prisons there are escapes (I've read the reports myself) and their route could very well be this. That woman is harboring renegades. One of the problems, we can't see inside. The fences are high around the garden and the yards. The back end of the gardens (the last one is a grove) runs into open

> meadows. I do my best putting our men (male and female) inside, as if looking for servant work. So far no success. The lady said to each, she doesn't need them. I don't know if it's true or she is cautious? I am convinced, she takes in rebels. Proof or no proof, I have to get in! I'll make my move in a week or so. But I need more men."

Here, the letter ended. Magda folded it in two, and put it back to the table. "Now, I understand!" she gasped. "That's why he goes out for hours, and again, during the night. A police informer! This is what he is! Working for the Austrian secret police. He is spying on somebody. But on who?" She left the room, but could hardly walk. That letter, and the man who wrote it; appalled her to the degree that she felt nauseous. "If I think that I feed him and give him shelter in the last three weeks, it makes me sick . . . what a lowly character!"

Sometime soon, right after she and her daughter finished giving lunch, Magda became very concerned. "How can I warn this somebody? . . . this woman . . . if I don't know who she is . . ."

A HOUSESEARCH

Erzsebet and her entire household had been frightened into a wake by a thundering bluster one night. Getting up, it took seconds to recognize the noise: gunstocks against the gate! A group of armed men! "Oh my God! What's happening?" The pounding was continuous. Still in panic, somebody from inside was running towards the main gate, and getting there found himself grateful the guns weren't yet fired before he had a chance to open it.

The ones outside-about eight or nine armed men-were immediately squeezed in by just pushing aside the startled old manservant, who managed to ask: "Who are you? What do you want?" But getting no response, or a desire for mutual introductions, he gave up on appearance. It was impossible to rescue the call. Besides. Almost nobody, only few in the house, including the mistress, suspected what could this violent intrusion be all about. "The police," they summarized. Others, mostly field workers, could not make out a reason for the visit, so they went on guessing. Whether groundless or justifiable, was still argued when these armed policemen made their way inside beginning the search for guns and fugitives.

Erzsebet kept her fort by holding a gun against the raiders, who disarmed her in matter of seconds and had a good laugh in her face. Then the one acting as someone in charge, came forth proclaiming, "Madame, we are going to search your house!" Erzsebet had no options other than finding the right composure that she thought might have a calming effect.

By taking a deep breath in a second it was there (thank God}, so she looked as confident as ever, asking very politely: "Oh? At this hour? Why? By the way, would you tell what is your rank? Or, are you a civilian? Judging by your appearance, I assume . . ." She was cut short.

"No. I am a lieutenant. It's besides the point. It is a police rank," he informed her.

"Yes of course . . . Well? Lieutenant, do you have a search warrant?"

"Yes Madame. I have it. Right here!"

Erzsebet looked at it. "Yes indeed, you have it. Well. Can I ask why are you so interested in our house, in the middle of the night?" Now the child started crying in the next room, and Erzsebet went inside to pick him up. For the men, this was the perfect moment to proceed with the search. They had no time to lose. Going by their command, those already inside started with the inner quarters.

Three men stayed outside and gathered the workers to keep them at gunpoint, meanwhile four other policemen checked out the whole Garay property, by getting through their various separated gardens, before they would go on to search every building, including the stables, the barnyard, the pig styles, the granaries, with the result of waking all animals, which inescapably only added to the general confusion and noise.

By then the neighbors were wide awake as was probably everyone else in this part of town. There was shouting outside, the way people exchange threats and insults, not to mention the dogs still on leash, barking in their wild rage, protesting against what went on, but mostly, that they were kept abeyant, kept from their job of tearing unwelcomed strangers to shreds and pieces, for which they were entitled and well qualified.

Those policemen working inside searched the house diligently, going to all rooms one by one, opening cupboards and cabinets, getting to the pantry, to the kitchen and the washroom, to the food storages, and finally to the attic, where they carried a torch. To no avail. It was a fruitless search. They saw nothing revolutionary in the building, found neither fugitives nor guns, or at all ammunition for any kind of soldiering. Finishing the job, they left empty-handed, without apology.

On the following days everyone learned what took place that night at the Garays. Needless to say, it roused the whole town. "Have you heard the news? Erzsebet Garay's house has been ransacked by the secret police." "Why?"

"They were looking for renegades!" "What on earth? Renegades? Really? Well! Did they find them?"

"No. I don't know."

"Do you think there are renegades in that house?"

"Why not? You never see what's inside a house, do you?"

"It could be, that it is a House of Renegades!"

"How do you know?"

"Well, you just never know."

Five days later on a quiet evening they came back. All of them. And the same men did the same search once more. This one was violent because the stable boy has been beaten up. He happened to oppose the search in his quarters. Afterwards when he came around, said: "Nothing is worse than taking it. At least I've knocked his jaw."

There was another victim. Kati, Erzsebet's maid, couldn't resist giving them one of her free advices. "The last time you forgot to look into my sewing box. I keep a rebel there. I used to lock him in my silver thimble. You missed him. I let him out just this morning." Her insolence angered the officer who slapped her rather strongly. She lost her balance, fell, yet made an effort to stand up. Her nose was bleeding. Erzsebet ran to her, and turned back to the policeman: "How can a gentleman hit a lady?" For the generous question, Kati screamed: "Because he is a perverted sadist . . . and a skunk."

The policeman stepped closer to them. "I could put you in prison for this, you know!" His face was red. Kati sent her last shot. "If you have left place . . . your prisons are filled with good men . . . and you, the lowliest of you, are running free . . . poisoning the air . . ." The officer left the room, possibly in fear that he might shoot her.

Erzsebet thought best going after him. "Look here, lieutenant. These intrusions of yours cannot go any longer. You leave me no choice but to report you to your superiors. As a matter of fact, I go to Buda, taking my complaint personally to Archduke Albrecht*. You

* In those years, the Palatine of Hungary.

simply left me no choice. What you do is unlawful. We should get back this country to law and order. Because what happened with me and my people, I call atrocity!"

The lieutenant was pale. It took some time until he replied: "Madame, we had reasons to believe you were harboring rebels. Escaped prisoners . . . and that sort of . . . element."

"What an idea! I? What for? Sir! I insist, you apologize!"

"Well, hmm . . . Our surveillance was incorrect. We made a mistake. We won't disturb you anymore," he said and left.

As soon as the premises were cleared from intruders, Erzsebet went down to the stables and asked the man to bring up the beaten boy to the house. The women tended to his bruises, and he would stay in the parlor for the remainder of the night. She wished to comfort her maid too, but Kati didn't take the whole thing too hard. The young woman created this idea of herself some time ago, of being invincible.

An hour later the three were still talking, sometimes crying, sometimes laughing. They recalled the last month when the secret passage was built downward from the chamber, going underneath an old wall and all through the garden, until it ran into a deep ditch full with stones and stickery bushes, where nobody ever goes (only the ones who have reasons to escape).

"It was clever, wasn't it?" asked them Erzsebet.

"Sure it was! It wasn't the first time I was beaten up," reported Kati, and summed up how she felt about the new underground. "Yes. I loved to do this gardening business . . . carrying the dirt in fruit baskets. Yes, I did. Now, that I know these rats, whom we still call people like our gentleman caller tonight-who will never get wind of how did we outsmart him. Sure. Sure, it's worth it. Beating and all!" And Kati, despite of her badly swollen mouth, gave out a giggle.

Erzsebet had been proud. Neither the secret chamber, nor the tunnel gave them away. They were saved.

By closing the chapter on the Revolution and by inserting an epilogue, it is appropriate if one talks of the men who gave the most . . . The best of their generation, who fought a war for their country, and were treated at war's end by the winning side like common criminals.

Twelve generals and one colonel of the war were executed by hanging, at the Southern town of Arad, on October 6th, 1849. Since then, their names are carved in the annals of History, as "The Thirteen Martyrs of Arad." They are: L. Aulich, J. Damjanich, A. Dessewffy, E. Kiss, K. Knezich, G. Lahner, (Count) K. Leininger-Westerburg,

J. Nagy-Sandor, E. Poltenberg, J. Schweidel, I. Torok, (Count) K. Vecsey—generals, and V. Lazar—colonel.

Later, other high-ranking officers were also captured and executed. Count Batthany who served as Prime Minister during the Revolution, after imprisonment in Pest-Buda, was sentenced to death, by hanging. But on the eve of his execution, Batthany cut his throat to the degree, just to prevent a proper hanging, so his sentence would be modified. It was: He would be shot on the same day-on October 6th, 1849. His bravery was such, that he asked for no blindfold, and gave order himself for the execution squad to shoot.

The greatest of the Hungarian poets, Sandor Petofi, fell on the battlefield at Segesvar. He died the same death he wished for, as it was so movingly conveyed in his poems. He was twenty-six years old.

The world-famous revolutionary, Kossuth, has fled the country just in time, and went into exile. He lived forty-five more years, travelling, writing, and mending in world politics, for the "Magyar Cause". He never returned to his country . . . only after his death.

Chapter 5

Adjustments

HOME AGAIN

Being released from prison and heading home in the second half of 1850, Arpad saw difficulties down the road, unless he was to make quick plans on reorganizing his estate.

It was a new world out there . . . Serfs were free now and had to be paid for their services. Luckily two of them came back for work as soon as heard the news of their master's return. All three of them knew, this time it had to be a tough bargain with the new terms on unchartered terrain, but eventually both parties agreed when one of them had the guts to come forth with a sensible offer: "We don't mind receiving part of the payment in food and grain and firewood . . ."

It was fine with Arpad, for he was not sure now if they will have enough profit from the medium sized land, after he paid the taxes. In those months, there was no way of seeing what could one afford.

But there came the good news. In 1850, the long-lasting trade embargo was lifted by Austria against Hungary, making it possible to seek market for grains, livestock, wool and various other products.

With all the changes implemented, about two years had to pass when Arpad could claim his estate was in good order.

He did nothing sensational, only producing grain and raising livestock for their meat, which went to the market. That was his adjustment to civilian and rural life.

Since his return, people noticed a gradual change in him. He was resigning in public, careful with politics, but who wouldn't, considering the times. Arpad became a man of quiet pleasures in those years. By spending his days with a growing family made him immensely happy, and if he could revise his writings on the Revolution, or could extend his thoughts in the War Diary, it made him feel content.

Sometime after that he would start to design ornamental furniture (especially cabinets), which he liked to do so much that it became a passion. The first one was a cherrywood chest that would be commissioned for his sword, and another one which followed, was for the rifles.

"The passions of a post-revolutionary hussar!" he told jokingly to his wife, whenever a piece of furniture would be shipped to the house.

THE HOUSE OF ARPAD

It was never a question, that Arpad loved his wife and children and was devoted to his family. Having lived the heroic age of the Great Revolution, even if the glory was short-lived and mutilated by politics, he was still conditioned by it. But perhaps as a result, he maintained a heightened sense of loyalty. It has meant a lot to him. When he was just a boy and learned to ride a horse, Arpad imagined to be one of the Magyar tribesmen who were crossing the Verecke Pass of the Carpathians, a thousand years ago.

As a grown man he fought in the Revolution for his country and lived through the fear of losing it. His feelings were less romantic then. Especially that year, when he found himself in prison. There, he had time to think. The recognition was clearer then, what it means to have a country. He could still hear it: "Don't forget how our fathers fought for it. Our duty must be defending it. Teach this to your sons too. If they lose it one day, they could start again the wandering. Looking for a homeland..." These were his father's words. And Arpad agreed. Now a grownup, he could think of his ancestors as far back as those tribesmen, who settled temporarily in Baskiria, Lebedia, and Etelkoz, until they would get here to the final destination, indeed after long wandering. What a faith they must have had, knowing they will find it!

Arpad thought of the great kings, who came after them. "The charismatic kings in the "House of Arpads" gave us good rulers, and many saints." Which all suggested, it won't be a problem finding names for his children. His mind was made up years earlier, they will be called like the kings of this dynasty, even the girls, if his wife agrees to it. And Erzsebet did, herself being named after the daughter of King Bela IV.

When their first son would be called after the great King Istvan, who in the year of 1000 was crowned on Christmas day, nobody showed surprise, knowing Arpad's grand design. Inevitably in a few years, people in the county would refer to the couple and their children, as to "The House of Arpad" (without the plural: s). Certainly, they would do it with a smile, for the Garays by then would be known in the town of K. as some wildly eccentric family.

AND THE DEVENYS

There was too much snow that Winter, one could hardly go anywhere. So he stayed indoors, often for days. On one of those mid-mornings Zombor Deveny opened his journal in which he would write thoughts on History and Government, or his observations on a languished culture. He also put down aphorisms he liked, but those went in a different booklet.

Today was a good day to reflect on his writings. Here was for instance an essay, that he wrote a year ago on the "Hungarian Character". It went like this: "Having an Eastern sensuality and the need to acquire the things to satisfy it, is mixed with the will of the Western man, who has a desire not only to conquer and control the outside world, but making it work. Indeed a strange combination, because work has a major importance in his makeup, through which he can express himself, his vigor, talent, and innovation. All these in one man, or in one country, can create considerable strain. If these, for any reason are not balanced out but still measured by the realities of every day life it would make a person, as well as a crowd miserable. And also, if time and again there is an insistence for personal freedom against all these, dark hours will follow. The fact is, we Magyars are not very disciplined. or, if some of us are, even then we don't make a virtue of it. (It's like going against the blood).

So it seems, with this character we are better equipped to break the rules, than make them."

Zombor Deveny put down his journal. "Well, that's how it is!" he thought. "By reacting to the outside world, our nature is torn between two opposing forces; the heights of exuberance, and the depths of misery. There is no way to go around this, even if one tried. Because it's imbued in our character, and became part of our soul. It is present in each of us, including the most disciplined men I know, who are a step ahead of the crowd, with their efforts to counter it.

By making these forces more plausible, we have the need to project them through our deeds (good or bad) but above all, to express them emotionally and verbally, but always with a fatalistic overview. We have no middle ground there. What we have is energizing, and scattering at the same time.

But while some of us fight these forces-in fear they could paralyze willpower-most of us don't bother and even refuse to temper them. I must admit, the worst part of this raging war is, the balancing act. For being the ultimate test on our character and morale, not to mention our frame of mind. It puts strain on the person . . . . or on the people with the same streak, if they have it.

"Well, that's the national character; all right!" says the average Magyar with a bit of pride, which sounds much like an ostrich, with head in the sand: "I see everything very clearly!" Perhaps it's not too wild to speculate: my fate is the consequence of my character. But how is it for a nation? Well, I think it's applicable, if we the people make up a nation. History doesn't just happen with us . . . unless we are so damn passive, to succumb our overactive mind to our pleasure seeking Eastern laziness, while make attempts to resurrect the glorious years of our past . . . to think, they'll take care of the future. But will they?"

When Zombor Deveny decided to put down some of it in his journal, he realized, this streak in the national character was nowhere more glaring than in Count Istvan Szechenyi. "The Greatest Magyar" who would start the Reform Age in the 1820s, for Hungary.

"But to think it now, it all really started with Ferenc, his father who in the 1790s raised his children by replenishing a keen sense of appreciation in them, towards their environment. As one example, he would invite his serfs over the main hall of his palace at each year on New Year's day, to properly thank their year-long work and loyalty. After his speech, and after the gifts, he expected his youngest child to kiss the hand of his eldest serf, so he would learn early something about respect.

Yes. Well. It was the right step, in the right direction! And Istvan Szechenyi grew up in that spirit . . . He was a man, bigger than life, a great man with raging inner wars, which could be so fiery that they had to consume him at the end.

And he was the best of us. "The Greatest Magyar" . . . ,

ARPAD'S FAMILY

It's neglectable what triggered Arpad's interest in fine woodwork if it kept him out of trouble, or if proved that hussar colonels are as profuse with innovations in retirement as they are in active service. An enthusiast of custom-made furniture, Arpad made sure different cabinetmakers worked for him, each on a singular piece, like a drawer, a cupboard or a cabinet, from walnut, cherry, pear, maple, or even rosewood, before he could decide who was qualified to make him a dining set.

His taste suggested to furnish the house with rustic simplicity, knowing the whitewashed wall will emphasize the heavy dramatic pieces. Now he had a cabinet ready for his gun collection, and a showcase for his sword. Because of his children, he would keep this room closed, but would open it for a visitor, when Istvan, his eldest son too could walk in. The younger ones were not yet into this sort of thing, but obviously Istvan was intrigued by the sword, and elated by the prospect that it will be his one day. He would touch the pistols that were kept in their luxurious velvet-line box. The boy was so impressed that he asked, who would use them next, or if they would be used in a duel. Arpad frowned, and told him, "Let's hope, they remain a showpiece!"

Duels wouldn't sound half as bad for his son's age, for he liked to be reading the novels of the great romantic writer Jokai, who was so prolific that turned a whole country into avid readers (and their offspring as well, for the next hundred years). In these works an era was resurrected which shouldn't have gone, thought Istvan. His mother felt the same, and so would others, who read them through. The boy had an active mind,and as years went by, needed books which had the capacity to teach.

Being born on August 13th of 1849-on the Day of Surrender-Istvan considered the timing a bad omen, and was wrestling with it all his life. "When a revolution aims for independence and ends in defeat, and the nation is forced to her knees, it must be-by any standard-a devastating day," he told to his wife years later, to whom he had to explain why wouldn't he hold birthdays.

His parents suspected how he felt as a teenage boy, when at first began to understand the role, as well as the pressure of History, something he tried to come to terms with. He realized, even his father

Arpad who fought the Revolutionary War and was sent to prison afterwards, preferred to recall only the elevating aspects of the fight.

Family life had its rewards. The Garays enjoyed each others' and their children's company, and of their evenings together. They both made efforts to beautify their home, Arpad with the grand design, Erzsebet with artistic details. They decided, every room of the house should be white, which gave austerity. Apart from the ornate furnishing of the parlor, other rooms were relatively simple. In the master bedroom a pair of canopied beds were put in, a commode, two night tables, a chest, and a table for the washbasin.

There was crucifix on the wall. Erzsebet and Arpad had a happy union, but each generation took its turn in this room . . . by making love, conceiving children, bearing them or losing them, letting them go . . . until they themselves had to go, to give place for a new couple. so they too could start the first whispers of lovemaking . . . and going through the stages of family life their predecessors were going through, till one of them gave out a last sigh, leaving the other one bereaved.

YOUNG ISTVAN'S MIND

Istvan the firstborn grew up hearing the brutalities of Haynau, and lived through the following "Bach regime".*

As a child, he could not justify such a repressive foreign rule, if the country was capable of running her own affairs. As a young man, he found the idea of Independence a comforting one. With his parents he had daily discourse on personal freedom. In these talks his father impressed him, who advocated personal responsibility, as the key element to the welfare of one's country. Yet Istvan still looked for solutions. He wanted to understand the great movements of the 18th and 19th centuries, their diversity, and if possible, the reason behind their failure to attract a greater following as they have had. He was less impressed by the way Enlightenment proposed the role of History. In this, Istvan fiercely opposed his father, who took the idealistic and progressive view. Our young man had this to say: "I am not convinced man craves progress. Or, cares about it. Nor does he work on a common good. Man is out for himself. For his own interest. If it happens to be a hindrance for others, so be it! Father, we all just want to be strong.

* A political era, named after an Austrian Minister.

Don't you think? For our own sake! Ideology steps in much later. So we could look winners if we found a suitable ideology while we were pursuing our own interests. Well. That's how I see it, Father."

Willful as a boy, but still with more restraint from others of his age, he shouldered the responsibility of being the eldest. Once Istvan told his younger brother: "One day I will do something big. Something, that cannot go wrong." It was typical of him talking this way. Even then. Istvan admired his father. He looked up to him, and at the same time envied him, for Arpd could put faith into elevating his country, and also he could go fighting for it. His father witnessed a golden age, was intrinsic to the Revolution, even if it was doomed from the start. Thinking about these for a long time, Istvan went as far as to prescribe its outcome, maintaining the patriots were weaker from the ones who came up against them! He tried, but could not change his mind on this. He never could.

THE COMPROMISE

It was told for years, Habsburg Absolutism cannot last forever, it has to end one day, and indeed it had. Istvan came of age at the time of the "Compromise". He was then eighteen years old.

In 1867, the "Compromise" created the "Austro-Hungarian Monarchy". A long peace had followed. The Compromise and the new Monarchy was chiefly the work of Ferenc Deak, the lawyer, statesman and diplomat. He put the country on equal footing with Austria at last, politically, economically and legally.

Deak served as a representative at the National Assembly, or "Diet" in the 1820s and 1830s, and as a Minister of Justice during the Revolution of 1848.

In the last decade, Austria has been weakened by lost wars with France and Prussia. Also, she was losing more of her acquired territories in Italy. Deak could seize the moment for negotiating with the Habsburgs. Even though it took a couple of years working out the details of this new alliance with fine points and clauses it is attributable to the fact, that neither Austria nor Hungary faced a better choice at the time. In reality, they both only benefited from it.

The Dual Monarchy was the result of a mutual compromise between Austria and Hungary, in which the Habsburg Emperor has been given a double role. He had to become the King of Hungary as well. With the crown of St. Istvan on his head, Franz Joseph was not only a consecrated ruler of Hungary, but more importantly with this act he was obliged to rule this nation in accordance with her ancient laws.

With the Compromise, inevitably a new era has begun. And the Revolution? Was it forgotten? Those who took part in it fighting, many were imprisoned, or the thousands who were forced to serve afterwards in the Austrian army, fighting unpopular offensive wars hundreds of kilometers away and could return only years later, would say in resignation: ". . . the Revolution? Maybe the next generation will resuscitate it. We are tired . . . and old . . ."

It has been clear that Istvan wanted a different life for himself. And even if he cared to, he could not make up for Arpad's dreams, which were lost in 1849, after the Revolution. Istvan was cut out to do his own thing. He didn't get excited about 1848 March 15th, even though in principle he agreed with it. But the young man had neither his father's dreams, nor his temperament. He was more pragmatic, most of the time looking for square-fair solutions. In all his youth listening to his parents talking on ideas (no doubt, for keeping the spirit in one another), well, ideas of king and country and honor and virtue and duty and glory, Istvan preferred to see life in simpler terms. He admitted, the words they used were magnificent, full with fire, finding the way to one's heart. Yet something was wrong with them! If these words meant to aid one's orientation, they failed to draw a map to it. There were no instructions on how to set goals, or how to achieve them. There was no mention of how to be strong. Really strong, so one can withstand anything. Not as noble losers do, but the way winners do. As they find a way and follow it, never giving up. Istvan believed there was a raw energy in the world and available if used for something big. He wanted to tap this energy, and also planned to be ready if there was a need. He dreamt to be strong like a bastion. Not somewhere in the future, but here and now.

Chapter 6

The Strongholds

A YOUNGER DEVENY

The majority being established in the lOth century, the fifty-two counties of Hungary began as fortresses. These original strongholds of the first Magyar state were organized by Geza, a king, whose son Istvan, the first Christian King of Hungary, greatly benefited from it by continuing and reinforcing the same. From this time onward to later centuries, townships would spread around these fortresses while building out a well-structured economical and social power that would fuse their political interests. By this covenant the counties were there to support the king and his central power, to guard against invaders from East or West, or from the Balkan if there was a need. Well, this institution worked well for centuries, oligarchs and governors stood for king and country, except when found reason to stand otherwise.

These counties-or better called county-states-were sprawling on the land like small kingdoms, being governed with local wit and flavor, some of course with more, others with less, but all with identical inference of a sovereign statehood.

Finishing law school and trying his teeth in politics, Zombor Deveny Jr. was glad to serve his native southeast. "For a young man going to the Assembly in any capacity is a great honor!" maintained his family. So his father made sure the son would be assigned to the county-seat, which was then a typical Southern overgrown municipality. Established possibly a millennia ago when other peoples would still roam the Plains like the Avaric, and later the Hunnish tribes (who also occupied the region from the 3rd to the 5th centuries), the city was layed at the crossroads of ancient trade routes. Going by documents, it has always been and would be still in Zombor's time (and long after him) an important meeting place. Indeed an earlier meeting point for the caravans too, and later in medieval times a marketplace, when map-making or writing were not yet essential parts of daily life, unless one thinks of the king's court, half a country away. Oh well. There was no need for maps, anyone could get here on horseback, on a buggy, on a horse-drawn coach, or on a mule. People found the way. The town kept close to the river, to the only one in fact that would risk taking a ride in this corner of the South.

Upon getting here Zombor realized the township still hosted cattle, horse and swine, and of the annual grain markets and the shows, just as it would for centuries.

Naturally roads were overused and spotted with bumps and potholes at early Spring each year. Travellers were taken aback-as would young politicians be-those years, for the town was lacking a good hotel, or at all that polished quality and refinement other places were already letting in.

Young Deveny-who fashioned himself a cosmopolitan (mainly because his wife-to be descended from the Northern Highlands of Hungary) didn't yet know what to make of the place. He only knew he had to find himself if his father insisted on entering politics. Zombor wasn't sure of the vocation either, but with a law degree that's what one was supposed to do.

But then, there were the clubs for comfort, where the gentlemen could lay back . . . Oh, but why would they, when they could do more politicking in those never-ending relaxed afternoons? "Considerably more!" thought even Zombor Deveny Jr., as soon as he learned to tolerate their company.

Well, that's what men did here. Discussed casually the nation's past, present and future soon after lunch when offices and the shops for a few hours have all closed up.

Zombor at first just listened into their loud conversations while tried not to detest their inconsistencies and platitudes. It went on for awhile, until one day he saw a new face in the club. The man was a talker and when our young man entered, he already had the floor.

". . . don't say that to me! No, no! Can't you all see our weakness in politics? We seldom study our enemies, gentlemen! Well, how could we? For us, the most important issue remains: What is my opinion? And if we figured it out, we go to take it around like a flag!"

Most gentlemen shushed him down, but by disregarding them he could carry on. "Also, we like to think our cause is justifiable, and theirs is not. As if to say, the enemy's claim is irrelevant. And when we say: "I never liked them anyway!"-I think we hit rock bottom . . ."

At this point no one could tolerate the chap. "What is he getting at? What does he want? Obviously what he says is gibberish. Someone has to tell him off."

And that's exactly what they did. "I don't rightly know what's wrong with you, Sir! Here, we don't circumnavigate." "Sure. That's the talk!" cheered others in the room.

Still, the man who challenged them all, didn't give up. "And here comes the black soup. We take defeat badly, Gentlemen! We acquired a very simplistic view of the world, if . . ." He couldn't finish his point, because now really everyone started talking.

Our young man, Zombor Deveny, happened to be the only one who was impressed, since he himself planned to tell them a couple of things. Things about Lajos Kossuth, their hero, who was a champion of all that was mentioned above, by way of working up people's emotions-a nation's, in fact. Well, that's how it was. He sedated their reasoning and went to war against the Habsburgs, and was surprised to lose. In spite of his brightness, he neglected to study both or more sides of a situation, even if the fate of his country was at stake . . .

That's what Zombor Deveny Jr. thought out and hoped to tell, until the general confusion made him change his mind: "What if they stone me? I can't talk of Kossuth here on a critical tone! It's still a sacrilege. It's best kept in."

There was loud noise in the room. Less and less people paid attention to the man now, who provoked them. It was far best anyway if they considered him a fool, and shut him out. Just when they did, Zombor knew he had a friend. "Perhaps the only one I'll ever have in this town?" he wondered, while rushed to the street to catch up with him. The gentleman was twice his age it turned out, but he took kindly that someone else too was thinking on his line. So, for the duration of their stay, the two of them would often meet to exchange their views.

Years later, being retired from politics they would still run into each other. The same happened again on the day they both came to solve disputes of jurisprudence to the very same old city. Today, after mutual greetings, they agreed to have lunch at the Golden Bull.

"We could cover, or give new meaning to the so-called blank years, can't we? So, why don't we meet at noon?!"

Well, the restaurant was rather noisy, but the juristic crowd could always get a better room. After the soup the old barrister took pleasure only in his recollections. "My dear Amice*!" he would start, "the thing you did, you learned law. There at least they taught you to think. Somehow you survived Latin, and Greek too. But you kept a clear head and tried to stay sober until the final exams. And years later, even if you diverted from your father's plan and didn't really practice law, just in name, still you were somebody . . . You could drink, if this was what you wanted. A lawyer without practice had more respect than just a drunk. If you soaked your brain in liquor, that was good too . . . well, if someone picked up the tab. If someone paid your bills . . . Only the poor gentry is aware of his sobriety. If he doesn't marry the rich girl, he needs employment. And to whom do you work if you are somebody, and have a good name? You can't work for anybody less than you! For God's sake . . . It's preposterous already, that you have to work . . . So we all say: "It is an honor to serve the government." After all, we all belong to the same club. We are the elite. Yes. Well. Aristocrats, great magnates, and the nobility go into politics as a way of expression. We like to arrange things, and have a say in what's happening in the country . . . This was, and is a passion, a necessity and a habit for us . . . Doing politics. We did that for centuries. The same people. Sure, we had oftentimes different interests, fights, serious wars even. But we all belonged to the same club, Amice. "Look at this upstart!"-we would frown, if an overly ambitious bourgeois decided to join us. Take for instance this Kossuth fellow. I say, he wanted to have it all! "-here the old gentleman was cut short. His boiled beef with horseradish sauce made it to the table, and everyone knew, it was his favorite dish. From here on both concentrated on the food, and wouldn't get back mentioning politics till Tokay was served with those tiny but handsome savory bites.

The old gentleman started to talk of the Lieutenant Governor in a manner, as if citing an old-fashioned poet. ". . . mounting his horse, he rode in the land . . . ," he said, and drunk to it which made him step out of his poetry for the sake of a different tone: "Of course, what he did to his cousin . . . The world hasn't seen such foolishness since the last duel in this county."

"Why?" thought Zombor. "It shouldn't be that difficult making a point, even with a sanguine personality . . ." He realized his old friend's outlook had changed. He was less sharp, and more irritated.

* Friend (Latin).

"Maybe it's the wine. It makes him moody," explained away Zombor Deveny Jr., who became better and better at tolerating everybody and everything, like other Devenys before him, who all made a conscious effort in the mastering of this family trait.

"Don't forget, Amice!" forewarned the old barrister, a bit too fervidly. "No Magyar with just a so-so brain reckons, a strong central government would serve his interests. No. It won't do. Not in this latifundium* anyway!"

Zombor was far and away in his views. Yet he knew, his old friend too was right, regarding the deviance of the 52 county-states in changing the law. "Yes, I grant that Sir, what you say," he replied thoughtfully. "I remember my father saying, it struck him as a young man, that these lands were too backward here, as if did nothing but sinking in doom and mud for centuries. He . . . had hopes in the Reform Age, which was a good thing, good for the country. Well . . . ten years after the Revolution, my father decided to send me in politics . . . where he had no taste to go. Oh but it was twenty years ago! So I went, as you know Sir . . . to the Assembly . . . but it's not what I envisioned to do. For the first chance I married, went home to my forest, my farming, and my horses. Since then, my old man had a stroke, and . . . we lost my mother. That's how I live now. With my family. I have a brother . . . a bachelor, who started a fruit grove. And I have a son. Well, my son Zoltan has an interest in Philology."

"Ah? Does he?"

"Yes. He could be a scholar one day. But I press him to finish Law."

"Very good, amice. And? And your father, old Zombor. How is he these days?"

"He recovered some. But retired from work now. He just sits in his tusculanum in the length of the Summer, smoking his pipe, taking a nap, and when the dusk is finding him on the veranda, he thinks of old wine, and young women I suppose . . ."

"Very good. And why not?"

"Well, that's how things are these days," finished younger Zombor his summary, and bid farewell to his old friend, without sharing his view on strong central government.

In the sense that he too could keep his thoughts, he was like his father more every day.

---

* Province (Latin).

Chapter 7

Second Generation

Motto:

"My generation enjoyed the longest peace. We weren't tested if we were heroic. But everyone had the choice of doing what he did best. We liked to work and we prospered. It was a rustic life. One couldn't spend time daydreaming. There was always work."

—Istvan Garay

THE VISITS

What is ten years in the life of a family? Or twenty? The passage of time has not changed the Garays, only made them older. And wiser? Maybe . . . In the town of K. things went as they would with other families anywhere in the second part of the last century. The Garay clan lived like everyone else, following a tradition. Children have been born, old people died-as had Arpad's mother-and the others in between lived as they could. Loved and hated, worked and rested, and when it was time, they visited each other yearly if they could, their brothers, sisters and cousins. Not all of them were highminded though. Come to think of it, only very few.

Such visits proved to be the best time to get on each other's nerves, to pick a fight, and make peace on the same day, or get separated from the rest of the crowd. Not that it was practical . . . To what end? Be an outcast? Oh, no. Why do it permanently? So, they came and stayed. Often for weeks. And had a wonderful time. They tried out each other's horses and buggies, liqueurs and cigars, and recipes and embroideries. While women exchanged gossips, men spent long afternoons to construe the politics of Europe, and with the remnants of their passion they would look into closer ranges of things right home in Hungary.

The hours were flying for the guests! Some took interest in Arpad, speculating if he changed his views. "I dare say he is smooth now. What is it? The old rebel lost its bite?" So they tried him out with the latest in politics. "What do you say cousin, to the Andrassy* plan?" they asked, by way of testing him. Arpad had to tell, he liked it. The truth was he really had.

A gracious hostess, Erzsebet would not lose faith. Composed as ever, seemingly it wouldn't occur to her the obvious: "How much longer will they stay?" But of course that was decided by the weather. Always. And those days lasted forever for Erzsebet to feed them, and for Arpad to bear them. But it couldn't be helped. As long as the roads were wet, the guests were stuck!

"Back then, Winters were hard!" The old ones say, "They were not made for sissies!"

FALLING IN LOVE

It happened early in the Spring of 1874, sometime before the leaves came out.

"No. I won't wait! The next time I'll propose. I just wish we were left to ourselves," said the young man. "I can't risk the weather to clear up either . . . or, her aunt to say: All right, Julianna, let's go home. Because then I might never see her, and might never know if she has feelings for me, or the whole idea is only mine. Yet I know this. Today she looked at me as if . . . So, I'll come early tomorrow, and I propose! On the veranda. I'll call her out . . . and there," decided Istvan on his way home, as he carefully tiptoed down the garden path between the two neighboring gardens, what has otherwise been soggy from the constant rain. It talked for itself how he memorized the shape and size of each stone while attaching deserved or undeserved significance to it. No wonder. He passed the path twice every day! Istvan became a

* count Gyula Andrassy, Hungarian Prime Minister, and Austro Hungarian Foreign Minister (1871-79).

frequent caller to the Vargas' since the girl arrived to them a month ago. Usually she travelled with her aunt, they told. Lucky for him, the old lady took Julianna-the favorite niece-along her round tours whenever visiting relatives, from which they had a steady supply all over the land, including Transdanubia.

"God bless the benevolent woman!" declared Istvan on the first week. He was presently twenty-five, by his estimation the perfect age for falling in love with the girl one hopes to marry. Yes. He was pretty sure now. He no longer believed it was just in his head.

In that year the Spring turned out to be inordinately long and wet, being apostrophized "a typical carriage—confining weather". The rain started two weeks earlier, stopped for half a day and then went on for another week, pouring down and cascading like a river. What was bad for anybody in the vicinity, was particularly bad for travellers. They were stuck where they were, trying to accommodate, or making up for lost time which didn't come easy, if they found no one to blame other than God for the weather, and the Governor for his neglect of county roads.

For a while, the visitors could only suspect what locals knew all too well. It was an occurrence happening most each year when the roads would become impassable. When there is no way to get in, or get out, unless of course in an emergency, when one's vehicle is removed, or pulled over by a double team of oxen. But it wasn't always that bad. Let's take this year. Considering, these very events kept Julianna in his town, Istvan wasn't about to complain. On the contrary. It made him optimistic and joyful. In his assessment, there had to be a sign to the visit. It was no accident. Her aunt provides an opportunity for her to come, and the pouring rain forces her to stay. She is in fact tied here . . . What does it tell me? "That she was sent to me. A godsend."

Istvan reached the corner of their house, but wasn't in a hurry to get in. A major issue had to be decided once and for all. "Yes, tomorrow I'll tell her!"

He had a vivid dream that night . . . Istvan saw himself alone, standing on a freshly plowed land what was vast, but had no horizons. Then a voice of a woman called him by name. He felt elated . . . and walked to her but she disappeared. Here, the dream ended.

In the morning, he didn't know what to make of it. It was too mystifying. But this day had to be a day of action. True to his words, Istvan has got around it and talked to Julianna and from then on things looked bright. Especially when learned, the young woman felt the same for him.

A week later Istvan could go as far as to confide in her. "I didn't plan a speech, because I knew what was in my heart, and . . . I wanted to say you that. But when I saw you, I just bumbled, I couldn't say it. It was so awkward. I am afraid, at first I looked like a fool." Holding his hand, Julianna smiled, thinking her heartfelt duty was to protest. "No, Istvan. You did not look like any of those things. Not to me. It is not easy to say the words. I couldn't either, until I didn't know that you felt the same. You see, for a month or so, I believed it was unrequited love. My girlish imagination. I am glad I was wrong."

And so, at the last month of Summer, just before the foliage would change into the livelier colors of yellow and rusty red, have Istvan and Julianna been betrothed, and in 1875 be married.

After the young couple decided to live in K., Istvan bought a modest house close to the ancestral home. The move would serve young and old. Arpad for one, was eager to share what he knew: "To establish yourself as a granger, you need land, money, connections, and informations on trade. For that, you must meet people," he said, and took him around a few times in the county, in one of his handsome buggies.

Meanwhile back home Julianna Garay would visit Erzsebet, who was very much taken by the young daughter-in-law. And Erzsebet would come to her to pamper Almos, the first grandchild a year or so later, when he was born.

But this perfect picture, and the harmony between the generations would soon end. In 1877, while out driving in their fancy carriage, Arpad and Erzsebet Garay have had a brutal accident. There was a mishap, they say, by the crossroads. Their horses went wild, which overturned the carriage and they would be crushed underneath. They both have died on the same day, due to internal injuries. Erzsebet went first . . . And Arpad would wait for his turn, like a true Southern gentleman.

Hardly recovering from the tragedy, Istvan and Julianna moved back to the Garay home, for they had to take care of running the estate and helping Istvan's siblings until they could stand on their own, or could get married.

Well, this is the story of Arpad and Erzsebet Garay, who despite of all what came to pass, seemed to stay in that house . . .

Perhaps to watch over those who were yet to come?

K., THE TOWN OF THE GARAYS

K. has been a much older settlement but gained municipal status and got incorporated as a town in the 15th century.

During its long history, K. endured flood and fire and of being sacked by the Tartars earlier, and also a long Turkish occupation later on, but reemerged in the 17th century as a strong agricultural center with grains, tobacco and substantial livestock. Townspeople had huge, well maintained gardens here for vegetable, flower and fruit, and of course a main yard with a covered place for the carriage and buggy. There were also granaries, the stables, the barnyards and pig styles, which all had been separated from the gardens and fenced from the living quarters and of the inner, or flower gardens.

Apart from its practicality and the need for security, privacy too had to be maintained. As a rule, every lot was fenced around with lumber or layed brick which also prevented others peeping into one's domain. Therefore each house with its system of yards and gardens and its other buildings looked like a fortification, on a lookout for new wars . . . which of course did not fail to come. Well, that's how townspeople lived here. This was the tradition. Dating back to the 17th century, by way of taking a burly and irregular shape, the town was spreading from the center with routes to the farmlands, and one to the town's municipal pastures. The pastures were divided for cattle and sheep and swine, each attended by herdsmen who would be kept on the town's payroll. People would be taxed then, according how much animal did they send out.

At each season, except in harsh Winter the herd was driven out, and back again to the village before sunset in a noisy and slow procession which would flutter the dust of dirt roads into clouds over the streets. Then windows hurriedly had to be closed, while the gates flung open to the homecoming beasts. Some people who were better off and had a homestead close to their farming lands, would fence a paddock for pasturing, or exercising animals, what would be kept out year long. It applied mostly for horses, since equestrian life has been part of the quiet pleasures. Also, they keenly followed the hunting grounds with its own peculiar seasons, and would walk from fields to woods, or down Eastbound to the marshlands. A large part of that was dried in the last hundred years, but some was still saved with its unique wildlife which included magnificent waterbirds.

Apart from the hunt, Plainsmen felt strongly still of their beaten and disbound army comrades who fought the Great Revolution. For them, the marshlands did offer the last refuge from a punitive and extended army service, under a young, and yet hostile Habsburg Emperor. People say, villagers in those days would guard a narrow path in and out to the wetlands, in an effort to aid those poor devils.

Regardless of its history, and of the fact that K. had been a regional center of produce and commerce for over two centuries, and that the "burgers" took pride in their work, activity, culture and tradition, still by some it was perceived as a flat and boring village. Whoever jumbled such deduction, he wasn't from the South! If city folks came in business and brought well-rounded lies and weren't welcome, the so-called "adventurers" had even worse reputation in old farming communities.

The challenge here clearly was staying put, and being useful at it! In the seasonal work of growing food, this made the most sense to the Avars who also occupied the Basin hundreds of years before Hungarians. The found in their graves attests to a once great wealth, a reputation that grows in the sight of their exquisite gold, now kept in museums.

To own land was a blessing, but in this century the ones who couldn't, were perhaps the ones who wouldn't. They were free, and in need of something else. People thought they were the restless, the vagabonds, the riff-raff, who just had no understanding of the land.

At one time the town would be even called "peasant nest" by those miserable travellers who had to endure muddy roads for half of the year, and clouds of dust in the other half, when the months of Summer dried up the shadeless roadside, which made them wonder why the trees had to be in such poor shape. (One assumes they haven't met the town's herd going through there twice a day!). People thought, it's almost certain the labelling came from pushy city folks who talk too much to sell their smart side, while patronize everybody on these awkward visits. Each time they came, they left convinced, country folks were ignorant, stubborn and backward.

But who cared? Nobody. Here they were outsiders, where most residents took pride in this world, that was hard but rewarding with its wealth and its own beauty. They didn't much care how the rest of the world defined good life, or beauty. Theirs was attainable, and ideal. There was even a rhythm to it. The golden days of Summer brought wealth to the region and to them each year.

Chapter 8

A Very Hot June.

THE BIRTH OF TASS AND HUBA.

The twins showed up early evening on a hot day of June in 1890. With remarkable timeliness, just when the church bell struck seven, Huba came last to be the seventh child of Istvan and Julianna Garay. "What a day! What a glorious day! Two sons!" exclaimed the father, hardly containing how moved he really was when hugged Mariska, the old relation of his wife who carried to him the news. Istvan, by then formed this habit of naming his sons after the seven chieftains of the Magyar tribes who came over the Carpathians in the ninth century to claim the land, and to build a nation on it. That's how the twins came to be called Tass and Huba, the follow-ups to the fifth and sixth tribal chieftains.

"Yes, we can tell, as of today, Istvan is as happy as can be!" concluded Mariska, since the couple had seven children now, even if one was a girl.

Oh, no! He had nothing against girls! This girl, his daughter could be a blessing if he looked the other way to distance himself from the fact, the seventh chieftain, "Tohotom" was still not in their midst. On this very hot day of June, in 1890, the last chieftain was only a thought. A desire, at most. "Oh well. He shall come next year!" cheered Istvan his own self, and went all the way to their bedroom, planning to visit his wife as soon as the midwife was ready, and was about letting him in. So, the happy father till then just stood in the hallway. Granted, it was a tiresome, long and eventful day, and that woman whom people called "sergeant", wasn't in her best mood, so Istvan had to be patient, thinking all the while what Julianna was going through.

He waited and waited still at the door half delirious even now, an hour and a half later as the results were out. He paced back and forth the length of the corridor three times, went out to the yard, smoked a pipe, came back and repeated by walking through thirty more times.

Fortunately, there is a time for everything, and the door at last opened to the women's domain. And closed again. Istvan couldn't do much, so he stayed right there, in front of it. Soon enough the midwife came out with soiled towels and a bucket. After she instructed the maidservant to remove those, Istvan expected she will tell something. Something good, that is. But it didn't happen. Seemingly, the woman took pleasure out of her temporary usefulness, and from being in charge of his house in large parts of the day, on this very important day, when he, the master, could gain two new sons. Istvan assumed, with things done and giving up the power she accrued for a day made her upset, more than she cared to show.

"Sore woman. You never liked men, did you? Too bad. You can't control them, unless they are babies," thought Istvan, and still had no trouble to act the polite host, by asking: "Ma'am, I gather you can use some rest now? Well, I suppose as things . . ." She gave him a stern look, which compelled the master to stop with the niceties. The woman went in, but soon reappeared, so he could ask: "How did it go?" He just asked what other husbands invariably ask in front of similar doors.

The woman looked at him. At first she did not reply, as if wanting to make him wait and suffer, if only for a moment, like that poor creature did inside for hours on those miserable sheets.

"So, tell me!"

She sent an angry look, by blurting it out: "What do you expect? It was too much blood. A double trouble, I should say!"

"But she is doing fine, isn't she?" he asked, this time placing his right foot in the door. He wished to hear a short affirmative no doubt, most likely a "yes", but couldn't wait for it, so he preferred to step in to see Julianna, this beautiful pale woman whom he dearly loved who still could look like a flower, after her seventh child.

Yes, she was the same Julianna, the young woman he loved from the start when she arrived to town some twenty years ago with her elderly travelsome aunt.

"Unbelievable how time flies!" said Istvan and this time he really stepped inside.

Meanwhile that other woman with the sheets who left the room to give command, still had this to add: "You men! Pigs. All you care is, to put it in!"

Already in his wife's room, and alone with her, Istvan embraced her, before he would pronounce: "God bless you my love!" and filled the vase with gardenia, Julianna's favorite flower, so it might take over and chase that smell of iodine from the room, a smell she could not learn to tolerate. He looked at the boys, stayed awhile and left only for letting her sleep.

The next day was a busy one. In the morning he took upon his traditional role of receiving a stream of well-wishers all day long and to drink a toast with each of them in the parlor. Everyone came and Istvan was getting drunker by the clock, until he was ready to convince the last guest, that all of his children were boys.

Istvan then went to bed with an idea to enlarge the house. He dreamt, where the new house solidified, but had problems with it, so he walked around twice and still couldn't find the marital bed. That, he found strange. Even in a dream state. In the morning, by fully awakened after coffee, he decided: "A bad dream! What can I expect with this hangover?"

These days were running too fast, when Istvan's delight of having the twin-boys unexpectedly turned to sorrow, because Julianna died of fever immediately after the fourth day of her giving birth. Well, he was devastated . . . The last thing she would ask, was this: "Will you forget me?" which for Istvan sounded quite impossible then, or later.

On the first day, just by looking at her cold body, Istvan mostly sobbed, and wandered aimlessly in an otherwise empty house from where the children were promptly removed. Seemingly everyone else was present from doctor to priest, and the women who dressed her up. He vaguely remembered afterwards staying out with some of the men who slowly, one by one disappeared. It is said, hours later the women too left the house with a claim: "Your wife is prepared for her exit now, so we can pray for her soul."

In the flicker of candlelight he took notice of an opal rosary being coiled about her clasping fingers. All of a sudden it made her death look irreversible, so he had to challenge it: "My Julianna, how is it, you helped the twins to see the light, the very light which was turned off to you? Why you of all people are denied? Why you? Lord! You should have saved her, not the children!" But when he realized how his words could connote sin for the conventional and religious mind, or to anybody not familiar with Hell, Istvan out of respect wouldn't repeat what he just said. He couldn't revoke it either as long as its content burned his mind and heart and flesh. He felt like anyone feels about the truth in moments of despair when one stumbles against the core, to converse to it unashamed.

That's how it was with him then. Till Julianna would be sent to her final resting place, for his endless questioning answers were in short supply.

The funeral came, and this time the gardenia was made into wreath.

And again people came, lots of them, relatives and friends and the whole town. Ushered by relatives there were the children, heartbreaking, holding hands, dressed in white.

This day too passed, but after the funeral Istvan just vanished. He returned a week later though, oblivious of the pain he caused to his older children, who were convinced the world must have come to an end, if both of their parents could so disappear.

What happened to him? Where did he go? What did he do? How little they knew . . . They couldn't; it was a missing time for Istvan too, a blackout really, something not even years later could he reconstruct as a memory. From then on it became apparent to everyone how much he changed, seemingly losing an ability (or interest?) for speaking to the rest of the world, as if being severed from it. Most of his sentences those days fell into a void, failing to resonate the frequencies one associates with human speech. From this time on, he never quite knew if it made sense what he tried to convey, or it relapsed into a mere presentation of arranged words drained of intent as soon as they left his lips. For the best solution was to avoid the crowd, even if it made him a loner. And so, as years went by, people had to see how the loss of Julianna turned around his life. Regardless of all his troubles throughout by raising seven children without a mother, Istvan still would not consider replacing her. He never could.

THE INFANTS

Still in the year of 1890, with two newborn in the family, at first life was in a disarray.

The baby boys needed nursing. The relatives made effort finding such woman in a hurry by taking turns and asking around, in at least four villages. Finally a young woman, some twenty kilometers away in employment on a large estate as a maidservant, had been located and eventually obtained. Her name was Anci. Her husband also worked there as a farmhand.

The couple's main reason for not minding a change, or a new residence, was the death of their first child who lived only for a week. It all happened recently, the loss was severe, and Anci wasn't even back to work. Yet hearing this new offer, they both seemed very willing to come.

The relatives too were glad to retain the couple for a better wage for similar work than what they were doing before, with the difference that the Garay family's holdings looked considerably smaller, and their way of life (including their habits) were modest in comparison to that of the previous employer's.

The Garays did not belong to the upper class.

It was on one of the hottest days of July when the couple came to them, and also the busiest on the fields considering that year the reaping could start early in the region. That's how one morning after eight, Peter Kis and his wife Anci arrived at the house.

"This is the "House of Renegades", folks! Take a good look at it. Something to do with the Great Revolution, I reckon. People came here hiding from the law . . . even a general. Or, that's what folks say . . . You get every kind of . . . . "So would the coachman describe the Garay residence with this unfinished sentence, because at stopping by the gate triggered to shift his mind for unloading the couple and be on his way to the inn where he could get his second plum brandy of the day which provided him motivation as well as calories. So have the newcomers found themselves at their destination in front of a house that didn't look a bit fancy; instead it gave the impression of a small fortress, by being dense and sturdy. "This is it!" they said, and stood there quietly, until after the first knock, knowing someone will show up to let them in.

They were right. Mariska came out hustling. She saw the young couple at the gate, next to them on the ground a wooden box that must have contained everything they owned. From this, she knew immediately who they were. At first glimpse, both of them looked slumbery, but she had no time for other people's business, having her own multiplied since her niece Julianna died, leaving her poor husband behind with seven children, but most of all her, the poor relation, to look after all of them, children, husband, household, fieldhands, everything. Mariska had no time for trivia.

And now that the reaping was under way, it has meant everybody on his toes, working hard like an ox. She did the same, having been overworked by the usual things, the household, the children, the newborn twins, the extras and everything else . . . but mostly the heat! "Why these poor folks came today? Oh! What am I saying? This is the best time they came!" Mariska came to think of it, that they could start working right away as soon as she oriented them, and fed them. So in a hurry she ushered the couple inside, offering them breakfast. Fried bacon was ready, put aside on the stove, she just had to tell one of the servants to fix them scrambled eggs, and cut two full round slices of bread from her homemade loaf.

Except of this interval, Mariska really had no room for trifles, and was lacking the vim for cheering up anybody, considering they were hardly two weeks after Julianna's funeral . . . Besides, she was the only one home from the family with some of the younger children, and she had to deal with the cook who happened to be an impossible woman with a big mouth, but thanks to the Lord, she was hired only for the summer, when more people worked for the Garays and had to be fed in the house like everyone in the family. This was how Istvan wanted it. And now, because of the crowd, the handmaids were supposed to divide their help between herself and the cook. So far it couldn't be done without daily quarrels . . . "But let's hope this Summer won't last forever." Mariska was with these thoughts, when she saw that Peter the new man, was already outside, heading to the granary for finding work, and Anci, the young woman, just came up to her asking to show her duty. "Oh, yes . . . come with me! Here they are . . . asleep now. But not for long . . . the poor little darlings. The merchant's daughter . . . lives two houses away, feeds them with breastmilk. She has a baby girl. Thanks to the Lord, she has milk . . . but still, these two need a wetnurse . . . a nanny . . a mother! Do you have milk enough? They need you!"

And with these words, Anci has been introduced to Tass and Huba Garay. "These babies need me," she kept telling to herself, and for a second she felt like crying. "Two babies . . and they both need me!"

MARISKA

Mariska was the poor relation who had no means of support other than the Garays. She was a good woman. Living with them since her husband died (who left her penniless) was something she came to accept and held no grudges. The bad part was only, that now her loving niece had passed away.

Apart from the twins there were five more children to be raised anywhere from four to sixteen, mostly boys, and a girl who was nine years old. No wonder, these days she asked the Lord to bless her with extra strength in case Istvan would decide for her to raise the children, but could never finish her prayers without falling asleep.

Pushing sixty, Mariska came through as energetic and tireless. She was rotund, but still had good muscle tone. Owed to her good nature, the children loved her, and some perhaps took advantage of her, for she had no idea how to discipline teenage boys. Istvan in his turn was a stern father who said, by expecting her to follow suit: "Aunty, you are being too lenient. Trust me! My sons respect a slap more than they do a hundred words!" Well, it was an accurate observation regarding the Garay boys, but Mariska armed herself with the smile of a strong woman who withstood worse and was ready to take more as part of her defense against poverty, meanwhile proving her own worth through her daily self-monologues: "No! It wasn't me. No, no. It was him. His weaknesses . . . and irresponsible actions. Not that I didn't warn him. I did. He was just lousy at everything. The reason we ended up like this. Beggars! Oh, well! I shouldn't have married him. Everyone said so. My sister married the right man. She became rich, I became poor. She wasn't better looking, or anything. It's just, she was smarter. Yes, yes. I was crazy going after him . . . just because he knew how to serenade a girl. I was a fool. He promised me: "Mariska, you will live like a princess!" Sure. And there I was, lived like a frightened servant for years and years . . . Oh, well. Only when he passed away have I gotten this chance. My niece . . . this fine creature, God bless her soul. Oh! How sad! Well, anyway . . . but at least since I live here, it's different. I know who I am. These kids love me . . . quite a handful, I must say, these kids. Well, in any case, I have a family!"

CHAPTER 9

Closing A Century

THE WIDOWER

Istvan stopped having dreams. The work, and being out at the farmhouse was the only thing now . . .

On these days being too tired he could fall asleep as he was, and the next morning would wake facing bare walls and through the window a generous slice from the sky. But then there was a change . . .

One morning something came back, something he lost for so long. He couldn't quite say with words what it was, only that it was around. Another good thing, nobody asked him. Later on that day it struck him, he was home here where he found peace. Right here out of nowhere, alone, not where he was supposed to be, in his house in town, with the children. He tried to change this-God, he tried-but couldn't really make it work. "Next year I might!" he kept saying. But after the first Summer without Julianna, Istvan would never miss the comfort of their big house. Here on the farmstead he had no running water, only the well. Basic furniture was put in though, but still he had no intentions to install curtains or rugs. Since the place was ideal such as it was, anything would be of excess-he felt-and ultimately a bother. He liked it simple. He liked it enough for starting his life afresh. Thinking out a new beginning which might lead some place?

Normally Istvan, who woke early, soon after dawn began with a quick wash at the well. Then he went inspecting the crop. At the time the workers had breakfast, he returned from the fields, by then knowing what's going to be the work. With plate in hand, while eating he walked up and down, and assigned the work of the day. They discussed the job, and afterwards everybody went to do what had to be done. In the hottest of hours, from noon till two, they had lunch break. The work stopped around seven in the fields, but still the animals had to be fed.

After dinner Istvan liked to finish his day the way he started it, by taking a quick dip in the water-filled barrel that has been warmed by the Sun. At sunset, he smoked a pipe on the porch, took a short walk, and turned in for the time the dark was getting deeper and the Heavens were closing the sky.

KOSSUTH'S FUNERAL

Still in exile at ninety-two, Kossuth died in March of 1894. His remains had been returned from Turin, Italy, where he would spend his last years. Almost everyone wanted to be at the funeral, for it was a day of mourning for the nation. "Paying last respect to the great man is the least my generation can do," thought Istvan, and decided on taking all his family to Budapest, including the twins, who were four years old at the time. He bought hastily for each a Hungarian "Attila", the black braided suit one used to wear on formal occasions, and the black hat that would go with it, and it's indispensable addition of egret feather, just like their fathers or grandfathers would have it, whenever similar conjunctures have prompted them to dress up like good Magyars.

The major part of the journey was taken by train. The trip opened up a whole new world, for the youngsters had not yet been travelling on a train before, which made them inquisitive and fluttered. But soon they both would fall asleep, while their sister Julianna peeled off their new urban attire from them in exchange of a lighter blanket.

On this day everything was new and awesome for Istvan's family. Most particularly Budapest, the thriving metropolis with its wide avenues, magnificent palaces and public buildings all of fine architecture, the bridges over the Danube, the parks, the Castle Hill, Buda . . .

Of course, there were hundreds of things to see, but . . . this wasn't their reason for coming here. They all came for the great man's funeral. People gathered here from every part of the country with the same thoughts. Not thousands, but millions of them. The procession was so long and wide, that it seemed the last rows could never get to the entrance of the Kerepes cemetery. Since the crowd still expanded the children had no idea what else to do other than cling to their father, the only man they knew in Budapest or in this giant convergence.

Not minding their good dress, some young men climbed to trees only to see a black river of people as if comparing the overview here to the Danube from Gellert Hill, where one sees neither beginning nor end to it, only a frightening volume of water flowing from Black Forest to Black Sea, as it was today with this endless procession of mourners. Istvan was moved to tears. This day had significance. Growing a bit older, now he saw Kossuth gave a definite direction to his life, more what he admitted when he was young. Denying him led nowhere. This man still-this time with his death-pushed himself for taking a central role, just like he did in Arpad's life or through him in Erzsebet's life. Did he still aspire to be a conscience of the nation? Looking around here today the answer came easily and Istvan said yes. On this day he was acutely aware how his birth coincided with Kossuth's departure, and that of the surrender. "I was born on the day you left your country. I wanted to be here when you returned to it. At last . . . you came home," thought Istvan and wiped his eyes.

Lots of pictures were taken. Special photographic machines were attached to roofs, and to the gates of the cemetery. This way the crowd could be photographed too. Istvan must have liked the whole idea, because the next day on their way home he said, "Now you can tell your children and grandchildren, how it was at the funeral." When they arrived to K., a family picture was taken and then pictures of each child in solo. The twins took the stand together. Later, they joked naming it our funerary picture". It didn't take long before the Kossuth albums would be published. Several of them. Istvan himself mail-ordered two versions. On the last pages he was proud to see the bird view pictures, where the boys attempted to find themselves in the crowd. But later, arriving at the age of adolescence (or, age of disrespect?) the twins would compose poems like: "In the picture we are in hat, and Kossuth is dead," or "We had a picture when Kossuth was dead and we were in hat." Somebody must have reported this to Istvan, because their father cornered them, asking if it was true. He slapped both young men twice and locked them in separate rooms for a day with no food. The next day he asked them: "Answer me only this. Do you want to grow up and turn into criminals who end up in prison, or want to be respectful, clear-headed men?" The boys said they wished to be the latter and apologized. As a matter of fact in a year or two they both were ashamed of the poems. Only their old aunt, who thought they were funny, urged them to write poetry. Mariska had good judgment. Also, she was fairly good at organizing the servants of her household and by taking care of the fieldworkers, considering the Garays provided them food and shelter. During Summers, her work was tripled because more people would be employed, which made her feel they were running an army barrack, from where only the cannons were missing. But of course the Winters were different. Then she had time to read books.

Either by accident or design, the twins were raised collectively. Well, everyone had a say in what they did or how they did it. So the boys learned to be content with each other's company. They were much alike, with a notable difference in their temperament. Huba was an explorer, who would take the lead. Tass was his follower, the one who would work out the details. And so, from early on there was a bond between the boys. By growing older, they gradually came to grasp what their birth must have cost, and how their father might feel about it. As years went by, they had an understanding that their mother won't be replaced, and they would always be an incomplete family. That's why deep within Tass and Huba looked for ways to please their father . . . as if there was a chance to make up to him.

Their only sister Julianna was nine years old when the twins were born, and she became their little mother almost from the start. Pretending they were hers, she spent a lot of time with them. They were her pride. She liked to take them everywhere when she wasn't in school, played with them endlessly and taught them things they would understand. The three grew close.

Nine years later Julianna had married the new veterinary who came to town that year. It was love at first sight, and not even Istvan found basis, in where he would oppose the only son-in-law; which of course made everyone happy. On her wedding, Julianna promised to her young brothers: "You come and see me every day or, any time you feel like it."

Well, the boys kept coming up until a year later, when their sister suddenly passed away. She was nineteen, and the twins only ten. She gave birth to her first baby and died soon afterwards, in the complications of childbirth.

It all happened in 1900, when Mother Earth bore a new century . . . .

Chapter 10

The New Century

GENTRIES AND ARISTOCRATS

At about the time a new century began to wear on the firmament, a transformation has been unfolding on the Hungarian political scene. On a dramatic tone it might also be termed a change of guard between two classes, the aristocracy and the gentry.

The gentry, this very populous class had finally emerged from a deep sleep for getting involved on more than one level in matters of state, in the government, legislation, and in the judiciary, obtaining active roles in most of these. Coming along by the thousand, they filled up nearly all administrative posts, and were creating positions hundreds of thousands more by the time their offspring were ready for office. It would be done not just serving the government and getting a stake in politics and power, but to build out their own network at last (in their final hours), as it happened before them by the aristocracy, or after them by the bourgeoisie, or by the proletariat long after the gentry has gone, which departure was almost as swift as sad, since they were eliminated by terror and force.

But at the time of our story, this old class has just came of age and was on a march to be a new social and political force. So the gentry-this landed middle class with some form of noble title-was planting itself everywhere from the capital offices to the county-states. This move was no longer about maintaining a lifestyle, nor about proving their worth to the magnates, to the peasantry or to the bourgeoisie. They had no desire to prove anything to anybody. They were secure with themselves.

Then, what was it all about?

Understanding their purpose, the shift had much less to do with saving an era that had vanished long ago, or of the lifestyle of a Magyar nabob, which has been a far cry from their own. These people experienced losses, and by this time, some even tasted poverty.

Even if their move has a conspiratory clang to it suggesting some unfulfilled social longing, one has to point out, such longing has been dormant in them at this stage. They had other reasons however, each more serious. This class had recently went down and was on the verge of losing everything, if only its members wouldn't come up with a survival strategy. They were poor . . . And because of it, the gentry went to work. This time not only on his own land, but to work for a common good which launched him in government service. It was a necessity they found jobs with regular salary. The situation was grave; they could no longer be financially solvent as they learned, under the new economic rules of the world, of Europe, and of the Monarchy! They were also finding out year after year how the heavy land-taxes brought them down, preventing them to keep their estate intact, or at all staying afloat, and at the same time supporting a family. How could they under such conditions preview the future in a progressive, optimistic light?

For this economically declining class, survival was the first step, and the second, making a comeback. Obviously they had to implement changes within, and to learn aggressive maneuverings before thinking of success.

Altogether their survival coincided that fortunate juxtaposition in time, in regard to the stabilizing needs of a monarch, who was fed up and tired of costly wars. The Emperor had his own agenda no doubt, but still he looked for people with whom he could meet halfway. Give or take a concession, he looked for a new support group which wouldn't pose political risks in any embarrassing fashion.

He saw to it, these people were active, and ready to help to raise a country to prosperity. That they were able to project a homogeneous front, was another prerequisite. Franz Joseph I. recognized the gentry to be a substantial class with a quarter of a million people or above it (just in Hungary) if he counted their children in tow.

The Emperor, who thought it all through, wouldn't let them down, or (as was in their case), to let them slip deeper. To a degree, he stabilized their existence by giving them a chance to run and maintain a bureaucratic apparatus, something he would watch to grow, until every corner of the Dual Monarchy would be governed with equal efficiency and fervor.

Needless to say, these years have set off an often invigorating and sometimes tiresome new game between the "K. und K." (Kaiser und Konig), and of Hungary. The Emperor of the Dual Monarchy had his good days though. At least he hadn't had to endure the Magyar aristocrats' further bickering at court. This time, they were replaced and kind of left out from the business of running Hungary, even if it was their birthright, secured for so long by ancient law.

Well, it seemed an entirely different era was in the making . . . Indeed, a very different century.

ISTVAN THE FATHER

If harvest was over, in a matter of weeks Winter could be at the door . . .

Even though old Mariska warned them just last week: "Pull yourselves together. Your father comes home any day now. He won't like it!" How useless it was to warn them! In any case, she told it once, and gave up on it. Prediction or no prediction, by Thursday afternoon Istvan returned, to find the house upside down and not only the boys' rooms. What he saw angered him, so after dinner he proceeded to give a speech to his family, which to his children sounded like a synopsis of all his previous lectures.

As Tass and Huba would recall years later, these were the closing words: "If your shabbiness will become a habit, and takes hold on your lives, then I can ask you nothing but this: Do you wish to end up with the Gypsies? At the end of town, there, behind the cemetery? In that dirt?"

The boys wouldn't dare to look at him. By examining their lap, they sat in silence. Still, Huba didn't find particularly threatening what his father just said. Not sharing his view, he didn't think the Gypsy row was such a bad place. He had a friend from that district who used to join them playing football. By the way! That boy was very good at climbing to the roof, to any roof for rescuing the ball if it would get stuck up there, and certainly the most alert, when they have got in the mood, trapping a prairie dog in its pit. They had so much fun flooding the poor thing. Zsiga was quick, and he was funny. It is true, he has been constantly hungry, but so have they, considering how much energy they would use up, just getting through the day.

Gypsies? Sure, they looked kind of down and out by the standards of wealthy farmers who owned the lands and a farmstead and a house in town with huge beautiful gardens.

These Gypsies had none of these . . . "But probably it didn't bother them," thought Huba. Because any time he went by looking for his friend Zsiga, his people seemed to be in good spirit, laughing or just being altogether in an easier state of mind, compared to this fat, rich town, where people smiled once a year if they had to. Huba did not volunteer for telling his observations to his father. He kept quiet about it. In these years—understandably-Tass and Huba were biased by their fellow townsmen, because the neighbors objected to the boys' overly loud conduct. At first, people would complain to their old Aunt Mariska. And later, somehow all of their daily shouting, screaming and fighting had reached their father's ears directly or indirectly, but always much sooner than they would have liked.

If Istvan had put it in retrospect, most of his sons were unruly at one time or another but were urged to grow out of it. Well, he made sure that they would. Istvan was very serious. He trusted his visions about his family's needs. "At this stage of their development, one has to guide and advise them. They cannot possibly understand themselves, nor the world, in such early age. So, I better watch out for them, for the future is at stake. And their morality."

Also, he was convinced, children benefit from a father's strong hand, therefore he wouldn't think twice before slapping them if they deserved it. In raising children, he trusted the old fashioned tools. They were reliable. And discipline was among them. He would say: "Until they feel the benefits, and conquer those dark corners . . . we all have! Until they play by the rules. Because there are rules we all have to learn and obey. Only then can one say: "I grew up. I am a man, who is responsible for his actions."

Chapter 11

The Acquisition

DESIRE NOT TO HAVE

Kuki Baranyi's inheritance reminded those who knew him of a flowing river both in profusion and obstinacy. His three aunts who were not married and were short of a suitable heir, made him inherit vast lands, forests, a lumber business and a grainmill. Having been replenished with such responsibility, Kuki felt overloaded. He did not need this inheritance! It went beyond his personal needs, and far beyond his concerns.

As a young boy he wasn't sure if he could measure up to the family's expectation. Apparently his father, without being aware of it, only reinforced the potential impostor in him, for lending this piece of advice: "Don't say what you want to your aunts. It won't take you far. Learn to tell them what they want to hear . . ."

Kuki still remembered the years when he tried eluding his aunts at all costs. Not that he had no high regards for them! He had. But he was uneasy, one day they find him out, saying: "The dear nephew was the worst choice for the continuation of our business and a nightmare for representing family interests." Kuki was not looking forward to this kind of an unveiling ceremony. Yet he knew, it was going to happen.—It was just matter of time.

Meanwhile, as if postponing the inevitable, he travelled in Europe a good part of the year, often making vague references about foreign studies, or suggesting that his mind was engaged in new methods or it was worthwhile studying Technology and Machinery. As a result, his aunts lived in the hope, Kuki will come home when he is ready, filled with useful experiences he gathered abroad and soon, very soon, he will take over the business. "Perhaps he will run it better than we did?!" Also the ladies liked to tell one another: "I am sure he is planning to bring new inventions here . . . I can tell you, he is very much unlike his father . . . he has character!"

Even if it has not yet been obvious to everyone, Kuki had a legacy from his father. They shared the talent of getting rid of any wealth for which they never worked.

One might think, when means of livelihood is secured for someone in such fashion, his worries are seldom existential. The same thought applied to Kuki. He felt fine, as far as he was entertained. Yet he had to shield it from the ladies, of whom he was obliged to visit once each year. By growing older, they kept to the only life they knew. Their philosophy was rather simple. It said: "Be puritanical and work!" Of which Kuki thought: "Easier preached than done." The old ladies' affirmations were made up by a long list of abstinences, that they would follow to the letter. Well, two of them would, competing, and the third one had no choice but to go with it.

As a child, Kuki used to spend a few weeks each Summer in their villa. Still he could recall the austerity of the place, by entering the building. It was like being alternately hit with a club and a bucket of cold water. The house had its air of forced modesty. Any sign of grandeur was banished, warding off dissipation and squander, the very last things this family needed.

Kuki as a boy had felt a strange kind of guilt after the first week, that only kept growing till he stayed around them and relief when at last his father came to fetch him. The last day wasn't any better. He had to witness the fight between his father and aunts on life's meaning and the proper manner of pursuing it. The ladies fought bitterly with their only male cousin, and parted in such disagreement that it only enhanced, not merely postponed, the mutual aversion they seemed to have, for yet another year. Oh, that bickering! Kuki saw it useless, like carrying water in a sieve, yet it has been the only day of the year when the ladies had a chance for a tete-a-tete talk on the morals of somebody who was wearing the Baranyi name. He was reminded of his responsibilities in connection to his individualistic whims. At last his reputation was discussed, and his father withstood it all. Still, the day served young Kuki well. (As it should his father.) But somehow it ended, and the male visitors left with refreshed memories on what they should do, or should not do, but mostly on what they must not do.

In their carriage on the way back, Kuki asked his father: "How can I convince my Aunties? They dismiss what I think . . . They don't listen at all . . .

His father calmed him: "Well. Don't pay attention to them. Quarrelsome women . . . but very rich . . ."

DESIRE TO HAVE

As weeks have pushed months into years, filling up again a calendar, so had Istvan built an aspiration for a large piece of land, which belonged to Kuki Baranyi, the gentry.

The Baranyis were an old family. In the last two hundred years they lived to the South of the lower banks of the Tisza, the long river with even longer delineations, ascribed to it by historians, reformers, poets, or by people from the Highlands to the Plains. These people, and the ones farming by who knew the Tisza so well, claimed to meet the soul of the river.

The Tisza traversed from Russia to Hungary. This was always the "Most Magyar River," for getting its substance here in the Carpathian Basin where this nation gets hers.

Anyhow, the mighty river was full with mysteries. People still remembered in Istvan's time the talk of those bargemen (the drifters) who would take one or two rides a year on it, for having this the only way of transporting timber from the Highlands to the heart of the country.

In this region, the Baranyis had vast holdings; among them a good sized riverbottom land, not yet cultivated. If rivers change courses, new generations in old families do the same. So it's safe to say young Baranyi was not an exception. Though at first his relatives put up a fight. In their effort to guide him on the right path, he was replenished with ideals, inspiring and noble, of which he didn't care for, and didn't follow. Instead, akin to a river's passage Kuki made himself known by drinking his way through the county, and far beyond. Doing this effortlessly for twenty some years, Kuki saw no reason to stop with it now, when he had established himself in every drinking hole. In these places he would be greeted like he was coming home! Hmmm . . . probably even more.

Only, this would not be all. Kuki was in debt. By putting it bluntly, up to his ears. Unfortunately the drinking, card playing and womanizing have lasted long enough for taking their toll, and not only on his estates. His willpower was in equally bad shape. But still, Kuki wouldn't give up this lifestyle to save the last crumbs of his wealth. So, no one was surprised if the relatives endlessly referred to his one-time beneficiaries, his three aunts: "The poor darlings. Have they lived to see how Kuki squandered their estate and the business, they would put him in chain! This failure has ruined the Baranyi name."

Well, the news travelled in circles. And since everyone knew of the squeeze, most everyone drew pleasure from discussing it.

Istvan was not interested in gossips about Baranyi, yet heard enough to maintain, soon he has to make his move. His concern strictly remained that good piece of Baranyi-land laying by the Northeast section of the county. "It's going to be mine!" he asserted, and began taking surveying trips to the scene. Istvan would leave town by cutting across the meadows and using that narrow trail to the North, before he could get to the main road, from where it was fifteen kilometers ride. He didn't mind the distance. Never met anybody while he was there, saw little animals, nice group of acacia trees, clearings and savannah-like vegetations alternating, as they made up the characteristic beauty of the region. Istvan could never resist to pick up a handful of dirt from the ground. It was random and impulsive the way he did it, then grinding it between two fingers, he would decide: "Dark, alluvial deposit. Good for grain. Perfect for what I want!" It not only had a good touch to it, but smelled surprisingly good. At this stage Istvan had to guard himself not to be too emotional about his discovery. The time was not yet ripe for it. Nonetheless, from then on he had this habit of going to the "Baranyi Puszta" and staying there for hours. There, he could work out the next step.

IN THE TOWN OF B.

People liked to know Baranyi's affairs, and so far he would not disappoint them.

In the town of B. nothing went in secret, where nearly everyone cited the latest of Kuki's scoundrels, among them the young apprentice from the bakery. Like this morning, when the boy had to quibble over a minuscule detail, standing at the back door of the Golden Crown Hotel, where he was supposed to deliver three basketful of bread twice a day, every day of the week. Just as he was to explain to the new kitchen maid how Kuki has been caught "in flagrante," two minutes later one of the cooks showed up to discredit him. He took the liberty of brushing off the boy's version, in order to present his own. The type who claimed to know everything, this time posed as some Baranyi expert, even if self-proclaimed. Obviously the boy from the bakery did not like this, so he turned to the girl, "I must be off. My boss . . . gonna to skin me alive if . . . Well, so long Marika!" he said, leaving them at the door. The girl was upset. "Why doesn't this idiot leave us alone? He ain't even the cook! That's what he brags about, but he ain't that. Trying to look like somebody? He stands there all day, chopping onions and cabbages. The cook tells him what to do!"

At this hour the back alley was crowded. The local producers huddled here, offering vegetables and fruits for travellers. The rear of the hotel would also open here, with its service entrances. Suppliers, delivering general goods to the storage and kitchen would come here daily, which turned it into a non-official gathering place, with those inevitable dubious deals. Of course the management wasn't too proud, knowing this. "It's an embarrassment, and we must force them out! It's not what we are about! It gives a false picture to our guests. As if . . . they were on the Balkan some place. In one of those noisy, rat-infested cities!"

The building-a three storey high Baroque palace-stuccoed in pale yellow, looked impressive from the street. The guests who used to stay here, would confirm much the same: "The hotel stands for Southern refinement, in the old style. It's comfortable, discreet, quiet. The management is eager to serve you. So, why shouldn't I come here?"

Needless to say, the facade only enhanced this image. At the front, between the second and third floor, a writing, cast in gold had spelled out: Golden Crown Hotel. In consideration to travellers not quite up to semantics, the real thing would also be there, to speak for itself. An oversized gilded relief, a golden crown was placed on the building, slightly above the balcony. True, it was the only balcony the hotel could show, but was fit for an emperor where he could wave or bless his subjects with crown and everything, in case matters of state would force him to come to this (by reference to his scale of existence) "humble but proud town of ours." These were the visions of the hotelier on His Majesty Franz Joseph I., Emperor of Austria and King of Hungary, in relation to the crowned balcony. He talked of it often, saying, unless His Majesty actually comes here to stand on it, it leaves them-all good patriots-with a sense of exclusion from this corpulent Monarchy.

Istvan was nearly as dusty as his horses on arrival to the Golden Crown Hotel at mid-morning, the place he would stay when he came to town in business. Today of all days, annoyingly, he had not found the reception in best order. His luggage was taken in, but could not see even one of the stable hands at the main entrance. So, he got out of the carriage and went around the building to trace them, grumbling. "Where did they go? They disappear like camphor." Working himself through the crowd, he spotted one stableboy standing at the steps by the kitchen door, being immersed 'in the listening of the boy from the bakery, and of the cook. Stepping closer, Istvan could hear what it was all about. They were gossiping on none else than Kuki Baranyi, so Istvan was supplied with two versions of Kuki's latest, without really asking for it.

"When you are finished here young man . . . would you mind getting back to your duty?" he called out, for which the boy came to his senses and ran to the front of the building, apologizing in earnest. "Sorry Sir, Mr. Garay. I came for my cup of coffee to the door and . . . I stayed. I'll feed your horses in no time. Yes Sir. Clean them too. I mean . . . it won't happen again."

After his carriage was properly parked in, and the horses were taken care of, Istvan wanted to get a breakfast. For that, the hotel's restaurant was the best. In the morning one could find here every kind of bacon and ham and a variety of sausages, made of different meat with Magyar paprika and fragrant spices. And also the Southern headcheese was served here, cold and thinly sliced. Some people had only this in the morning, taken with a sip of apricot brandy. They used to have freshly made potato and egg pie, cheese, coffee, and sweet cakes, more of the traditional kind. For breakfast, Istvan preferred only slightly smoked meats baked in the oven with sauerkraut and fried bacon on the side. By his standards, each meal had validated the good name of the restaurant. Most everyone agreed, its reputation was well-deserved for feeding out-of-towners and insiders alike, such as the juristic people, the county officials and their administrators.

After his breakfast, Istvan settled in one of the corner rooms, washed, and changed in half an hour like someone who still had a lot to do. From his window he could see the town flat and wide as it was, with its avenues dusted up by the constant coming and going of horse-drawn carriages. Some of those, weren't only finely crafted and fashioned by the latest styles, but perhaps were a bit too flighty for his taste. He had to think of his father, "How much he would appreciate these! . . ."

Istvan liked this town and took long walks here whenever he could. Just about everything made him realize this was the stronghold of the county-state. The mighty "Varmegye*". Here, buildings were sturdy and well-built, were always renovated at the same time, and exuded an air of rustic elegance, which Istvan thought was not only typical of the region but also most appropriate in this fast growing city—town. "Why not getting rid of anything outmoded in the pace these new handsome carriages appear? Why not?" he asked once more, and felt like a rebel.

After breakfast, Istvan was on his way to the land office. The secretary who led him to the registrar, closed the door and from then on could hear only undulated words from the discussion. They sounded like: ". . . inquiring . . . vicinity of . . . put my name . . . on sale . . . if foresee . . future four hundred . . ." The whole thing went faster than thought, so Istvan could attend other business. He checked his pocketwatch and walked to the bank. The director waited in his office, making time as long as thirty minutes to his client. His partners would be also there, talking on a muted tone until Istvan would enter. The bank, this oversized building gave an impression that huge deposits of money were stacked up to the ceiling. The clerks climbed the ladders to get it, each time someone borrowed, or withdrew money. In case someone deposited, they climbed up and put the money neatly back. Well, of course it wasn't so! After stepping in, one discovered the main hall was of an overwhelming space to its relative emptiness. It would also be cold. In any season of the year people sneezed, in the first five minutes of entering. The last disappointment one had to face, was the money or, the lack of it, that it was nowhere in sight but hidden somewhere in the safe.

When Istvan was in, they shook hands. They showed him a seat and one of them offered cigars. The director, a quickminded man, began to talk. "Mr. Garay, you did business with our bank before, you are a valued client. Tell us, how can we be of assistance?"

Istvan got straight to the point. "Gentlemen, I intend to expand my business. I have short and long-range plans." "Hmmm. Very interesting," said one of them.

"I am not in a hurry though. But, to someone like me, who has a big family, it makes sense to expand."

---

* The word is medieval, meaning fortress, with the surrounding towns and villages. In the text, it means a county-state.

The bankers-two of them brothers-smoking their strong Havanna cigars, absolutely agreed. Istvan continued. "The market is growing, I intend to produce more grain."

For this, they all went into the discussion and analysis of the current grain-market, and of the stabilizing factors, which kept the prices high within the last two years.

"I am thinking to invest in modern machinery, down the road," added Istvan. "But obviously, I need more land. I want to buy a substantial portion. Let's say, a 400 acre piece? If you know someone selling, let me know gentlemen."

The bank director was invigorated. "By all means, Mr. Garay. And how much cash do you have?"

Istvan told him very slowly: "I should say . . . half of the price. It depends of course on the sale price . . ." He talked like someone, who wasn't pressed by anything to the least.

"Mr. Garay, we have knowledge of two . . . or three lands of such size, being on the market. one is right in this county. When you decide which is your choice, or perhaps a third one . . . well, we'll draw up the papers. Knowing of your stock's value and your liquid assets, and your present estate, I don't see a problem. Lending conditions are good this year. Should I say, this year is the borrower's market?"

Istvan was smiling. He forgot to reply, as he was thinking. "I hope, you don't lose money though." But at last he said. "Ah! Very good gentlemen!"

THE TIME TO RELAX

With most business done, Istvan Garay headed back to the center. By now the mild weather has brought more people to the Corso. He still planned to see his solicitor, who advised him on property matters. That's why he sent word to him with the bellboy, earlier this morning.

When Istvan returned to the hotel, the receptionist gave him a letter. It read like this: "My dear friend, I have a nasty court-settlement today, which takes longer than anticipated. But late this evening I'll come to your hotel. Yours, Dr. Rakay."

It meant he had time. So, Istvan had a coffee in the foyer, ran through the papers, and with the afternoon still young, he thought best to explore the city. Strolling on the main street gave a chance to witness the changes since his last visit. There was fashion, for instance! The mode, women dressed up for going out. "My world! Those hats. How can a woman carry such a bulk on her head?" They put on a large hat, not far from the size of a millstone, and even put up there some dried fruit, if my eyes don't fail me, or a basket of flowers on top of all that." He frowned, and tried to get over it, which wasn't easy, considering later that afternoon he saw a lady's hat decorated with a stuffed bird, birdnest and twigs. Istvan would not believe if someone had told this. But he saw it. "Well, I never knew much about trifles or fashions. Women! They can surprise anybody!"

After dinner he stayed at the club room, where around eight his solicitor-has finally showed up.

The next morning was set aside for the steambath, and a visit to the barbershop.

The town had been famous for its thermal waters for centuries. When Hungary had broken up and divided at first into two, in 1526, and then into three in 1541 with the Turkish invasion of Buda, the Turks stationed here for an unprecedented length of time, and began constructing a minaret right away, and the Turkish bath, finishing both and using them for three generations, up until international politics forced them to realize the Ottoman Empire or what's left of it, had to fit back again into Turkey. They left, and the Mussulman buildings stayed; still in these days in remarkable shape. Other baths were built. The curative streams attracted travellers mostly with rheumatic aches and pains, who gladly spent a day or two sitting in a muddy, steaming water. "You come here crawling, and leave us running!" was a popular motto to one bath-house, by capitalizing on the water, the mud, the steam, the doctors, the nurses, the masseurs, the manicurists, the pedicurists, and even on the faith of the patients.

Quite close to the streams and to the small curative lakes, a botanic garden was planted by a Hungarian magnate and patriot. Acquiring these fields in the 1820s he created a smaller tropical garden amidst the big one, utilizing the thermal vapors, which would provide a microclimate to such plants and trees as frangepania, magnolia, jacaranda, lemon, orange, and the African flamboyant tree.

Istvan used to take only the steam, as he would today. Afterwards he was massaged, showered and ready for the barber. The barber was a funny man, who could handle anybody and anything with ease. He didn't mind sharing his views either which kept his customers from falling asleep. He also gave a good haircut. "Oh, what a day, Mr. Garay, what a day! I already cut three heads."

Istvan rescued saying: "Well, I hope you spare mine. I'll take a trim and a shave." The barber went on talking while he worked on Istvan's whiskers. "And how do you enjoy Sir, your visit? You know what happens in the world? There are every kind of news . . . Pardon me, turn to the left. Where was I? Oh, yes, have you walked down the Corso?"

"As a matter of fact, I have," replied Istvan. "And what do you make of the latest ladies' fashion, Sir?"

"Well, it's not my job to tell. But those hats. They are really . . ."

The barber jumped in on the subject. "You are quite right Sir, Mr. Garay." All together he had a lot to say about the weaker sex. "Those hats! These days women dare to put anything on their heads. Every kind of fabrication and idea goes-should I say-on and in their heads? How can they carry all that around? That weight? The weak creatures. And it's not only that. Oh no! If I may say so Sir, in these days, women do what they please. In dress, in behavior. Their talk of independence is a laugh. The "woman suffrage" opened a beehive to the'world. That door had flung open. For what? They say they wanted voting rights! I am asking what is so good about voting? Their rights? Nobody is bothering them. Men don't go to the kitchen. Why should they? I dare say if they keep doing this, one day they might decide that we are the enemy. Men! But I am asking this. Who is going to protect them if we are the enemy?"

BEHIND CLOSED DOORS

People assumed life was stable, and things went well at C. county-state. And why shouldn't they go well? After all, it was a stronghold! Regarding the basics, everyone had something to eat, because plenty of people worked for it. Business was good. Producing grain or raising livestock was steady, commerce and trade was ever so vigorous, but so was corruption which was followed by scandals and gossips. Though it couldn't be too serious. If it was there-one generally believed-it wasn't as yet visible on the foundation of feudal Hungary. As tradition had it, occasional cracks could be plastered over in this powerful city, where most everyone had a weakness to feel either mighty, or prosperous.

Let's take the bank for instance, which handled Istvan's request in the last few weeks. The directors here mulled over the paperwork, while conducting an informal chat: "Lend him the money. If he goes down in one year, we are foreclosing in two years."

"Oh. I don't think he goes down. No. He is not your new son-in-law. No. He knows his trade. He is a peasant . . . this Garay."

"Well, you never know. My wife likes to brag how our daughter married the baron, but keeps silent of my money. If it wasn't me, and my daughter, the baron would be a titled pauper now. No more. A nobody . . . a . . . a landless figurehead. You see, we are a family of strong ties . . ."

"Sure you are! Hold on to it. So? What's the verdict? Should we lend the money to this Istvan Garay? And then see how much profit can he plow? . . ."

"All right," they said, and in an hour or so, all three signatures were on it.

From then on, things moved fast. Istvan bought the land (at first only one-third of it) and started putting broomcorn in the place where the drained marshes used to be. He worked harder than ever. Only after he secured a buyer with a five year contract did he lean back. "Now, I have a crop which pays. Good for a start, anyway." He also had sorghum, poppy seeds and sugar beet, considering these too sold well.

So in six months time, Istvan would also be "weighed" in another quarter of the city.

This one took place in the club at the county-seat, where for a gentleman was inconceivable making money from money. Yes, it seems the idea of barter was still closer to the members' heart, than speculation at the Burse would ever be.

Heavy in design with Dorian columns, the club was an old manor house. By the entrance, ancient symbols were carved in stone, the griff, the dragon and the stag. Spacious and inviting inside, the building had its own grand library, packed with rare books in Latin, Greek and German (still in the Gothic alphabet), some of them dating back as far as the 18th century. The dining room wall has been decorated with pewter plates and serving dishes while the cups adorned the shelves. An aquamanile stood at the door and was believed to be from the 15th century. Regardless of its beauty, the vessel was illfitted to the place, but the members insisted on keeping it where it was, saying: "The Archbishop wouldn't have an eye for it." Well, let's just say, they didn't think he deserved it. So the object stayed much as they have, for they were all quite stationary.

Following lunch hours the gentlemen were still smoking, and some were taking a nap, until the conversation had some lift to it.

"Kuki Baranyi went down, I hear," someone said.

"Huh! Not surprised. Are you?"

"Not particularly. But the new owner . . . who is the chap?" "Who? Who bought the land?"

"I tell you. He lives down South from the county-seat. Has a house in K. I hear, his father was the Hussar Colonel, Garay. He is the son. Sure you are familiar with that renegade story! The colonel's wife, you know. Great Lady."

"And so, what sort is this chap?" joined a member in, who just made himself available upon terminating his nap.

"What sort? I tell you," someone replied. "He is a Seven Plum Tree Nobility."

"Oh well now. That's an improvement! A surprise really, that Kuki's lands didn't go to a Jew."

"Sure, that's good news. And a surprise."

"Yes. Yes, I suppose it is."

When the matter was thoroughly discussed and closed, one of the members made a motion:

"This Garay chap. Why don't we get him in the club? We have to get him in."

"Quite. Why don't we? Get in touch with the man. And he has to come to the hunts too . . ."

"By all means."

Just consider! For a man of new means such distinguished offer might have appealed, or could have sounded as the right thing to do, only Istvan has never been accommodating to anybody. This quality was not part of his makeup. Besides, he was hardheaded even to consider that he should belong to any group. Istvan wasn't a group person. He preferred to do his own thing.

The cigarsmoking gentlemen couldn't possibly guess as yet (what they would learn in due time) that the "Garay chap . . ." doesn't care, or give a thought for their social register.

This wasn't why he bought the land. Well, he bought it because he wanted it.

Chapter 12

The Garays and the Devenys

A FARMER

When at last Istvan Garay bought the land, altogether 780 acres (in the first year 250 acres, and in the next two years twice as much), in five years he would enlarge his estate four times to its previous size. He pushed himself to buy at the time when others, by reasons of high taxation, were forced to sell. If larger lands were idle, they went down in those years. Istvan saw the solution in producing grain, or anything which had good market value. Having been committed to modern farming, in the first year his main concern was to make the land ready for it fast. Hiring was not difficult at the time as people were free to come and go. He asked the reliable ones to stay, to bring their families, of which some were glad to accept. There was a chance to make a new life there, while turning the wilderness around for profitable farmlands. By then his plans were ready for the house, the workers' quarters, the well, the farm buildings, storages, granaries, barns and stables, yards and silos. To begin with, he ordered new farm equipment, bought six of the heavy-set Murakozi horses, and two pair of oxen, so the land clearing could be set in motion. "If I produce, and double my product, the value of my land goes high. Not that I intend to sell it. God, no!"

Himself an orderly man, Istvan respected nature for its order and illusory simplicity. To a degree he was excited about experimentation, but then realized things followed a course anyway, without interference from man.

Puritan life appealed to him, which in some way put work in the center. In the work there was structure and that's what he needed most.

"Aren't you lonely out there, Istvan?" asked his sister-in-law once very unexpectedly.

"No, no. The work, you see," he replied a bit embarrassed by her bluntness. He felt out of place still, if others insisted he should in any way be part of a conversation. Without letting them know, Istvan was stunned how some people could talk for hours about nothing. Well, he didn't mind it, only made him think of that other place, and of his evenings alone on a clear night watching the sky. Such evenings felt as if a universal truth would be portioned out. He kept still then, thinking it might disappear, and he could end up feeling robbed.

Of course, Istvan would die first than tell this to anyone.

Ever since Istvan moved out to the new place, only the latter days of Autumn impelled him to come back to the place of good and bad memories, that he just left behind, literally distancing himself from it.

The house in town was occupied by the children and their old aunt. But it would be full far too often, to accommodate relatives and cousins who came to town. If they dropped by for a week, or just for a day, it made no difference, because by this time the house began to look like a train station anyway, with someone always coming and going, unpacking luggages or doing the reverse, like packing and leaving. It's safe to deduct, "The House of Renegades" could easily pass for an inn these years. No one had a feeling of home there, if the interior lost character by the hundreds of coarse changes. It happens to any house with willful adolescents in it, who learn the growing up game with absent parents.

But the boys didn't seem to mind. Their days were their own, ruled by their temper or mood. No one was there to restrict them. Not until late Autumn, that is. Because for the Winter their father would move home. By finding a new life, Istvan found himself no doubt, but things were more complex, if not downright convoluted when it came to his family. Back home, everything reminded him of Julianna. He knew, from that loss only the young ones could spring out virtually unhurt and healthy, like young animals who have great hunger for life. For they come to take the world with untamed curiosity, energy and will. He also knew, children were not concerned with the past. Why should they be? In their childish dreams, the seed of their future was slowly gestating into reality, yet were waiting some, till their arms would be strong enough to carry it.

"They will have their own life soon," told Istvan to himself, who did not want to be in their way now, or ever. But still, he wished he could influence them. That's the reason all the boys had to come to the farm at different times, to learn the trade whether they liked it or not. Learn about land, farming, grain producing, soil, irrigation and generally, about cultivation. Luckily the youngest ones got hooked on it, who planned to follow their father's footsteps. The others already were engaged elsewhere. One was about studying law, and two went ahead pursuing careers in the Army. About these years he would tell to his sons: "Remember. If someone gets rid of his property to cover gambling losses, that's all to him. He did not respect the land. He knew the life of pleasures and how to spend money, that others made for him. Someone had to work for it once, you know, sometime. But for him, it was easy. Always there. It's different if you make it. Working for it. It makes you feel like a man."

When still young, the twins Tass and Huba wondered what was the force pushing their father to obtain that much land? What was his reason? On Summers when they took turns in working on the farm, they could see how it was out there . . .

His farmstead was like a well-run kingdom where everyone knew his duty. Everyone was useful. Everyone worked for the land like a slave. Most of all Istvan.

"A strange kind of ruler!" they thought then, with irony.

A SCHOLAR

The Devenys' house was built in 1901 by Zoltan, when he would be in his twenties. A year earlier he moved here to N. to start his law practice, only not quite sure on what venue. Looking into the future, it seemed a good idea if he bought an existing building in the very center of this small town, in which he could build more rooms, in order to create that spacious urban home he often envisioned to have. He would change the facade to Classic Greek on this old house, which served well for a statement, as well as for an exordium to anything he believed in, or stood for, both professionally and privately.

Many urban homes in the last century would be built in Baroque. Those who could afford them, built it. Some, among the nobility, who couldn't, merely repaired the cracks, or touched up the exterior in some accepted style. But they preferred decorating in Baroque, or used its regional alterations. Evidently, years later a good many buildings of the area were viewed as an assortment of the Peasant Baroque. The traditional country-home of the gentry, either with Dorian or Ionic columns, still kept to the Greek Revival. This has been the favorite. Elsewhere in the country, in public buildings regardless of regional taste one could find every architectural style from Renaissance to Eclectic and the then modern Art Nouveau.

Well, young Deveny didn't mind the move to these provinces, where Romanticism has been transformed to a Southern mood, indicating more of a lifestyle and a state of mind which came with it. At the time young Zoltan Deveny was ready for practicing law, this locale projected a more commodious existence in contrast to the North. Apart from his professional plans, that year he had two reasons moving to this corner of the world. "I had to start somewhere, and I like the Plains," would be one, as he was shedding light to future plans with a tightlipped sentence, that made him sound grim and elusive. His second reason for the move would be his uncle's will. We have to talk of the good man now, who left a well-tended and profitable orchard to Zoltan, his nephew, who happened to be his only relative. There was also a sizeable land, maybe good for grazing cattle, but not substantial for farming, as it was spelled out in the deed, of which Zoltan carefully studied.

"Being an uncompromising bachelor, my uncle's passions (if any) were channeled into his gardens, no doubt," said young Deveny, who regarded his inheritance,the grove, a viable enterprise. He decided to run it as it was before and by the same people, to whom he later confessed: "I had neither training, nor experience on this field."

Locals in N. did not understand why would the new proprietor of the grove put up residence in the village. Why not in the country? His claim: "A house in town is a good choice for my plans," caused a wild uproar, but of the best kind. "Why indeed! We should be happy. A most eligible single young man is moving to the village!"

So much for the news. Arriving freshly to the South, Zoltan Deveny the young lawyer buried himself at once in Philology and historic research to the dismay of local matrons, who, in the last two hundred years employed their maneuvering tactics with brilliance as they were directing the social scene. We must report, Zoltan knew nothing of it. Even though he should have understood the simple fact, these ladies had daughters to worry about. Worry is the best word when one's mind is focussed on one desperate goal. Wedding! Yes, wedding. The main theme of a woman's life.

The early years of this century would still sustain those allusive ambitions in womenfolk, who haven't been yet reading every kind of revolutionary ideas on what women can do, would do, could do, should do, or shall do, until this century was out.

If we bend just an inch towards the judgment of these local mothers, we will sympathize, or even agree that in the category of "hopefuls," the young-lawyer has been a disappointment. A huge one! To begin with, he was away most of the year. At first, many believed he went away as a lobbyist, for having the good sense of getting deeper in politics, like anyone should in his standing. Who knows? Maybe his mind was not yet on women. Which is to say, there was hope, he may choose a wife from this very locale. Gradually and painfully however, they had to learn who young Deveny was. Well, he was a loner, kind of hopeless case . . . Really. Who was this man? For the social circles of this tiny town, his enigma 'was not yet resolved. Men found him difficult to talk to . . . but again, who knows? After all, he is from a good family. "An excellent family!" It was told at the Gentlemen's Club in the capital city of this county-state.

"We have to take into consideration, not everyone is a great storyteller. Just as well. Gentlemen, it might be an asset, if some of us can keep his thoughts."

On that day the gentlemen finally agreed: "The Deveny fellow is a listener!" When their conclusion reached the young man, he did not object. Considering his not so social uncle, who was called "The Hermit," he did better.

In the meantime, especially after harvest, Deveny took lengthy trips to Budapest, where he would spend days in the "Szechenyi Library", working on reasearch. Being there, he couldn't help dreaming and planning that one day he too will leave a library to his village, just like Count Ferencz Szechenyi donated his to the nation. This man inspired his son Istvan Szechenyi, who in return started the Reform Age, in the 1820s. It demanded constant work, and money, and effort to launch his countless projects, that would go on, till the fall of the Revolution. "What a man he was, what a man!" sighed Zoltan. "A great man. A very great one!"

Deveny was aware, his idea of a library was too modest in comparison, but felt it equally inspired. He played with this thought: if the proceedings of his orchard could finance it, he would be out of the woods. Just now out on the street he felt slightly dizzy, and decided to take a walk. Zoltan talked audibly when at last he knew the plan: "I can work as an attorney. It will cover my needs and expenses. And I can give free legal advice once a week, each week for the poor, and still won't go hungry!"

And there was another thing. A great desire to spend sufficient time on his writings and research! So when returned to the village, Zoltan came with large wooden boxes, all filled with books. The books kept coming most of the year for forty years from all over the world, for he could read Latin, Greek, German, English and French, would correspond in German, English and French, and would use Latin in legal matters.

If he travelled, he did not discuss it. To say he wasn't impressed with the world, is highly hypothetic. But it's fair to say, nobody knew what he thought. A close friend in the South who knew him for years, once elaborated: "The man was dropped in the wrong century. Never at ease with anyone, friends, family, or strangers." His other friends, certain he was distinguished in many ways, weren't sure if it wasn't a burden on him.

True to his words, the young man who previously spent years in Budapest now set up his office in N. and did there what was needed. He wrote letters, inquiries, complaints and just about anything on their behalf on that "one day" and took no payment for it.

That's how he became locally known, really known. Through his deeds. Which made him almost transparent . . . Well then, why was he still so mysterious?

Chapter 13

The Third Generation

Motto:

"The world was an exciting place. So my brother and I took a plunge . . . to see, what was there for us?"

—Huba Garay

THE TWINS RETURN FROM SCHOOL

It was the Summer of 1913. The students left in flocks in the last two days, emptying the part of town where the university and dormitory buildings were located.

For Tass and Huba the two years here used to feel like eternity, yet now that ended . . . they were a bit daunted by it. At the same time their longing for home was stronger than anything. The twins boarded the train and were sitting with outstretched limbs, immersed in their thoughts about manly pleasures like hunting or horseback riding back home, on the Plains. How much they missed these, in the confinement of school! Their thoughts went ahead of them, ahead of the speeding train.

They were returning from Germany after finishing their education in Agriculture at the Hochschoole of M. Huba studied Horticulture and Soil Management, Tass had interest in Aquaculture and Forestry. They both began to do research in the school and had plans to do their own, sometime soon . . . Maybe this year? Of course a lot depended on their father. Will they agree at least on the basics of Agriculture? Or, he will oppose them? When the twins came of age, Istvan signed part of their inheritance in their name . . . It was a good start, since in theory they were free to do what they wanted with their land. On earning their degree, somewhat later they testified it was good to be away from home because outside of Hungary, they learned to be better Magyars. More appreciative, they thought. However, such indexing at the final review turned out to be of secondary importance, for the primary goal was the study itself.

The school had a good reputation even on abroad. It expanded to teach and host different kind of students who would come from all over Germany or from the Monarchy.

During the first year Huba and Tass oriented themselves to the international crowd, all the more reason they were lodged in the same building and started taking language courses together. Also they met plenty of students in the canteen at mealtimes, some curious, some friendly, some indifferent. The rules and activities of fraternity life took up a lot of their time. Having lived in dormitory, sitting downstairs by the fire and taking active part in debates with fellow students at late evenings, opened the door to friendships. The twins attracted people. They were called the "Magyar-set."

One of their best friends. who had great vitality and talent in sports, came from Croatia. Another one (from Slovenia) would entertain them in the dining room with a variety of verbal skills, which included mimicking the professors. He was the center of attention, but as times passed the twins discovered more common ground with the Polish and Moldavian students. The football playing was best together, if their athlete friend gave a professional touch to the game. He had a lot to teach them about stamina, or about one's energy staying at the right level. For early Spring of 1912 (after their first year in school), theirs was considered a strong team, called "Foreign Students Team," playing opposite to the "German Students Team."

Obviously, they had little room for boredom. They would take short trips as far as classes could permit them, and once visited the North coastal cities of Bremen and Hamburg. This journey satisfied the curiosity of the twins, as well as justified an amazement of those, living in a landlocked country. "Wow! Now we can tell how the North Sea really looks like!" they said, by looking over the harbor. Their lives were full . . . Tass and Huba even took up fencing, or continued taking classes in Germany too, since a one-time champion ran a fencing school, famous for its technique and style.

By living in Germany they began to understand how in this country every aspect of life was serving a purpose, and if possible, the same one. Ideology, plans, growth, had great importance here. Just during their stay, the industry would grow considerably. Heavy steel, shipbuilding and trade, expanded to proportions not imagined before... "Strength" was the word the two young men kept hearing everywhere. Even in the school. The growth in economy permitted political strength, which in return permeated an ideology of expansion, not only physically but in self-importance. The feelings of supremacy were beginning to take forms.

For Tass and Huba, who were subjects of the Dual Monarchy (which equated considerable power in every way) and also being the citizens of a kingdom with early medieval roots, found it impressive that Germany, this relatively young country, formed by the previous principalities, was already a great power. Perhaps on the way to become a super-power.

At the beginning, Tass and Huba would frequently compare the two nations. They noticed, the main difference was in temperament and obviously in attitude. "Hungarians live for different ideals," said Tass, who wasn't too enthusiastic of what he saw there. "Tell me. To where this new sense of superiority leads people?" Huba replied swiftly: "It gives them a chance to grow" Somewhat later he added: "Expansion is quite good, until it stays within one's border . . ." "See? That was what I referred to!" said Tass attentively to his brother. Once when Tass noted the difference in their ways and sentiments, his brother complained: "They don't pursue freedom like I do. I wish to be free and belong to something bigger than me . . . without being run by it."

In their letters home, Tass wrote to their father: "We appreciate their method, for they combine strong agricultural studies with new research. You will be surprised father how our superficial knowledge has changed on land-management, soil, irrigation, or planting." As time went by they missed Hungary, the Great Plains, and their father. All those things they associated with home... but now, riding on the train, the brothers had time to muse between two borders, crossing from one world to the other. Huba was in a talkative mood: "It's hard to say how it is with them. I know, one needs discipline. Without it, nothing really goes . . . But in this country they don't mind if it is decreed . . . by an authority . . . because they seem to . . . want to mold in fully. To the "Fatherland". That's . . . Listen here! Tass! I just realized we say "my mother country" for homeland. See the difference? For us, Hungarians, it is more of an emotional tie. For them too, but . . . it is a masculine thing. A duty. As if the Fatherland tells them what they should do. And they do it And sometime later, all is explained why they had to do it." He stood up from his seat. He found their compartment too small, opened the window and continued. "With us, it is different! Almost in reverse. We, Hungarians, need inspiration. Then, we think about it, emotionally digest it, and at last live by it. If we agree on it at all! But, we move only if we are forced to. All in all, I don't think we are good followers." Huba stopped here. Leaned back and watched the landscape, as the train was leaving cattle, farmlands, barns, houses and trees. He used up his steam, yet felt easier that his views were declaimed on the subject.

Sometimes it was obvious even to them that living in a foreign country meant living by comparison, with their reference point remaining back home.

Next, Tass was deliberating on German practicality and how new inventions were put in use by wasting no time. "I admire their organizing talent. But, if I put things together . . . what if this talent and technical advancement won't let boundaries stand in the way? After all, Germany is becoming a naval power . . . on the lookout for colonies? I don't know. Who knows how they use all they have? And for what end?"

Just before noon the train would stop in the last German town. It was a busy station with incoming trains, with travellers standing by the platform, waiting, or running to catch a train, the one already pulling out. Newspaper boy, candyman and conductors all shouted their own verse related to the trade, thus creating a dissonance not at all unpleasant to listen to, until their crescendo had broken up by an incoming locomotive.

"This awful, awful noise! Who can take this?" frowned a young woman who was running the whole length of the platform, for she had exactly two minutes to board her train. The conductor did his best to orient her, telling her everything he knew. "Yes Miss. This is the one to Pressburg. We have exactly one hundred and twenty seconds from departure."

In a second the hoarder pushed a cart next to their wagon and started to load on some luggage. A few minutes later the same woman finding her way to the compartment that has been occupied by the twin brothers, showed up in her elegant, but loose attire. The brothers had an impression that this woman must have dressed in a hurry, having no chance to finish that prescribed look, that dictators of ladies' fashion usually dream up. Therefore, she was coming and going through the day unfinished, somewhere halfway from looking perfect. It could be possible too that she didn't think much of fashion if arrived to that tranquil simplicity, where appearance loses meaning.

"Gentlemen, can I use the remaining seats, or somebody . . . ?"

"Oh . . . yes. By all means!" They both jumped on their feet and helped her to get in with all the luggage, altogether six of them, including a food basket. After some exchange of politeness, she settled down. As it came to light, the lady travelled alone and was also heading to Pozsony, before she would return to Vienna, where she lived. In Germany she was just visiting. "Yes, I have relatives here too!" "How lucky you are, Miss!" one of them sighed. She has been open and friendly, but was not the type who could be described as "pretty ". Tass and Huba tried to guess her age, but couldn't. Could she be a woman who is ageless, who manages to look much the same at eighteen as she would at fifty-eight? Possible. But considering her flair and ebullience, the twins suspected she was young. Tass and Huba noticed how she talked, by being able to lead a conversation about general subjects "like a man," with her striking grown-up poise. The three of them became friendly very fast, a bit more than convention would have it though. But train journeys often defy conventions. They even made plans for the next day . . . why not? Since all of them will be in Pozsony! And later? Who knows? Her full name wasn't revealed as yet-only "Miriam—but the three have been eating her sandwiches for lunch, and of course by now the twins approved her idea of travelling with a full basket of food.

It was told Miriam never saw Pozsony before and was about to visit friends of her parents there. "I am lucky, it is true. I am well-acquainted with Europe, because of relatives here and there." Her life was unfolding as the train had run across this hilly and rugged terrain what would be called Sudetenland. The two brothers listened to every word she had to say, and she had a lot to say . . . For a year she studied in Zurich, meanwhile lived with relatives who own one of Zurich's many banks. She liked that city and found Switzerland "gemutlich" with everything in its proper place. Yes, Miriam realized how privileged she was to take courses at the best schools of Europe, but she assured them: "I know it sounds strange, but I prefer simple life. Simple life is good for the mind. It can stay focused on things. Things, which really matter . . ." The young woman neglected to mention what were those, because she was explaining the next step. "On the other hand, it would be foolish to deny from myself what life wants to offer me. Don't you agree?" They both did.

In the midst of lunch before they would start eating the candied fruits it was told she is Jewish, and at home they speak Yiddish. Her father who owns a jewelry store in Vienna, is very much for keeping the orthodox faith. "My father believes in progress, as far as it is in our interest. But doesn't promote mixing. He says, everyone has to maintain his traditions. If one denies his roots, his soul will shrink, and won't survive. So, he believes in that kind of balance . . . He says, we have to have that, who live in a diaspora." Suddenly Tass asked the young woman: "Do you feel the same way?" "Well? I wasn't tested so far . . . so, I don't know. Not yet. I can't see through it all . . . at this age. I should think these concerns come later. Young people are daring. They want to try their own ways. Don't you agree? I suppose it is the same with me."

Now the time came for coffee. They rang for service and soon a waiter showed up pushing a cart, with the aroma of freshly brewed coffee. After service, she picked up the conversation where it was left. "I am close to my mother. She is a genuine caring person. She is quite beautiful, you know. We go to Paris each year with her and my sister. My mother buys her gowns there. Hats too. Yes, I speak French and I love to be in Paris, because something very important is happening there always. Is it Art? or Literature? or, Philosophy? Everything begins there! Paris is the capital of the cosmopolitan world!" In a second, as a result of her wide and sudden gestures, her coffee was kicked over and spilled on her skirt, for Miriam there was a need to coordinate her enthusiasm with both arms. Now, she did make only this remark laughing. "My father says I talk like a windmill." The stain had the size of an apple, yet she didn't seem to care. "Who would notice a coffee stain? Tell me! Nobody!"

"The last time I was in Paris, my cousin told me of a group led by Raymond Duncan. And so, I wanted to meet them. It is very important what they do. They intend to revive an organic way of living, which is self-supporting. And he teaches how to grow your own food, cultivate cotton for its fiber and weave it, and to raise sheep to make your own wool, build your own house. It is a beautiful philosophy . . . You know, his sister is this gorgeous girl, the dancer, Isadora Duncan. She designs her dance on similar principles, saying, dancing is a way of life. Quite natural in fact. An expression of beauty, some sort of recollection of it . . . It is the revival of a Preclassic Age . . . I find it most inspiring. I really do. Apparently this organic revival is what Steiner says, and before him Goethe, philosophically expressing . . . and of course Madame Blavatsky, the great Theosophist . . . At any rate, I must know your address, so I can send you some of these books. Where in Hungary do you live? In Budapest?" The twins gave out a short laugh. "No, no. The place called: The "Nagy Magyar Alfold." "Meaning what?" asked the girl. Tass replied. "Great Hungarian Plains . . . the Flat Fertile Basin. The Breadbasket. That is where we live!"

Miriam's excitement grew. She clapped her hands: "I want to learn that name in Hungarian. Say it again . . . "Nagy . . . again . . . Magyar . . . again . . . Alfold."

The journey came to an end. Since they stopped checking their pocket watch when Miriam boarded the train, nothing had indicated the length of time they spent together, which went rather fast, nor the closeness of the city, to where they arrived. "We take you to an historic city tour of Pozsony tomorrow," offered Huba, who was no less captivated by her as his brother . . . "So, it's an easy goodbye." "I can't remember when did I have such nice fellow passengers!" said the girl in return.

Tass and Huba stayed in a friend's house for three days as guests. This family happened to own one of the old townhouses close to the Bishop's Palace and to the old "Diet" building. That part was considered the center of old Pozsony.

They discussed the day's excitement before going to bed. Huba brought up the subject teasingly. "Well? What's your guess? How old is she? Twenty? Thirty?" For some unknown reason, Tass didn't think the question was funny. He said: "I suppose it's all right with her. With her, one doesn't mind beauty at all . . ." He paused here, and continued: Besides . . . if you marry a beauty, you can watch her grow ugly." Huba couldn't miss saying this: "But with her, there is no such danger!" On this, they both had to laugh. Sometime later Huba finally said: "She is a fascinating woman. You forget everything else when she talks." "Yes, you do," agreed his brother fullheartedly.

Tass, Huba and Miriam would spend the next day sightseeing. Part of the day was dedicated to the castle and to the historic inner city. Tass wanted to be the first guide. "This city took the role, as the capital of Hungary from 1526, he began. "This is a terrible date for us. We call it the disaster of Mohacs. In 1526 at Mohacs we lost a battle, a king and two-thirds of a country to the Turks. It resulted in the partition of Hungary to the Ottoman ruled region, to Transylvania, and to Royal Hungary, under Habsburg rule." "This was the darkest period of our History," added Huba. "The situation lasted for 250 years, with minor changes here and there . . ." Tass continued, "Yes. It ended only in 1789. But the Hungarian Parliament continued working here, until 1848 . . . until the Great Revolution." "Also . . . the first university was established here, back in 1467," joined in Huba. The three of them were able to see certain old documents on display in the City Hall. The next walk took them to the Archbishop's Palace, a Baroque building, what has been hosting and witnessing the change of command many times. The famous "Peace of Pressburg" (Peace of Pozsony) was signed in this building by Napoleon and Francis II., after the battle of Austerlitz."

"I am sure the French visitors have more fun with this document than Austrians have," remarked the young woman teasingly, who showed great interest in everything on their tour. "Pozsony, Pozsony," repeated Miriam playfully. "City with many names. Hungarian, Slovakian, German versions. Pozsony, Bratislava, Pressburg! I feel the cosmopolitan flavor. Don't you?" Now they all were getting tired and looked for a place to sit down. So they had lunch in a small restaurant. After they ordered from the menu, the cook himself came out as he usually would, to discuss the finer details of roasting and the selection of herbs to the gravy. "Basalicom? Dalmatian Sage? So be it," he said and disappeared in the kitchen. Until the food was ready, the three of them had wine. Through the window they could see the street and a small square, the people passing by, and the coaches while they could hear the rhythmic noise they made on the cobblestone.

"I love when you talk of your . . . heritage," said Miriam who sipped her wine rather slowly. "I feel . . . or . . . seem to feel the suffering, this place has collected. I try to imagine how it was, let's say 400 years ago!? And of course it's not all. There are much more." Tass found himself very outgoing today. He was stimulated by their companion and possibly from the red wine they have been drinking. "Centuries of strife," he said. "For trying to keep what we used to have when we as a people started here. And . . . it is not easy. We have glorious times and grave losses. Like any other nation, I suppose." "It is true." replied the young woman. "If we keep the flame. It gives a . . . sense of purpose for people . . . As I was listening to you in the last couple of hours, it made me realize how well-grounded you both are. And I wonder . . . is it because you, as a nation, had to go through a lot? Or . . . are there other reasons too? What we can't understand, because they are hidden?" None of them talked for a while. Eventually Huba said this: "I always thought, the position . . . of being at the gate of East and

West made our country vulnerable. And it . . ." The other two could never learn the end of his sentence because the food was delivered to the table. It occupied them fully, so they could forget about Tartars and Turks and Habsburgs. Life seemed perfect as they raised their glasses to everything life was yet to offer. They were drinking for the future. Their future.

Before day's end, Huba and Tass invited her to visit the Hungarian Plains. "Why don't you come at early Autumn? We can all go out horseback riding, and . . ." "But I never tried horseback riding. You know, I am a city girl." "It's time you learned it. We have good horses. Father's pride. We would take you to the "Puszta", or "Steppe" if you will, for a day and a night, to sit by the campfire. Where the lights have this curious way to change . . ." explained Tass. "Change into what?" asked Miriam. "Into . . . dancing shadows with this open space around you. And the stars! The sky teaches you a great deal. And if you are lucky, during the day we might even see a mirage." "You are quite a poet, Tass. When it comes to your Puszta," told the young woman. She was moved. "That place must be a far cry from Vienna. And even though I would love to come, I am not sure if you would want me as a friend?!" "Why shouldn't we," asked Huba vehemently. "We do!" Her voice changed when she replied: "I never had such a good time with anyone like you two. Truly. And I want to thank you for it." Huba seized the moment by confirming it more than asking: "So? You come!" Miriam looked to Tass waiting if he repeats his brother's gusto, but he didn't. "Doesn't he ask me to come? Could it be, he has a sweetheart back home? Oh. But, why am I so emotional? He already asked me to come. What more do I want? I can't be this foolish!" Miriam realized there must be an understanding between the brothers what is running deep, negating the need for words. If one said, "Do come!", the other one has meant the same.

That night Miriam didn't go to sleep fast. "These Magyars! Interesting people. I want to know more about them, and . . . and I am sure I will!" She was thinking of the twins. The first notable difference between the two was their temperament, and use of language. Tass was not very talkative, but when he talked he carefully crafted what he said. He was more reserved than his brother, also reflective, and had a good grasp of reality. Probably he liked to spend time thinking and analyzing, concluded the young woman. Huba talked plainly and effectively. It showed a man of action, who gets into anything without fuss, solving problems as he meets them. "How perfect!" she thought.

"They are complimentary. One is fiery, the other is calm. I understand why they are so close!" Miriam still couldn't fall asleep. She was getting a glass of water, put on the light and looked for a book. She returned to bed with a German translation of Balzac, his book of "Old Goriot." She read it in French, still in high school and became one of her favorites. Yet tonight she wasn't tuned to reading. The happenings of the last two days kept her awake. The brothers! "Interesting people! In their behavior I see no pretense. They could be wild, exuberant and a bit sad. Almost at the same time. They reason with their heart. They involve you. They involved me!" Miriam has read about fifteen times the famous first sentences of the Balzac novel, but never could tell what was she reading. She remained widely awake, thinking through half of the night.

Chapter 14

Back Home

THE PLAINS

Here, everything related to agriculture. The rich fat lands surrounding the rural towns of the Plains reflected their thoughts, their storages, their corporeal bearings. People who lived here were impressed of things that could be weighed, measured, and sold on the market. It didn't matter for the locals if a person came from Paris or Vienna, or if claimed to see the "world." Here only those earned respect who were dedicated to rural life, took interest in farming, or in raising cattle, were running a dairy farm, raising pigs or poultry, breeding horses or dogs, or were busy with bees. From Spring to Fall the work was constant, and for events, there were the horse and cattle shows.

Anybody, who came here and bragged to be a cosmopolitan was regarded a bore. Some people went as far as to say, a stranger is at best an upstart, at worst a vagabond!

To sum it up, here, people had as much pride as other people had elsewhere in the world. No less, no more.

The twins were glad and very moved to see their father, who seemed to be pleased on their return. Only, he couldn't find a way to demonstrate it. As a result of constant strain and physical work Istvan was worn out, but wouldn't listen when his sons told him to slow down. He still lived away from town, on one of the homesteads (from which he had three now). So years later whenever Huba talked of his father, a profound sadness moved on his face. "Poor father! With my brother we talked about it all the time. We didn't quite understand him. He was a late version of some barefooted king, who built his kingdom and became a slave in it. But this was his ambition! I could not explain it otherwise. The least to myself . . . even though I tried. He was part pariah, part landbaron. The first served the second. The wealthier he became, the more he was the slave of the land. He wasn't a free man! Did he enjoy doing it? He must have. Else, he wouldn't do it. So his family had to come to terms with being wealthy, without making a show for it. I used to think on these a lot. Mostly as a rebel . . ."

A COURTSHIP

The men were discussing Sarajevo. It happened just days ago, and by now the news was everywhere, in every newspaper of the world. "Franz Ferdinand and his wife were assassinated in Sarajevo." Not that anyone in this country loved Franz Ferdinand, given the reason the Archduke had been a loud "Magyar-hater." Still, his hatred wasn't reciprocated enough to kill him for it. Not in this country anyway, for he was assassinated by Serbian extremists, in Serbia. Still, it was bad news. What will the Emperor do? How will he react? Will he send troops?' Where does it lead to? Will there be a war? It was a hot sunday afternoon, and the men talked for hours now . . . of the same thing. "Poor Archduke!" said Huba. "He wasn't very insightful selecting his enemies, was he? Would someone tell me why did he go to Sarajevo? To be shot at? He surely knew the Serbians' claim! And the rumor of their organizations! Yet he took his wife too. Who understands this?" "Yes," someone else added, "He walked into a trap . . . I wonder if the Pan-Serb movement will be halted, or . . . altogether aborted, now that . . ." "If we are dragged into a war . . . then, let's keep in mind that our "Kaiser und Konig" has an alliance with Germany."

"You mean the Triple Alliance?! Since Italy joined them in 1882 . . . "Yeah! That's right. They got to go together now, don't they? Hand in hand." "Think of it. Franz Joseph sought out Russia against the Hungarians in the 1849 war. When he was a young man. Now he is an old man. Abandons Russia, for the sake of a German alliance. I wonder which one is better."

Huba had been seated with the men, but was looking at Franciska all afternoon. It was his sixth or seventh visit in the last two months in a brand new capacity. Now, he was an official beau. Going by Southern tradition, he had to seek her parents' consent for seeing the girl, who happened to be their only child.

Huba knew the family and knew the girl before, who all of a sudden . . . well, grew up. When the twins returned from Germany and saw her the first time Huba couldn't look elsewhere. Franciska turned into a beautiful woman, which gave reason enough for young men like him coming to their house. By early May, however, he knew it wasn't just an attraction. It had more to it. He was falling in love. But since he couldn't be sure how the girl felt, he had intentions finding this out on each visit . . . He was a man of action, and he had to know. But until he could, it was a must that Huba did court the whole family . . . which in Franciska's case would construe a long list of aunts and uncles and cousins, next to her parents, and the grandparents on both sides.

Mellowed by the beauty of the garden, and relaxed in each other's company, on Sundays all her kin liked to gather under these shady old trees. Here, nobody forced them to prove anything, so they could pass the time of the day as they saw fit. It was a picture to behold-them together-which tempted Huba to feel, they could be carved from one block of stone.

The surrounding was magnificent and very peaceful. Except for Huba now, who had to think: "I am sitting here with you, instead of Franciska. I should court her, not all of you! But so far she eluded me. And now I better do something." In that moment Franciska sat with other women in the shade of the huge oak tree, perhaps the biggest one in this whole "puszta" where their homestead would be enveloped in a medium-sized wood of about three hundred trees. They were mostly of acacia, linden, walnut or sycamore. But outside of it, one could be overwhelmed by a sea of land which ran far to meet the horizon. And it had. This was open country. This afternoon the girl stood up when her mother told her to, and walked around with a jug of lemonade to fill up the glasses of their guests. It was the only afternoon Huba loved lemonade because he said yes to her the third time, and held out his glass, so he could see better this beautiful but shy young woman. When Franciska came closer she looked at Huba and blushed instantly. Her eyes were large and blue, almost like cornflowers. She had unblemished skin, dark blond hair, which she usually kept back with a blue ribbon. How old was she? Seventeen or eighteen? She was young and mature at the same time, small built with massive bones. Huba turned his head again to see her, as she walked into the house with the characteristic gait of those women who are determined and industrious, who would concentrate on duty rather than thinking about themselves.

"I talk to her!" And by following the sudden impulse, Huba sprung up from his seat to go after the girl. He caught up with her at the veranda, that had been ran over with wild grape, by giving adequate protection from the sun, or from those outside in the yard. He too stepped in the shade and started telling to her: "Franciska, can I come in too?" She blushed, looked at her shoes and said, "If you like," and left too soon, before he could say more. "Hmm-there is something about her which says 'I want to make it right.' This woman has quality. I am going to marry her. I am. Soon. Before someone else will. For I think of her all day . . . It means only one thing. Only one." His thoughts were interrupted. The girl returned with a plate in hand which has been packed with gingersnaps and some light sour-cream cookies. Huba took the plate from her, and put it down to the table. He took both of her hands into his. "Franciska, I suppose the time came when we ought to talk." The girl didn't mind they were holding hands. Huba went on. "I am sure you know the reason why I come here . . . in the last three months. I . . . I wish to marry you. Because . . . ! love you. Tell me . . . what do you . . ." Franciska ran inside. Huba had no idea what did that mean. "Was I too straightforward?" He went after her. The house was cool inside with the shades down, and he had to accommodate his eyes to the relative darkness. On the left to the entrance, a door has opened where he heard someone crying. "Franciska?" Huba stepped in. "Why do you cry? Say something." The girl came closer and said, "Yes." "Yes?" asked Huba, who embraced her strongly and passionately in the twinkling of an eye. "Yes? oh! You made me feel so . . . Oh! I am on the top of the world!"

Well, that was all to it, so at the same evening Huba could ask Franciska's hand in marriage. He was lucky again. Her parents did not object to the young man. It was dark, and the first stars had already lit up the sky when he headed home. Huba felt he should shout into the night. "Now I don't care even if the war comes. She loves me! And I marry her."

He could think of nothing else on the next day, only Franciska. There was something about her that he did not understand. A sadness? "Could it be this beautiful woman is so afraid she won't be accepted? Why is this anxiety? Where is it coming from?"

Strange, isn't it? After their marriage, he would still ask these questions. For years. "Where did the hopes of this young woman go? When did she lose them?"

THE PRECEDING OF WORLD WAR I

What did really happen, preceding the great war? The Balkan War hardly ended, a new Pan-Slav movement flared up in its place. It had been an outgrowth of a policy, in which the Slavs had inferior political status within the Austro-Hungarian Monarchy. Now Serbia wished to secede from the Dual Monarchy, persuading other South Slavs to follow suit. Events would not stop there . . . unfortunately. On June 28th of 1914, Franz Ferdinand-Franz Joseph's heir presumptive-has been assassinated by Serbian extremists in Sarajevo.

For this act of provocation, Franz Joseph decided on war. But many spoke against it. The Hungarian Prime Minister, Count Istvan Tisza have met the Emperor-King, proposing other measures. He believed, sanctions against Serbia would be enough. The main concern was the following. Should the Monarchy engage in war, where would it end? In a local war, or it would escalate to a full-scale war? And then what is the consequence? The escalation could come easily if the Russians and Germans would decide to take part in it. The arch-enemies . . . In a way, Austria has got assurance from Germany, that Russia would not be involved . . . Because if she would, then Romania would get in, in hope for territories . . . And God knows who else?!

A month later, on July the 28th, 1914, the Dual Monarchy declared war on Serbia. Within days, more countries expressed need to play a part in it. And soon, almost all countries of Europe or of the world would be engaged in war.

Thus, the First World War began.

THE VOLUNTEERS

Inseparable as young boys, the twins tried to discover a world that might have been designed just for them . . . Sometimes they thought one only has to figure out the game. As we know, Tass and Huba were complimentary in nature, in talent, in temperament. What was missing from one, was there in the other. Huba was assertive, inventing what they should do and Tass made it work. One had inspiration, the other had patience. Together the twins perfected plans, of which neither would do alone. They were a team.

An inch shorter from his twin brother, Tass has been a pleasant person, softer in manners and body, had dark blond hair and moustache, arched eyebrows and blue eyes. He didn't talk much, only as the last resort, or when had important things to say. Tass liked to observe what was around.

Huba did the talking. He was lean, muscular, had brush—like dark hair, and a crew-cut, that he favored all his life. He was not particularly handsome, yet women liked him, reacting well to that unpredictable streak in his nature, combined with an easygoing ruggedness. Or perhaps they couldn't resist his fair skin and grey eyes, that sometimes had a tint of blue. He, himself, never quite learned which worked better and to what end.

At the end of their finishing studies in 1913, they returned from Germany as grown men. When years earlier Elod, their older brother had left for active military duty, the twins had a touch of envy. But in 1914, the war broke out, and these two took it as a great chance for bravery. "Why don't we? Do you want to go? I do!" they boasted almost at once, and went hurriedly to sign up. Well, that's how it was!

Istvan, their father, didn't know what to make of his sons' euphoric enlistment. He had two sons in the army already, one a career officer, and the other one being drafted. And now the twins. That's four. The twins . . . weren't they too young? Days later conforming to it, he would still say: "Well, I must admit, it's a fine deed. It's quite something to volunteer for king and country. Well. They made a fine choice. But aren't they too young?"

TASS AND HUBA IN LOVE

"Well? You see, I couldn't wait," explained Huba to Tass. "I asked her hand in marriage. True, it's a short engagement, but in a month Franciska and I will be wed . . ."

Tass did not understand it. "Wouldn't you rather wait? Now, that we want to fight. Getting to the front. Doesn't she mind?"

Huba looked at him. "Mind . . . mind! Of course she minds!

But I didn't ask that. I asked her to be my wife. Eh! We beat the Serbs in a month or so, and we are home. And if the war gets bad, even then it's over in six-seven months the most. So? I don't get it. What's the big deal? I can't risk that some sleepy idiot comes up and asks her to marry, while we are away. I can't, can I?"

On the same afternoon, they both were drinking with the rest of their friends in town, most of them very young, who were just as eager to be enlisted as Tass and Huba were. The notions of heroism, loyalty, honor, fighting spirit and love filled their hearts to the tilt, that they were ready to explode. It was much emotion for a day. They acted out a new enthusiasm and determination, saying more or less the same, so it hardly made a difference if nobody listened. Who is there to listen when everyone talks and shouts at once? "Sure we go! Men go to fight. That's the thing. A man doesn't sit home by the fire! We beat the Serbs or the Muska (Russian), if he wants to be licked. We beat the hell out of them . . . so they can go to Mama, crying." Others were only saying, "When you are young you want to go. We go to war!"

It was getting late when the twins went home, feeling just a bit tipsy. On the way they already passed the church and town hall, realizing they still needed plenty of fresh air. Neither of them spoke now. The pavement was covered with hundreds of petals from a straight line of planted acacia trees, so one could smell the fragrance of late Summer everywhere. Huba was who broke the silence. "I wonder how he takes it?" "Who?" "You should know! Father. I have to tell him." The thought on it's own, sobered him up. He turned to Tass. "And? What about you, my brother? Huh? Shouldn't you fall in love before we go to war? I already have, you know. I figured, when we come back, we are changed men. No doubt. Our heads will be filled, let's hope not with shrapnels, but with concerns of the real world. Idealism? Let's face it, by then it will go. But if we find-or found-our sweethearts now, then someone will be there for us, to think of us. Someone will be waiting until we fight. It makes the fight all the more . . . how should I say? Worthwhile? Maybe! It is nothing like a woman's love when you are a soldier. When you fight for your country. Think of it! She puts you in her prayers. She wants you to come back. Come back to her! And if you will, she will appreciate you for it. Always . . ." Silence fell between them, and Tass thought the time came to tell his brother how it was with him. "Huba, you might remember Miriam. Our travelling companion and friend?" "Yes, yes I do. What about her? Sometime ago, she wrote us a letter." "Sure. And I wrote back. Since then, we are exchanging letters. Just the two of us. She and I, well, how can I put it? We feel the . . . same for each other. So . . . I proposed to her . . ." "You did? Well, well. My big brother! Then, you don't have to look for romance, do you?" "No. I've found it. I sure have," replied Tass with a certain relief that the secret was out, and there was no need to carry it alone.

A FATHER

Now four of his sons were still waiting for their command, and he, Istvan was already waiting for their return. "This is how a father is, I suppose," he shrugged. Istvan felt ambiguity about this era. Where was it heading? His generation was doing without war. The Dual Monarchy enjoyed the longest peace and prosperity. "What will this decade produce? Disagreements, wars and strifes?" he asked, and went on convincing himself. "All right. I have to realize it's a new generation, with new concerns. Yet it seems to me, their politics have a tendency towards radicalism. One hears every kind of radicals. That's right! One hears them, for they are screaming loud insults most everywhere against any establishment. Some of these young men are passionate on ventilating their dislikes, yet offer no solutions. They seldom work for anything. The least for solutions. Eh! We will see! I just have to take it how it comes. Slowly . . . waiting out the age of iconoclasts . . ."

Istvan had a great sadness for letting them go, and was short on the right words for telling how much he cared for them, and that he loved them. So, he just said to the twins while seeing them off at the train station: "You must know this: I am mighty proud of you, my sons!"

Chapter 15

In Vienna

THE BUMBERGERS

"How should I start? Tell them straight out and see what comes? How is the least shocking? Papa won't forgive me anyway . . . so I could even tell them I was pregnant . . . No! No pregnancy. It's too brutal! Marrying a gentile will be enough for Papa . . . the ultimate tragedy . . ."

Miriam was rehearsing for days on how and when to tell them. This anxiety went on for so long, so she thought. "It must be this evening . . . I just give them the facts. I won't ask their permission. Because I don't want a flat no. I just tell them. "So and so, these are my plans." So? When? "At dinner . . . If I tell them in the morning, then I'll have a whole day of shouting and cursing. And crying! As far as Mama goes. Mama? Poor dear! She tries so hard! She tries to be everything for all of us. I wonder, where will she stand this time?"

It was afternoon, her mother came back from a tea, she heard her voice. Miriam looked at her gold wristwatch, and realized she hadn't much time left. "Perhaps my last peaceful hours in this house . . . before I bring in the storm."

The first part of the meal went smoothly. Not much talk, except for her father. Mr. Bumberger liked to examine his children at dinnertime. This was the meal they had to sit through. No excuses. It was family time. They were supposed to take part in the conversation but worst of all, supposed to pay attention to their father. Tonight he wanted to know why doesn't his son, Mark study Chemistry, instead of Physics? In Chemistry there is future and . . .

Miriam couldn't pay attention this time. Besides, it was a fruitless argument. It used to be like that. Her brother Mark had his reasons, but apparently not good enough for Mr. Bumberger.

"Now tell me what business opportunity do you see in Physics?" he asked. Mark made attempts to explain. "Well, it's not really why I took interest in it. I like Physics. It is able to grasp the obvious truth in the material world. It has great potentials. But it's more interesting than Mathematics. Even though they heavily rely on one another. Or, should I say, they correspond?"

"Yes, yes. It is all very well. But it didn't answer my question. To my judgment, any scientific field has to establish a connection to some industry. If something useful was invented, it has to go out and be sold. This should be a major point in science. I don't know any country who can afford useless scientists, just for the sake of science, do you?" "Father, Physics is not useless . . ." "Of course not. Not per se . . . but Chemistry . . . it has much more clout . . . more chance. A real need for products . . ."

Miriam lost them, somewhere here. She couldn't follow the conversation. Miriam didn't mind to obey, but tonight it had to be different. As she sat by the table, anything that was said came through a screen. She had the sensation of being there, and also being someplace else, where her family could not reach her. It felt safe. Well, so far. Because the dishes were removed . . . Which made her feel dizzy. "I must tell them . . . must. Right now!" The young woman drew a deep breath. The maid already took the plates and returned with a handsome little silver brush and the matching plate. Miriam looked on, as she worked with it, and thought: "The same is happening with us. We are nothing, but crumbs . . . to be brushed off." The crumbs were removed and the table was expertly rearranged for coffee with a fine china. Miriam was staring at the cups and saucers, and couldn't tell their color. The maid placed the coffee pot on the table and brought in a small tray of dessert, before leaving the room. Miriam grabbed the table with both hands now. "This is my time. I can't wait . . ." In that moment when the only solid matter in Vienna was that table, a very pale Miriam took another deep breath, exhaled it, and began to talk. "Papa, Mama, I want to tell you something. I hope you will understand me."

In an hour the war between her and the rest of the Bumbergers raged in that proportion that Miriam envisioned since the day Tass Garay proposed to her. The head of the family was beside himself. He walked up and down. Everyone in the house had to hear the insults he would shout to his daughter. "And what do you think he marries you for? I tell you! For your money! My money! But he won't get it. This gentile, this nobody, this fortune hunter!"

Miriam pleaded with him, "Father, please. It is untrue!"

He continued. "Landowners, you say! A bunch of peasants I say... whom, I gather never crossed their county-line! Some kind of inbreed! Hah! That's what they are... who... who sleep in the barn with their sheep. With their boots on... these bunch of..."

"Father! Please stop! Stop it! It is all untrue." Miriam ran out crying and her mother went after her.

By recounting decades later the crowding fluctuations of her life, for Miriam, a figure surged to the forefront stronger than anyone. Her long dead father still dominating, if not the scene, then the remnants of her guilt, and that ever-present inadequacy of which she tried so hard to outgrow.

The rage of Joshua Bumberger lasted much longer than they all thought it would. "A lifetime wasn't enough for Papa to come out of it. A lifetime!" Given the fact he suffered greatly for having such a daughter, at first he wanted all his family to suffer, reminding them what was at stake: "You better listen! My child, part of my blood is going to mix herself with this gentile? How dare she is. Shame on her!" It was only the start. The next week couldn't resolve a thing, and a week after that, he still worked on persuading the young woman. "Don't you see it all leads to disaster? Come to your senses, Miriam! Have you any idea how many prosperous fine families, even here in Vienna would be glad to have you for a daughter-in-law? "Yes, father, but only the Jewish ones."

"Oh, no! This is where you are mistaken. Even nobilities with no money! With my holdings you could become somebody. You can have any title you wish for still. But I would never let you marry a nobody. You can't say I am a bad father... you can't say anyone was hurrying you. Your father is not that cruel! You... you had the time of your life. Freedom! Too much freedom. So, we are stuck with this tragedy! You... you jump in bed with a... with a..."

"Please, father! Stop it. I can't listen what you say! It's terrible. Try to understand me father. I just... wanted to marry someone I love! And now I have found the man I love!" Out of exasperation she came close to crying, but Mr. Bumberger had no intentions of giving in, or the least to give up so easily. He still had to present this argument by taking long strides in their living room, occasionally hitting a table or a commode with a fist. "Love!" she says. "Where do you live, daughter? In the clouds? She is in love. With a gentile of all people. A gentile! Did you ever think what will become of us if we all get loose in this fashion? I tell you right away. It will be the end of us. Yes, yes! If we let these things to happen! But I won't! As long as I live, you won't do it. I won't consent!" A day later he informed Miriam, "If your mind is so contaminated, I'll have to take charge. I can't just watch how you drag us down. Your own people . . ."

Miriam tried to explain she had no such intent, but there was no use. The fighting went on for weeks and they saw no end to it. Owed to the upheaval, Mr. Bumberger was neglecting politics and his social contacts and even his business had to take a backseat. Sarah, his wife, reported to her family. "He is less concerned of the coming war now. That just shows how much he changed. I am terribly worried how it all ends . . ." And so, for months and years the matrimonial plans of Tass and Miriam held the promise of tossing two families up and down and sideways, weren't there a raging war in Europe doing already a good job at it.

For some reason, everybody opposed the marriage. Not only relatives or friends but everybody formed the right to interfere. Trying to talk them out of it, they ventilated the cliches: "Mixed marriages never work. Why don't you give it up? You will see later how right I was! What makes you think you will be accepted anywhere . . . as a couple?! You will thank me later that I warned you."

Still, the two weren't about to change the plan. Miriam had her fight in Vienna, and Tass had his on the Plains. That is, until he went to war. And after . . . when he returned.

Chapter 16

The Great War

WAR

The outbreak of the war and its escalation had become a terrifying presence, a threat, and an impending force to change the lives of people forever. Millions were engulfed by this growing monster, but mainly the soldiers who were forced to look at it at close range. We are talking of the thousands here, being sent to the front to learn the art of killing, and perfecting it, as long as it was a command. By sitting on transport trains, they must have felt to be driven into dangerous rapids, where their knowledge of the world proved to be outmoded and useless, in view of the despicable things they were yet to meet and endure, like all other soldiers who go to war.

And the war dragged on for four years. Men fought, died, or stayed alive, back home the women prayed, worked and fed the children, and were grateful if their men returned. Because some never did . . .

From the one million and four hundred thousand Hungarian soldiers who went to war, more than seven hundred and thirty-four thousand were captured and sent to prison camps.

Somewhat more have been wounded, and six hundred and sixty-one thousand have died, fighting in it.

Among them, two of Istvan's sons . . . Elod, a career officer in the rank of Captain who fought with the lancers on the Eastern front, was killed at Przemysl, in Galicia, in 1917. In his last letter to his father, he wrote: "After weeks-long duty, I have a day off. So I can write to you, and Etelka and the children. Here, the odds are against us. Their fortifications are too strong, yet we try our best to break them through. We pay with terrible losses for this struggle. My men are dug in, and so am I. After the great offensive I am promised a three week leave. I think I can use that . . ."

As it was reported later, one night they were blown to pieces. Their undermined trench had been detonated, explained the letter. Elod had a wife and three children. Soon after this-just in a matter of weeks-the Eastern Front has been eliminated from the war!

A peace treaty was signed with the Russians, or rather with the new Revolutionary Soviet Government, at Brest-Litovsk. In addition, the Russians did let go of the Magyars from their prisoner of war camps due to the fact, that Lenin and his Bolsheviks had trouble feeding their own populace let alone foreign prisoners, following the new embarrassing development (which was desirable only for the Bolsheviks) that they, the Reds, and the White Russians (officers of the old army) were now engaged in a civil war, burning up most of Russia.

Kund, Istvan's fourth son, and second to be lost in this war was killed in action on the Italian front, at Doberdo.

It was a terrible battle, owed to that rocky and barren mountainous terrain. One has to mention the noise cutting through the brain, and of how hard it was to take cover against bullets hitting the rocks close to their face, and at the same time being prepared for flying pieces of splinters and broken stones, as it all occurred everywhere by the damaging stray bullets.

The twins, who also served with the artillery, fought with Kund's division in 1916, in the war against Romania. The Hungarians won this campaign. Later, however, the brothers were separated by new assignments, but back then, in his usual easy-going manner, Kund would still joke with his younger siblings: "The smart thing about war, you won't resent Hell that much, now that you have the sample! All right, you two. I like to interpret life as some comedy! A dark one, I admit. Laughable only here and there."

It all happened after the time when a great deal of maneuvering took place in international politics.

For instance, Italy had a change of heart . . . Regardless of the pre-war Triple Alliance in 1915, Italy decided to withdraw as such, so she can go to war against the Dual Monarchy. It resulted in the opening of a new front . . . the Italian! Sometime later, Tass and Huba too were to fight in Italy, at the area of the Isonzo river, close to Slovenia.

AT THE ITALIAN FRONT

It was on one of those dark and cold nights, when Huba stepped inside their temporary headquarters for a quick report. "Evening Major! I have a report to make. I am back from the reconnaissance mission. With all my men."

"What did you find Lieutenant?"

"Sir, we explored the region in the last week to the South and Southwest of the river. We can't report major troop movements."

"What about villages?"

"They are guarded, but calm. Telegraph lines are down, poles damaged."

"Anything else Lieutenant?"

"Yes ir. I suggest changes on the map. Because of the heavy rains, my men reported two more creeks. We found it here . . . and right here . . . If there won't be more rain, we can cross them with cannons. The water level of the Isonzo is about twenty centimeters higher now since the last time."

"Very well Lieutenant. Next time try not to be cut off from your main unit, will you? Not with such low supply. How did it go by the way?"

"We rationed bread and rum. And slept under the foliage, sir."

"Very well. You may go Lieutenant."

Huba left his superior officer, who called out immediately: "Sergeant, do come in, I dictate. Put this down to the Colonel. And take it to him: "Dear Sir. Recent survey of the river suggests relative calmness. If we go forward to South, and want to ambush one of these villages, this is the time. I recommend surprise attacks."

A month has gone since and they would still be in Italy, with November right on them. By then the troops were tired and above all, cold. Even though the supply sluggish, ammunition and food was still coming, but not enough warm coats or blankets. Men could not be motivated by words any longer, for the war has turned into its fourth year. But they still liked the smell of the mobile kitchen, or of the morning rum in their hot tea. It cheered them up, if only for an hour, or so. Otherwise they must have felt locked up, because there was no room for maneuver since the enemy came closer, and in spite of thinking out the best strategies, the enemy still looked twice as big. Well, it almost made no difference now, for tomorrow at dawn, they were to fight! With the big day getting near, now the second half of today could be used up by the usual, ritualistic preparations. Soldiers wrote letters, looked at family pictures, some told his best jokes, or drunk, or played cards . . . Anything was better than thinking. Anything. Officers did their best to maintain appearance. They finished shaving, pulled on back the shining boots, not that it made them feel better. Behind their disciplined and polite demeanor, there was a lot on their minds . . .

Tass recalled the last ambush about a month ago of being separated from his men, when enemy soldiers were after him.

The best choice he had was getting fast to the camp. His feet took him on the speed of a chased animal, who in every second of the day knows one thing, the only thing that matters, and in that second, it was how to run. There was no past, no future, only going forward. He kept repeating: "If you shoot me, not my leg! . . . not my leg! . . ." He said it several times, and it sounded very much like a mantra. Then he heard one shot, and felt to be hit, but could still run. Luckily, his men were up close and could return the fire. It worked! In a minute, the enemy soldiers disappeared in the woods. Later, the bullet was removed from his arm, and he recovered. "That was that. Nothing. But tomorrow. Tomorrow is the big day!" concluded Tass, and wondered if anybody in the camp could sleep with an easy mind.

There was some shelling during that night, and then it was quiet. At dawn, Huba was up, thinking on these: "Why do I feel it now . . . with the combat getting closer, that . . . I could run into my own death with the same careless jubilance I felt as a child . . . running through the door . . . just getting out! Be outside, so I could play!" He was surprised to discover how little the heart of a grown man does change.

It wasn't yet morning, but it was time. With the artillery in position, the range still had to be calculated. Commands were shouted and the action started. And the men did what they had to, none of them knowing if it took minutes or hours. Was it panic or a state they all have been in before, being able to do what they were supposed to do, forging ahead, running, aiming, shooting, taking cover, and aiming again.

The liquor and the excitement of the fight took hold of people's brains. They forgot how to think. In any case, something took over their will, so they could do what was expected and could also hold on to their sanity.

The fight was on when it began to rain. By looking up he discerned the sky became much darker, and for moments Huba couldn't tell when this whole thing started, today or yesterday. Was his unit around the same field fighting an infinite battle, or he was in a delirium? Or they all were? Participating in a common dream from which only those could wake who fell to the ground . . .

Very suddenly a shrapnel next to him shook his senses, urging him to crawl back. It made him realize the artillery was heavy on both sides. When the shelling was partly over, he found his men and they took the chance to retreat. It was already dark.

Back in headquarters he gathered and patched together the things he knew. Where was his commanding officer? Nobody saw him. The position was not yet clear, losses were still not known. Some of the wounded were treated already, back at the medical tents. He went to see those men. Almost all in the tent had serious injuries, bled heavily and looked quite hopeless. "One possible amputation . . . maybe more" told the doctor who was rushing from one operation to the next. Huba stepped out, and by just standing there, he was thinking of the dead. "Poor devils. My comrades. They tried to stay alive . . . but couldn't."

The night, following the battle was shorter than other nights used to be. His mind was still on them, couldn't let them go . . . not just yet. Before turning in, it came to him: "Who is next? Tass or me?"

But the war could not go on forever, it had to end one day, bringing the twins closer to home. Only, they wouldn't come that fast . . . Subversion, mutiny, and complete confusion weakened the morale of a beaten army on the Italian Front, from where soldiers were deserting in growing numbers. They would rather go in hiding, they said, until the armistice would not be officiated. Thousands made this choice. At least Tass and Huba have waited out to be discharged, only then did they come home.

Despite of the ending of the war, the year of 1918 has been difficult . . . Only the two following years, 1919 and 1920, could be regarded more traumatic. And they were, not only to them, but to an entire nation.

For the Garays, their grief was over losing two brothers to the war.

The Monarchy also lost the war, with grave consequences for this country. The winners shamefully imposed everything written in the book, from sanctions to all the way to the amputation of territories.

For Hungarians, there was a new test: to endure and witness one of the deepest political, social and economical turmoils, that this nation could face in her entire history.

In spite of it all, on coming home, Tass and Huba had to put their own lives back from how it was, to what it should be.

HUNGARY IS CLOSING THE WAR

And now, we must take a look at what led to those internal turmoils of postwar Hungary!

Franz Joseph I. died in 1916, and was followed by Charles IV., (also, from the House of Habsburgs). Right on the second year of a World War, and at the start of his reign, Charles, the new Emperor-King of Austria-Hungary thought necessary to modernize government and state affairs, something he immediately forced on to the Prime Minister of Hungary.

The King wanted electoral reforms at once, without considering the current problems of the country.

This misunderstanding prompted the Prime Minster Count Istvan Tisza (a highly accomplished politician and statesman), to resign.

(Strangely, the King's signature on this resignation would lead to his own fall from the throne of Hungary, soon after he was pushed down at first as Emperor, by his own countrymen).

There was a greater problem however, and a more immediate one. After the King's decision and Istvan Tisza's departure in 1916, the country's internal struggles were left exposed, and have gotten wider, without the Prime Minister's balancing talent.

These forces manifested themselves, partly through the Nationalists, who were the opponents of war for Hungary (they still were!), given the fact, it was in behalf of Austria and Germany. Also they were wary, that this country might be furthering these countries' interests. Then, there were the nationalities of Greater Hungary, who (not surprisingly) wished to have their own autonomies.

And, there were the radicals, who in 1917 had their chance to fall in love with the Bolsheviks, while could start dreaming on that line.

So it was the best timing for Count Karolyi to ventilate his socialistic views, and his solution for all the ills of Hungary-internal or external-in public.

By then, the war came to a close. It was 1918. Before the King (who found himself on the losing side) would sign the armistice, he appointed Karolyi as Prime Minister of Hungary, renounced his own right to participate in politics, and by pressure, he declared Hungary a Republic, with Karolyi, as provisional President, in an almost leftist government.

It all took place just in a couple of weeks . . .

The end of the World War was far too turbulent for Hungary.

Romanian, Serbian, and Czechish troops pushed themselves into Hungary, so Count Karolyi the President had resigned, by letting the leftists to take charge.

In March 21, 1919, indeed a new government (this time a Communist) formed itself in the Bolshevik fashion, and called the nation: "Soviet Republic of Hungary."

Bela Kun was the man who ran the show, which altogether lasted for 120 days, which gave them a chance (amidst ongoing foreign invasions) to eliminate a couple of 100 (or perhaps thousand) Hungarians. Their rule was called the "Red Terror" which explains all too well how the populace was taking it. In early August, the Communist "blackjackets" (mostly the top men, though) fled all the way to Soviet Russia . . .

By then, the Allies asserted themselves inside the country in some peace-keeping mission, with provisional governments, and negotiations in sight.

The giant confusion would taper only with the entering of Admiral Miklos Horthy, in early March of 1920. The Hungarian nobleman crossed the border with an army, for aiming to get rid of foreign invaders as well as internal ones, like those leftover henchmen from the Communist regime.

Soon, Horthy was elected as the Regent, (after all, Hungary was still a kingdom), and also as head of the state. With this step, he began to reinstate normalcy, appointed a prime minister, who then formed a coalition government.

Chapter 17

Post World War

AN "ANGRY ANGEL"?

The war ended and it ended badly, by unleashing an unhappy string of events and a tidal-wave of bad fortune. While it suggested to think over a commonly shared fate, people stopped and listened to the words of Ady the poet, who proved to be prophetic more than once. He said, an "Angry Angel" was flying above the land, punishing a whole nation!

There was something to it. The reality-that Hungary was about to lose two-thirds of her-was too painful to bear or at all to express it in any form, be that artistic or diplomatic.

The hard facts were already known, but in 1919, weren't yet sanctified. So, everybody, amidst a bitter struggle with the leftist radicals, everybody at his right mind, serious politicians and diplomats, made efforts to prevent these annexations of mainland territories, till there was a chance, and time.

THE "PEACE"

On his return, Huba has been already the happy father of a three year old baby girl named Helen, who was born in 1915. But Tass, determined on marrying "that woman" had yet to fight his own war, because apart from his twin brother, nobody supported the marriage of Tass and Miriam.

"Don't worry," would Huba occasionally calm him. "People change . . . if not exactly how we want them, still they change. They get another prejudice. That's how they improve. So, what do you care? Why should you ask the world? Go ahead with it! Do what you think best!"

"I know!" was his brother's response. "I'll talk again with father." Considering today held no more promise than the one four years ago, when he mentioned the marriage plan the first time, he could easily be discouraged not to go to him, but it just had to be done.

Istvan never forced his children into a wedlock they wouldn't desire, but learning from Huba that Tass was still serious about that woman, he risked saying: "I was kind of sure he gave up that plan." Huba went straight to his brother: "Be prepared. Father is not yet in your camp." Being as prepared as one could be, Tass crossed the corridor on his way to Istvan's room thinking: "These days father is the only one who thinks he can divert me from it. Well, he just has to curb his ambition." How well he remembered how it was four years ago, when his father didn't ask him to sit down, knowing well in advance, the meeting will be short. True to his design, Istvan did not let the meeting to develop into a conversation. He would ask only these: "Austrian and Jewish? Couldn't you find someone from your own kind? Or from your own country? If you go through with it son, what will your children be like? Living between two worlds in a limbo? Did you think of that?"

Before Tass would open his mouth to explain what it was like to be in love and to tell the so-called wrong woman was the right woman, before he could build his case in Miriam's defense, the audience was over and he was dismissed like some juvenile in bad need of discipline . . . well, that's how it felt like. He couldn't say a thing, for Istvan who had only questions, simply walked to the window that opened to the flower garden where the snowball bushes were in full bloom after an hour long heavy rain. The clouds lifted since . . . In the fresh vapors each big flower-ball transmitted a strange greenish-white fluorescent glow, ultimately turning them into these unusual festive lanterns, something neither men could see before.

Apparently the "lanterns" failed to reflect the mood in the house. The father, showing his back to his son, stood there for a long time. "He must have been taken by it!" occurred to Tass at first, who was getting angry for just waiting there like a lackey. He couldn't help to leave the room five minutes later, frowning all the way: "What makes you think, I don't exist?" From then on there was a gap, if they were ever close, which they were not.

Tass decided afterwards, he will manage not to show how hurt he was, neither would he confer in this with anybody. Not even Huba. He wouldn't easily get over it though. "How typical of him! He asked six questions. This was his answer! Forget my answer!"

Four years have passed since and there was a war. And the losses which came with it. Tass was somehow convinced that this time his father will be different. After all, he must be grieving to lose two sons and dealing with the widowed daughter-in-laws and the grandchildren, of whom he supports generously with provisions and money.

Today, Tass opened the door to his father's room and said the same he did four years ago: "Father, I am going to marry the Bumberger girl from Vienna." Only, this time he was to add these: "I didn't change my mind. I saw no reason. You asked me before, to think it over. Well, I have. The war gave me the time to do that."

Istvan looked at him and said very quietly: "If you must, then I . . . ," but did not care to finish the sentence.

MIRIAM CONVERTS

At early December a peculiar little news reached the Garays, what they only half-expected to hear. "Miriam Bumberger became a Roman Catholic." What they did not know as yet, the young woman acted entirely on her own accord, without consulting Tass. In fact she hoped to surprise him by this so-called "removal of the first major block" between them, which by her estimation had the highest potential to grow into a major disaster down the road. Talking of roads, she figured everything neatly out: "Let's take the first step. To the altar. How could I possibly take it, without converting to his faith?"

Has it been up to Tass, he might not have asked her to do it, but she was firm. "It's my marriage! If everyone has a say in it, so have I!" Upon learning the news, everybody wanted to know why this young woman was getting into such predicament. From where they looked at it, they saw a woman on her own, standing on a rope bridge suspended between two worlds that only few people care to cross at either direction and those who do, have no claim that it made them happy.

Only, Miriam knew better . . . she pointed out, it was time she started her own life. Being very much in love and wanting everything to work out, she forgot about obstacles and roadblocks. She seemed to be optimistic, implying everything was for the better, and whatever happened, it eventually improved her station in life. Miriam went as far as to interpret everything with a new edge. When walked into problems, she would take pride in them with a renewed zeal, saying it was her business alone, and her choice and destiny and karma (admitting it was a mixed bag), but still she had to have the guts to handle them, or ultimately shake them off.

"Did she really convert? Is she now a Roman Catholic?" asked Franciska in excitement. The Garays didn't know what to say, except that it was a giant step, that should be recognized. "A person changing religion for love, is very, very serious. Well . . . and dedicated. I mean . . . she is really into it." It took days to catch their breath. On the first day they were stunned and surprised. Later? A bit embarrassed. "Of course, we accept her!" would repeat the cousins and aunts in due course. "Sure we do. Well . . . think of the sacrifice she has made. That poor woman. Ahh! What am I saying! She is a rich woman."

THE AFTERMATH OF THE WAR

At war's end the Monarchy fell apart like a rusted cage. Those parts worth salvaging were thrown to a runaway pushcart which made quite a crowd on the losing side.

That's how it must have looked to a neutral agent if there was one, because there were only two sides then, with hardly anything in between. The other side did consist of the winners. Omnipotent, as well as fortunate, they would not listen to reason (other than their own) nor to petitions presented to them every day. Instead, they came forward and by right of conquest, rearranged the map of Europe. As early as in 1918, the new super-powers were seated at the bargaining table with a goal to work out the new treaty. The conference, headed by the representatives of the U.S.A. had had it's shortcomings. Though it was a long sit—two years—still not everything could be ironed out. The pretender (with an army of aids), making bold decisions in behalf of an ailing American President, lacked the foresight of European History. Others joined in, and this allied superficiality opened the Pandora's Box of future politics.

Paradox as it may, the seeds of World War II. were sown right there and then, under the table, where the "pacifying" documents of World War I. have been signed.

It all happened in Paris, in 1920. Huge territories were now on wholesale. Those relegating the conference gave away the countries of the losing side to those on the winning side, and to their allies, if they wanted it. Hungary is one example from where everybody took a piece, all her neighbors: Romania would get Transylvania, while Yugoslavia, Czechoslovakia, Austria and the Soviet Union were also rewarded.

All in all, with the Paris Peace Treaty over, Hungary ended up by loosing two-thirds of her . . . In 1920, this was the price of peace.

Chapter 18

The Bumbergers

CONVICTION

By pressing her forehead to the window, she could tell Vienna lost it's beauty. Completely! "How dare he is talking to me like that? Papa takes me for a criminal!" True, so far Miriam wanted to win. But these days everything crumbled. Seeing his mother in constant tears made her realize, she inflicted too much pain on her. Come to think of it, on her father too, even if he had a different way of showing it. Markedly different. Always. Normally, such display of emotions made Miriam nervous, and more so, if she had to be the target of it. "What does he want to accomplish? To defeat me, so he can rule my life as he used to? Now that's over, what can he do? Punish me? How? . . . Well, that's easy. He will find the way . . . by taking revenge, I suppose."

At early afternoon Miriam had to take time out for reorganizing her thoughts, and it seemed best if she was taking a stroll in Vienna.

By getting downward on the slightly sloping Schuler Strasse, Miriam would reach the Ring in no time, just to experience the usual city traffic and the hassle on a grander scale, and be part of it.

She used to enjoy this convenient and long thoroughfare, the buildings, people and the happenings. Directly or indirectly the Ring followed up the vision of the late Emperor Franz Joseph I., by way of connecting the outer settlements with the old city. From here, one could get to any location without experiencing that sense of loss, some people tend to have in a big city. It certainly would not apply here on the Ring, since orientation came easy even to those who weren't born Viennese, and were only passing through. But one has to add for fairness sake, this is what locals presumed. As of what-if anything-Miriam thought on this issue, remained unclear for the duration of the day.

She would not stop at the Bristol either, for devouring her favorite "Esterhazy Schnitte" (far the best cake in town!), instead she crossed the road in front of the Opera in haste, and continued on her way, so she could get straight to the Burggarten. In certain hours (preferably with a clear head) she liked to come here for taking endless walks on the curvative pathways. When less frequented, she would get inside the Imperial Greenhouses and stop for a moment in awe, before she could look at the plants to appreciate the beauty, and could inhale the fragrance she found there at each visit. so, we can say on most days Miriam felt rewarded simply just coming by. Except today. It seems nothing did wonders, nothing worked. It wasn't her day. She had to go.

Paying no attention to what the world was up to, she took long decisive steps, went through the Hofburg coming out at Joseph Platz, and returned to the Graben without realizing why was she there. She noticed nothing out of ordinary on the streets. If the city reflected a postwar mood, and the confusion over losing an Empire, which perhaps combined with the guilt of letting a young Emperor go, if it was at all in the air, Miriam hasn't got wind of it-well, in any case not today—since she had her own burdens to carry.

She couldn't exactly tell how did she get to the far end of Singer Strasse, or how much time she spent out, but saw no reason to continue for another hour now, that she found herself so close to home.

Actually she was glad for the chance to see her mother, and talk to her. From an early age, Miriam preferred people who were refined and sensible. Her mother was like that. Elegant, polite, beautiful. Impeccable always, the way she looked or behaved. She dealt with any problem or crisis with dignity. Like this one for instance, that they were struggling with right now. "What . . . I brought on them!" As far as Miriam remembered, this was the greatest one they ever had to contend with as a family. "Catholicism." This one brought down the Bumberger house. Well, maybe not the walls per se, but still it proved to be painful to them all, and presently Miriam saw no way out. Sure, there was a way out, but not a clear way, or a nice way. And now, as of today, it was over, definitely over to repair this damage, or to undo the "shame." It was predictable her father might cut her out (she thought about it for months), and so he had. Just yesterday. "And he . . . oh, no!" It was too painful to think of it. This afternoon Miriam acted it made no difference, but secretly she was hurt and felt cheated to be disowned. Yesterday evening, after their big scene, Joshua Bumberger disappeared for hours and at last she had a chance to console her mother. Today, this afternoon she hoped to find her in the house, even if she had a disposition, Miriam had high hopes, she could make herself available to consult her. And it just happened so. An hour later, they had coffee together. Sarah Bumberger did not change. She was sad, but kind and considerate. Her voice still carried the same quality what Miriam admired as a child. It could smooth her fears or agonies, in fact it transformed them. Perhaps she still had this power!

"Mama. Tell me, really tell me what you think? Deep down. As a human being, a woman, a mother . . . and . . . as a wife." She looked at Miriam trying to smile. "Well, he cannot help it, dear. You know Papa. He is not a bad man. But darling! You went too far. Too far."

"Maybe so," agreed Miriam, "but not far enough. I don't understand. Why does he humiliate his own daughter so? Why?"

Her answer did not come too quickly. "You just don't understand him, dear . . ." Sarah started to say, and came to the point of not understanding him either, after yesterday. Getting all worked up and shouting to his firstborn the things: "What are you waiting for? Go! Go! Go in exile for all I care. Die in poverty! You know what? I wish you did!"

Miriam then thought, this was the culmination of their evening. Well, she was mistaken. On the same night, her father announced "My oldest child is dead!" And then he tore his clothing. It was terrible. The whole scene, everything. The women helplessly cried, and later during the night neither could go to sleep. They both came down with swollen and red eyes the next day, not to mention their tormenting headaches. They both looked somewhat relieved when learned Mr. Bumberger left, for having his breakfast in the neighboring cafe. So at least the women could have some peace, but that leisurely, easy-going feeling of their mid-mornings together, was no longer there. It just vanished . . . Miriam was having tea, and she sat in silence. Regardless of the night, Sarah Bumberger still looked stunning, but was very quiet. While put a drop of cherry preserves on her freshly baked kaiser roll, she had these thoughts: "Where did Joshua go after coffee? Did he go on with his business, or rather . . . he went to seek spiritual advice? Or . . . legal one? So, he would prepare himself, in case our daughter goes through with this "savagery", how he terms it . . . well? What am I going to do? She is my daughter. I didn't bring her to the world to watch her downfall! So I just have to . . . to think. To think hard."

When in a week the young woman could recover her youthful optimism and could look at things with a new eye, she realized worst came to worse, and even that went to pass. Her parents weren't taking the journey to the Hungarian Plains, after all. This idea collapsed, killing the possibility of a cordial, lukewarm relationship between the two families. So she realized was best, if left things, and directed her energies to the future.

In the years ahead, Miriam was lacerated on their break. And never learned (not the full extent of it) that her parents were divided on this issue as early as the time of her wedding. Sarah, concerned about her daughter's dowry, took steps to correct "the mistake we do with our own kind," as she once dared to phrase it in front of Joshua Bumberger, who admonished his own daughter for life. She also pronounced: "I won't let my child to suffer!" and refused to give a hint on how she planned to eradicate their "mistake."

Chapter 19

The Sisters-In-Law

MIRIAM ON THE GREAT MAGYAR PLAINS

She had so much freedom then . . . before her marriage, Miriam could travel all over cosmopolitan Europe often on one day's notice, without worrying on money or language or accommodation or company. Yet one day this independent woman moves to that remote part of Southeastern Hungary "for no good reason" other than her own. Supposing she knew what was she getting to, Miriam wrote to her mother: "From day one I have to watch out on the Great Plains, so I won't confuse Plains with plain! I have to watch to live my life exactly how I wanted it. So it won't be plain, as it is for Franciska, my sister-in-law. She knows no better, I am afraid. Tass and Huba are different. They are vibrant and exciting. I am going to have that kind of life too, whatever it takes! Mother dear, as soon as I understand these people here, I will be content. I am sure of it!"

That's how Miriam summarized the new place, two weeks after the honeymoon. But then, with all said and done adapting to the new country . . . well, by her own admission this took at least ten years.

It's not easy to start a marriage with a curse. But it gets increasingly difficult, if only the curse is familiar and everything else is new, unknown or seemingly hostile. Miriam didn't suspect that having a new family, country, religion, and language will be such an unfurling tribulation, so on her better days she has to ask, "If I get over the first year it means I can stand anything?" On other days she was more abiding, for she realized how this all came about. "Yes, I asked for it.

So, I swear to God, I make it work. Oh, not only that! I make the most of it! I will! Eventually."

Tass was the only family Miriam had now who fulfilled multiple roles, like checking the Hungarian grammar his wife so diligently picked up to study. Miriam could not speak fluently in the first year. Understanding the natives was still beyond her, but could produce little sentences and even longer ones, each surprisingly well-composed. Also, she could follow what was" the conversation about, if only these plainsmen hadn't have a tendency to use words she never heard before. Their dialect didn't give an easy dissection for a stranger.

"Oh well, Miss Miriam. This is the most difficult language of Europe. And the most isolated. By now, you can tell why, can't you?" cheered her Herr Schwartz, the so-called tutor back in Vienna during the war, who had the task of introducing the basics to her. From there on, they slowly built a conversational Hungarian, in the manner of the Viennese coffee society, relying on the old ladies who would speak it in their prime. Miriam was encouraged to talk to them of which she daily did, but needless to say later learned to regret it when came to live on the Plains to speak the language with the natives, where it was a matter of survival if she put theory in practice.

She was a determined woman who did not agree the language was "unapproachable" as others would vilify it who tried and failed. Now, on the Great Plains even if it broke her tongue she produced sentences like: "The cows are grazing every day in the Summer. But they are not grazing in the Winter. There is no grass", quite unexpectedly by opening a conversation, which of course made Franciska burst out with laughter, but dazzled her husband and his brother, admiring her courage and appreciating her interest in rural life. Sometimes Tass would offer her: "Why don't we speak German?" where he had a disadvantage, but she declined each time: "No, I don't want a day off. I am a Hungarian now. I live here, and I am going to love it here. At any rate . . . I try!" Miriam was no fool. This strange land and the people on it were a far cry from Vienna, from her urban-minded, well-to-do family and friends, most of whom were Jewish. "I am married now, and a catholic," would repeat Miriam, while trying to be best in both. "I just hope they won't think I denied them. I hope they understand how much I love my husband. If I would make a demonstration of my heritage here, well . . . it would be out of place."

Tass thought of it differently. He was concerned. "Isn't it too much? All at once these changes and restrictions!" So he said to her, "Give it some time. Just don't overdo it. You don't have to, you know."

"Oh dear, easier said . . . ," thought his wife. "If I gave up a lot for my marriage, not everyone applauds me. For some, I am still a stranger. My father-in-law is one. That Franciska woman is the other, and only God knows the cousins' mind."

What she didn't yet know, Istvan was distant to everybody. And Franciska? Well, it was a different game. Miriam hurt her feelings as much as Franciska did hers. They did not like one another, not just yet. There was a rivalry between them. Miriam judged Franciska inferior to her own level of sophistication and refused to look deeper if indeed this was the case. Her sister-in-law knew it and suffered from it, inventing her own weapons. "That ugly woman," she would say at each turn. "That woman is lucky to get married at all. Poor Tass. I am convinced she is older than he is." This one came back though, with the help of a cousin who disliked both women. Miriam was furious that her Hungarian wasn't advanced enough for fighting this out. "I hate her," she said to her husband, and Franciska said the very same to her husband. The brothers didn't like this, and left them out from socializing until they would comply. Neither did it willingly, for it took a decade until their relationship would improve.

FRANCISKA, AS A CHILD

Her first memories were funerals . . . The vicissitude of having lived through a diphtheria epidemic that was to claim her brothers and sisters-all five of them in two years-might explain Franciska better than anything; certainly better than words.

She was very young then, but it's fair to say a social persona began to emerge in the months ahead by the discovery: "I am the next one to go," which became sadly justified on the day she too fell ill. That year Franciska was all but six. By then she completely forgot to smile, yet by eating and sleeping well, empowered her to sport a massive constitution. She had a sweet round face with tightly closed small lips and those unforgettable blue eyes, that reminded everyone of the Southern fields of Summer, where cornflowers pop up and ripple in a sea of golden wheat.

On the day Franciska was taken ill, apart from this central question, everything lost importance: "What do we do now?" Her parents gasped in panic with good reason, for the little girl had rising fever and some of the symptoms they knew all too well. Her mother, devastated as one could be, came to her senses (well, some might argue, she was losing them) by refusing to take the child, her last child to the doctor. She yelled, "We have no use of him, don't you see? Franciska cannot die!" After confronting her husband, she turned to the last resort. This was what she said. "We must call the Shaman woman!" And was surprised how the father of her children at once agreed and how swiftly he went to the stable to get the horses, so they would not lose time.

The Shaman was revered and as far as he knew, terribly old, perhaps getting close to a hundred. "I should say, a hundred!" he would confirm a couple of minutes later, already on his way. "I remember my grandmother mentioning that 'old' Shaman woman. Now that's old!" As people said the way he recalled it, she still lived in a shed out in the woods to the West and had to be brought in town with a carriage or coach every time there was a need. She took cases the doctors deemed "hopeless" just to redeem them with fairly good results, using drastically altered measures, largely in disaccord with Western medicine. The true astonishment came at the end of her treatments! People had no idea how to be grateful, or settle their debt, for she would display a remarkable purity by her refusal of taking payment for her services, be that money, applause, food, or clothing. By all means this was the hardest to understand. But then, one had to consider she was a Shaman who knew things, saw things, and fixed things. She wasn't like others. She was an enigma.

Franciska's father found the woman at the clearing not far from the hut, who by his genuine surprise, seemed to know in advance of his coming, as well as the reason for it. He also found it queer how she made herself ready for the road, before he would ask her to. "What an old witch she is!" would comment normally the girl's father, but since that day was out of ordinary in every sense, he had to keep silent. Just merely looking at this little old thing in his carriage made him aware she was capable of doing anything on any day, like performing a miracle. "Let's pray that she will!" In an hour they arrived back to the house that was packed with relatives in an attempt to calm their fears, and for keeping vigil as one does when one runs out of options, no longer trusting his learned wisdom, nor the wisdom of other mortals. Well . . . except of the Shaman woman's, for being the only one whose reputation was not yet tarnished in matters of life and death. "We might as well face it, she has an impeccable name. That's right. Regardless of her hocus pocus. Well, we used to laugh at her, but she is the only one now! I must trust her," concluded Franciska's father on their return, while opened the gate and helped the old woman down from the coach, ushering her immediately in. He stayed out for a short second, so he could draw a deep breath. The sharp pain was still there in his stomach. He couldn't eat all day from the fright and of the self-blame. It made him sick for having failed many times over, for having failed protecting his own children from such an early death. By this time the house inside was getting transformed. Wasting no time the old woman took over the duty of treating the child with an herbal potion. There was another, that had to be boiled at first on the stove, a concoction of some unknown substance to which she called Franciska's mother to attend, up until she saw how the second liquid begins to set loose strange bluish opaque steams. It also gave out an aroma that no one could identify, filling the kitchens as well as the inner rooms with it.

Everyone was motionless, waiting for what will happen. In spite of reticence, now the old woman released the tip of her finds: "Blue. This is the color the child needs . . ."

"Well? This is the color? The child needs? What does she mean? All right, blue. But what does it say?"

"Meaning what?" risked to ask the father, but he wasn't heard. The Shaman did not see them, she was concentrating. The young mother was asked again to help with the pans, the towels and the basin. They had to keep the blue liquid hot, while cotton towels would be cut up to be soaked in this solution, to be placed around the child's neck in order to heal her throat. This would be repeated in every five minutes, for about an hour. For that time, the fever disappeared.

The Shaman then requested brandy-the strongest in the house-so she could give it to the child to gargle. Taking in account the little girl's age, she asked the mother to demonstrate it, each time she was supposed to gargle. Then quite unexpectedly she put down a finger in her throat, successfully removing a stubborn slimy residue of the illness, affecting the child. The operation took a second, the girl cried a bit, but when she found yet another soaked cloth wrapped about her neck, she went to sleep.

The time came the Shaman sent everyone out, allowing only the parents to stay, put out the petroleum lamp, lit a candle and canted a magic verse to the spirits. Franciska's father noticed the rhythmic sound to it, resembling his mother's voice when she prayed the rosary. Or . . . was he too tired, and suspectable for harboring every God under the same roof? He wasn't too clearheaded on this, considering the hour. But he knew, they were still watching the girl. The Shaman would do it until midnight, then by standing up she said: "This child shall have a long life. Long life. Only . . . has to beware of fire." When it was all said and done, the Shaman wanted a warm soup. She lay down on the carpet afterwards and at dawn she asked to be taken back to the woods.

When the sun came up, the morning promised new beginnings to the couple. Franciska recovered, gained back her strength and in a month could get out anywhere she pleased.

Her choice was taking up the daily walks to the cemetery with her mother, to where the two would take violet and daisy and later some other flowers in season. Even if these visits slowly made her understand the larger part of their family was no longer home, but out there, still she could not grasp the idea of loneliness. One day when her aunt commented:

"Little Franciska is a lonely child." She did not know what to make of it. Why? She had her parents and relatives, some toys, and the trees in the garden, the dogs and the cats, the birds and the picture books . . .

A world, real or imagined was there. It was there to take . . .

CHAPTER 20

Learning Married Life

TASS AND MIRIAM

Miriam who saw her surrounding in a new light, would soon write these to Vienna: "Mother dear, it's not that difficult to love this place. Here, people are temperamental and excitable. But I love it. Despite of it, or because of it? I really can't decide."

She realized, the people of the Plains were good with horses, liked outdoors in every season and physical work in its time. The majority was medium-built with fair skin, high cheekbones and dark hair, which is to say they obtained most physical characteristics of the Huns, or the cumans, who lived long centuries ago in Hungary. Miriam found the mixture very exotic. But there was ambivalence in her as yet; for not knowing, which aspect of their nature will be on display.

In her next letter, she would share this discovery: "Tass tells me a great deal what it is to know. It touches me, when I learn about a country and its people. I am getting closer to them now, and I seem to feel their sentiments. Mother, just think! Our ancestors ventured far on the Globe, and felt right at home where they were. Why shouldn't I have the same resilience?"

And so, after the first two years, life became easier. By then she understood more the Magyars, had friends and knew half of the village. Just a year ago, she would say, their love of land was an obsession, but now she saw it with a different eye. These people lived here for over a thousand years, for twenty generations more or less. Some of the lands were granted by a great king, or a poor king who would bestow their nobility. Others bought it if they were in trade, or fought for it in some old battle. Inherited, or bought, in any ways these lands had great value, because the grain in it had the highest quality. Everyone took pride in it. Everyone talked about the soil, the crop, the weather, the reaping . . .

Miriam recalled her days in Pozsony, after the three of them had met on the train. The twins talked about it even then. "So, how come I don't miss Vienna," asked the young woman now.

HUBA AND FRANCISKA

It was not until after the war in their first year together, when Franciska could find herself, though Huba felt she was still waiting. "Just as well I might give up for what, for it can be anything!" he said then, more to himself. "Is my wife an insecure woman, or she still rehearses this tightrope act we call marriage"? Well, why not?" he thought, since most of it was ahead of them when he returned from the war. "Some women know from the start what they want. Security or status; money or happiness; or like the grabby ones-let's have it all!-but Franciska, thank God, is different."

So far Huba, who wouldn't mind learning his wife's secrets, has been a superficial observer when it came to women. Besides. He was too involved with the building up and running of his estate. So it took time realizing what kind of role his wife did long to play, or at all, she fostered something in her heart. Well, as it turned out, this something for Franciska would be motherhood! When played with her doll at six she had a desire to be a mother; a real one with a real child one day, which she even knew would be granted. Then she could be happy to play the role of her life all the way until sixty or eighty when she still would be a devoted mother. It all sounded reasonable and beautiful, but one has to ask: how did her husband fit in the picture?

Perhaps hardly at all, one has to add. Even if he paid no attention, Huba had to recognize as early as his brother Tass married the girl of his heart, the kind of intimacy these two-Miriam and Tass-have had, won't be there in his marriage. Confident from the start, they as a couple set a different tone. Huba didn't need intimacy, and Franciska didn't seek it. If anything, she needed distance. Huba had no objection to this, unless we count his many moods, when he could be pressed to learn the secrets of his woman's heart. On those days by outdoing himself, he would shower her with gifts. But couldn't do more. Franciska stood it all; the good and bad moods, while she took refuge in her own world that would be furnished with plans.

From the very beginning, she was a cautious young bride, wised up by women who for years used to come visiting her mother for conferring the things their men, or his family would do to them, while forcing them into dreadful arrangements of every kind, under the aegis of marriage. Listening to these would empower Franciska to exclude the dreams and illusions from her own marriage, saying she needed the substance and foundation built in reality.

She tried to avoid her future self somewhere on a very dark day with yellowed wedding voile in hand crying as most women do, as far as they tell . . . and they do; because she heard them. It couldn't be helped, Franciska was a realist. All she had to do was taking a good look around. No wonder she came to this marriage convinced, a woman is better off trusting her offspring above her man. This man is never really her own. It is a mistake to believe he is. If one's husband was a stranger once, he could very well be one again, as soon as he gets bored, while one's children . . . even at their worst, remain one's own. On the day Huba proposed marriage, similar thoughts breezed her young mind: "This man is a taker, and we both know he can take me. All the more reason I have to define a territory of my own. Otherwise . . ." Well, this girl didn't want to end up badly. Yet at their engagement she would quiet her earlier doubts to say yes. Looking deeper in her heart, she concluded: "I would have said yes anyway."

Huba wished to see her every day, and this made her happy, for it was the proof, his love accelerated. The planning of their matrimony went fast. But the young woman needed to map out the future, at her own pace.

Concerning-their union, there was an incentive from the start. Huba wanted boys, Franciska wished to have girls. She recalled the closeness with her mother, the affinity they used to have, something she hoped to repeat with her children. A bit daintily, she thought: "Most likely, I'll be alone in the house, while Huba is away . . . roaming, like men do."

The two were opposites. Could it be the reason they fell in love? The first time Franciska laid eyes on him, she saw a keen young man who was going after what he wanted. Huba did not look the type who gave up on anything, and Franciska was attracted to this kind of energy and attitude. From then on, falling in love with him was easy. He had been friendly and tall and handsome with his bluish-gray eyes and brown hair. She liked his new crewcut the way he ventured off to the war. And she liked it, after they returned. Franciska loved him how he was, regardless of telling herself: "It's better if I temper my love."

Being aware of how others love to plan their wedding, Franciska took more interest in what comes afterwards and started concentrating on the years of a married woman. Even if she trusted their upcoming marriage to be long and stable and prosperous, she was prepared for the times when they will disagree. In view of the fights of married couples, she was putting down the founding stone of her own domain.

A TERRITORY DEFINED

Never a romantic dreamer, Franciska lived in reality and on the subject of children she had these thoughts. "If I'll have a son, Huba takes over. The child hardly grows, they'll go out riding or playing football, and he will teach him hunting. They'll have their own world, their own secrets. And I won't be part of it. Huba demonstrates to withhold emotions the way he and his brothers were trained, and obviously ended up with the same idea of manliness. No doubt, Huba brings every decision about him. As years go by, the boy goes to war, if God forbid, there is a war. Leaving me in tears. If God allows him to come back, he falls in love and marries right away. Yes, it happens all the time, but sometime before that, he alienates gradually from his family. This is how it is with sons.

If I'll have a daughter, it is different! She remains mine."

Alongside of this reasoning, another notion was taking root which maintained, only women have talent for friendship and loyalty. Only they are capable of giving comfort for those in need . . . This was the bottom line why Franciska preferred girls. But to achieve this one needed a scheme. Her mother once told her: "In a marriage, your satisfaction must come from having your own cards, something you shuffle and play behind lowered curtains and locked doors."

Franciska agreed. Marrying this man was listening to her heart, but the future needed a cool head. Planning her pregnancies had to be the first step. Only, it was a secret. There was an ancient method, that Franciska during her childbearing years would follow to the letter. Well, she didn't do anything wild; only would concentrate on the feminine phases of the moon, a reoccurrence of two to three days respectively, while the celestial bodies are rotating in the wheel of the Zodiac. Franciska made sure to let her man close on those days. That was all to it. If ancient people used it, so could she! Notwithstanding, the last person Franciska would let into her wisdom was her husband himself. "Huba? Why would I worry about him? If God would not grant him sons, there isn't much I can do. I realize, at the end it's God's will."

By Franciska's admittance, Huba liked to challenge his fate. As if saying: "It's not up to you! It's up to me. Just wait! I'll show you." He fought a continuous duel, and the choice of weapon was his. Always his! Up or down, Huba was ready for the next fight.

"Fight! Why do men fight? What for? Pushing to the limits? We women are not like that. Our wisdom comes, when we learn to stand it."

THE NEW HOUSE

While plans for the new construction had finalized in his head in 1920, Huba did order huge quantities of timber from the lower alpine region of the North, that quite shockingly was annexed to Slovakia, and became a different country overnight.

Evidently the new situation has brought on new rules in foreign trade, therefore nobody understood why he insisted on buying there.

Timber in these parts was too expensive to build with, and he was aware one had to make the best use of it. By starting with the old structure that was brick, Huba wanted to utilize the new one around it, from wood. At the same time he knew, the interior would be panelled in nearly all rooms on the ground floor. So he made sure the sturdy brick structure remained in the center, that he wrapped with rooms and corridors, as if in need of stratification for some unseen catastrophe.

His father Istvan, who decided not to hinder his youngest son's building genius, had nonetheless these thoughts on the matter: "He puts much effort in masking this homey labyrinth. Huba reminds me of my mother . . ."

When they were ready, the main living room dominated the ground floor. A new vital center-similar to a grand station-was to play a similarly complex role. To the right the library opened, to the left, the parlor. There was a main door to the hallway, leading to other rooms, and also to upstairs. But there was a smaller door, concealed with the same deep terracotta lumber, as the rest of the room. This had a narrow staircase behind it, which led the Garay couple up to their own bedroom.

A double door opened to the dining (what was a spacious room) and next to it another door to the kitchen, via the pantry. From the living room, it was at least four ways to reach the kitchen, or for that matter, any other room. Huba wanted to ensure a noncongested traffic, when drew up his plans to modernize.

We can't leave out the door which led the lady of the house and her daughters to a room used for fittings and sewing, especially when the seamstress moved in with them for a week. Next to it a plain guest room opened, and right after that, another one, and a bit further the office of Huba with the telephone. There was a door opposite to the main entrance, the one next to the back terrace on the North, a Summer room, furnished with wicker chairs, small tables and flower stands, making it a pleasant sitting in hot weather. And the very last door had to be the door to the bathroom.

One couldn't be sure if this house was perfect to be lost in, or provided the best escape routes to anyone in it. Their visitors thought of this more than the Garays. "Franciska dear! Those doors! Don't you lose your way in this maze? You must feel like the Revolutionary grandmama, in her topiary garden . . . well, do you?" her friends would frequently ask. (Her youngest daughter, Julia said when still young, that it was always an unsettling room. Whenever she came home from the conservatory, she pointed out its strong electromagnetic field. But since the piano was there, she played there. Later she said, it helped her playing, but could never rest in that room, or could read a book in peace, without being aware of the currents.)

Since the building became such a puzzle, Huba took great pride in his home, and often cracked his own anecdote in it: "One morning I woke to find a stranger sleeping downstairs on my leather sofa. I go to him, wake him up, asking why is he sleeping? He says he lost his way and got tired, and gave up. So I ask: "All right. Get up and drink this silvorium. Have a game of 21 with me. So we played till half past four, and he lost badly. So I said to him: "If you were a better card shark, you could bail yourself out of this jam. But now I take you to the Gendarme Major." Here, he started to plead. "I can work for you for a couple of days!" "O.K." I said, "how about two weeks?" "Deal!" he said. So I said to him, "You can send more, like yourself. Reaping is not that far. Tell them, it's easy to get in." When Huba could get this far, Franciska invariably informed the listener, the story was made up. Of course, Huba didn't understand why would she . . .

Chapter 21

Attila the Hun

ISTVAN, MIRIAM AND SARAH

At first, it was a daily exercise in good manners for Istvan to accept Miriam. While his association with the new daughter-in-law set the tone of cordiality and respect, it made him aware she was not one of them. Miriam had a different position. She wanted to marry his son, and wanted to come here. She wished to be part of their world, and wished to assimilate. Swallowing her pride, she took extra steps each day trying to fit in, so she might be accepted and recognized. She thought: "One day I'll be even liked!" Well, Miriam has got her wish. In a year or so, even her father-in-law was fond of her. But never, not for a moment did he consent to the marriage, as "some good idea". He would be cross with Tass for the rest of his life for causing such a stir, which in the long run will ruin him, and also his children and his wife. He couldn't resist to think of the future, to foresee, that this poor creature who came over and converted for her husband's sake, will suffer at the end for living on foreign soil, far from her own people, alone one day.

Istvan couldn't help divulging what was yet to come . . .

A year after Miriam's marriage, in 1920, Sarah Bumberger's mind was made up. She was putting together her daughter's dowry. Also, secretly consulting a lawyer and her brother who gladly helped to draw up the papers, she transferred her holdings on Miriam's name. It also helped that she came from a banker family. Still it took a whole year to arrange it, making it legally sound, without her husband's knowledge.

Whether he knew it or not, Sarah and Miriam would exchange letters regularly, using another address in Vienna. In the last year, Joshua Bumberger noticed a change in his wife. Sarah adopted an extravagant taste and a lively interest in jewelry. She often visited her husband's store, letting him know if a diamond ring, or a bracelet, was good enough for her birthday. Obviously, she could have them, for Mr. Bumberger adored his wife. He understood perfectly, the time came when Sarah appreciated jewelry not only for its beauty, but for its worth. But then, why did she forget to put them on? If only women weren't so scatterbrained! "Ah, my! I just put them in the safe!" they say.

This was the back game allowing Miriam eventually to claim a beautiful collection of her own jewelry. Sarah didn't trust, humiliation was a good lesson. "Life is lesson enough as it comes. I cannot punish her, Joshua, because your pride was hurt. I must protect her, even if it is from you." She would say it over and over, rehearsing it, so one day she might even get the guts to tell him. Well, Sarah wouldn't push things far. She understood him too, not only her daughter. Joshua was not a bad man . . . perhaps just stubborn.

ATTILA

Predisposed or not, in a year Miriam too was deeply in it . . . She was fascinated by their history and learned the facts, that between three and four hundred years after the Huns, the Magyar tribes came along to occupy Attila's land. In lessening number, the descendants were still around, mixing inevitably with those, who time and again came to conquer them.

In any case, by now Miriam understood why Hungarian plainsmen were passionate about Attila the Hun, if their country was named after him, and was the least surprised if they still expected to find his mysterious burial place. She even counted her husband Tass to be among them. "Sure! It's here some place, in this region!" he would confirm it. "It shouldn't be far!"

"Why don't you tell me the whole story?" asked his wife. "Books I read on History don't reveal the good stuff. Well, they should. Rather than be careful and scientific and boring. Most of them fail to look behind the scenes of great actions. I miss that. It's only me . . . I suppose. I am a reader who looks for blood and fire. Or, more precisely, for the man who strikes the match! Excitement is what I am after. You should know."

For this kind of invitation, Tass was more than willing to get back to the Huns. "The way we know it, is this. He was buried in the Tisza river. No, no! Not just dropped in. The concealment of his burial place is the greatest scheme one can think of. Hundreds, if not thousands of his slaves worked on digging the grave. Some grave . . . the Huns diverted the river to bury their dead king! What do you say? Awesome, even in its own time. To think and act on such scale! Anyhow, a curved part of the riverside had to be excavated as deeply as the supposed riverbed. We shouldn't neglect to mention, hundreds worked on it. Hundreds! It is also recorded, while the ceremony advanced, people overcame by grief and there was a-mass hysteria. Considering the conditions of his death, I am not surprised. Since he was a great king, a ruler, and the conqueror of Europe, hundreds died with him. Did you know that?"

"No, no. How?"

"Most committed suicide during the funerary rituals. Well, it was told by his sons how most of this happened, you know! The proceedings-by today's standards-were most peculiar. His body was prepared and placed in a triple coffin, each containing the other, one gold, one silver, and one copper. When the time came, this enormous coffin was lifted and lowered into the future riverbed-his grave-the one, his people freshly excavated. Then, his sons ordered the slaves letting the river run through. So the Tisza rapidly flew over Attila's coffin . . . It must have been a great moment. I imagined it often as a child, you know.

When it was done, the former riverbed could be filled and the surface smoothed over. With the groundwork finished, well . . . his wives and concubines were put to death."

"What? Were they killed?" Miriam was astonished.

"Yes . . . well, it was customary then. Ancient peoples had these rites. The wives went too."

Miriam interrupted her husband once more. "So, these poor wives had to make most of their marriages!"

Tass asked her very seriously: "Shouldn't all wives? But wait! What do you say to this? That Attila died on his wedding night, choked on his blood."

"My God! It is horrifying!"

"There is another version though, explaining his death. It says, nosebleeding killed the man. Obviously, my dearest Miriam, it would be the end of Hungarians if we consent to that. How could a world conqueror die from a bleeding nose? No way! No Hungarian at his right mind falls for that. It is preposterous. Would we occupy his land if it was true? We prefer this one: his new wife killed him. A foreign princess."

"The bitch!!" shouted Miriam. She did it rather passionately for an Austrian.

"Yes, I agree and so does everybody. Especially if we take in account that this was the end of the Hunnish Empire. Literally the end. His sons divided the kingdom and were trying to run it, but couldn't, because they were competing, fighting and killing one another. The country broke to pieces, and wars followed. Soon, stronger people came . . . Remnants of the Huns either scattered or stayed, never rising to prominence again. There went the greatness," Tass said, finishing his story.

"But it is shocking," picked up Miriam one loose thread. "I mean, this abrupt ending! So, the Hunnish Empire was the singular talent and will of Attila?"

"Yes, you can say that. Almost. He inherited parts of that kingdom. He and his brother . . . But he was the one extending her borders to "half of the world" of that time. He did challenge the Visigots and threatened the Roman Empire for many, many years, invading it from North to South. From the Northern cities, people were forced to flee to the lagoons of Venice, which was assumed safe from the Huns. The "Scourge of God" took subsidies from the Romans for some twenty years! Tremendous sums of gold . . . Imagine, a thousand pounds of gold, the "golden solidus", was paid to Attila annually. It is recorded, the weight always depended on the last peace-treaty. And they didn't collect only from the Romans. Others paid him too. Half of Europe and the Balkan. But then, in 453 A.D., he died. And as we know, his Empire went with him. Went down." Tass finished the lecture, and stayed with his thoughts. For whatever reason (could be respect for the dead king?) they did not speak for a long time. Only later Miriam broke the silence. "So, this is the connection? Your people and his? Or what's left of them."

"Yes. Sharing a country . . . In this region you know, people like to think they are of the same line with Attila. Of course, we will never know. We have no conclusive written history of that age, so we can't tell how the continuity applies. We can rely on their contemporaries of Roman and Frank historians however. And on the diplomats who travelled to his court. There are references of Attila and of his doings as a ruler and conqueror and also mention of the people who populated these countries around, from East to West or North to South. They are the best sources of getting closer to the 5th Century. But still there is a puzzle, or a question, that could be answered a thousand ways. Who, or what, made these ancient Magyars come here to the very spot with an idea that it was "rightfully theirs?" as it is expressed in the legend. Could it be, some tribesmen were here before? Or the other version, the mystical one has the truth, suggesting the will has been originated in a dream of divine inspiration. This was what prompted them to go, to find that land. They obeyed, found the land and claimed it. Well, there is another explanation to this. Upon his father's death, Attila's son Csaba fled with his people to the East of the borders and settled. He talked of his country all the time, he planned to return; later his sons too kept this idea of "coming back". But they couldn't for generations. Later they wanted the Magyars to join them, who were a strong tribal community, living in their country, called "Etelkoz", at the Kuban region of the Caspian Sea. So, when the Magyar tribes migrated, they were talking of "coming back to Attila's land, to the land of the Huns". This was their destination, no doubt.

But here, we have a new puzzle. Why did they have to leave that land? Is it really owed to the conquesting Bolgars pushing the Magyars to the West? Or was it the time of the divination in the dream promising the final homeland?

Historians, the studious, the respectful, the cynic, all had (maybe still have) a hard time to decide where is the truth? Let them stick to their finds, and we stick to ours, by learning what do people have to say . . .

It was late night when the couple were sitting at the table, not realizing how much time they spent with the Huns. Tass thought it was a good idea to go to sleep. Miriam didn't agree. "Not yet. You know, the complexity of it hunts me, that in either way, these people had to end up here. I . . . that's what I call destiny. Not only that. It's a beautiful story. Poetic," marvelled his wife. "And the funeral? This is the most extraordinary thing I've ever heard."

"Oh? The funeral? Did I tell you . . . well. I didn't finish that one, Miriam. Somehow I was diverted from the end . . ."

"Well wasn't it end enough that the Tisza closed on him?"

"No, I didn't finish. We were at the groundworks, weren't we? What the slaves just completed. Well. Listen to this. When they finished, they found themselves in the middle of an arrowstorm. They were all killed. It was part ritual, part politics. Out of respect for the great king, secrecy had to be insured. Also, Attila's sons wouldn't like witnesses. So, at the end, only they, and very few privileged men would know of the burial place of Attila the Hun."

Miriam picked up from here: "It is amazing! That triple casket of precious metals . . . am sure in the burying of the gold he possessed . . . if it was customary . . . is down there some place. I am sure of it . . . some place close."

Tass looked at her. Realized or not, Miriam was already speaking like a Hungarian! Now he said the final words: "After these centuries, the whereabouts of Attila's grave remains a mystery. It can be any place where the Tisza flows, or even far from it, considering the river changed courses over and over several times since the Huns were here. You see, it can be anywhere on the Plains. The Tisza is a mysterious river. The most Hungarian river. The Danube is international, everyone can drink from it. The Tisza is ours. A mighty river . . . moody and capricious. Keeps our secrets from us. There are reasons we love this river, you see. It reflects our soul."

Chapter 22

Work

TOBACCO

Of being a granger, Huba produced wheat and for a special project he cultivated cigar tobaccos and the "Tobacco Rustica", that was safe for business. From the very start he would grow "Burley" and "Virginia" and later the Havana type, since his interest stayed with the development of aromatic types.

After his military service. Huba built a research station. But before starting mass production on the fields, he had to have separate seeding beds. Recording their development, their resistance, or anything remarkable until they could eight weeks later go out to the fields, was the next step. By then, of course, the soil was prepared, but as always, the weather had the greatest say in their growth. Huba soon learned, the riskiest time for tobacco came at mid-Summer, when the combination of heat and humidity can ruin the crop in the course of an afternoon. The most essential part was to cover the flowers with muslin nets before pollination, to fertilize them with the desired culture and to label them until harvest.

For two decades he tried to come up with a different hybrid in the pleasant aromatic varieties, that would still retain the strength and resistance of the original culture. Perhaps needless to say that each year Huba kept a portion of his best cigar tobacco for private use.

With the product on the market the works eased up, so he could start an aromatic curing of the leaves, the process he would alter year after year. Of course these recipes had to remain a secret. When all were dried and cured and ready, a worker would cut and roll out his handmade cigars, which he labelled with "Huba Garay", before he boxed it. Huba later offered them to his guests, or just smoked it alone. It had a nice smell to it, but Franciska never missed the chance to comment on the habit: "Your favorite cigars will kill you one day!"

RIVALRY

If only Huba knew right in the first year, that by declaring, "Miriam is a fascinating woman!" he will set off a bad chord between the sisters-in-law which won't cease for ten years, then he would keep quiet, given the fact, this "fascination" was no more than a word, and a very minor point in their lives. But he said it. And Franciska, who had no self confidence, didn't take it well. Gathering her wits afterward, the poor woman would look at him and ask faintly: "Is she? I should say, she is a sloppy one. Only an occasional draft cleans their house. How can Tass put up with it?"

By then Huba was aware it was wrong to praise her vis-a-vis in such manner, and wished he could take it back, but instead he quipped: "I am sure he doesn't mind!" and left the room, thinking: "These two will eat each other alive if I am not careful."

There was no need to worry that Miriam would be victimized though. She was a bad candidate for it, by choice. The reason perhaps why Tass too entertained similar thoughts very recently, similar to his brother's, that is. Miriam had so intensely disliked her sister-in-law, that she would casually use remarks like: "That mean woman. Plain and stupid. How can Huba stand her?" attacking Tass almost daily with it.

At first, the twins did not know what to think, and the least of how to solve it. Yet in months the situation has worsened and went out of hand. If the brothers attempted to put an end to it, it was in vain. For having no ultimatum to give, at about the same time they both kind of gave up, saying: "Look! It's between you two. I won't fight my brother's wife. Make peace. If you don't, we don't wish to hear your squabble."

Well, that's how things were and for years they would not change . . .

Remaining on this line one should mention a chapter in their rivalry, which began when Franciska asked her husband one day: "Have you seen that woman's earrings and bracelet? Utterly ridiculous in this village, how the jeweler's daughter is showing up!"

One should report, by then Huba learned more about women and of the quiet maneuverings of those crucial moments (in which, some men are graduates). So, instead of berating "that woman's" taste and ill sense of propriety, he ventured off to the city to purchase an expensive piece of jewelry to his wife. It was the best move, for he made her quite happy with the gift even if Franciska grumbled: "Where? Here? I cannot possibly wear them here!" But all the same, she would open the box quite often, just to take a look at it. Well, that's how the jewel contest began . . .

Ostensible, long running and public, the feud and the bad blood between Miriam and Franciska might have been going forever, hasn't there been a family matter to interfere. And so the time came when it had to stop, just when after ten long years of warfare these women were getting really good at it, when it would bring not only tremendous frustrations to their private lives, but provide good entertainment for both, if one could outwit the other.

But it was time to make an end. And the way it happened, someone helped them out of it with his death.

TASS'S ENTERPRISE

Being aware-acutely aware-he couldn't come up with less, Tass was eager to demonstrate his projects to Huba. His philosophy was: "an idea should be put in use", yet became overly irritable before he would practice what he preached.

In the early 1920s, he thought about a rice plantation on a larger scale. "Why? It's a perfectly sound enterprise!" would go Tass, defending his position. Huba didn't think it was very smart, neither did his father: "And where do you find buyers? These flatlanders here produce the best grain for the best bread. They are meat and potato people. And they eat bread in between. Why would they buy your rice? Besides, why on this soil? Rice likes tropics. Torrential rains. Think of Asia, son . . ."

Tass had, and since they both talked against it, he changed his mind. Not only his mind though . . . he decided to do it big, by going as far as to change certain conditions in his way, even bending nature, so it would cooperate. Tass was pretty sure, if man demonstrated willpower and did follow through, nature had to respond to it. After all, this was Agriculture supposed to be. So he came up with a new idea, that would keep him occupied for months. He started ordering books (at least ten of them) on water management, soil engineering, irrigational methods and such. He wanted to learn how to get water, how to regulate water levels and how to keep it intact. Then consulted his textbooks on vegetable producing. So when Tass obtained maps on the chartered grounds, by then the project in his head would be ready.

"What do you think if I'll build a small reservoir?" he sought out Huba afterwards, which made his brother very curious. "How do you supply water?" "I'll find the way," replied Tass, who wouldn't yet volunteer to say more.

A month later Tass came to see his brother, while carried a large sized county map. "It's a good thing I went out duck shooting. I've met this Varga fellow. You know him? Never mind. You fall asleep when he talks to you. But has lands to sell. This is the bottom line, not those damn ducks."

"And?" pressed Huba. "Did you make a deal?"

"No. I am not the rushing type."

"Then? What's this map. doing here?"

"Oh, that. I can show you the place. I tracked it down. And figured all out, how to supply my reservoir. See? I spotted a small stream. About three to four hundred meters from here . . . which did lost somewhere. If I am lucky, it's somewhere here underneath. I asked a geodesist and an engineer. We must figure out something, to get that stream."

Two weeks have passed, in the meantime Tass presented an offer, studied the surface and the structure of the soil, so he might get the proper drainage. But the owner who was keen on selling, seemed reluctant on making the deal. Tass, without changing his offer, decided waiting it out. "I'll have capital on the groundworks, if my offer is still good. What I save on the land, I can spend on engineering."

Ten days later the deal was done, and the brothers went to the site.

"So, how did you get this whole idea?" would Huba turn to him. "I mean, this place."

"What do you mean?"

Huba couldn't wait with his main objection in the matter: "The place is next to Devil's Gap, for God's sake! I wouldn't invest here. It is not called Devil's Gap for nothing . . ."

Tass disliked the patronizing tone: "What of it? They had to name it somehow."

The terrain was no good for riding, so the brothers had to dismount the horses and to take the reins. They led them carefully up and down to the bend, by the side of the new lot. There was a rocky opening at the borderline, tall enough to project as a natural gate, from where one could see down to Devil's Gap. Huba couldn't resist the comment, "As far as I know, this part has not been used for anything. Not even for hunt. Animals don't come here. Hmm . . ."

They were silent. Tass decided to wait this out. Opposition, everything. His brother finally asked: "What did father say?"

He said, "Why should I withhold your share, when you need it? You get the money." He also said, "Son, If I say, don't o it, you do it! So it's up to you what you make of that damn place!"

Huba was quiet. He didn't like this whole business. Well, he didn't like the place. They walked back to the trees and led the horses once more to the edge, where a long cloud like mist has formed since, about three or five feet above the gorge. It wasn't there, when they arrived! . . . Now they both paused to take a look at the fuming vapors below. Huba tried to speculate the interpretation his brother could have on this. "Tass, frankly doesn't think, it has significance . . . And he won't listen anyway . . ." Tass, who was ahead of him, called back now: "Look! Do you see the bend? That missing part? The first thing I'll do, I fill it up, making the lower part safe. It will serve as a floodgate. Those people on the other side-whoever they are-have to feel safe from the water. They have no idea as 'yet, somebody starts a construction up there, pretty soon."

It was getting late. A breeze came and found them, and the shades began to grow. They walked about, and Tass went on with the presentation: "The dikes come here! Really thick ones. Well, the geodesist sees no problem finding the spring. He gets a dowser. And then, we know where is the vitality of the spring. Then we just got to free it and contain it. So it won't escape. I see no problem here!"

DEVIL'S GAP AND THE MOUNDS

"Devil's Gap" has not at all been popular. Far from it. The so-called gorge took on an irregular shape before it widened into a ravine and finished off in a sunken ditch. It was not a good place to go. Apart from various accidents people were disturbed most by the common discovery, the ditch has been emanating strange energies. Some felt this, and some knew, and in either case they did not let their children to get anywhere close.

Around the top of this ignominious stretch, wild horny bushes snatched themselves downward to the reddish-brown laterite soil, from where occasionally a goat had fallen to the deep, after an ill-fated attempt of taking the last bite from an enticing shrub.

"And? So? What of it? Disappearance of animals happens every day! Everywhere!" anyone could argue if only reason would apply here; but here things were less tenable than elsewhere, considering anything or anyone falling into a ravine of such magnitude with a wide-open crust, had to fall terrifying depths, which of course explains the name, the scare, and the lore of Devil's Gap.

No wonder everyone kept away, perhaps with the exception of those who were committed to crime. There was another group, made up by the few who lived within a quarter of a mile, that has been quite a distance from any town or village. Well, who were they? And why there? The reason was simple and down to the point. They did not belong anywhere and had nowhere to go! They weren't looking for eagles, were not watching the sky, forgot to dream, or if they haven't, ignored it just as well if the dream was void of heights and victories. Here, people took no interest in discussing heroic ancestries or great conquests as it has always been part of the national pastime, and a pleasurable part at that. They were not taking pilgrims to burial mounds of ancient Magyar tribes, where any chieftain, or man of rank has been prepared and was made up in his grave-whether to please the gods, satisfy the spirits, or to impress his own burial crowd-is open for dispute; or, rather to wait for the next call, for the next chance to get up and go, yelling: "Geee—yaaaa—yaa!" and jump for the first sounds of the "trumpet", as great warriors all do, by mounting their horses in full battle gear, quite ready to go! There would also be his household installed in the grave, including wives, concubines and the slaves, and a good amount of treasure, which all must have secured him good standing in his time, and at the end, an honorable death.

These isolated spots, the mounds and graves of the Plains were indicating the zenith of a nearly great age, a bygone era one knows so little about. That greatness, or (by taking more realistic measures) near-greatness must have come as close as it could in any given age-that is to say-having been missed out by perhaps just an inch.

Lending a unique and powerful presence for the region, some of these mounds retained their height and shape to an extent, till the twentieth century. Their power must have lay in their secrets. On certain days, as people still attest to it, the sounds of their silence carry far. Perhaps in constant search for remote times, they pick up the tunes that must be there, beneath. In time other graves would be found, some by accident. And it turned out the burial places were talkative by way of heralding other peoples now turned to dust, who came here and left also in distant History, like would the Scythians (from 600 to 300 B.C.) and the Romans (from the 2nd to 4th century A.D., ruling two separate parts, then named Pannonia and Dacia) and of the Huns at their height (from about 360 to 470 A.D.) in the 4th and 5th century, and so would the Avars in the 6th century; all gaining recognition by their military might, all prominent by exerting power in politics, in their organizations and social structuring, in their wealth and artistry.

They all had an empire! They all occupied the land and were cut apart only by narrow centuries, before the Magyars showed interest and made their move.

Exactly how many large groups have settled here before cannot be stated with absolute certainty, even if one has a list of people like the Thracians, Macedons and Gauls, after the time of the Scythians, or, of the Gepids, Vandals and Ostrogots, who came briefly after the Romans. Only one thing can be proven-regarding certainty-that the Magyars came, settled and stayed, raised towns, built a country, kept the place and kept the dream.

Yes, but whose dream?! One has to realize, the elevated aspects of History seldom occurred to those who lived outside, like for instance the ones here, at the edge of the ravine. These people who did not belong anywhere, did not think of the Devil. Only those who lived in the towns and villages were wary of Devil's Gap. The way they explained: "Them ancient folks . . . knew the place! . . . 'cause they left." Well, Tass Garay was the exception. He came back to it.

STARTING THE PROJECT

As we mentioned, regarding his new endeavor, Tass Garay ignored what others knew. His mind was made up, he bought the land.

Coming over to inspect his acquisition, he also walked around the first day to check out the new neighborhood. The lot next to his own was a scarcely populated county property, with huts and sheds here and there, but mostly at the end of the dirt road that came very close to his property, to the very spot where his reservoir was supposed to be.

Some of the shelters seemed to be abandoned here. "What kind of people are they?" Tass wondered. "Only the squalid could live here . . . the destitute. The people with no prospect. Well. I don't mind to employ them when it comes to it. In case they want to work."

As Tass has learned in the following months, a family came there with several children, but the rest of the tenants appeared to be single men, drifters or just plain derelicts. And a woman was there also, who lived alone in a shack. They-the grownups-would do occasional jobs, like cleaning latrine or septic tanks, or sties, or chopping wood for a few pennies, so they could live.

Things would start to pick up for Tass as soon as the dowsing guided them to the vital spots of their underground stream, enabling them to obtain water from the subsurface!

"A high powered pump is what you need next," said the engineer, shaking Tass's hand, "and a generator to run it."

The new owner's plan was to strengthen the upper walls of the rock at the edges, with long metal rods, and a thick dike. In case the water could overflow, he planned water collecting ditches to lead excess water right down to his land. There was no chance, by the way, a flood would occur unless in an earthquake, if the water level was controlled with pumps in the reservoir. The design was not to fill it up ever higher than half, or two-thirds the most.

The phases that followed were clearing, groundworks and the excavation for the reservoir. The removed soil was used to build the dikes. Then just in a couple of weeks a team of experts arrived to build the reservoir and seal it too.

But soon the year came to a close, and in Winter, the work had to be halted. Again from late February next year, the farmland could be prepared at last, by way of attending to the desired angle of the surface. After that the soil could be evenly flattened and the trenches cut and cleared.

Making it all, took two years for Tass! Only then could he start planting his first vegetables into the ground.

Chapter 23

On the Homefront

AN INHERITANCE

"Five o'clock? Already?" she asked, when the motorcoach, or "bus" rolled in to the main square. The center, normally crowded at this hour was best avoided, so Miriam crossed the street. This was when she heard: "Mrs. Garay! Mrs. Garay! Ma'am!" Since it was her name, she turned around. A young boy ran after her, who explained on a sign language, she was needed on the main square. It seemed a matter of urgency he said, so when they walked back, he revealed the nature of it. "A stranger, in a nutty hat, is in town. He is no use. Can't even speak Hungarian. He is kind'a talkin', but can't say what he wants. My Mama saw you Ma'am, and says, you talk to him."

"Me? That's an honour!" She burst out with laughter and said, "So! Let's go!"

When Miriam reached the bus stop with the boy, the stranger had already been posted in front of the Catholic Church in the hope, the good priest might talk German.

"Go after him! I am coming too," nagged Miriam the boy, who was more than willing to run. "Wait there, Mister!" shouted the boy. "The lady will help you out . . ." and while looking back and forth, he held out his arm, pointing to the lady in question. It worked. The man stood still until Miriam too came close. "How can we help you, Sir?" she asked in German.

Rescued at last, the stranger took off his hat and told them somewhat cautiously: "I am here to locate certain Mrs. Garay. Mrs. Tass Garay. Perhaps you could orient me . . ."

Miriam again started laughing: "Pardon me, Sir. You see, it's not a big town. I am the woman you are looking for. I am Mrs. Garay."

After mutual introductions, Herr Winkler informed her, he has been the power of attorney for the late Frau Eberhardt.

"How extraordinary this is!" exclaimed Miriam. "She was my great aunt."

"Mrs. Garay, my mission here is to hand you over certain documents . . . Shall we go?"

Not until the same evening when everyone concerned (including a minimum of two witnesses proficient in German) were sitting in the drawing room, would Herr Winkler approach and conduct the official business he has been entrusted with.

It all started with a speech . . . We ought to point out, it wasn't entirely his fault if the usage of numerous unknown legal terms made his presentation hard to bear. Did he realize, this environ lacked familiarity with the thriving legal jargon of Vienna? He probably didn't, for it failed to build the desirable effect he sought. Liked or not liked, his audience had to get over it. If the presentation seemed overly done on the surface, on the whole it was precise and well-orchestrated.

The second phase aimed to concentrate on the documents. All eyes on him now, the man cleared his throat and put down an oversized envelope to the table. The next action started with a touch on his pockets and a removal of a letter from it, which was then placed to the right side of the previous document. Stretching the moment a bit, he looked to his assemblage, paused, inhaled, and proceeded in a loud voice: "Mrs. Tass Garay, nee Miriam Bumberger! I hereby hand you over these documents, containing the final will of Frau Eberhardt, in the presence of two and plus witnesses. I have been entrusted by the deceased, who by association was your maternal great-aunt. Now I ask you to read this carefully," he said, and handed the smaller envelope to Miriam.

"Aunt Alexa's letter!" she sighed.

It was dated two months before her death. The letter was short, handwritten with lilac ink. It said:

> "My dear Miriam,
>
> Since I am childless, I decided to make you my heir. I thought about your life, what your dear mother described to me. Congratulations! For marrying a Hungarian. Once I loved one, you know, and I too began taking language lessons.

> But it was a half century ago. Since then I discovered, reason doesn't warm you when you are old and live on memories. I am glad you had more courage. I wish you happiness and a long life
>
> -Your loving aunt, Alexandra
> Vienna, 1921"

By reading it through, Miriam couldn't talk for a minute. "Such generosity."

The second document gave details of Frau Eberhardt's estate, a house, lands-much of it in Burgenland-stocks in mining, and a livery. In her youth, Aunt Alexa liked horse race activities, and the old lady "amused herself with horse breeding" (as her envy-ridden relatives would invariably put it), spending considerable time in the Hungarian horse country, at Mezohegyes, as well as at Babolna. But being old, she died, and it all came to one thing. Suddenly, Miriam was wealthy . . . And also all too suddenly there was a lot to deal with. For clearing up financial complications and checking the legalities, she needed a lawyer at once. That's why Herr Winkler was hired on the spot, and was Miriam travelling to Vienna a week later, to see what can be done.

She met her mother, sister and brother too, but couldn't come to the house. Her mother, while fighting her tears, told her: "He won't know you, dear." Miriam also tried hard not to cry. At this time, she was astonished to see how her mother was getting thinner, losing weight, as well as the beauty of her skin. The glow has gone now, and there were grey circles under her eyes. She looked ill. Obviously, Sarah Bumberger reassured her daughter that she was well and healthy, but Miriam suspected it was getting every day further from the truth.

Being in Vienna, Miriam tried to forget the worries, in order to look after her own affairs. Getting in and out of different offices was what she did most of the day.

There were obstacles. The first one, the estate she inherited, was in Austria. Since Miriam previously became a Hungarian by marriage, the Ministry of Finances in her native Austria objected of her being a "foreigner".

The second one, her aunt's will was contested by a far relation, who later had to be bought out, which Miriam couldn't settle out of court. This experience, and of coming to Vienna occasionally, taught her many things. Seemingly the good old days have gone for the bourgeois class, being replaced by their constant disagreements and legal battles, which only permitted a new class to emerge from their own midst, a financially secure army of lawyers.

Definitely, it was a new world since the Dual Monarchy came to an end. Miriam didn't take notice of it earlier, living on the Plains by being busy to fit in where she didn't belong, but in these visits to Vienna, she realized the same, having less and less to do with them, because the people she met sounded selfish and narrow in their world view, and spoiled and provincial. "How terrible it is . . . Terrible for me, that I don't like them any longer. Why did they stop to grow? They think, I live in a backward place. I think, they are backward . . . in spite of the place . . . the balls and the concerts. In spite of their money."

Given the excitements of the last one and a half years with similar concerns she could definitely say, things have changed. Austria and Hungary were separated, but they had little to do with each other anyway, other than sharing a Habsburg "who could sit two thrones with one behind"-the way she and her brother Mark used to clown, or to pay homage to the double monarch, years ago. They weren't a speck of royalists back then, but now, that both countries denied their monarch, it was kind of sad, lamented Miriam.

Only, her own life had to be taken care of, and urgently, she realized. To close a nearly two year long legal battle to get her money, Miriam sold the properties to an Austrian. What else could she do? But wouldn't sell the movables Aunt Alexa left to her. And so, after her last visit, she could return to the Plains with an easier heart. Getting home, Miriam playfully threw money to the dining table, declaring: "I am a rich woman! We can buy anything we want, and build anything we want!" Well, true to her words their house in town was modernized. They bought a large and comfortable second house in the country, where the couple planned to be most of the year. There, Miriam insisted: "We should build a double tennis court. It attracts people . . . They want to come in the season." They bought a new car. It made them the first luxury car owners in town. Miriam couldn't rest. From then on she travelled frequently to Budapest, ordered a grand piano, several string instruments, gramophones and records by the dozen. She had in mind to organize musical evenings in their home.

"Yes, I understand," murmured Tass, "to attract people. But I don't know why? Or, why that many?" For him, it became obvious Miriam wanted to get in Southern society, even buying her way in, if her charms would fail her. "Well, I understand her. But why the hurry?" But soon Tass had to realize, his wife wasn't doing badly. In a couple of months, she was considered a friend of Anna Deveny, the wife of

Zoltan Deveny. "Do you know him? The noble man, the philanthrope, the lawyer and scholar. Do you know him? You must meet him, Tass!" urged Miriam her husband. "He is really somebody . . . Very impressive. I mean, absolutely upper class. The way he speaks . . . he moves . . . everything. It's just there. Everything!"

Tass couldn't remember, his life plan would be getting closer to the Devenys. He vaguely recalled an argument his brother once had with Deveny. That's all. "No, I don't have animosity towards them. Why should I have? But I am not sure, it's essential to get close to them . . . merely because they are "good society". Well, I suppose Miriam likes that, and she likes them. I just don't understand why is she so ambitious? Why?"

No, Tass wouldn't say this to her, only thought about it. He also saw, Miriam couldn't and wouldn't stop now, when things went so well. She gave money to the local school and planned to give a substantial sum next, to the Catholic Church. Her husband thought then: "Miriam is ready for big time."

As soon as Aunt Alexa's personal belongings, furniture, porcelain, paintings and Persian rugs arrived in several oversized trunks, Miriam hired a decorator. When he came to the house, she hurriedly instructed him: "I want a new milieu! Some . . . grand design. Make it Eclectic! And make it quick . . ."

FRANCISKA, HUBA, AND THE GIRLS

By warding off depression, Franciska worked long hours in the house, that very soon, fulfilling the duties of the day became an end in itself. Even she knew this, but still the best medicine was work, with vague redemptive qualities attached to it, like: "I did this for my family." She assumed they appreciated it, so there was no need to go around and ask them.

While still young and in this strange mood, Franciska wondered of the years still ahead. Oh, she was a realist! Not very clearly though, but she could see herself alone one day with her daughters gone, all married, and Huba still out of town a lot on business. She imagined losing her beauty like most everyone in that age, and turning into a disgruntled woman who takes refuge in fault finding, who discovers the same in others she has within, but strangely, hers would be less magnified. There was a muddled future over there, awaiting, in which Franciska could picture her own self as an ordinary person.

Not at all better or happier. When she realized people in general were not happy, the imagery of the future was getting stronger, in many instances showing pictures of it. The thought felt about as comforting as a prediction about the weather: "The snow will get here. Maybe tomorrow?" And it would be there.

Huba regarded his wife to be a good woman, who (for reasons unclear) was filled with anxieties, the kind men never think of, and rarely comprehend. "If I find her perfect and beautiful, why can't she? Why is she so uptight? Well, I gave her a free hand for ruling our home which she . . . well, instead of enjoying it, converts into a "house of duties". Why does Franciska look for penitence, when she could as well look for pleasures?" Huba, fiery and active, a man looking at the sunny side, has been her opposite. If anybody, he knew how to have a good time in most everything he did. He loved his work, his experiment station, his hunts, his journeys, his horses, his dogs, his tobacco. His . . . his . . . his. Everything was "his". His house, for instance. When Huba was home, the house was full. Vibrant with energy! Everyone, from Franciska to his daughters to the people who worked for them, responded to him. He was the master . . . Franciska was his shadow . . .

If there was any space, she just had to utilize it. This opportunity came with the children. By then, Franciska was in her element. This was her orbit: "At last I can say, "my daughters"." It was all true when they were small and around "Mama", they were hers. But the girls have grown and became different from one another, that people who didn't know the family, wouldn't guess they were from the same parents.

As years passed by, only Helen would stay close to her mother's heart. She was the one to bring back Franciska's sedentary dreams. And so, consciously or subconsciously, they both began to build Helen's future on this foundation, smoothing and weeding the ground as she slowly grew into the envied role of a debutante.

Kati, or Julia? Oh, they were just the girls. Younger than Helen and "not particularly interesting", neither had been easy to raise. But for different reasons. Kati had far the strongest personality among the three. She was headstrong and impudent, almost impossible to handle when was slapping doors on her mother, or provoking her with arguments with no meaning (Franciska wouldn't find in them, anyway). All of these usually led nowhere other than exhaustions. This girl however, was tenacious; who followed through anything she would get into her head, fighting along for every sentence (often for every word!) until she would be recognized, or in some fashion, justified. A few times Franciska has been worn out by these, and would ask Huba to intervene, but at the end she had to punish her, because Huba didn't know how.

Julia, the youngest child, was the most sensitive. She had a delicate body and soul. There was no doubt. Her shyness must have been related to the illnesses she picked up before adolescence, the time the girl became withdrawn, which just made her mother more worried. Franciska had to invent for her a special diet, and Julia still looked worrisome. Once or twice she would be taken to get the mountain air to the North, but came back pale as she went. Julia's delicate constitution didn't help to erase the poor image she created in her mother's eyes. "My poor little mold-flower," she would think, by looking at her. "She is so unlike Helen. Not at all pretty." Well, Helen was the one who mattered and for a long time, their mother thought, Julia was quite without spirit or drive.

Later Franciska would criticize things in Kati and Julia, but her target would be their adopted son, Geza, who-right or wrong-on the most part was indifferent of what others thought of him.

Chapter 24

The Patroness

THE "PASSAGE"

This Sunday was no different . . . The bell tolled the second time, so Miriam could open the church door. Her disarranged look suggested a busy woman, whose mind was either made up, or preemptied on the topic of dressing about a decade ago and in these days nothing could stand in her way to be a natural. She was unremitting in this. Miriam could not be forced to check outfits in front of a mirror for anyone's sake. Not even on Sundays-for God's sake-which by Earthly measure have got here once a week. In the knowledge of all these, her style-if any-might have been considered blase, even in minimalist fashion circles.

But stepping inside, by now everyone could tell, today's outfit on her was not only mismatched in color or fabric, but altogether it belonged to another season. Some women in the church thought: "Why? She should be wearing those things in late Autumn. Not now, in late Spring. Well."

Being inside, Miriam stood hesitantly for a moment, to figure out where to sit. To the men or to the women? All of them were on speaking terms with her. Women talked about her, men talked to her. Is that such a difference? These arrivals each time felt twice as long as they really were. People would turn their heads, Franciska would whisper her comment, so that a smaller crowd in her circle could hear: "She looks sluttish. What's on her head? A hat, or a pot lid?"

Even though each Sunday Miriam was praying the priest would be in time standing at the altar (where he was supposed to stand) sharply at eight, but no. Most of the time he wouldn't. If he would, she wouldn't have to endure her habitual church-entrance-passage, providing a hell of an opportunity for people to whisper and giggle behind her back. She knew, she had large feet and she wasn't really for wearing hats, but it was too much fuss made over her by townspeople.

On these mornings she wished them to mind their own salvation, for they were stuck for it in the right place. Holy Virgin! Why is the priest so late?"

Due to his faulty, old pocketwatch, the good man was nowhere. Not inside anyhow. But if and when the priest, this chronic late-runner was in, he could stand with clear conscience there, personifying the good pastor in body and soul. Everyone knew that. He wouldn't only deliver powerful sermons on his heavenly baritone, but would sweep clean the church aisle from floor to ceiling, by purging and cleansing negative energies or shameful thoughts from people's heads, catching and knotting the mongerings, the gossips and lies to each repentant soul.

So did the man of cloth lift his congregation after he arrived. But he didn't, and now for Miriam enough was enough. These Sundays compelled her to hit back! She didn't wish to drag herself through the main aisle for fifty more years in this crowd, if it could be helped.

So, while waiting for the priest, she worked out a plan. An idea came to her. A very good one. "There is this inheritance from Aunt Alexa. What if I purchase an organ for the church? And pay of course for the interior repairs. There would be . . . well, only one string attached. An easy one. I might persuade the pastor with it. Or, I'll go to the bishop. He might grant it for me. What do I lose?"

THE GIFT

Miriam's plan was building a pew. A private seat at the side for her family and access to the entrance with the altar boys and those who gave church service. She was willing to pick up the bill, she said, and waited. But lo and behold, with a surprising speed, her wish was granted on both levels.

"Yes, my daughter, you can build a side pew at the altar and can use the private entrance." She was ecstatic to receive the bishop's letter, of which she showed to the priest with no delay. "Please, Father," asked Miriam, "let me contribute to any repair you need. I have only one favor to ask. Would you be punctual from now on?" and she took out the new wristwatch, that she bought for him.

On her way home, she was amused by her benevolent scheme. She also expected, the nasty remarks will stop. "Even if they won't, I will be far from the crowd, removed from their wagging. My money will get me out of my misery."

Miriam was right. But even she couldn't foresee the effects of the pew. Well, at first we better discuss the garden party that has been preceding the interior construction of the church. What on Earth? A garden party here? Whatever for? The pigsticking feasts one understands. or weddings. Even funerals. or, the village fairs for the church patron-saint. These things were customary. But a garden party in this neck of the wood? Yes, why not? If Miriam displayed generosity to a new organ, she felt similarly about a garden party. It was for the whole Catholic congregation, usque seventy-five percent of town.

The party, which was held in the shady churchyard on a pleasant afternoon, turned out to be a success. Everybody seemed to be there. When the time came, the priest made his announcement to his flock, with the following words: "Instead of the small, out of tune pianinos which we use ever since our organ was destroyed in the fire, now, within a month, our Catholic Church will acquire a new organ, one of the best built these days. Yes indeed. It is time. It feels like Johann Sebastian Bach comes to town! This instrument will be ours, through the generosity of Mrs. Tass Garay. Without her donation we could not buy it. She also helps in our restoration of the interior walls. The Garay couple is going to stay in our prayers."

Well, that was something! People were moved. They liked what was said about their church. Splendid! Getting a new organ! The Garay woman is donating it. The one who is from Vienna. She is the one who converted. That's right. How generous!

A retired captain, first in the line, has approached Miriam, clapped his heels noisily, and said: "Permit me to kiss your hand, Madame. I am honored." When he did what he said, he also said: "You are a great lady." Then he turned to Tass and added: "My friend, your wife has valor!"

The captain's worldly manners must have inhibited some of the guests, making them realize they couldn't speak so decorously. So they just stood there, drinking and talking among themselves. "Townspeople are short of words my dear," leaned Tass to Miriam.

The townsladies have got over this donation business faster. Right now the ritzy hors d'oeuvres kept them guessing what was inside of this one, or that one, or how they were baked.

A gentleman farmer, a confirmed bachelor, came over to the couple, who used to talk exclusively to men. What he said now, he said it to Tass, gathering he would translate it to the wife if he wanted it: "I am sure, my friend, you have a hand in it. One or two gold, heh? Heh-heh! Good sport, I must say. Heh-heh. Rather."

A group, under the oldest wild chestnut tree, was loud and excited, by talking all at once. Standing around their priest, they were the people who alternately played the church piano. Only one or two could play an organ well, though.

"It's a different business. Well, well, how different it will be!"

"Yes," picked up the word the priest. "Our church will sound like a big city cathedral."

It was a promise they all believed, for he looked truly content on this day

THE PEW

The blessing and initiation of the church organ was a great event. The bishop, who in the last hour cancelled the trip, still sent his well-wishing words which were read out loud to the congregation. All in all it was a joyful morning. When the music teacher (also an accomplished organist) played several pieces and finished with Franz Liszt's "Missa Brevis", there were no dry eyes in the church. As of: "Music comes from the Heavens" seemed to be confirmed by many, on this day.

When going home on the same morning, people were a bit ruffled. They recognized, Miriam offered a hand. Yet not all of them were ready to clean the spotty corners, while thinking on it. "Well, she is generous and she is rich. That woman can buy anything she fancies! Oh, but it's not my business . . . I should do well listening to what the priest says: "At last we could replace our organ."

Beyond the presence of such instrument and its soul-lifting vibrations, yet another change transpired in the church, even if not ever so powerful. Just as the king of instruments was built in, and the interior restored, and then the new side pew was installed . . . the remarks have stopped. They disappeared! Oh, Miriam understood perfectly how the pew brought her respect. In fact more, much more that the new organ ever could, even if their price was incomparable... She recalled how badly she tried fitting in, and for how long. She still tried. Deep down she asked, how could people be so impressed with wealth, even if she knew the answers to it. So, what was this game about? On her part, being sufficiently hurt, Miriam removed herself from the rest, and not only physically it seemed. She built a social barrier with the pew, which-like it or not-people always recognize. Even if green with envy, they are impressed. "The pew of Mr. and Mrs. Tass Garay." But then Miriam always knew people would fall for money. The time came to ask, what only a fool would ask loudly: "You wanted to cast me out, did you? Well, the joke is on you now!" Yes, the pew signified an important step. In people's minds, the place and those sitting in it had to be distinguished. If the time came for Miriam to be respected, the town was ready. If townfolks looked at the altar, she and her husband were framed in one picture with the priest and the altar boys.

And so from that year on, from 1925, everyone attending Sunday mass began to look at them, as being part of the altar piece . . . "Mr. and Mrs. Tass Garay."

CHAPTER 25

The Garay Children

A FEARLESS GIRL

That Kati should have been a boy everyone in town agreed, but still when in 1925 Huba and Franciska adopted Geza, a nephew, the girls did not consider him a threat. For them, the change was only this: the favorite cousin on his parents' death, became a favorite brother.

Getting along with him was easy, and the first year ran fast as the Garays with the three girls set out to alleviate his grief. In that year, Geza was seven and Kati five.

Huba was the happiest among them. He used to have a nephew and now had a son. A mutual affection developed between the two, but it soon became evident the boy was his own man. Huba lived with the desire to have sons-or just one-since the earliest days of his marriage, so it was not surprising if he built up a creature in his mind who encompassed everything a father wished in a son. This boy began to grow dreamlike, years before Geza's time. But eventually fate arranged him to face both prodigious sons, one the figment of his imagination, and the other in Geza's person. Things might have been perfect if the two could be molded in one, the phantom-child and Geza in person, but it did not happen and Huba gave up on it. "You yearn for children who agree with you and imitate you, but they won't. If one does, it's a white raven."

He had to see, the image and the boy were on parallel lines, taking separate courses just like the two men have, father and son in later years. Destiny seemed to arrange their journeys apart, the way it started them.

The years following Geza's move to the Garays helped to unfold a personality that was to take surprising turns. The boy adapted well, and appeared to be happy on the surface. A loner, he read a lot, disappeared often, and engaged in conversations with grownups, dazzling them with his brilliance. Geza did not seek physical activities or outdoor games as much as others of his age. It was Kati who would play boy's games, unafraid of bruises or getting into rough fights. There was indication from early on, she took the role Huba assigned to his adoptive son. She was barely six when learned to ride the bicycle on a grown model all by herself on a peaceful afternoon, when her mother visited relatives and her sisters stayed home, content with their dolls. Kati kept to the bicycle, fell a couple of times, but still wasn't giving it up. By dusk, she knew how to master it, landing safely, taking turns and riding straight. She learned to swim with the same tenacity. Having no need for witnesses, she ventured off one afternoon to the smaller lake. Two of her schoolmates-boys-were in the water, pretending they knew how to do it. By nightfall, she could swim like a dog, very smartly, even in deeper waters. On the same evening when at last Kati came home, she had to be punished, because Franciska imagined her drowning in the lake and it made her cry running down the street. This was where she collected and slapped her all wet and cold. "Why are you doing this to me?" her mother asked. "On a day, when your father is out of town you run away like this?" But most things out of ordinary used to happen anyhow, on these days.

Kati climbed the trees too, to which her sisters couldn't add much, only their awe: "This is amazing. How do you get up there? How is it you don't fall down?" or "I say, better come down, because mother will faint if she spots you that high . . ." She couldn't remember when did she learn skating. Only the year when she coached her sisters who discovered skating was ladylike. By then Kati developed to be a strong adolescent who would stay out day long doing physical activities, just like a boy. School bored her but did well, well enough to have good grades. She was noted by her early teachers as "Kati Garay, who likes challenges."

At fifteen, her father taught her to shoot, so she could participate on the hunts as an equal in the party. The reason for Huba's concession was his disappointment in Geza, who declined his father's repeated offer, who tried to make a squire of him, but couldn't. So he made one from his daughter! With the boy, it was hopeless. Even Huba knew it. All the reasons were lined up on how to keep balance in nature, at no avail. It would not work for Geza. He said to his father: "When rabbits and facans come close by, and start eating our neighbors, then I might be convinced to intervene. Because then, only then(!) did you convince me Father, that balance in nature is not on our side." So most of the time if Huba went for a hunt, Kati joined him, unless she was away at school. But the Winter-hunt would be the most interesting. Everyone shared this view, including those who wouldn't hunt. Many of the guests travelled from great distances, bringing family along, and it wasn't uncommon, that after the hunt some of these people stayed for over a week. They usually came from Csanad, Csongrad, Szabolcs, Szatmar county-states, making it look like a flatlanders' jamboree, where the hunt means a field-hunt. For men, this was the most exciting time of the year.

Kati who shared her friendship with horses early, began horseback riding at six. So, by age ten everyone predicted, she will be a first-class horsewoman. Despite of her frequent early falls she has been the least cautious or at all concerned, which gave an impression of a risk-taker, who was fearless of physical injuries. It was true however, she could be angry in a second . . . until that anger just as fast would fade.

Older people found it striking how she never complained or cried. Men admire that in a child (especially if it is a girl). Without discussing further, they concluded: "She has character . . ." So it seemed Kati secured her place among grown men who maintained, sporting life was about endurance, and not about pleasure. Was it an incongruity in some way that they welcomed her in their world? She couldn't tell, for it happened much before she understood how rare it was. Kati had no explanation for it then, and would not look for it later. It felt natural to be where they were, or to behave like they did. She didn't have to pretend with them. And it felt good.

With girls it was different. The girl, who looked like a boy with her shortcut brown hair, who would be a good sport on the hunts, had difficulty making her place among them. They knew things, she never thought about. They had secrets, they knew how to dress, how to look pretty. Somehow they knew what to do with their hair. So far Kati had only vague, or erratic notions how to do these. They were a bother anyway, better postponed. So the day when Kati declined to go out with the girls who giggled in her presence, when she gave up on being one of them, that day her life became easier (more simple); the day when she said, "I can't look like they do, and I don't see the point why should I try, for it makes no sense!" That day has set her free.

A REFINED BOY

As Istvan grew older, he liked to spend more time with the boy, thinking: "This boy has something that none of us have." His grandchild Geza reminded him of his late son Almos, the boy's father, who died in 1925, just two years ago, going after his wife. If it wasn't for Huba and Franciska, the boy would be an orphan, thought Istvan, who assumed it is owed to the happenings, that the child was still so sensitive. "Should I say too refined for his own good? Let's hope he will grow out of it though. Oh, well. He is only ten."

The old man's favorite pastime was still duck hunting, and did not hesitate to take the boy, for the family had a shortage of boys. His other grandson from Tass and Miriam was just seven and already a bookish child. On top of it, Zoli had a doting mother, which-by Istvan's standards—did more harm than good.

But Geza? He liked him. He liked him with a tender heart. Did Istvan think he could make a hunter of him? Well, most probably. The boy liked to go out with his grandfather, and this morning was no exception. The sky began to gather some clouds, but they were not yet heavy. Istvan was quick to remark: "Later today we will have rain."

Wild ducks flew above them. Geza was about to say that he felt for the ducks, but there was no time. Istvan raised his weapon and aimed to shoot. In that very moment, the boy started shouting to the sky: "Get away! Get away fast! Fast!" he yelled on a shrill voice and clapped his hands. His grandfather, regardless of this disruption and of the child's protest, shot out his gun . . . but wasn't satisfied. He took a side glance to the boy and turned away. The old man walked towards the beaten track which took them to the woods. Geza looked up to the sky tracing the ducks, which were taking quite a distance. Then, he followed his grandfather. Neither felt good about what happened.

HELEN ENTERS CONVENT SCHOOL

After considerable lament on finding a proper school for Helen who turned thirteen in 1928, mother and daughter have chosen "Ecole du Pure a Priere". It was one of those small convent schools with good enough reputation, which daughters of the middle or lesser nobility would prefer. They came here to study for four years, or less if they changed course in midway. Whatever the consideration might be, they probably had a thing in common. Getting equipped for none else than the great event of their youth, the "Coming out Ball". Some didn't mind getting an education too, if it was necessary, but only as a byproduct, for not every girl could be fooled in this regard.

The location was convenient for the Garays, that Helen would be in a neighboring county-state. The first weeks were the most exciting for the girl. And the place! Having been run over with ivy, this Renaissance brownstone building had a garden with planted sycamore, willow and birch trees, a small park and another garden for vegetables and various fruit trees. Somewhere far was even a pond, a good place for daydreaming. The town was medium-sized and the convent was at the edge. Their ownership consisted this large property, a forest, a mill and more land. Since it wasn't far, Franciska felt good about the place with Helen in it getting a taste from the outside world, rightly so, in this protected corner.

Soon after orientation and introductions, students were allowed to choose roommates. They ordered uniforms, received them, and went right on with their first assignment. So Helen, like others, would embroider initials on garments including her stockings and underwear, for preventing mixups in the laundry. Before serious studies, getting acquainted with the principles of Catholic education was a starter. And of course, chance was given to the girls to sign up for extra courses or taking up special interests.

In her first letter to Franciska, Helen would write: "The school is fine, I already like it. The nuns aren't difficult. The one who teaches French is nice. There was a test, just a play really. And when I asked her, she said, my basics aren't very good. I need to take it seriously. She meant my grammar. I've signed up for lots of activities . . . Next time, I'll write you what they are! Give my love to Father too. Your daughter, Helen."

Helen's enthusiasm filled Franciska's heart. For days she thought of her. "We are getting somewhere, after all." She imagined her daughter entering society, as a refined lady. "When? Five years from now she is a lady. Not just a country girl with a dreaming heart, that I used to be."

Huba did not participate in the choice of schools. By the time his oldest daughter reached the age of thirteen, for him it was apparent, Franciska owned the girl. He could detect her reason, it wasn't inexplicable. His wife wanted to have something or somebody of her own, namely Helen, whom she would nurture and form, until the young woman was perfect.

From early on, it had been tossed and turned in Franciska's head, that Helen was capable of being somebody. Yes, she could see her as an embodiment of her best dreams. "Helen will follow them, not giving in halfway, as I have," she promised to herself. Franciska thought out opportunities for Helen, which she takes with no hesitation or fear. Through the years she built Helen's sense of importance and the confidence she herself was lacking. "Have it all, you are exceptional!" was Franciska's message, and Helen had no problem adopting it.

Two years have passed since the young girl entered the school, and it was already 1930. Mother and daughter have frequently wrote to each other of this time. Some letters were more, some less memorable to the girl, who would read them over on rainy afternoons, when her roommate did still study, occupying the table. There was a letter she particularly liked. Franciska gave advice in it, a very good one. It read like this: "If at the beginning you please people who could be useful to you, later on they will do anything for you, you will see!" There were more, but this one stood out. It was practical and clever . . . It just reinforced her feelings. "Mother is my best friend. She is the only person I completely trust!"

Today, the rain would not stop, it was hateful even to look outside, and she could do but one thing. Going to the library . . . to get some book on romance. "Something very light," thought Helen, "and glamorous. Something to get me away from this . . . this "every day the same thing" stuff. I need something very romantic." So decided Helen, and left the room.

With her mother's many reassurances, the girl remembered having a good start in the first year. She was amused now to think of it. That morning for instance, when looked for the academic director of the school, Mother Clara. "Could I ask you a personal favor?" she would begin. The nun stood in the door, waiting. Helen went on. "I was wondering if I can use the library, apart from my assigned readings? I am so used to our library back home, and here I would love to feel completely home. But only . . . if you let me. What I mean . . . the library. To use the library."

Helen could see from her face that Mother Clara was flabbergasted and pleased at the same time. In the last five years almost nobody in her academic directorship would approach her, asking a favor of this sort, unless . . . "Well. To think of it, there was one girl, but she has been a sickly creature, wore glasses, thick glasses. She was a bookish girl," Mother Clara recalled. "But now, this . . . this quite pretty one?"

"Yes, of course, child! You have my permission." She thought when the girl left the room, "Hmm. I am taken with this kind of dedication. Very rare. Hmm. Other girls mostly giggle, gossip and think of nothing but boys! This girl is different."

Helen was right. Owed to that morning's visit, Mother Clara was soon holding her an example for an entire school, and she thought, "Not bad."

THE "MUSICAL" CHILDREN

It doesn't really matter if it was true or not as long as was recognized: "These three, are the most talented children in town." Well, that's how Miss Carola, the music teacher saw them anyway, and the parents weren't about to protest. Ever since the Mizur boys took alternate roles to accompany Julia at her first solo recital, Miss Carola was diligent on working with their parents behind the scenes on the next step: the preparation of their musical careers. With the boys playing the violin, and Julia the piano, made them look "irresistibly cute" on the stage, people said so. So who could blame the mothers, whose ambition ran with them each time (with teacher in tow) as far as the town's square, for they were against raising higher hopes or unrealistic expectations in the youngsters, at such tender age.

At the time being they were content as things were: "Those three look so cute on the stage," which said it all. The problem started only when a local benefit concert was planned, and the two mothers signed up the children to participate. It made Julia cross (the first time in her life) that her mother would not consult her, regarding the new threesome arrangement. She insisted on a solo recital: "I won't play with them. I play alone, or not at all!"

Franciska was upset: "How am I going to explain this to Ella? She was so looking forward to it! Julia dear, the Mizurs are a good family. And the brothers are so musical. They are going to make something of themselves, and I think . . ."

It was all in vain. Julia was not taken by the boys, even if they were from this so-called good family, to whom musical education was a must. In her response, Julia put two words in quotation marks. The "good" and the "musical". "Mother, if Miss Carola would teach a cow to play the violin, that cow would learn just like the Mizur boys have."

Later that evening, the girl realized it was rude to make fun of their clumsiness, but wouldn't compromise on the list of her objections, saying they were stupid and sly, whose mind lacked elevation for being busy to figure out what to eat next.

Franciska gave it a thought. It must be something to it if Ella, Mrs. Mizur, (who happened to be a close friend of Franciska) complained of this: "Oh dear. They eat like wolves, these boys. Franci,—I tell you this in confidence. They came after my mother-in-law."

There was a week-long misery for mother and daughter, but Julia kept her fort. Eventually at week's end, that's how nine-year old Julia presented her argument to her parents. "I don't wish to associate my name and musical reputation to speed-players. They are famous for playing the Hoffmann-Bloch collections the fastest, among Miss Carola's students. One of the reasons I dismiss future stage appearances with them. We are not on the same level."

Julia left her parents speechless. What could they say? That was that. Julia had principles.

The next year the Mizur boys stepped out of Julia's musical life. They gave up violin. And Julia acquired musical education elsewhere. Also by this time the Garays realized this girl, their youngest child, was cut from a hard but fine substance if she had such uncompromising qualities. She even let them see through it all, which could have reminded them alabaster by the way, if they really looked.

A YOUNG MAN'S MIND

A fairly good student, Geza did not find school invigorating. Or, was it just an objection to local boys whose interest revolved around chasing the football day in and day out? Yet he had to sit it out until a major change presented itself and could go to convent school at the Order of St. Benedict.

His adoptive parents were not too keen on letting him go, however. "What if the boy gets lonesome living that far?" But given the fact the school was his choice, Geza didn't mind going. There was a need to distance himself from provincial thinking besides, and to be engaged instead with a temperate and sharp training of the mind. Regarding future studies, he wasn't optimistic at the beginning, if some of those could or would not change him somehow, but at least he was hopeful that his cluttered and moody days were over.

During school holidays, he satisfied a deep curiosity by reading through the library of his family systematically, starting with books at the bottom row, and going upwards to the heights, where one reached the volumes with a built-in ladder. Geza was a fast reader. On those days he would read for hours and then rove absentmindedly in the house, till he could catch a glimpse of Julia. Julia was his only confidante. With her, he could talk freely about anything, and most particularly on what bothered him in this world.

At fifteen, for Huba's astonishment, he made this remark: "Western Civilization forces us to think in fragments, don't you think, father? Contrary to Eastern thinking and philosophy, which seems to be suggesting that absolutely everything is part of a greater order." He went on: "I must say the Western Civilization has a lot to fix . . . Something went wrong quite early there, father. Don't you think?"

Huba didn't suddenly know what to make of such broad application of his son's discontent. Finding no immediate solution, he just told him: "Well, when you read even more, it might bend your opinion back a bit? Heh? Shouldn't we get out for a ride? It is not so healthy to be with just books, you know. One has to keep the muscles going! I am convinced, outdoor life teaches you almost as much as books do . . ."

Chapter 26

Two Homes

"OWL CASTLE". IS IT A BETTER NAME?

He couldn't quite escape it. Townspeople named his new house (just as they would the old one seventy years ago) and Huba couldn't be that surprised, for the two oculus window implied the name. With the modernization and rebuilding, he hoped to alter the image of the house, so it no longer would be called "The House of Renegades".

By building an additional floor and adding two mansard rooms, the volume and shape of the building had considerably changed. It became a very big structure.

The mansard rooms would be occupied by Geza and Kati at first, who both loved to stay up late, by working on their studies or reading a book. Then Julia moved up, taking Geza's room, right after he left for interim school. And now the name. Since the upper windows were cut in two half circles and were lit for hours late into the night, they suggested an owl's eyes to the people, living opposite. So the neighbors began to call it "Owl Castle". Huba didn't like the name more than the old one, but resigned to the fact: "It's safer. It puts the Gendarme Force to sleep."

With the house ready, it was painted for rust. An unusual coloring in that region if one travelled through the Plains, where one saw only white houses, or perhaps a high class villa in pastel yellow, or an official building in the palest of grey. But the favorite has been the white with red ceramic tile roofs, or sporadically those thatched roofs in very small villages. Not a golden rust house! "Rust? For a house? Nobody heard that in seven counties added up!" Well, Huba had. He liked it as it was, in "statu quo antebellum"* (even if it was an afterthought). Maybe his exuberant spirit came through that house and its color. But still, for years the public mood would be mercurial. Everyone was commenting on it, as if the building would be raised from public money.

The house, beautiful as it was, looked so changeable! On a sunny day, the various hues of rust exuded warmth, which by early afternoon assumed the color of gold. Later it changed for copper, and when the sun hit the horizon, the house would just be plain brown. This would be the final phase, where those earlier colors had to lose themselves for overnight.

The Garays had a workshop, that Franciska named "Asia Minor" in the twenties, for the constant confusion one faced there. It hosted run-down furniture, cupboards and shelves to the ceiling, baskets, butcher tables and boots. One came here to clean guns, to shred cabbages and to marinate fish, lamb or beef. It was good for everything. It felt and looked like a bazaar with its own disorganized freedom. Also it was neutral ground, which attracted people.

When Friday evenings Huba invited his political minded friends from the village, they would end up always in the workshop. Women didn't bother them there, so this was the right place. One could smoke there, chew tobacco, spit to the floor, all the while one discussed politics, like a true gentleman. "Asia Minor" was a perfect place. Sometimes even felt as the most solid one in the whole of Europe. Well, maybe it was; despite of its turbulent history.

ANXIETY

The stamp showing through their letterbox indicated mail from Austria. "Mama wrote to me!" yelled Miriam, and her face lit up. She opened it and read it twice, but the letter troubled her. She was quiet all evening, and only at night when they went to bed did she bring up the subject to Tass. "Mama wrote! She tells me a couple of gossips, things about friends and . . . the family. They are all right. She . . . Mama, took a trip to Paris, for a week only, but this time alone. But . . . you know . . ." Here Miriam stopped, got out of bed, went to the drawer, took out her letter, as if she planned reading parts of it loud. Then, decided against it. After all, the content desired explanation.

* of how it would be before the war.

"What is the matter? Is something wrong?" asked her husband. "Well, no. Not really. Only . . . Mama tells me, Papa participates in some sort of political meetings!" she said, and looked worried, until she was able to blurt it out. "Tass, it's the Zionist movement. So far he kept it a secret from Mama. But he is an activist!" "Listen to me!" he said to Mama. "In modern times Herzl is the only man who did great service for us Jews. He was right! The Jewish question is a political question. We should be all lining up behind him. You too, Sarah! And I am serious." Mama is terribly distressed over the whole thing. She asked him not to do this. But Papa was firm. "I want to represent our people, Sarah!" was his answer. He is uncompromising. This is the word Mama actually is using. But he was always so. Well, the point is, she is fearful, really fearful, because it's dangerous, Papa could get into trouble . . . She says, they had a bitter argument when she confronted him: "You ought to be content with your family and business," she said. "We live a very good life here in Vienna. What happens if they won't tolerate us any longer?" She says, Papa retorted with a speech. In essence, he said: "We have to show them, we are stronger. Then they leave us alone!" He said this over and over as if . . ." Miriam stopped again.

"As if?"

"Mama says, as if he would be obsessed with it, repeating: "I do it for our people, Sarah!" Well, anyway, this is in the letter," said finally Miriam, "but . . . I really don't know if times are right or wrong for this kind of demonstration . . . this show of force. Or, at all, if the times necessitate all of these? You see, it could easily be taken by the authorities as the worst kind of dissent. You just never know . . ."

"So, that's why you were so worried when I came home?" asked her Tass.

"Yes. You see, Mama cries a lot. And I am afraid she is not well."

Miriam went to the mirror to brush her hair. She was too nervous to talk. Only sometimes later would she turn to him. "You know Tass, I used to think on the History of the Jewish people. And I have to admit that he is right. But, what Mama told him: "Think of your family, and how good life we have here in Vienna!" Then, I think Mama is right."

With brush in hand, Miriam walked up and down, contemplating. "I don't know how do you feel about all these? Of course, you are an outsider. You can't feel what I feel, but I guess I too try to make up my mind on who is right and who isn't. Maybe I go on trying to understand it until the day I die . . . It is very difficult to be Jewish, you know."

"Well, I am sure it's . . . not easy," contributed Tass his wisdom to the subject.

"Yes. It's . . . like being in a boat somewhere in the ocean. A very uncertain feeling . . . you just don't know a thing . . . but of course you pretend you do. It's very Jewish too . . ." she said.

"Well, yes. But don't you think it's a basic experience? That we all have it? . . ." asked Tass.

"I am glad to hear it, if we all have it, and if it's not only in the mind . . . a kind of hysteria . . . taught by "historia!" replied Miriam. "Well, I suppose we all have our own baggage, don't we?"

She decided to finish the subject for today and rather go to bed. Tass took her in his arms. Neither would talk, but both had a lot on their minds. Tass Garay, who couldn't come up with an easy answer, held his wife tightly. He kissed her, wanting very much to tell her that being together was what mattered most. Unfortunately he couldn't control the rest of the world; but still on this very night after the town was to turn to its other side, he had to confess an open secret to her. And that was his love, ever since she boarded that train in Germany. With the same deftness she occupied their compartment, she would occupy his life, his heart, his mind and his future. Well, as of why did she show up, was no accident on that day. Their paths were supposed to cross, and were meant to continue as one. "Yes, Miriam, I love you from the day we took our journey in 1913. And as long as I am here, you don't have to be afraid. I can promise you that!"

Chapter 27

No Scruples

PLANNING A SCHOOL BALL

"Have you heard it?" "Yes, I have! But when?" "In May. The first Saturday of May!" It was the ball, this annual event that made everyone so excited, especially now that the date was announced. The student ball, a joint venture of two Catholic schools (the high gymnasium for young men in the city and the convent, where Helen studied) used to be held during the Spring.

In view of the dark years of world economy, and of Hungary, the organizers wished to keep this whole affair, if anything modest and understated, while putting forward a rule they had in previous years: "Only for students of the two schools. No outsiders."

No wonder most girls have discussed their upcoming ball in the dining hall at mealtime. Everyone had, until quite unexpectedly Helen, even before touching the second course on the plate, rose from her chair and asked permission to speak. As it turned out, she had a proposition: "Why don't we all wear our Sunday uniforms to the ball?"

Well, it wasn't the kind of proposal anyone expected to hear. Not from a student anyway! All the more reason Mother Irena and the sisters were delighted by such exemplary suggestion. Especially Mother Irena! "What a splendid idea!" It ran through her mind. "A chance to demonstrate simplicity. Not only preaching it. Which is very hard if the pupils have no inclination. And now? Here it is." She was electrified and said it loudly: "Why? It is an excellent thought, Helen! Here, at "Ecole du Pure a Priere" we try to teach you values by which you hopefully live your lives . . . And if we reflect upon such thoughts, we recognize, this ball is not about vanity! It is about something else. The recognition of . . ." but it was impossible to learn more, particularly what were they supposed to recognize, because Mother Irena's words faded into the growing noise of a hundred students.

Everyone was talking. The dining hall sounded like revolution in a beehive. Her chance to elaborate further was already lost in the middle of this uproaring demonstration. Words of disbelief were shouted from every direction, and words of dislike. "What's wrong with her?" "Is she out of her mind?" "Helen is crazy." "What is she up to?" "In uniform?" "Lunatic!" The majority of the girls couldn't grasp the necessity of this whole idea, they felt it unjust, and were expressing their anger. But the sisters could not tolerate more. This was quite enough from emotions. "Dinner is finished! Everyone leaves the dining room! Understood? Well. So. Shall we say our grace?"

Those assembled have said grace, but this time their heart was not in it. With that, the matter on how to dress to the ball was considered closed. "There are more important matters to reckon with," told sister Vera to the girls an hour later, soothingly. "It is not the end of the world."

If not earlier, by bedtime they understood, there was nothing they could do about this "double-dealing Helen." That was that. If the nuns wanted her version, her expose, there was no use to resist, was there? Already in bed, one or'two girls still mumbled: "I wonder, why this stupid Helen wants to look like a nun at the ball?"

Yet it came. One morning everyone awakened for the same yells: "The ball is today!" Someone opened the window in one of the upstairs bedrooms, and called out with such triumph, that even the gardener could hear on the lawn below, while tending the hyacinth bushes with a trimmer. "Il n'y a pas classe aujourd'hui!*" In that voice, there was a happiness of youth, or so it sounded to the man down in the garden who turned to see the girl, who by then disappeared.

One can never be sure what kind of powers are in work to flip things and threw them off balance, to challenge or surprise with the unexpected, as they were on the day of the ball. One can never explain why the ball turned out to be a spectacle, but some inclined to say, planet Saturn had a hand in it. Whatever it was, one thing was sure. The nuns have lost control over the ball without even knowing it.

* "There are no classes today!"

THE BALL

And now I must tell what did really transpire before, during and after, this much awaited great ball.

Just when the girls woke from their beauty sleep, and when the frenzy would start, in the last hour's excitement a student, named Helen Garay has swept off a full box of talcum powder by accident with her elbow from the commode top, to her Sunday uniform. By making it worse, a glass of water went with it. So, in matter of seconds the dark blue dress became soggy and soiled like a floor cleaning rag, which looked irreparable on the spot! Naturally, the girl couldn't do much other than crying on her misfortune. Well, going to Mother Irena was the next step.

"Mother Superior, please, listen to me. I am devastated . . . by . . . by losing my chance to go to the ball. I am so unfortunate! And I love to dance. I really do!" cried Helen.

Those in the office, all sympathized with her. They also had to face, there was no time to get another suitable uniform, and definitely not the seamstress, who could alter it. No, it was late for that. But in the meantime the nuns tried to make her stop crying: "Look here now. It's just a ball! A trifle. What does it matter?"

"It matters to me!" replied Helen in tears.

Eventually Mother Irena had a solution:. "Wouldn't you find something to wear in your private wardrobe? A visiting garment?"

For Helen, the time was right to cut short her sobbing. Seemingly, she had to think what she had there, before she could reply: "Yes, I think so. I might . . . Now, I remember. Mother sent me a dress not long ago. She thought . . . that maybe . . . maybe that would be . . . good for now? Well, I don't know."

The nuns in the office showed relief. Time was in their heal. Downstairs in the ground hall the music has already began. Mother Irena had to do something, so she encouraged the girl: "Now, now. Don't be so upset! Go and put on that dress. Don't let this talcum powder ruin your evening!"

Well, what could be done? Because of the happenings, Helen had but one choice. To wear a perfectly beautiful custom-made evening gown, that was made just for her a couple of weeks earlier. She went ahead to arrange it on her Wednesday afternoons, when students had time off, which they-from third grade up-could spend without supervision in the city.

Now, that I gave away Helen's tactics, it's perhaps needless to inform the reader that Franciska, the good mother, sent the money for the dress, as soon as her daughter would conceive the plan.

More than one way, the ball has remained an unforgettable night for everyone . . .

For the majority of male students, a girl made it unforgettable, who looked like a dream in a long taffeta gown. Wearing a color between peach and pink called "blush", made it easy to mistook her for a flower in the background of a hundred girls in their dark boring uniforms.

By the nuns' recollection of the ball, one of their students was dressed like an angel, or a perfect likeness of it!

In the memory of female students, there was a violent (and justified) interference with the soft refined hues of peach, pink, blush or flowery. And for the mention of "dream" or "angel" or "lovely" (in this particular context, that is) they made themselves ready for breaking Helen's nose, were they getting the chance for it. For them, a word surged to the forefront-deception-and the bitter taste that comes with it.

And what could this old building-"Ecole du Pure a Priere"-tell if asked, for witnessing so much of everything? Perhaps nothing new. Being saturated with joy, pain, purity and trickery, the walls keep quiet . . . to retain their dignity.

Chapter 28

"What More Could A Woman Want?"

THE DEATH OF A FATHER

Well into his seventies Istvan Garay would still cut the grass as if to prove he was in good shape, and would move to town with Huba and Franciska for the Winters, often reluctantly.

He slowed down perhaps but kept well until 1930, when a tumor did develop in his right lung which claimed him later, in that year. He was eighty-one.

The twins, then forty and close to middle age, have been squeezed between youthful dreams and their accomplished selves, did arrive at a crossroad. "What else is there for me?" they seemed to ask, while recalled experiences one gathers from a tender age, some of which one coercively puts aside.

In spite of the distance he kept, they admired their father; yet his death signalled a turning point and the chance to make up for lost years, including a guilt-ridden and awkward childhood when they had to borrow his sense of duty, through which they both learned to please him. But doing it for thirty some years, the formula has thinned out. After Istvan's death the cloud lifted and with that the guilt too had disappeared.

GEESE, FEATHER AND ALL

1931 wasn't pictured a fat year to anybody! Certainly not to Hungary. Well, perhaps only to Franciska. But for her, it hardly mattered what was the year, it could have been 200 years earlier as things were going. Time moved ever so slowly down on the Plains, making it appear nothing has changed. In traditional households certain works had to be done, and feather plucking was among them, that no woman could avoid. Well, this might have been fine for others, but not for Franciska. She wasn't cut out for farm life. Though the general idea of running a large house appealed to her, but having no robust physic for it, she could get tired in no time. Of course, here in the country this could be regarded an inaptitude at best, or at worst the epitome of laziness, if only she wouldn't put up a fight. Even admitting to herself at first took time, which makes one understand she never advertised it, and the least to her husband. For a long while she would have bad conscience on being so different from the rest of these women though, who pretty much liked to do what they were supposed to do, and on top of it, could display a gleeful strength in the process. Was it all sincere? Who knows? If it couldn't improve her stance, why should she care? In any case, that Franciska could not resemble them, was obvious.

In response, she lived with an unremitting desire to get away from it all, from this rural life, that has surrounded them since generations, but could not see how. Although in the last couple of years running a big house has become more and more debilitating to her health and physic, she still continued doing what everyone else had, and did not complain. Not openly, that is. So she snagged herself into a pattern of perpetual work and fatigue and guilt, and again would repeat the same like someone who has virtually no control of stopping it.

That is why in 1931, she was ready for something new. She thought it was up to her that certain things should change, like for instance feather plucking, towards which Franciska developed a specific long-running dislike. "It's time I readdressed what I hate, before I refuse it altogether. But I am no fool. It looks better if I gave one more try. I am sure I'll survive . . . and even set myself free. Well, from this one anyway, which is far the ugliest task."

Anybody running an old-fashioned household knows, geese feather has always been valued higher above all feathers. That's why Franciska saw, it made good business sense to start a geese farm, and sell the feather in bulk. How come the whole idea of making it big (and with feathers) came from none else than Franciska? Why from her, who hated it? Everyone knew her reverence to the fine plumule, that floated all over the place when they had to restuff the comforters and pillows. Each year she would be more troubled by the tiny clusters which filled the barn like a fake snowstorm. By getting rid of this nuisance was another story, something that could be done only in days.

So this year, Franciska thought out a new strategy: "If the air is so utterly filled with it, it might as well bring in some profit. If I put up with it one more time, there must be a trade-off in it somehow!"

There was another angle. Banishing goose and duck-raising from their spacious town residence might help them to be more urbanized (she hoped), but couldn't possibly bring up the subject to Huba in this form. Still, her mind was made up, and the next day at breakfast, Franciska would present her case.

"Since your poor father passed away, we have the farmsteads not much in use. Huba, why don't we move out the animals . . . and keep only a few around here?"

"What do you mean, Franci? You want to move out?" asked her husband.

"Oh, heavens, no! It's just, out there we can raise more and sell them, and not having them around year long. It makes sense, doesn't it?"

"Hmm . . ."

"Let's take geese. I mean raising them. Getting into business. Raising them for their feather, as well as for their liver. What do you say? It's just a couple of months work, and it's over."

"Hmm," repeated Huba, who thought, in the year of crash (for Hungary!) one had to jump into anything which might bring quick money. Because grain prices had fallen, and could hit bottom in a month, or later in the year!

"Think of the profit," went on Franciska, "and of course, the livestock, the pigs, the cows, the poultry could be all moved. To be in one place. Doesn't it sound wonderful?"

"Yes, but if we don't live out?"

"Huba, don't be like that. I mean, somebody we hire will move out. Just like your dear father resolved it."

"I'll give it a thought," he said to her. So on that day Franciska couldn't be sure if her husband was going to comply, or her plans will go up in smoke. So she waited.

Huba understood well his wife. She had a desire to prove how practical, strong and capable woman she was, who could handle more what she had to in her everyday life.

So, a couple of days later he agreed to it, being aware he had to contribute not only money, but also time, until this whole venture could start, and stand on its own. It has meant time away from his business and farming and tobacco research, but it wasn't such sacrifice if Franciska wanted to be a business-woman. "Anything that makes her happy, is good for me."

Planning took about a month. During this time Franciska learned everything there was to learn about "those damn geese", including how to select the stock. They calculated the price of feeding, attendance and extra care. "Organization is the key element! And to see who is responsible for what," informed her Huba. "Also, we have to have precise figures. If you want your geese for meat or liver, for how long do you raise that?"

"For nine weeks," she would reply, "and I can sell them right away for their meat. But if I go for the liver, I have to forcefeed the birds after this nine weeks."

Huba was impressed: "So, we hire strong, experienced women, who can take this sort of . . ."

"Right!" she said bravely, "quite a few. At first someone who prepares the food. Because every six hours they have to do the noodling . . . which goes for three weeks. You fatten up the fowl so much-for fifteen pounds? And this goose has a pound and a half liver. But so far we were discussing the meat and liver goose. The feather of these birds has no value."

"So, you want that too?" Huba asked anxiously. "Why not? If not I am the one who does the plucking!!" replied Franciska. They both smiled.

"So. Tell me. What makes them so feathery?"

"You raise them with the rest until the eighth week. Then you separate them, and in the fourth month you start the plucking. From Spring through the Summer, you can pluck the same goose four times. It yields eight grams of feather at first, until it gives from a hundred to two hundred grams. Then it's an old goose."

Huba was amazed how much his wife knew. "So, we just have to coordinate somehow the two."

Meanwhile possibilities were discussed on yield and production and the importance to secure a market. Huba was glad to seek out the contractual buyers. Within the week, he would leave town in an excellent mood, and would return the third day like somebody who had good news. On this trip, he arranged the following. He made two alternate contracts with two well known county-hotels in two different towns. The Garays were bound to supply them with meat and the exquisite goose liver, and also the downfeather. The latter would be transported in one bulk for each client. The contracts were drawn for one year.

For Huba, the transportation raised no problem. It could be worked out, reaching both close-by towns, so each hotel would get its supply the same day. Huba or Florian would take either the truck or the transport wagon in the morning and be back by the same night.

"Doing it once a week for a couple of months is no big deal. Nothing to it, really," he said. Luckily, he and Florian happened to know the shortcuts to both towns, assuring Franciska they wouldn't mind at all that much travelling. From the onset, it sounded the business was advantageous even for Huba. Why of course! In this year, one had to try everything.

True, the close-by farmstead was not built for comfort, except for the cats who slept through the day after their usual feast on mice. But as the geese-farm began operation, some hired workers stayed out overnight, or stayed for the season. Some came for the plucking, others for force-feeding.

Eight people attended works in the first two months, until one-fourth of their stock was cut and cleaned each week, and the meat production would be over. Then it was time to concentrate to the next phase. To the liver. One person would all day mix and grind and soak the corn with oatmeal and other grains, to make the "noodles", something the women would stuff into the birds.

Well. That's when it all began. Though Franciska merely supervised the work, she became gradually sick of it. The smells, the blood, the entrails, the feather! Everything. She has got ill at mid-season which forced her to stay home for two weeks. The doctor had little insight on what could originate her ailment. To stay on the safe side, he recommended diet and rest. Huba was worried at first, but while his wife rested, he kept the reins.

Two weeks later, he would report to his wife: "Franciska, six more restaurants signed up for the liver. think we can double our production next year. Still, we wait out the feather, though. But I am sure this is a good year!"

Franciska tried to take part in the conversation, as before: "Isn't it nice? I think of those hotels. Now they can make their own fine duvets. It's smart. I am beginning to envy their guests. Of course . . . the liver. That brings us a good profit. From Monday . . . I'll go out working!"

From then on, everything went like clockwork. Everything, but Franciska's health. She returned as promised, partly because she had to be present at the last feather—bulking as a way of seeing off a once terrific plan. But soon, very soon, she became seriously ill. It was in evidence she couldn't cope with the atmosphere of a large scale-or of any scale-poultry farm.

Huba was determined to go on finishing the year and planning for the next, saying: "It's really a gold mine!" At the same time he comforted his wife: "Don't force it, Franciska! You don't have to go out there if it bothers you. Why? Florian will keep an eye on them. So do I when I am out. Besides, these women know their job. Why should we intervene?"

Huba left in an upbeat mood, not realizing the effect of his words on his wife; who became terribly upset: "Everyone can do my job but me. Why can't I do it? Why am I so unfortunate?"

She went out the last time, spent there three hours and returned to town. By the time the cutting started and the liver could be weighed, she strictly stayed home. Franciska took pity in "those poor innocent geese". There were so many and she couldn't look at them. She couldn't look into their eyes! If these wouldn't be enough, she also developed an allergic reaction to feather. Unable to conceal it, she spoke to her husband: "I could not do another year. I beg of you, not to renew the contracts!"

Well, Huban didn't know what to say. But it goes without saying, Franciska couldn't touch another liver in her life, raw or fried, the very thing which fared so well on the gold (pardon me!) . . . goose market.

Huba was still concerned. "What if the dissolution of her business sends her right back where she started? Who can tell what it is all about, but Franciska gets easily depressed." Huba noticed this in the last few years. "As if she could make it happen. or, if not that, then it's painful just to witness that she can't run away from it, even though she tries. With her business, she wanted to tell me: "Look here. I am a strong, capable woman!" And by saying it, it undermined her health. Now, she will blame herself . . . even though there is no reason. How can I help her? I can't let her feel disheartened."

Huba thought of these when visited his wife, who was now put up in a sunny room. "I want to comfort her. But it might not be enough. I want to make her feel happy. Yes!" he muttered, and opened the door.

Next morning, Huba had to leave early. So he left this note to Franciska: "I am off in business. I'll see you in the evening. You must rest. Read a very romantic novel and listen to some music on the gramophone. It will cheer you up. Love, Huba."

It was late, sometime after ten o'clock when Huba came home. He opened the door carefully, expecting her to be asleep. But no, Franciska was still awake, searching for something in the drawer.

"Tell me, my rose, what's in the box!?" he began. She turned around, a bit surprised. What does it mean? Oh! A riddle! He is joking. Huba gave her a riddle. He asked again: "What's in the box?"

"What box?" she asked. "Is that what you hide at your back? Huba! What is it? Don't tell me, a puppy!"

Huba laughed. "No. It isn't. But it is yours. I couldn't wait till Christmas. So, it is yours now," he said, by handing over a large oblong shaped velvet-covered black box. Franciska was just looking at it, having no courage or nerve to open it. Huba came to her rescue. "Do you want me to open it?"

"Yes," she said faintly. "Please do."

He opened the box, she looked at it and started immediately to cry. It was not only a surprise. It was also very beautiful! And a fortune! To her? It was the most sophisticated, precious jewelry she has seen so far.

"Is it for me? For me to wear?" she kept asking. "Huba, tell me, it's not a joke."

"No," he said, "it's dead serious."

The gift was a magnificent emerald set, consisting of a necklace, a pair of earrings and a ring. The emeralds were lustrous and large, and were studded with round full-cut diamonds, more than ten carats in total weight.

Franciska was ecstatic and that night she went to bed with a new thought: "Really. What more could a woman want?"

CHAPTER 29

"What More A Man Could Want?"

MISS GIZI

It was 1933. Two years have floated off like downfeathers and nothing has changed; some people stayed put, some were restless like Huba, who still travelled a lot to nearby towns in business. It was Autumn in its youth with the days pleasingly warm, though shrubs and trees with less protection from the North were rusty, and in a week ready to fall.

Huba was bored with the journey till he could stop the coach and step out by the backside of a once ornate building. It stood a bit further and to get inside, he first had to cross a smaller pasture and a garden. He strolled on the foliage and kicked lightly the fallen leaves on the way as if asking them: "Why do you give in so soon?" meanwhile his brother Tass continued the trip to the center of town. In less than two minutes the church-bell tolled. Huba by then crossed the pasture and jumped the broken fence like someone who knew his way. He passed an old pear tree, heard the bees buzzing underneath while taking hold of the fruits on the ground. so he picked one pear, the latest of the season.

The building didn't show much life. The only noise came from the kitchen window, where someone was grinding coffee. "Probably Mari the cook," the visitor thought, "she is preparing breakfast." (At noon? Well, yes. In this house, late breakfast was customary). Huba stood close to the window and whistled in. "Master Huba! Do come in!" called outMari, and opened the door. She, who was never idle, talked rapidly: "How glad I am to see you, Sir. The boy from the grocery was just here. Doggone. He forgets something each tirne . . . Eh! Never mind. Coffee? It's fresh brew. Miss Gizi is in her office. Works already. Just go right in, Sir. I'll bring the coffee on a tray."

Huba, as asked, walked to Miss Gizi's domain by crossing a large dining room which had high ceilings, and went through an oversized parlor that wasn't yet cleaned, even though all windows were open. Perhaps only for a second, it occurred to Huba, he saw a different room now, that he used to see . . . Unlike on most evenings, decors and colorings were unfavored by the Sun, as if this light was making them look calculated and chimerical . . . For Huba, this wasn't reason enough to stop. He proceeded to a side room, where a lady of great beauty was sitting at her writing desk as the slightly opened door could permit him to see it.

When Miss Gizi recognized Huba from his steps, she quickly stood up, smiled and came to the door. The two embraced one another as dear old friends would. She greeted him in the manner of a self-assured woman, the kind who could afford to be generous. Miss Gizi was about thirty years old, tall and graceful with a perfectly coiffured reddish-blond hair. She carried a fully developed figure on both hemispheres from her waist up or down, and a pair of shapely legs. For the sake of those legs, men would travel a hundred miles one way often just for a glimpse-and this is the truth-and another hundred the way back in utter misery. But when one took a better look at her, it became obvious it wasn't just sex-appeal in the works, this woman has exuded warmth.

This day however, the lady came up with too many questions as she drew up the plans. "How long will you stay, Huba? Would you stay tonight? I will arrange a "Black Jack" and later a game of cards. You tell which . . . All right? Wednesday is good for business. Safe. Usual customers. Town's upper class, which isn't a crowd," she said, and gave out a healthy laugh.

Mari came in with the tray and the two cups, the saucers and a steaming coffee pot. "I brought fresh cream too," she would say, leaving them again. Gizi served their coffee in a contemplative mood. "Tonight my girls give all their time for these gentlemen. They won't be overworked at last. They like it! And so do I. Wednesdays feel like a social hour. A party. A real party . . . Well, if you would stay, I could tell Mari to prepare pheasant. I ordered your favorite wine if you . . ." she stopped here. In the last sentence, a touch of anxiety brushed her voice. What was it? Could she be just a little precarious?

Yes, he too sensed there something. Huba looked to the trees outside as if consulting them, before he gave a reply, somewhat hesitantly: "I will stay . . . until dawn."

Gizi let out a sigh and smiled at him. Now she too was ready for coffee, since started her working days in the mornings, doing bookkeeping.

"Until tonight then," stood up Huba minutes later, taking his hat. "My brother and I have to attend our Association meeting. Before that, I'll go to the bank. But from early evening, I am a free man."

EVENING

Just as Miss Gizi would indicate it, it was gentlemen's night. After seven, many of the local luminaries came to this impressively posh bordello, that was upgrading itself to be pairless in seven counties (or so they say). One really doesn't understand their motives, but a couple of hot-blooded gentry advertised the place in other parts of the country as well, as if they were a voluntary brigade of some sort. Behind their all knowing boyish smile there was a hint: "Look old chap! I am a possessor of great secrets. What we are all talking about here, is the story of Miss Gizi."

Consequently, these gentlemen liked to tell the story of Gizi, whenever the conversation took turns from politics or money to the third most obvious subject, gossip. In that cigar smoke, after considerable amount of brandy, they just had to. They knew, in those not so deep but useful social contacts, knowing more piquantry than one's neighbor is an asset. Or even a virtue. Well, maybe not that. But in any case, it makes one sound an insider.

"Oh yes! Sheee iiis diviiine!" as the retired colonel once started the roaring. "She is a goddess, I tell you. Did you know she was married to a Count in the Ukraine, when she was just seventeen?"

"You don't say! Was she?" emerged the question from one of the curious faces, waiting in the circle.

"Yes! But! Listen to this. Pssst . . ."

Our talker here retreated to whisper: "Her husband, the Count, was forty years of her senior . . . arranged marriage. Presumably her father had some . . . financial mess something or other . . . At any rate, they say Gizi the young Countess, was seen frequently with the stable boy. Well. The stable boy worked for both of them . . . or . . . should we say . . . he stood up for the old Count?"

Here, exactly here was the place for a blaring laughter, that never seemed to fail coming in time. Then someone asked from the group: "What did the Count do? Didn't he shoot this imbecile? He should have, you know! Why? On the hunts . . . to get done with . . . once and for all . . . why?"

"No, no." Would our speaker resume the floor. "He couldn't do a thing! It was a scandal. Even before those two could run away. Which made the Count falling apart. Totally. As for the Countess? It didn't work out that well, being with this brute. She was used to luxury. And that sort of thing . . . and so, she went back . . . to the Count. But, Count Bruvazecy shot himself with a pistol, before they could reunite! What a pech*!"

Here, a chance was given to the audience for lucubrating over the couple's harsh fate. "Poor Countess! No wonder she is a . . . a . . . a lady of the night!" commented one of the guests after some thought. "This is where you are wrong, my good friend. The Count left half of his money to charity, the other half to her. When the Countess was left a widow, she reached a decision. She put her life on that track, where she felt it right. That is why, and how she bought that old mansion, and turned it into a dazzling center of night-pleasures. There are days when it doubles as a club, gentlemen. Well, of course we shouldn't forget those ladies. You must come and see them for yourselves! It's quite a brothel, nothing like it in the whole country. This woman has style, my friends! After all, she is a Countess!" Finally, a great ovation came about. "Bravo! Bravo for the Countess!"

"She is smart you know," remarked the tall and senile one-time under-secretary of state, "because the Bolsheviks took all those lands in the Ukraine. They would take it from her, if she weren't smart . . . very good . . . and lucky too!"

Well, he (the one-time under-secretary of state) wasn't so senile after all! He had some clear hours.

PATE DE FOIE GRAS

Miss Gizi had started a tradition some time ago by serving buffet dinner on Wednesdays, when a large table would be set and decorated in the dining room. Covering the feast, one should begin at one corner with the crystal dishes that were holding salads and fruits of the season,

* Bad luck (German).

or compote, pickled and hot melon-the kind men like-and sauerkraut from Vecses. In the next row, on the finest porcelain trays of Herend, different roasts were placed, pork, veal, fowl and stuffed chicken, along with chopped liver and mushroom pates. There were various local breads, crusty or lean, white, whole grain or rye. All presliced. In a round porcelain dish was the famous "korozott", a goat-cheese spread made with cream and sparkled with paprika, cumin and plenty of shallots. Mari would start to do it early morning when the Sun came up, and put aside to cool it for the rest of the day. This has been the favorite. So much so, that by late night nothing was left of it. Next there was a rectangular dish, called "Eggs Casino", made with aspic and cream and cooked vegetable and stuffed eggs. After it was decorated and cooled, it gave a very good likeness of a Rokoko palace.

All this food on the table went well with table wines, as well with heavier ones. It posed no problem to make them ready, the house had an old wine cellar, and when it came to buying, Gizi asked only expert advice. As it is fitting, she had secret admirers all over, who would also send the best of wines quite regularly.

Opposite to the dining was a medium size panelled room, furnished as a bar. Cognac was offered only much later, when the homemade desserts were served on tiny delicate trays. Mari put hazelnut, walnut and orange bombs on the table, or chocolate frambe, at the time coffee and tea would arrive. It was not a question that gentlemen preferred brandy and cigar.

If the saying was true anywhere: "There is a proper time for everything and there is time for everything," then it was definitely true among Southerners. Being attentive to the pleasures of flesh was put on high pedestal here sometime ago . . . maybe since the Magyar tribes migrated in. And it was still holding! Enjoyment of sensual pleasures, wine, women, Gypsy music or dance . . . but then, also the love of land, and work, and horses and adventures, and family. Yes, all of it must have dated that far back.

Oddly, the new generation did not object either to this issue in any form. "Our love of pleasures might have dulled us into a solid mass of Southern old boys!" would ruminate Huba when occasionally drunk with them, yet couldn't do a thing with it because he was one of them, and he liked it. So did his brother, and all their friends. "We refuse to be anybody else." In their soul, it has summarized to be a bittersweet love, the love-story of their lives, and the love-story of generations. It could bring on years of laughter, and years of cry. Who would be such fool to claim that love is about happiness? No. No. No. Love is about love. And laughter and cry.

At the end of supper, the affluents of town and country have dispersed. Some went to the parlor, others to the dining or in the bar. They formed groups and reformed them when coffee would be served. The girls joined in and were everywhere, in case they would be in demand.

The gentleman pharmacist, for being a romantic as well as a piano player, started at once with the fiery tunes of "Csardas", but realized nobody was ready for dancing. So he switched to play softer melodies like "Hungarian Dances" from Brahms. "I sleep better if I paid homage to folk and classical music in one sitting," he explained to Gizi, who just delivered his cognac to the piano. The girls adored him. He was a nice man, a flamboyant soul and most entertaining with his involvements. Since started coming here, he already has fallen in love with five of the girls, and of course with Miss Gizi. The girls had a hunch, he never really gave up on "Madam", but life went on and he romanced the next in waiting. Beyond the capacity of his heart, it is said he was a first class pharmacist and, given the girls' profession, danger lurked in every bed . . . Why explain? Association with a medical man was a must! And tonight, as always, he was surrounded by most of them, all beauties.

Tass arrived later than the crowd when most guests were seated at the bar, discussing politics. So he joined the group here, even though cigar smoke has penetrated and clouded the room. Huba behaved at his most convivial, to which his twin brother provided the background, as well as the back to be slapped. Tass was used to it, that he wouldn't even notice the role.

A careless remark was made on the government now, that only Miss Gizi's appearance would dress up a bit, who came to break them the news: "Gentlemen, the gameroom is open!" Some of the guests eagerly waited for this, knowing gambling would go from eleven p.m. to one a.m., and then close.

That's how an average Wednesday night took care of itself in this old mansion sparkling of loud magnificence aided by candlelight, as if telling its guests through that delicate lace of smoke and soot: "Look. I am the best brothel the South could dream up. Stay! We supply the dreams . . ."

A GAMBLER

Having had so much style, the Contessa seemed to like casinos. She happened to be also a shrewd business-woman, who arranged the gambling permits for a limited number of games, but needed only two days of the week for it. On those days however, she would insist on a guest list, and that they sign up in advance. Without the signature, she would let in only exceptional visitors.

Obtaining gambling permits have cost a lot of money, and the bank advised against it, as soon as the director got wind of it, regardless that she raised the capital. Gizi still had obligation paying back half of the loan for her high-style bordello. "These are hard times, Miss. This is recession. What if you won't have as much guests as you expect? One doesn't take such risks in business!"

"But I do!" she replied, and could tell, the banker didn't like her attitude.

"All right then!" he said. "If you fail to make your payment just once, I recall your loan!"

Gizi found this repulsive: "The man of money and his threats." So she looked straight into his eyes and raised her voice: "Don't make me laugh, Mister! I am your security. I am your investment. Don't ruin it! It might ruin you!" She stood up and walked out, being certain she would win. Oh, well. Once she was desperate. Now she was a gambler.

The only casino worth tracking down on this part was further sixty miles, in another jurisdiction. If she could, she would frame that day in silver, when the thought entered her mind: "Why don't I seek out this proprietor . . . and do business with him?"

It was a successful thought, her new interest. So much so, that the two reached an agreement, the lawyers drew up the contract and have got into a joint venture in just matter of weeks. Since their services were markedly different, Miss Gizi agreed to recommend the other establishment to her clients, the ones looking for serious gambling. And Gizi's casino partner did the same, when it came to girls.

Well, the news ran fast. "Two days gambling on the premises!" It was so profitable for Miss Gizi, that in less than a year she repaid the loan to the bank, minus interest, that was due only in eight years, plus interest. By that time the bank struggled to keep inflation at bay, mostly if issued risky, long-term loans. Which it did. The finance business had to take a blow that year, taking many banks down . . . meanwhile Gizi felt she was wealthy and began to invest in real estate.

She liked the business; the casino provided equipment for these provincial and modest gambling hours, and lent two of its employees to preside over the cash.

Of course, the picture looked less rosy outside these walls, especially at daylight. Depression hit harder. There was panic, people fell into traps and some lost everything. The papers were filled with suicides. Lots of business went down, lands were foreclosed and confiscated . . . the government had to sell them.

People felt betrayed, making it hard to understand how things could get this far. At about these months, a saying would go around the "house," "Miss Gizi put her bank out of business, with a wink!" One day, a customer even asked its validity, for which she replied: "I wish my winks were that effective!" Later that day, Gizi recalled how it really was. "Oh boy! If you just knew how long and terribly painful this wink has been for me?!"

But let us step back, back to the night where we all were: To that social gathering. Oh, well. Back there, it was already closing time. And Miss Gizi still had a private guest to entertain. All others had left by now and Tass too decided getting back to his hotel to sleep, if only for three hours. "At five then!" told Huba to him, since the brothers wanted to leave at dawn. Now, there were just the girls, retiring more or less, and Mari, who drafted the lower rooms from the heavy smoke. Huba followed Gizi to her boudoir, where she poured their last drink.

"Huba, my cushions and beddings aren't the same they used to be. After all, this establishment is supposed to thrive on pleasures. And what happens? My cushions and pillows are lifeless and limp. No refinement, no fluff . . . my beddings are dead. Finished! I have all these problems, because . . . of your wife!"

"My wife?"

"Yes, Huba. Her. You know as well as I. Since your wife gave up the poultry business . . ."

"Oh . . . ! Don't bring it up! Please. She couldn't . . . she . . . had to give it up."

"I wish she hadn't! It's a shame. If I think of those pate de foie gras! Oh my! With dry champagne. And the dinners afterwards. I must admit, quite a few of my elderly costumers (you remember Dr. Verboczy and, and that what's his name that old colonel?) who came all the way to my house to take a bite from that goose liver pate. What an attraction it was! And getting the truffles? Hah! I had to hire someone to get it for me from Transylvania. But he kept the name of the forest from me. It is still a top secret. Some secret! Oh, it was quite a year. A boom year for me. It was a success! My girls, my gambling, my suppers, my beddings, everything! What a year it was! What a year!" Gizi reclined on her long armchair, smiling like a kitten. "Half of the credit goes to your wife, Huba. She must be a wonderful woman! I wish . . . well, I wish I wouldn't envy her that much!"

He let her talk. If someone else would hear this, might think the woman was blase. But Huba knew better. He knew everything.

Gizi sipped the last of her apricot brandy and still had a lot to say, of which she started with a roaring laughter: "Pate de . . . ha-ha-ha foie gras! Ha-ha-ha . . . I find it screamingly funny, that I didn't know what it was, you know. In my village, we ate goose liver, before it had a chance for making it into a pate. We ate it once a year. But since I became this high-class madam, I know better the small but significant labels we put on things, which obviously have regular names. But you better forget those. You keep quiet. You smile. And this, makes you a lady. Or, a distinguished courtesan who equals it, because she keeps those miserable illusions of human sexuality at hand like some marionette player, and pulls the strings when it is time. Oh! There is a difference, though. The figurines I pull, are real people who jump during the night, the way I make them. And next morning they won't know me. That's when I pay . . . At daytime it is their game. They pull the string, and I jump . . ." Huba noticed she had a great chance of getting depressed tonight, and he couldn't let her. "Gizi, you are tired. Don't upset yourself with such notions. You don't need it. You need love." Gizi looked at him and asked: "Do I?" and her face could not hide well her sadness.

ANOTHER DAY

"To you, I hate to say good-bye," confessed Huba to Gizi at dawn while buttoning his shirt, and trying to guess if Tass was getting here in time. Gizi put her arms around his waist, leaned to him, and waited. "I want to feel and hear your heartbeat," she explained, then released him, saying: "To me, you are the man I always wanted to . . ." but stopped abruptly, and never finished the sentence, as if was already saying too much, or went too far, where she had no prerogative.

He took notice and turned to look at her searchingly. Gizi seemed embarrassed. Huba didn't ask what it was, so she started to say other things, that were also true, and just as important. "You are a strong man, Huba. And kind . . ." She waited for a second: ". . . and not cunning! You are honest with me."

Huba looked into her eyes, quite moved. They both smiled. Yes, there was intimacy between the two, in spite of the many things separating them.

Now it was five o'clock, and his brother Tass has arrived with the carriage. After the last wave from the window, Gizi closed it again, as Huba was out of sight. She didn't know why her eyes got wet: "I am not impartial. No. But it doesn't matter. My bookkeeping will pick me up. After all, I am a businesswoman. I won't cry over a cavalier . . . eh! Men come, men go . . . I should know!" And Miss Gizi opened the bathtub, where the sober part of the day used to start.

Out on the road when Huba looked back to the house, a thought came to him: "Gizi . . . really, what more a man could want?" But the thought left as it came, just as lightly.

There was not much traffic in this early fog and the carriage could get on fast. They were already miles ahead when Huba took a glance to his pocketwatch. It showed quarter to six. The carriage top was affixed because of the chill, and a woolen blanket. kept him warm. The other one was on his brother, who slept in the back.

No, Tass by nature was not a wild romantic. Huba was the one who took the bites from this red apple people call "life". Tass was the type who could wait, and act later. By observing what went on, he asked: "Do I really need this?" and more often then not, said: "Yes. Why not?" Tass had tasted most what Huba wanted to taste, since he followed him still everywhere. But with only half the gusto, energy and desire, that his brother demonstrated since their childhood.

Neither knew why, but Huba liked women and Tass liked to sleep well. That's how they were.

The darkness has gone, the fog settled and a cold wind was coming, which he found invigorating. For a second, his thoughts went back to her, wondering on what she meant, just an hour ago . . . He wouldn't mind knowing the end of that sentence Gizi started and never finished. "Why didn't she?" Of course, he knew why. "I couldn't ask her . . . on what ground?"

By this time they reached the junction of two main county roads, and after taking the turn, it would be a straight long line to home. An easy ride. They used to say: "From here, a blind horse can make it."

Gizi faded from his mind. "Why would I complicate life that's running its course smoothly, like a river? These rivers. Do they jump out? Seldom . . . very seldom. Or if they do, they get back. Everything has a place . . . a course . . . well, a time even! Just the way it was set out."

He felt sleepy and had a thirst for hot coffee, but it had to wait. Huba grabbed the reins to speed the horses. "I am going to buy that stallion if it's still for sale . . . It's about time I take horsebreeding seriously . . . beautiful animals. Beau-u-utiful!"

The Sun has risen faster now, and the new lights began to change the landscape. He didn't have to think more of last night. There were other things in his life, and they were just as exciting . . .

SO? WHERE IS THE TRUTH?

Regardless of the frequency by which Huba did or did not think of her, there is another story to Gizi's past, that has not been in circulation.

So? Where is the truth? Huba met the girl in early 1928. It all took place in a pub, in Budapest. There was no question she came inside looking for clients. When they began to talk, it came out she used to work for a madam. "But I had to quit. Well, I didn't have to. But I quit, all the same."

"Tell me one thing," asked Huba, "what makes a beautiful girl like you to do this?"

The girl took her time before she would say: "Look Mister. If I know anything about men, I know this. The last thing they want to hear is, the story of my life." She shook her head when finished the sentence. There was something about her that appealed to Huba. Her sadness? She was a serious girl, and in spite of going after men (maybe, any men), she somehow looked untouched, or distant from it all. To him, she did not look a fallen woman. Huba couldn't yet give up. "What if I am different and want to hear the story of your life. Nothing else. Only the story. How did you get here? Because you don't belong to the street . . . Let me introduce myself. My name is Huba Garay. What is yours?" The girl still found this unbelievable. She shook her head and for a minute or so, tried to look everywhere but to this man. She must have thought: "Is he going to mess up my life? Playing the concerned or the moralist, who merely wants to look and analyze what's inside of others?"

For quite a while neither have said anything, but finally the girl gave in. "My name is Gizi Fodor. Do you . . . do you want to hear my story? That . . . why I've got here? I'll tell you, Mr. Garay . . . but you have to buy me a drink first . . . because it's not pretty . . . what you are going to hear."

Huba ordered the drinks and looked at her face, and believed her sadness foretold her story with better accuracy than she could.

After a deep sigh Gizi began, by asking this from her gentleman listener: "Do you know what poverty is, Mr. Garay?"

"Well, I suppose I . . . do . . ."

She carried on, disregarding how this obviously well-to-do man tried to conceptualize poverty. "I won't ask if you know what destitution is. I'll tell it myself. It was a bad year in 1925. We had no money. You see, my mother became ill. The doctor put her in hospital . . . So I came home from typing school to help my father with the land . . . he worked in tenancy. I took extra work at graintrashing . . . The doctors had to be paid. And paid again. And still, we made not enough money to pay the rent for the land. They operated on my mother . . . She didn't get better. My father went to the bank and borrowed against our home. Small, one room, one kitchen, one storage house . . . We couldn't pay it back in time . . . the bank was about to liquidate the property . . . I went in and begged. Told them what happened. Asked one year extension. The bank director said he would give it as a favor, if . . . I would also do a favor. I didn't know what to do. I said, all right. We couldn't lose our home! So, I said to myself: I have to do it. And I did. But this man continually pursued me . . . I said no! Once was enough. He got angry, shouting at me: "One day you come back begging . . . you little country goose." We lost the house. My mother was dying . . . and we moved to her sister. My father worked day and night . . . lost half of his weight . . . literally. He was so worried . . . that my mother will vanish, thinking he hasn't done enough for her . . . And my mother died. She had cancer, you know. From that day on, my father hasn't said a word to anybody. Not even to me. Then I came to the city, and . . . and I was offered into this . . . bordello. But one day . . . I still don't know who took him the news, my father heard what became of me . . . and . . . he hanged himself . . . You know the rest, Mr. Garay . . ."

She finished, looked at Huba and said to him, "I think I need another drink." Well, it was his turn now, so he said: "Miss Gizi, do accept my sympathy for losing so much . . . your parents, in such a terrible way. But . . . I suppose you have to plan your future. Now, it's only you. Yes. What would you do if somebody would offer you the money-no strings attached—in a normal businesslike fashion. You get into some kind of profitable enterprise, and build up financial strength . . . until you get independent. If you have that, you are a new person . . . hmm? What do you say?"

The girl smiled at him the first time, which made her more beautiful. "But Mr. Garay, I don't know if I have talent at all!"

Strange as it may, but Miss Gizi decided upon opening a brothel. "You see, there at least I can claim some expertise," and she planned to do it in the country. Huba suggested, "Why not the South? With my connections I can be useful." He was right and the girl was progressive. Their first meeting led to others and each time she gained more knowledge on the various aspects of her future enterprise, until she knew everything.

Huba kept his word and lent her half the money on a low mortgage rate. The other half was coming from a bank. The permissions arrived, and finally the license. Huba had good reasons suggesting the South. He knew plenty of influential men there, it was his turf. An attorney made the contracts, and Miss Gizi was on her way. Huba, the silent partner, asked ten percent of the profit for five years. Then he was out.

INVENTING THE "CONTESSA"

But still a few components had to be ironed out. There was a need to create a certain mysterious background for Gizi, where she was imbued in some never-ending fuss and whispers, when she became somebody who stirred the fantasy of men and envy of women. (Even if courtesans seldom seek the company of women or desire their friendships). Huba tried his best attending to every item, with here and there Tass helping out. When everything came together, still he had to launch her. And that's how he did it:

Huba Garay attended the Southern Landowners' Association back in 1930, as he would each year. The meeting would be followed by dinner, and afterwards most of them walked to the club. It was a cloudy, but pleasant night; the best time for daring actions as well as for launching a project, which in its ambitious future ride would also depend on a crowd. ('Well, perhaps on the same one).

Let's listen in, how Huba started the speech. "I wonder, if you've heard it, Gentlemen! There is this woman. A countess, I believe from the Ukraine . . . called Gizi. Well, she . . . she is . . . is aaa . . . high-class courtesan. Just came to the South . . . days ago?"

"Go on, Garay! Go on! Don't stop now!" urged him the men.

"Who is she? Is she really a . . ." asked somebody from the group.

Huba gave in, and told them what he knew. "Psst . . . All I know is, her husband the Count was forty years of her senior. Arranged marriage. Presumably her father had some . . . financial mess, something or other. At any rate, they say Gizi, the young Countess, was frequently seen with the stable boy. Well. The stable boy worked for both of them . . . or . . . should we say . . . he stood up for the old Count?" Here, exactly here was the place for a blaring laughter, which didn't seem to fail coming in time. Someone asked from the crowd: "What did the Count do? Did he shoot the imbecile?"

From here onward, the story went as planned, the way we read it earlier. Well, word by word . . .

By sharing the story of Miss Gizi and old Count Bruvazecy, and by including the brute stable boy came so naturally to him, that no one thought for a minute, he only made it up! The story went well, damn well, and what he said down to the tiniest details was not only destined to get into circulation, but was destined to prevail.

The way he told it was perfect (with keen attention on effects and dramatics) that no speaker since wanted to divert from it, or skip from it, or add to it, even though the story was repeated many times.

Well, he did it, she was launched, and Miss Gizi became a sensation overnight. So is the full story of the "mysterious" courtesan, the way only Huba knew it, and later I came to know it, or as you came to know it now. (And if you ask where the truth is, I better say, everywhere).

Chapter 30

"Consolation"

THE EMERALD

It's all very true, Franciska was misunderstood by those who looked at her with envy, who felt she should be a happier woman. But did they bother to see what went underneath, to sense her dismal, or her efforts to implement change? In any case, Franciska felt proper to hide behind the screen of convention as her mother advised her by the time she has got married.

Could it be then, Franciska had no talent for happiness? Maybe she hadn't. Since extremely few women can claim: "I keep a full emerald set with ten carat diamonds in my drawer," it's almost fair to say, the envy of others were justified. If only they knew enough! Notwithstanding whichever way these emotions would be played out, Franciska's perception of the jewel has changed. Considerably, one should say, by having misgivings of it sooner than liked. Yes, at first she was very much taken by the beauty and luster of the stones. She would open the jewel case every day for taking a glimpse or trying on one piece, till realized, "they are out of place, like I am," and would close the drawer.

But one day, something happened. By walking in the garden, a thought triggered an insight, by opening a separate line of her brain, which must have been waiting there for a future impulse, so it could be released. "The emerald!" she said. At first it was quite vague. But it came forward as a disturbing thought, to penetrate her like poison. And from that day, the emerald brought Franciska everything but happiness.

It's possible, the idea itself was fed by the lores circulating on precious stones since medieval times. Of course then, they were recognized by experts and kings alike, even though in modern times it's looked down and sniffed at, as a stuff of superstition. "Oh, but that's crazy!" one keeps hearing.

Franciska did not belong to the skeptics: "They don't teach anything worth taking in." She was convinced by a simple truth: "If these old beliefs could keep us spellbound—regardless of the passing time-then they are worth holding . . . Others do what they like! I don't care."

Emerald was believed to show the truth about the man who was sworn to be faithful to his lady, if she was the possessor of such stone. It is said, the stone changes its hue if the other is unfaithful, and even cracks at times, as it was recorded in the case of King Bela I*. The monarch was wearing such ring when he embraced his queen. Did the ring warn him for what he suspected, or already knew? In the court, the ring has got the credit by those who knew more on what went behind the scenes, and this version came down in History, via the scribes or "Deaks". The "Deaks" would be the worldly scholars in the secular world of medieval times, for being educated in Latin and writing, and also having acquired knowledge in music and diplomacy, making it a noteworthy resume to show in return for the King's employment. The monarch often asked them to witness and record anything outstanding taking place at the palace, where courtiers and ambassadors planned their clandestine romances with the ladies in waiting, or the more political minded oligarchs have got incited in plotting against one another, that is until their head was in place.

On her part, Franciska was convinced. "If it is recorded, it must be the truth." For her, it was valid that precious stones are curious in more than one way. Throughout centuries, they have been known to delight, to protect, to heal, to forewarn, or even to doom their possessors. If one was able to learn the proper attribution to each stone, one could not be caught off guard.

"I am surprised to see Huba for being so careless! It's out of character. Or . . . he doesn't know the lore of this stone? Which makes me feel, he bought me a keyhole, so I can take a good look into his escapades. And pretend . . . to know nothing. Nothing at all! How appalling!!!"

---

* King of Hungary from 1235-1270.

Franciska couldn't help it, the idea stayed with her. There were days though, when she could dismiss it. But the more she tried, the more she had to resign to it. As if she was lured into knowing, Huba had another woman.

TRUCE AND PEACE

The two women's heads were together. "No, Miriam, no. I can't argue with him. For Huba, temptations are opportunities. If he thinks like that, why would he bother to resist them? I don't know about other men, but he rather goes out to meet these, his so-called "opportunities", because he wants to have it all. But all he finds are the cheap substitutes of his dreams. Not that he admits that to you. No. When I ever confront him, he thinks it's clever to disregard my feelings. I don't think it's clever. To me it is heartless."

Miriam listened thoughtfully to her sister-in-law and agreed on most. "You see, Tass is very much like this. I just didn't see it earlier. I was blind. Blinded by my love for him."

"So, what are you going to do?" asked Franciska with concern and a bit of curiosity.

"I can't change him. Not now. I have to see if I can change though. It's hard to become a new person, you know. Who was born from a disappointment."

As we've learned earlier, only after Istvan passed away in 1930 would there be substantial changes in the Garay family, but hardly the kind the two women would wish.

A new era forced Miriam and Franciska to reevaluate the family, its values, its failures, and most particularly their role in it, if they were to save it. Both women wanted to start over now, by making a truce, forgetting and forgiving by working on the peace, or going as far as one day forming an alliance. Alliance? What for? Where was the enemy? Well, just around the corner. In any case, they had no time to waste. Spending fifteen years in the Garay family, neither could risk losing what she accumulated, be that love, wealth, or social status, not to mention that well-rounded, if a bit too transparent sense of security most married women like to sport as soon as they are accustomed to the idea, their man and provider is climbing in bed with them for life.

When he was alive, strangely, neither woman realized the extent of the hold Istvan had on the twins. Immediately after he was gone, his sons underwent a dramatic change, as if doors would fling open without anybody banging on them, for the reason of letting these two into an unexplored zone for harvesting the thus far forbidden fruits of sensuality in a bountiful, all which they could buy for money.

So, they had it in every variety of shape and size, sampling it unashamed, forgetting it the next day, or starting it over in a week, or whenever a thirst in their groins would grow, urging them to go out and get some more.

They enjoyed it a great deal and decided by changing notes, hearing about it was different than doing it. There was nobody to hold them back now. Not their wives, anyhow. Why? A Southern gentleman did not owe an explanation to his wife in such matters, so they thought, they were well within their rights by frequenting the whorehouse. Or the casino. Well, the wives should be the ones to exercise discretion. Times did not change!

Tass and Huba plunged into the middle of a nightlife, card playing, drinking, and more serious gambling. Sometimes they would spend only two days home from a week, as if by going home was necessitated by the change of clothes and shaving, or talking in a hurry to the overseer. Showing their bristled faces to their wives meant to be a reassurance that they were still alive. But on the rest of the day Tass and Huba were as good as dead, because they had to sleep off the wildness from the wild nights and the revelry, the alcohol, the music, or some of those good for nothing promises made during a sexual escapade, when the act and the word both disappear with the night, leaving only that bad taste in the mouth, something only the strongest brandy could rinse out.

That's how they felt of coming home, but still they were doing it. It worked like a forbidden game for a child . . . They both adopted new tactics by being demanding and inconsiderate, simply turning defense into offense when Miriam and Franciska would scream.

But what happened? In their thirties, the Garay twins used to be the picturebook of normalcy. People recognized two responsible, well-established men in their person, who fought a war with honor, were successful in their trade, each had had a good marriage and nice family. What went then wrong? Well, maybe nothing. But this nothing was too much for their women. And for the sisters-in-law, the first time in ten years the enemy ceased to be the other one, since a common enemy surfaced in such an ungainly form that it took the best of them to fight it. There it was; the sensual nature of two grown men kept on leash, now exploding. It was not uncommon . . . but still. Even if the twins were taking a curiosity ride-would reason their women-still there was reason to be concerned and worried, because they couldn't tell when would it stop, if at all it would stop, or it will one day turn into a serious threat to their marriages. This, of course, could not be known. It could only be waited out.

There was a tiny little gain though . . . Now both women could laugh it off how it used to be between them. The distrust, jealousy and pettiness. Franciska felt badly why she ridiculed her, but Miriam told she doesn't mind if dresses and hats and shoes disagree on her, or accessories were either too much on her, or something was missing.

Being aware how people looked at her when she started talking, Miriam enchanted her critics since she was a girl. Perhaps the same happened to Franciska now, who complemented her sister-in-law in earnest. "Miriam, you don't look a year older since the time you came here."

"I can tell you why. When I was ten, I looked the same. A little old child. Wait. I'll show you the picture. Here, this one! Doesn't it look like it was taken yesterday?"

"Hmm. And who is she?" asked Franciska, who evolved to be such a'diplomat that she could bite her tongue, instead of hurting "that woman".

Miriam seemed happy to talk about it "This one is with Mama. You know, Franciska, still when I think of her, I cry. The beauty she was! She was so lovely to me, saying I was special to her and . . . I believed it. She loved me more than anybody. Now I know! Everything was beautiful on her. She used to tease me, saying when beauty and schick were given out at the main gate, I must have wandered off, but stood twice in line for brains. She would talk to me like that when I was little, just to amuse me."

Miriam was still taken over by grief, any time she would mention her mother, of whom she lost three years ago. Franciska tried to talk of her own parents and how she lost them, and Miriam would listen, for in these talks they both had a chance to bring back those years that they would foolishly deny from the other.

CHAPTER 31

Helen, Kati, Julia

FINISHING SCHOOL

At sixteen, Helen was confident in everything she did, and after spending three years in a convent, in 1932 her family would send her to finishing school. So, the young lady in her usual pandemonium said good-bye to the nuns, packed her things and invited over some school chums for a week in the hottest of Summer holidays to the Garay home.

She threw a party just for them, a good old-fashioned girl party when they slept half a day, and what's left of it they ate whatever they pleased from fresh fruits to sweet cakes and double whipped cream on everything, saying this was their last year to pig out. The consequence, a few kilos on one's figure, was not yet big deal, if there was another year to get it off. They giggled and gossiped, smoked a cigarette, made promises, were telling their secrets, and dreams of the future. They felt half women, half children. Only one among them came up with a plan, saying: "I will be in society, and I will get a central role."

The Summer disappeared fast that year for Franciska, who cried a little while Helen stepped to the grounds of a new school. This one was located in S., the biggest of Southern cities, which after a devastating flood had to be newly designed. In this century, the place would be adorned with well-maintained parks and small cultured gardens, with promenades and wide avenues, which had the role to lead travellers in and out of this elegant city.

Being divided by the Tisza, the center would consist of an Old and New Town. Given the layout-with a very wide river in between-each part of the city had basis to affront the other side: "Just look at you! Why should we be one city?"

Meanwhile other girls had trouble getting used to the place, Helen (oddly) wished to know the hierarchy in the works, and overnight if possible. After that much schooling, Helen avoided episode players unless they could be of use, like the ones she approached for information in the first week. Her sources became older students, the housekeeper, the gardener and a very young nun, who gave the piano lessons. Whether these informations ran on the line of gossip, were fabrications or lies, they were informations nonetheless, something Helen did not plan giving out.

During school years Helen would excel in fields where she could get attention. Therefore, her favorite subjects were gymnastics, classical dance, drama and voice lessons. Academic fields did not mesmerize her, yet in some way or other, she managed to earn average grades in most subjects. Whenever asked to prove how much she really knew, her classmates would say: "Listen to this! Helen speaks her way out."

Inadvertently, on these days too, she had the limelight. Helen wasn't a group person. It wasn't in her nature. What would intrigue her in a group was how to be the center of it. Well, if she couldn't, she never joined. In general, she connected these years for getting answers. Mainly to track down if life was working in her favor. It was not surprising, how Helen considered schools as neutral grounds; that is, for each girl having the same chance the day of her entering it. In this world, inside as well as outside, the rules were different from the rules of the family. Something Helen understood quite well from the first day of leaving home.

"You start your day with exercise and you take a shower. But it does not end there. You take care of your skin, your hair, your teeth and nails. And your dress and shoes. Everything."

Most students were bored by Sister Vera's speech on health education, for it sounded all alike. Besides, Spring has been knocking on the window, the birds came back, a whole different message was written across the sky, filling the air with that something . . . But what was it? A substance? or a projection of one's desire? Who knows? Nothing was clear . . . "How strange! When Spring arrives there are new feelings one cannot explain. What is this confusion one feels? Why at this time of year? Is it because one is seventeen? To think of last Spring, things were none less confused. Oh! One just had to cry. At least once a week . . . even if there was no reason for it." At any rate, these circumstances were enough for most girls to think of love, this sublime and miserable feeling, which gets one alternately if one is not careful, but one is never careful, and the least at this age.

"Love . . . love . . . love. How incomprehensible it is in its entirety; could not be explained or taught, which must clarify the reason why most schools leave it out from their curriculum as the least understood subject under the Sun, or if not there, it is definitely in the realm of Academia."

"Take a look at Helen. How perfectly groomed she is," continued Sister Vera.

If nothing, this sentence reawakened most students. They disliked what was just said. Furthermore, it annoyed them, that Helen of all people was the one they ought to follow. "What's happening in this world? We know from fact, Helen is a big liar who takes advantage of everyone in the school, students and nuns alike. Something, Sister Vera ought to know, but whoever of us will blow the lid will be reprimanded and be considered "unethical". So, it's much better if Sister Vera will find this out for herself one day. The problem is, when will be the day? The day of reckoning when nuns can tell false from truth. Well, until then, one just has to wait. "Helen is brushing her hair!" So what? Just to hear this stupid nonsense, makes one nervous!!!"

Spring or no Spring, it seems daydreaming was over for now . . .

THE DEBUTANTE

And so Helen blossomed into a debutante. Since everyone was affected by it, "In her case this should be mentioned with capital letters," pointed out her young sister.

The last year in school was difficult. Helen couldn't keep her mind on her studies. In a letter to Franciska, she wrote: "I am fed up with education! I want to step into real life!" Helen had dreams of getting engaged and being married one day, yet right now she thought all right enjoying the "ball season" for a few years. And after that? "She dances her way into society!" would portion off Kati (the same sister) her sketches on Helen's taste, preferences, or way of thinking, which was far the best entertainment this family could get.

"It is no more than sibling rivalry," observed Franciska, who was offended by it. Well, wanting it or not, she had to forebear the child's bias explorations such as: "You won't catch me dead in a long taffeta gown. I'd rather die being thrown off by a horse," or "Why on Earth do you curl your hair, when it goes back straight? It's stupid!" These were just part of her tenets.

Franciska on the other hand has begun mental preparations for the "coming out ball", and to the ones that would follow. She organized everything to the last details to make sure, it was a success. Helen had to have the best dresses and gowns, so it was time to take a trip to the capital, for they needed new hats and shoes and suits-really good ones-but then . . . where were the best ones? In Paris. Where else? So, Franciska was working hard convincing Huba that she and Helen ought to go there. When, if not now? Really, when?

On previous Summer seasons the family spent time in a resort spa, located on the Southeast part of the country, where the waters had curative powers as much as the clay, in which Franciska was digged in daily for half an hour. It did wonders to her complexion, or so she believed. The children, Julia and Kati played all the time, were in and out of the pools, Helen was having a good time with young people of her age, Huba went to the casino to play cards. It felt good how everyone found a suitable entertainment.

But this season was different. Helen came first. She had to be prepared. After all, she was the debutante. Franciska went ahead and planned the trip to Paris, where Helen could speak French, to show up her knowledge. Things have progressed tickets, programs and hotels were arranged, mostly through the mail.

Mother and daughter were to take the Orient Express from Budapest to Paris. Before three days of their journey however, Franciska became ill with heavy bleedings. It came unto her in a drastic way, which just kept worsening each hour. The family was alarmed, called the doctor, who showed up at late afternoon. Emphasizing the urgency, he advised immediate hospitalization, saying Franciska had to have corrective surgery and rest in a hospital bed following it. "But you see doctor I can't go tonight, only early morning. There is an unfinished business I must attend to," replied Franciska.

Not quite understanding it, the doctor left frowning, and Huba came in. He was very nervous when said: "The trip shall be cancelled, it was just a trifle anyway." But Franciska would not hear of it. Of course, she cannot go . . . but . . . "Look here," she pleaded, already crying. "Helen has to go. For her, it is essential!"

Huba lost his temper: "Franci, you are worried about your daughter's wardrobe and at the meantime lose half of your blood. That should stop now! It went too far. The girls and I, don't know what's happening to you, and you are acting, as nothing is!"

"No, Huba. Listen to me. Please? Helen has to go. She cannot pay the price that I became ill . . . She was so looking forward to it."

Huba protested: "But she can't go alone! No way . . . unless we find someone . . . to chaperon her. But who?"

"Oh. Don't worry. I thought it out. There is no one but Miriam. Yes! Miriam. I swallowed my pride. Look! She really knows her way around Europe. We cannot disappoint our daughter, Huba. It means so much to her."

Huba took his time, before his answer came "I still don't like the idea. You could go a few months later."

Franciska noticed, Huba lost steam from his argument. She waited, and while holding her hand, at long last he gave in: "All right, if you insist. Miriam isn't a bad choice. But we have to call her. Asking what she . . ."

Franciska smiled: "I already have. I knew, sooner or later you will approve. You see, Helen mustn't start her grownup life with disappointments."

YOUNG KATI

How could her parents help if Kati's obsession for social justice has surfaced early, or if she gave voice to it in such manner that made them nervous, especially when they had company.

Being deeply passionate about such issues at thirteen was commendable "in theory", they agreed, but when the girl opened her mouth to use loud and bold statements-to provoke people who would come to the house-Franciska and Huba were mortified. Since Kati liked to test them, people just never knew what was awaiting them at the Garays.

Afraid to lose friends, Franciska was more embarrassed. "Kati acts, she is out to get them! It's lunatic. And I have to be ashamed, that I cannot restrain her!"

Huba, on the other hand, let it go each time, which just aroused Franciska's suspicion, that he was amused by his daughter's little speeches, who pushed her listeners to the mat where they could wrestle with "the social responsibilities of modern man," her favorite subject at the time. Women avoided to respond, but the male guests invariably ended up defending themselves with explanations or excuses, so they could be released from those awkward positions this young girl would put them. Though it was good lesson for both parties. At least, Kati could learn how very much men hate to be cornered.

But since every good thing (even in an experimental stage) once must end, when it was getting nasty, Franciska would yell: "Leave the parlor at once!" So, she left. But as soon as the girl reached her upstairs room, she would shout insults to the walls in her outrage, half-hoping, those downstairs might even hear some of it. "Assembly of idiots! You well-fed selfish creeps!" Only, when her anger has receded would she say somewhat later to herself: "I will show them one day. I'll find the way." And for a brief moment her future came by, for concentrating on that young defiant face, perhaps forming it for the days ahead, when she as a young woman would indeed find the way . . .

"The complacency makes me sick!" she would say, a year later. "It really does. As far as this class neglects the moral obligation to give . . . I mean to give to those who have nothing. But how can they? This class is totally self-serving. Totally. So, you are never going to convince me. Never! Don't bother. To begin with, I reject the milieu I was born into," she informed her brother. Geza listened to her just a little more, even though he came to her room only to get a particular book, a collection of essays, that he lent to her weeks ago.

As it turned out, today Kati was on the right path for changing the world once more, with a rage not yet tamed. "Perhaps she doesn't want to tame it!" occurred to Geza. "Or, just doesn't know how?" He had no idea which while displayed his patience as she went on. "I think, as far as responsibility goes, one should serve a common good, in which one includes the poor and defenseless! Not only his own class. I don't understand. How do they dare to speak about values?" She looked at Geza who just figured there has to be a way out. For him, that is. "Beautiful speech, Kati, beautiful. I envy you. The next time I'll born around, I try to be like this. This time it's late for me. I am already rotten . . ."

Kati picked up her head for the sarcastic tone. "Why don't you keep your mouth shut? Idiot!"

Wild as anyone could be, when Kati talked like a fieldhand and didn't even know it, the time came to put her in the right school. Or any school!

Against the girl's protest, that's what Franciska decided, who didn't trust local schools. But again, under the circumstances, the most the Garays could do was sending her to a moderate boarding school' which had this reputation of being just a bit too liberal with a curriculum permissible to pick up every kind of advanced ideas and thoughts, so the students can play with it. It sounded good and attractive enough, so she agreed to go, and for the parents the ultimate victory was that she went at all.

A SECRET ADMIRER

He would often watch her coming from the school . . .

Even as a boy, Geza loved everything about Julia, her voice, her scent, her smile. She was his best friend. He adored the way she walked, the lightness of her gait, that wouldn't have been too easy to describe, for Julia seemed to have a method by touching a minimal surface of the ground, which made her look like an angel who did not use ordinary gravity, but abided a different set of law designed for creatures like she herself appeared to be.

During the holidays Geza discovered he did not only enjoy Julia's company, but increasingly longed for it, which posed him a difficulty in the last few years for sorting out what attracted him the most. Her beauty, intellect, or personality? Why not all three, he asked one day, since Julia has been a far cry from other girls he knew. Their love of provoking bothered him at no end, and by finding it so very immature, he accordingly despised it, for which he was in the right age.

In comparison, Julia was natural and kind and comforting and superbly intelligent. It remains a question if he fully realized, that throughout the years the greatest asset of her friendship was, Julia provided the chance, as well as the direction to balance out the fluidity of his abstruse character. Usually the girl had sound advice to his countless dilemmas that would excite him at first and upset him later. He let her reason out most of these, so she could make him look at it with a new eye.

At about the same age, next to an intellectual curiosity, a new hunger began to grow in his soul, to find a soulmate with whom one can share everything. As soon as someone belonged to him, he knew his sense of loneliness would vanish. "It's very normal, I hear. Everyone searches,for his other half." The holidays spent together only helped him to realize, he found her, and this person had to be none else but Julia!

On his part Geza was ready but could not rush to inform the girl. How could he? There was a paradigm in that Julia was a delicate creature, but with such strength of character that could make others envious, and at the same time the only soul who understood him, and knew who he was. Yet he had to be careful, and had to investigate if she was taking at least half as much and similar interests in him, as he was in her. And he had to be cautious. Nobody could suspect what was taking place in his heart and learn of it other than Julia! Still, the sad part was, it couldn't be told to Julia, and there were a hundred reasons why. The first, Julia would get frightened, wouldn't know what to say, to do to think. Perhaps would start hating him, and he would lose her at once. So the best idea was to keep silent. "My emotions ought to be rationalized!" he thought afterwards, but saw the contradiction. "Emotions rationalized? It sounds stupid."

Geza decided anyhow not to tell her this Summer, and not even at Christmas, because Julia was still too young. Next year sounded better. By then he would gain time to analyze his feelings and understand them better. "Well, this is just as stupid. My feelings won't change by analysis or understanding. They will be there, and I'll feel them all the same." So, what was there to do? Waiting in the knowledge of an unmistakable certainty, he found his soulmate, his friend and his love in his cousin?

But he waited till there was hope (however remote) that one day Julia will return these feelings with the same abundance he had them. "Well, I wait. Time is on my side. After all . . I am sixteen."

Chapter 32

Terka, And Those Around

TERKA

When the Garays took her in, sooner than a year the half-witted girl furnished a private paradise with the gadgets she obtained in a string of village fairs, and also with the ribbons, buttons and shoes, not to mention her choice of clothes, and just about everything she felt essential putting into her domain, that was the small room next to the kitchen.

Terka had a trauma. She was victimized as a ten-year old child for being left alone during the big flood in the city, which time her parents have assumably perished. She spent two whole days and the nights on their rooftop with a cat up until the river began to recede, and finally men could be seen on barges who were out to spot survivors. She had an old aunt who took care of her after the horrifying week, and when this aunt years later died, people asked around in-the county, and the Garays decided to take Terka in. But by then, she was nineteen.

Terka wouldn't take part in conversations. No, she wasn't shy. She could offer strange, unfinished sentences quite suddenly instead, or things that no other person would successfully reconstruct, or otherwise comprehend. Nonetheless with no seeming inferential motive she pushed forward her remarkable thoughts and the end result reminded any person who carries a rational mind to a broken kaleidoscope, that people invariably throw out even if it still fascinates.

Instinctively knowing she was not one of the Garay girls who went to school and looked very smart, Terka fashioned herself after the first month as the "maid" and told to Franciska outright: "I'll do the fireplaces for you. And the stove. And things in the kitchen. If it is warm."

So in this first year, Julia put down the following in her journal: "The strangest girl came to us. I must think of her as a still wandering lost child of a Pantheistic age. She has knowledge, we only dream about. And it comes out in fragments. But it is hardly comprehensive . . . What can I say? People tend to look down on her."

Julia loved most how Terka used to sit at the fireplace transfixed and motionless for hours, just staring into the fire, listening to the crackling of burning logs and waiting for a salamander to jump off of the fire, as it came to light, something she even told with words, that made Julia decide, Terka was a naturalist. She didn't care to eat with the family. Upon a militant insistence, Terka had three meals, and all in the first half of the day.

Her breakfast consisted of porridge with shaken crystallized sugar and cinnamon, of which she waited to melt, and when they started to flow, she loved how they formed lakes and rivers. At ten o'clock, after some work she took a glass of milk with bread and a washed carrot. Not much after two o'clock she would have steamed kasha, as her last meal of the day. Each day the same.

Years later, Julia tried to divert her to do as others, which she did for a day, but on the next she returned to her old dishes. Which just says, Terka was her own woman, really a "terra incognita". That she was ageless, proves the same. If one said she too grew old, didn't make sense, since she never behaved her age. She remained a child. Waking at dawn, each morning after breakfast she was to explore the gardens, the stables and the storage rooms. When it was done, the rooms of the house (regardless of occupancy) had to be opened one by one, so the Garays learned to lock the bedroom doors in their own house, after a few of these embarrassing visits. Their guests were advised to do the same. And Terka, on her daily pilgrims, gave out those little screams at the door of each room, such as: "Oh! Julia's room!" "Oh! The big dining!" "Oh! The library!" and so on, until she would settle in Asia Minor, on the canape.

PASSION FOR POLITICS

Feeling better versed in matters of social justice and misconduct than just a year ago, Kati was back from school for the holidays to make known a few of her ideas on the subject.

"Don't they have the same right to own a property like you have, Father?"

"Sure they have!" replied Huba, who still had a lot to do on his daughter's re-education, regarding property. He felt comfortable with what the law decreed on it, and proceeded to talk as someone who wanted to be tolerant. After all, it was his daughter who needed to learn the facts of life. "Kati, you forget one thing. I own a property of which I inherited from my father, who happened to be an extremely hardworking man."

"Father! This is beside the point! What I am talking about is, rights and deprivations. So far these people-the poor-know deprivation only. That's why you and others. I mean big landowners ought to . . ."

Well, it was too much.

"Stop right there, missy! Don't you believe, this deprived state made them better from the rest of us! Or, do you think it gave them rights to our property? This is too strong . . . even from a radical!"

"I didn't mean it that way, Father. But something has to be done, don't you think, to improve the lives of these people?"

Here they had to stop. Franciska opened the door and called in: "Huba, someone is here to see you." So Huba left the room. In the next hour, Kati and Geza occupied the best corner of the living room, sunken into an endless discussion. Kati wasn't a vain girl. She thoroughly enjoyed Geza, the wit of the family, because he dared to tell her if she was too naive, concerning the great unsolved issues of mankind, or she had the realistic assessment on them. At any rate, he didn't let herself take too seriously. The two sometimes fought. But why shouldn't they? There were days-like this one-when they fought about his "non-involvement". "You puzzle me, Geza! If you do understand the interaction of politics and economy, and see how one serves the other and how bad it is to society by creating an underpaid underclass who is the most sensitive to the whims of this dangerous double game, and you see clearly that the money market pulls the strings, controlling economy and politics and as a result, the well-being of all society, then why aren't you more involved in getting things done in the right way?! I mean . . ."

"Because there is no right way!"

"What do you mean by that? Don't say this to me, Geza."

"Well, I say it . . . Things were screwed up at the very beginning, when man "invented" dominance. He didn't quite invent it. He had it. Built in nicely in his tiny little brain . . . And when the Earth began to be populous with at least two more people on board next to Adam and Eve, man couldn't resist to make this announcement: "I am the one who will run things here from tomorrow." And he thought: "And you, my friends, are the ones who serve my interests." But didn't say it. On that day, man invented politics too. This is what politics and power are all about. In a nutshell. How to use others to get me things I want."

The girl was not satisfied with this. "You love to divert my mind from the original subject. I know it's funny . . . or sad, rather. Not at all funny! But I am talking about involvement. If you see what's wrong, why don't you want to fix it? I . . . I want to do things for others. But . . . it happened already, that I wasn't much appreciated . . ." confessed Kati to him.

"If I am not mistaken, it's about your letter to the Lieutenant Governor? When you suggested the sharecropper housing . . . Well, dear sister, you were successful in embarrassing father. But other than that, the people said they don't wish to pay for permanent lodging. They didn't need it. You see, it wasn't what they wanted. You should have asked them."

The girl did not agree: "What a thing to say! I hoped, they want to be raised out from the hopeless conditions . . . Their existence is . . ."

"Sure. I know. Socialists and radical intellectuals like to inform the world about the "people's" needs. And they don't even know them. You see, you have to be one of them to understand it."

Kati was fed up with Geza's high tone. "You are cynical. I think of it like giving a helping hand. To make them understand, there have to be plans in order to reach their potentials. They are frightened and ignorant to think of their own possibilities. They need good leaders. Who speak for them . . ."

"You must be kidding!"

"Why would I? I am not."

"You say, they are distrustful. Sure they are. They were used in the past and will be used and mistreated in the future. Just as much. So much for leaders. Let's take this Lenin fellow . . . what did he do for the people? Nothing at all! He spoke for himself. He was a cheat! And you still expect the masses to march on, following a con man? I suppose, it's better if they figure out what they want."

They both were silent. It was hard for Kati holding back what she wanted still to say. Geza noticed it, and said it on his own accord. "I know. I know. I am not involved. I am cynical."

The only way Geza could stop irritating her, was by leaving the room. Nonetheless, later that day he thought: "She is a crusader. She really is. In the true sense."

The girls grew and for Franciska it was clear, the land and money were capable of making up for the lesser glories of "seven plum tree nobility".

She had no worries that her daughters wouldn't marry well. Why should be a problem if they had money, were brought up well, and were also beautiful? "Normally, they will be sought after. They could marry very well, and could occupy any position in society. Since we are well off . . ." summarized Franciska. "But in case anything would go wrong, when one might marry under her class, their dowry will provide a very comfortable life . . . even then." She used to think on these a lot. Like other mothers do.

A YOUNG MAN'S HEART

How different it was with Julia! He could talk to her and express himself with perfect clarity. What he said then was in accord with what he thought, and the core of it wouldn't be lost somewhere in between. There was no need to dress them up, nor to modify them. They came across in their original form, not bypassed by vanity, this hidden and not yet conquered desire he had, to impress listeners. Oh, it worked both ways and most people wouldn't suspect it was a game . . . But the only times would be with her when Geza welcomed the chance to become the person he felt was inside, this doubtful thinking man still in the making, inventing yet another, better or poorer self each day, by going along and ahead thoughtlessly like a fool, ignoring his potentials, for having no idea where does it lead or who could he become, or what direction, if any, should he take.

He couldn't tell if it was his youth, or his seriousness that gave a dizzying effect to his options which he saw in front of him. But there they were; a giant pool of his imagination and the pool of possibilities out in the real world tempting him to choose as many as one can take, and the same time challenging him to have none of it.

And a third option was also there; urging him to learn detachment from his visions . . . as well as from the visions of the real world.

A "FUTURE"?

"So? What profession will you choose? Did you think of it?" asked Huba one day. "You ought to make up your mind, son." It wasn't the first time he asked Geza to plan the future, because it annoyed him, that despite of all his brightness, his adopted son lacked ambitions, the way others had them. "Sooner or later most of us find out what to do and how to go about it," he shrugged. "Most of us, but Geza! He seems to be incapacitated by time. Being almost obsessed with it." Huba, who was concerned, had no idea how to counter it. "Time? We are aware of time, sure, but most men do something about it. Attempting to hold it back, or to slow it down. The smarter ones I know, take a ride on it. Any which way it's a good fight. Man fights, because it's his nature. Why would he make an exception with time? Fighting is manly," said Huba and made a fist, as if in need to demonstrate it. Naturally, he wished his son to be strong in his field of endeavor, whatever that turns out to be. But actually telling him all these was a different matter.

Huba wouldn't push Geza where the young man didn't want to go; but hoped against hope he would have time for a vigorous start. So when the carefully planned sentence was popped again, Geza's reaction was no more than a lost look on his face, which seemed to say: "I don't understand what's the fuss? Why others have this compulsion to shape things to their liking?" But after a long silence he issued a statement: "I don't know. Not just yet. I'll take what comes." He stopped here. He was tired to explain something that he himself didn't understand.

It was time for Huba to speak up: "Son, listen to me. You get into your inheritance in a couple of years. What do you intend to do with four hundred acres of land?"

"I might sell it!" replied Geza, apparently quite amused. "You do what? I know, I know. You are joking. But!" attested Huba, "You have to choose a profession. Farming? Studying law? Army?. Do choose a field son! Time is pressing."

It couldn't be helped. Geza wasn't sure if for him there was a "field". "These days one meets little experts of this or that field and they are blank for everything else. Do I need that?" But when he offered to elaborate further on it, his father, losing patience left the room with a bitter taste in his mouth. "These are your reasons?" asked Huba passing the corridor, and couldn't entirely get rid of his disbelief all evening.

And Geza? What did he nurture in his mind? Was he aware, a pattern just emerged to stay with him till the end? That he was looking for an exit before he even entered?

At about this time Franciska told her husband: "Something tells me, our stepson is going to end up a drifter." And Huba thought she must have spoken out of spite.

Chapter 33

A Horse Show and A Birthday

THE HORSE SHOW

Being almost fifteen, that horse show brought on more excitement for Kati than she normally would have in five years.

Even though the show was only in its third day, (just as their stay) the trip toM., to the Hungarian capital of horsebreeding, was a success. She was accompanied by her father. Others in the family were less interested in horses, except Geza who came over just today to see the race, and to learn if his father was really buying a mount. Other reason to come here was to meet a couple of schoolmates who also showed up with relatives.

It was an annual show. Everyone concerned seemed to be present from the South as well as from Transdanubia, which Huba found very stimulating. He let his daughter run around in her riding habit all day, regardless of the programs. Nobody was there to reprimand the girl to dress properly or to behave like a young lady since Franciska could not come, and Kati certainly made the most of her freedom.

Oh, but there was reason for excitement! She was riding in the junior category that day, and her number was scheduled for the morning hours. It meant, the night before the girl could barely sleep and decided to get up at four in the morning. At breakfast, she complained to her father: "I have no chance. I really don't !" Huba shook her up. "Kati, Kati! What makes you think the others did sleep?"

Later that day, Huba told to Geza how it was: "She didn't sleep, and thought it ruined her concentration. No way! She is a strong-willed girl. Kati does well under strain! Being tired and all nerve, just enhanced her performance. And, you know the horse! She feels what you feel. She wants, what you want. You win it together."

Geza agreed, and had to think of Julia who was elated when played music. Yet when played in public, it mortified her to start. But afterwards, by doing it she forgot the world. That's how it must be with Kati too. Both girls have this singleminded dedication about their talents. Obviously Kati is more passionate than Julia, for which Geza thought, "I wish it was the other way around." When Geza arrived at noon, he couldn't find them in the hotel. Not that he believed he would, so he went to the racetracks. About a thousand people were standing and sitting here, or walking around, looking for others. He headed for the stables. At about the fourth or fifth booth, there she was, sitting on a stack of hay, explaining to her admirers (Geza counted ten young men) a technique on how she holds back the horse when it's not yet time to go. Then she noticed her brother: "Hey! You there! Geza! See this?" she shouted, and was holding a medal high above her head. "I just won it! Why didn't you come in time?" "Sorry!" said Geza, "I didn't know when was the time. I mean, your time . . . It's terrific. Your medal. Let me see it! Congratulations, sister. It's great!"

"No big deal," answered the girl like a good sport, and changed the subject. "Where is father?" "I haven't met him. Not yet," replied Geza. "Then, I'll tell you where he is. He is . . . you won't believe this! Father is buying a Lippizaner!!!" The girl couldn't contain herself. She screamed. "A Lippizaner! This is the happiest day of my life!!! Everything! Everything is happening today!"

It's possible, there were tears in her eyes. "I am glad, surely glad," told Geza to her. "You deserve it, you know."

She was brushing off the compliment. "Not in the least. I guess, I am just lucky." Kati stood up, and went to the horse. Geza called after her: "You come to the reception, I hope? There are people you must meet!"

The girl waved back: "I'll be there!"

Her afternoon was just as busy. Predictable as it may, she came in her riding habit and stayed for an hour. Then Kati excused herself before leaving the two young men, who kept her company. "I must get back to the stables now. Was very nice to meet you." Geza himself not an equestrian, couldn't momentarily give out a better advice than: "Don't fall into horse manure!" The girl, pretending not to hear it, walked away. Slowly, the crowd dispersed. The refreshment booths were packing up, and the band played the last tunes. Most people were looking forward to the evening's ball, and women hurried to get a short "beauty-sleep". The reception was about to end.

Our two young men paid no attention to the comings and goings. They were glad to have a few more words. "She is quite a girl," pointed out Pali, who happened to be the youngest son of Baron Verkey, a Southerner, whose lands were at the Northern section of the Great Plains. Pali and Geza were school chums, back in boarding-school days.

"She is a good sport, isn't she? I love the picture she paints from the world. On her canvas everyone walks in white robes . . . It's most educational listening to her . . ." Geza explained briefly. "Yes indeed. I noticed she has some socialist tunes. Does she know it?" inquired Pali. "I am not so sure, she does! But believe me. She is an original. I wouldn't say, if she wasn't my adoptive sister . . . She found the cure for a couple of embarrassing situations, we have in the world. Glorifies the poor and blames the government. or, "society". My sister believes, people are innocent, or if they aren't, then someone didn't give them the chances and opportunities for embetterment. With her, it's always a social issue, not a philosophical one. I particularly enjoy when she says: "One man shouldn't make a slave from the other," as if we wouldn't see it happening all the time!"

The young man politely asked from Geza: "I didn't really know how she meant it? I was wondering on this, you know . . ." "Sure. She meant it socially. And economically . . . Yes. Well. I have this tendency to think, the same. In a broad sense. Quite simply, they make slaves out of each other more casually than we generally like to admit. Oh, really! How innocent this whole blaming game is! It isn't social injustice, that makes people act poorly . . . Don't you think it's more of a . . . conditioning . . . I mean cultural conditioning to act a certain way?"

"Indeed," pointed out Pali, who wasn't that political, but admired those who had concepts of different kind, and didn't mind the least expressing them. That is why he found Geza most amusing. "He always comes up with some groundbreaking idea, which compels me to think on it often for a whole day," thought Pali, and contributed this to the conversation: "Ghastly . . . isn't?"

"Yes. The poor does it as much as the rich. Exerting power and control is a basic need for a lot of people. They just have to have it. As a result, you can see any variety of slaves. Not only social, or economical. The argument of the rich: "You do this for me, or I don't give you money. Or, ruin you by the power of my money. The argument of the poor: "You do this for me, or I beat you up. Or, I organize against you, using physical power . . ."

"Absolutely! Oh, absolutely! That's how it goes, old chap . . . Well put." Geza went on: "We are enslaving one another. Not only socially,—or economically. What about home? In our private lives? Tell me. That's where most of them are. Slaves, who have no courage, or ability to break out. To break free from home. Tell me now! Which is worst?"

"I don't know . . ." replied Pali, after short hesitation. By now the reception was over, and the two walked leisurely towards the edge of town.

"Yes. Well . . . Isn't that a shame?" asked Pali, who twenty some steps later, succeeded in bypassing the topic. He wanted it back to young Kati, for quite sometime. "By the way! About your sister, old chap. I hope you bring her to the ball tonight. And anyways . . . If she is such a horsewoman, why don't you bring her over to my father's estate? Two weeks form now we'll have a "sport-field-day." For ladies and gents. I expect to see you both. And then . . . I might visit you. I sure enjoyed listening to both of you . . . She is . . . your sister I mean . . . is quite a girl. I saw her riding on the show. No lady stuff there! She rides like a man!"

The next day on the road to back home, between Geza and Kati, the following conversation took place: "Eventually you have to decide, you know! Don't you want to be a Baroness?" "Why should I?" snapped the girl. "Pali is mad about you. He might wait, till you grow up." "And, then what? I can't stand him!" "Why? Because he is a Baron?" "Yes! No! . . . Because all he talks about is, his father's estate, his father's houses, their stables, cars, their servants, and all that high-class pomp. He talks like a po'mpous ass. He wants to impress the whole world with his title!" "First of all, it is not true. This wasn't to impress you. He couldn't very well talk about his experiences on the "Mud-Row." He doesn't live there. He just talked about what he knows . . . Come, come . . . We do the same, don't we?" "Don't patronize me! I just can't stand these . . . these . . . spoiled people." "I know what's wrong with you. You are in love, and hate to admit it," teased her Geza. "Mee? Meee? What did you say? You accuse me of . . . of . . . ? You are blind. I never would fall in love with his sort. Never!"

"I know, I know . . . You will become a Baroness. And live happily ever after. His father, Baron Verkey is a horsebreeder. They welcome you, as the famous horsewoman. Everything fits. A perfect match. I'll better start to call you Baroness . . ."

"Oh-oh-ooh, shut up!"

JULIA'S BIRTHDAY

For Julia, Spring has landed early in 1936. The snowdrop bushes were ready to bud, and she took a round telling how the meadows exhaled an aroma that only the rousing soil could give out. Others, while cautious that this Winter won't easily step aside, Julia knew something important has already happened.

In these days she turned fifteen. If this age is tied to impatience, it could also be an age to bring forth confidence. Well, Julia felt ecstatic to be fifteen! For her, it was a milestone when confusions disappear in exchange for a dream, what one ought to see and pursue day and night. Her newly found age landed new determination and the courage to speak up, to seize the moment, before it would disappear like the melting snow in their garden, year after year.

With her family present on that evening (what would be her birthday) she came to the middle of the room, raised her voice slightly and announced for everyone to hear: "I wish to dedicate my life to music!" Julia looked around, smiled and blushed. All of a sudden everyone in the room took notice how beautiful she really became this year. The moment had significance on more than one level. Declaring anything that would be so out of line with her surrounding (which she dreaded to challenge or go against) has required courage. Lots of it. That's why the girl planned this announcement for months. So the moment was essential, no doubt, because she knew with an unshakable certainty, that her life was going to depend on it. To stand there was exciting, but when it was over, Julia felt relief. "I said it, and now the world knows." After her declamation at first there was silence. But when the reactions came, they were a mixed bag. Some encouraging, some concerned and some indifferent. Kati was the first to react: "I can see you as a great pianist, Julia. The audience is applauding and I sit in the first row."

Helen asked: "And what about marriage?" It was Geza who explained it to Helen: "Julia prefers the solitary aspect of life. She is an artist. She has the mystic qualities . . ."

Franciska had to confront her stepson: "Why would she? Why would she overlook what we all do? Getting married. But I am not arguing with you. This is Julia's birthday . . ." finished Franciska, while turned to Julia: "We shall see, dear!"

Huba would only remark: "Well, Julia, you have to study music. If this is what you want, go to the Conservatory." Almost everyone has got over it in days, but her mother. It stayed with her like a headache. She disliked the whole idea and didn't quite trust it as Julia's best choice. "Let's hope this nonsense will pass and she won't remember of it on her next birthday. Well, I suppose I should stop worrying."

Depending on her mood, Franciska could be caught off-guard for having unlatched thoughts on her children; some thoughts comforting, others perplexing, or even unpleasant and inconsiderate. Obviously Franciska restrained them and stopped them as soon as she could. But to get rid of them, she had to put herself in another role. From there she could borrow other notions, less turbulent ones. These days were easier. She could get the feel of a perfect mother, and could even analyze the role: "It's not an overstatement that a mother knows everything. I know their secrets. Yes, yes. My girls are like open book to me! Well, not all of them are that interesting to read . . . but I try. Even if it wasn't my duty, I would try, for I have to accept them as they come. Julia? She is a dreamer. So it shall be my duty to find a husband for her. In two . . . or three years Julia is a debutante. By then, she will change. I am sure she will." But it didn't quite happen the way Franciska thought it would.

Julia came of age when the W.W.II. broke out. It made her belong to a generation who grew up faster than the one before them. Their youth would not be about coming out balls.

Chapter 34

Old Deveny, And Geza

"OLD" ZOLTAN DEVENY

There was nothing casual about "old" Deveny. When in company, he didn't waste words, had no stories, or simply curbed the need to tell them. But his diction was remarkable. When he spoke he did it eloquently, drawing enthusiasts like no man in the region.

There was a drawback to his manner of speech, as a schoolteacher once pointed out. "He can become distant and transform the local tongue beyond repair, on which these people built everything and are almost chained to!" (Andromeda came in mind here and Perseus, but what's the point of scaring off the villagers, he thought, and stopped). So the teacher, who couldn't decide if Zoltan Deveny was doing service or disservice to them with his fame, just frowned. "It's not fair. Making the rest of us sound . . . what's the word? Inexpedient?!"

Fair or not, old Deveny's version of speech lacked the heavy emphasis on E's and A's, thus abolishing the very character of Southern accent, here, in the heartland of it. But there seemed to be no problem as far as his educated presence kept them in awe. Besides, they liked him. They loved his efficacy in public service and his way of expressing an elevated mind in simple elegant terms, while avoiding to call attention to it.

Owed to the fact that old Deveny didn't look like anybody from the region, people tried their best to portray him somehow, and only few succeeded. Any time showing up on the streets, he had the look of a rare solitary bird by way of wearing that loose-fitting grey suit-his trademark-that was quite ready either to take off or to follow him in some rhythmic fashion, if only it wouldn't with each step miss half a beat.

"It isn't wholly his appearance, making such impression, you know! But of course, you have to know him!" his wife Anna postulated so, and went no further explaining him. She just hoped people did bother to get behind the surface to see his true character, that happened to be far more significant and tangible than a look or an outfit. Yes, but what was it? Be what it may, still it's not easy to find the words, for old Zoltan Deveny happened to be an extraordinary man. People who knew him-including his family-invariably gave account to be in the presence of a humble saint, who came either too early, or too late to be effective, had he have the role of shaking up this thick-layered nihilistic world of ours, filled with ignorance, hatred and corruption and sin. Old Deveny was lean and tall, had white hair, blue eyes, and a weathered face lined with a hundred lines like a sailor's, who spends twenty years at sea. He looked like this now at fifty-five, or later when turned seventy, but a photograph of his at thirty revealed an old young man astonishingly the same, lean and tall with a lined face. At closer inspection he already possessed that particular remoteness that was there to stay, even following his marriage to Anna, and the birth of his son, Zoltan. Years went by with occasional new pictures taken if some of his endeavors called for it. Then he had to give in, to pose with a sad half-smile, like somebody, who had animosity and little regard for pontification. However, a photograph was there documenting on this line when he, the new corresponding member joined the Academy of Science. Dressed in their prestigious robe and in the matching cap, he looks dour on it. Just a faded snapshot, taken back in the 1920's, "really a long time ago," as his grandson in the 1950's would say.

There was every kind of speculation as of why he came back to the South, where after Budapest, he didn't have an enviable position by any means. Confiding in her friends, Anna often asked, "Would you believe I never knew his parents? Nor anybody, who knew him as a boy! When, or if at all he was a boy, it must have been a silly disguise. Which makes me think, he came like this!"

Well, old Deveny was certainly the most admired man in the town of N. venerated by all in the county, and respected a great deal in Academia. "A model citizen." People would so evaluate this erudite old man later on, who lived among them with an intensity of purpose by taking each hour seriously while making sure they were not spent in vain.

Anna believed unswervingly, that her husband was cloistered in his body by taking his skeletal outfit in haste for possible reasons of working on to fulfill a promise, or honoring the sacred agreement he had within, the one he might have made just before he came. Anna also thought, all these time he was aware, he could fly away, but he wouldn't. Later she came to be convinced, his departure has been delayed by way of imposing his own ties and strings, in need of testing himself by this temporary stay, even if it led to the clipping of his wings that must have been set out for greater heights. Throughout the years Anna did not change her mind on this. She felt quite the same, between the first and the last days she could spend with him.

A TALENT

Since the beginning of the early 1930's, Geza was studying Latin and some Greek and was taking up French as his next project. By then his professors encouraged him to go in this direction seeing an obvious talent for foreign languages. In a few years he would read French and English literature (in original), starting with the poetry of Lord Byron, Shelley and Apollinaire and Villon his favorites, and was reading the "Lettres d'un Voyageur" from George Sand with great delight, pointing out he never thought a woman could supersede the men of letters with such ease and elegance, as she had. Now he was not surprised that even Turgenyev counted himself to be among her fans.

German was planned for next year. On this holiday, he admitted to Julia: "Lately, I like less and less the idea of reading translations. I rather work myself through the real thing." Julia asked him: "But how do you handle Russian literature? Wouldn't you read Puskin as he wrote? The Russians are sublime. If I think of "literature" I think of the Russian writers and poets. I really do!" said Julia. "I can't agree more," replied Gdza, and after some calculation, he added: "No problem. In a year or two, I'll be glad to learn it! Hmm. Reading Dostoyevsky in the Russian! Think of it!

Whenever home from school, Geza did not mind taking his sisters to the movies. Their outings were a success, considering their entertaining potential, which often outweighed the productions they were bound to view. For the girls it was a thrill to go, because they knew Geza's interpretation of certain movies made them laugh more for one evening than they normally would in a year.

Once it has got that far, they were asked to leave the theater, because he innocently, but quite loudly inquired: "Is this booby supposed to be the handsome lead? Is he mysterious to you? Well, I don't know about you, but he reminds me of the producer's nephew."

The girls started laughing, and it soon shifted into a poorly concealed screaming, by which time they were removed. On the next day the theater owner let Huba know how his almost grown children dared to behave. Pouring his anger out, he charged: "Mr. Garay, it is preposterous! Your children are a public nuisance!" When he left, Franciska did get hold of them: "Is this the reputation you wish to maintain? There is no more movie this Summer! Do you understand?"

Huba, as always, was secretly amused by the incident.

THE MEETING OF MINDS

Each time he returned from school, Geza and old Deveny had fierce debates. "Are you aware, the Mystics offer a peerless explanation on the laws of dynamics, regarding purpose? I mentioned that to you once." "Sir! Are you stating, if the laws of dynamics in a given situation could be altered by will, then this superior force operates on a higher frequency, or operates by another set of dynamics? . . ." "Yes. Which is the same thing if you come to think of it! You see the hierarchy,working. One force is superior to the other . . ." "If it is so, I am bothered by the fact, one can't see beyond. One can't see the meaning of it. Only perhaps a very abstract structure. But not how . . . how it operates." "Well, there are manifestations, in order to grasp purpose . . ." "Let's stay with our first statement, Sir. What do they manifest? You have interpretations, I have them and the next person have them. Each is different. Maybe things around us are not manifestations. Things just are! Regardless of interpretations!" Some time passed, which made Old Zoltan curious if Geza could be persuaded. "You might consider taking up Metaphysics one day?" "Maybe. But Sir, these days I have problem digesting the New Testament. Well, if the premise of Metaphysics is the acceptance of a higher being, or intelligence, than I am a step behind."

He was already finishing his first year, and was more or less involved with Philosophy "in a bookkeeping fashion" as he liked to term it. They studied the Greeks and took the Middle Age in great strides, as if they were giving the students a taste, in general. On the following years covering the so-called "modern" philosophers from Descartes to Hume down to Bergson, he was influenced by most for brief intervals. At first, his reasoning was clouded by reverence to Descartes; his assessment still had the value of the novice, who took upon a voluntary devoir for spreading the word. But soon he questioned if a meeting place between soul, spirit, mind and body, was indeed as Descartes proposed. When he grew out of this, his old friend asked, still curiously: "What do you say to Spinoza's "Ethics"? He gets very close to the Mystics. Gets back to the idea of an omnipotent God, and structures his doctrine from this standpoint."

"He is a superb mind. But I search something else. Something more tangible," replied Geza. "Well, you might get back to him one day when taking an interest in Metaphysics," attempted old Zoltan. "Of course, you have time. There is no hurry."

Geza's choice of the next great was Lord Byron when he was swept by the Romantics, among them Rousseau. On him, his old learned friend had this to say: "I like his diction but I can distance myself from his persuasive power in no time. Rousseau is not my world." Geza was not yet aware, that his touch with the Romantic movement, or rather with their world-view, which included a contempt for money, had an effect of a headcold on him, costing him a fortune later on.

He found Leibnitz's "monads" too farfetched in regard to matter. "I can't accept it," he said. "His arguments are too speculative, giving too much unnecessary work for future philosophers, either affirming or denying it. However, his "possible worlds" is far more interesting. I like that. It shows his true intellect."

Then they both agreed on Locke's political philosophy. The young man found it remarkable. In his last year at the University, Kant had considerable influence on him with his "Critique of Pure Reason", so he could hold on to him longer than he would to others, not distancing himself completely from him even years later. Old Zoltan also read Kant and Hegel, but he preferred above all else the philosophy of the Classical Greeks. "They were great teachers in the true sense of the word. From them, one learns to think, and to distinguish between knowledge and speculation."

Eventually overfed, Geza found Nietzsche erratic on the account of common men, promoting the exceptional "great" man, who happens to know something better than the rest. "I am not a socialist, in any of my views," he snapped. "But Nietzsche goes too far in his eliticism! It smells something like self-adulation to me."

AND SOME MORE PHILOSOPHY

Throughout the years, their polemics hardly changed. Perhaps only ripened. But before starting the University, Geza was out on a limb.

"To me, the best drill is to think all day," he would inform his friend, old Zoltan. "To scan and avoid the traps of my mind which works like an ideal servant, collecting and delivering every kind of ideas, including my own. Mine, I take it, could be as devious as the ones out for grab. Just as well. One promises solution, the other comfort, mine mostly wants a way out if it can't have the ultimate answer . . . But there is'no way out, so I end up with my stupid illusions . . . and restart when I get this far."

"Well? That's quite something. It just says, you already found a very useful device. To get to the brim, and back again," acknowledged his old friend.

Geza looked at him and continued. "You know Sir, I used to ruminate on every kind of matter, to rack my brain. Not that it gets me anywhere! As a matter of fact, I am inclined to say, we walk on this planet with a similar sickness of mind . . . not understanding the why?'s, the how?'s, and the when?'s. None of it. So I can't stop wondering how did we ever get this far? I mean, this far back, or at all to this destination? And really, why? Anyway, it all must have happened a long time ago. Any anthropologist will tell you that. The millenias have passed, so have civilizations, with us being trapped in the same darkness of the mind. Why? Look at us, and decide. What are we? Apelike sophisticates, or handsome convicts? I don't think it's weird. Assuming things went havoc with the prototypes and was late to reverse or stop the experiment, makes sense. A planet taking the rounds out of control . . . As it is now . . ."

When Geza, as a young man had these to say, old Zoltan knew, he was tormented by the deepest kind of depressions. What could he-his friend-do other than talking about his own views, and as a last resort, lending him a Bible on the very last week before he would enter the University. Geza must have read it, following his uniquely systematic reading habits with a similitude of drinking a glass of water, taking it in all at once.

At semester's end he came home and visited each time the Devenys with great expectations. Old Zoltan noticed, the young man's paletta of reasoning became richer, but still he was fighting his own battle with faith, that has dimmed from his many torments.

The Devenys were glad to receive him. Always. "Come early!" Anna would say, when invited him for dinner. And he came. Before being seated the men were usually involved in some deep discussion. Anna, busy in the kitchen, could mostly hear the finishing sentences, as one time when Geza made the talking: "Too much expansion is followed by an explosion, making things to collapse. Whether into themselves or out, is beside the point."

When they were seated there was a short silence, and Anna hoped they might start with the soup. Both men utilized this time for contemplation, for something seemed to be unresolved. Well, it was, until the "old" man would quietly say: "In a broader sense nothing happened, only Brahma was taking a breath."

Neither Anna nor Geza knew what to make of it. Geza wasn't sure if he was ready for deciphering. He couldn't ask for explanation, because Anna thought, it was time they concentrated on the food. After dinner the two men had more talk. Old Zoltan had a quintessential approach to the theory of creation, that he wanted to share with the young man. "How do you react to the following?" he asked. "What if God is still working on Creation, finishing with the fifth eon, and has still two more eons to go? My point is, how can we be critical, until he finishes? Definitely, these are critical times for man, since the number five represents mankind as it is right now, in its way from involution to evolution. We arrived to a very crucial platform. Having our chance for improvement in the exact pace and rhythm as it was set in the grand design. The Bible says: God created the world in six days and rested on the seventh. Well, I have this to add. Maybe the "days" were confused with the eons in the history of man. Because of various Bible interpretations, the truth is still elusive. Perhaps one day a sage comes along telling us of the scriptures . . . And so, the divine message will come to man."

Geza was energized. He liked the whole idea. Especially the doubt, since he had more of it than faith. He just couldn't help it. So he said, "If we presume there was a Creation, then I am sympathetic to your point, Sir. He can't be through with Creation! Just look around! Everything is halfbrewed . . . still in the making. You see, here is another obstacle! We don't understand time. The message (if there was one) and the meaning of time in the scriptures must have gotten mixed-up. And so, we are living in a perpetual misinterpretation of the things contributing to our condition. Well, I am convinced, we piled up civilizations on false truths, gods, ideals. The worst is we know it by now, yet live with it as if we were bound to design or create, if you will, our own Heaven and Hell. As if this race-mankind-was banished to this planet to do whatever it is capable of doing with itself. I am sorry, Sir, this is the Creation theory I am willing to accept."

Chapter 35

The Young Deveny

A YOUNG POLITICIAN

"Hmm . . . It wasn't bad. He talked with clarity, used philosophical references, but kept them light. Oh. I think I understand! It wouldn't agree with him putting emphasis on his education. It would be vulgar," concluded old Zoltan, who tried hard to be objective about his son's first public speech, back in 1930. By his assessment, his son came across as some fiery young man in the clouds, who had this desire for public service. At this early stage young Zoltan did not follow any particular ideology of the times, thinking he had yet to come up with his own. Though he felt, and was even convinced, that his experiences weren't sufficient for understanding the need of the common man. Because he, who was born into privilege, didn't go out to ask them more than once, or twice. Still he planned visiting the hamlets and the homesteads where people lived with the real problems of every day, who most likely were pushed down by bad taxation, when they could barely make it to next year. Well, the young man suspected, their worries overwhelmed them. It was reasonable to guess even, how their prayers must have sounded. "Lord in Heavens, how do I make the next payment? How will I get the money? I want you to help me. Because there is no one else."

For young Zoltan, it was obvious. These people who worked and were poor, lived with a constant burden and worry, seeing no end to it. "They see no future, only the limited existence that we, politicians portion them out. No wonder. What we have, is ambition. We won't give a second thought in our haste, if this constant worry kills them some day. Well, it happens, in case of a bad year. Many die, as young old men. And that is why we must do something about their despondency. I wish, I wish . . . there were easy solutions," thought Zoltan, while knew, there weren't. "We, politicians ought to solve things straight on. But, are we ready? If we ask the wrong questions, we can't get the right answers! Yet that's what we do. We employ our misleading little platitudes, like: "How was your year, old man?" or "How is the donkey, he-he-he? Does it pull, or needs a kick, he-he-he?" making them feel impersonal, just one in the crowd. We prevent them from saying what's wrong, or how we should help. God gracious! If this is not the bottomline of politics, then what is? Going there, where help is needed, and giving it! Giving to those who can't help themselves . . ."

Young Zoltan was serious. He wanted to go out to listen to those, whose voices were not heard inside the thickening walls of County Assembly. Or across the main square for that matter, alongside the corridors of the Governor's office and of his many aids. At any rate, he was convinced of the following: "Until I won't hear what they want to say, or learn of their utmost needs, I am only half ready for the job! Someone, who is not good enough." There was another thing. Often he found this career easy-of which he tasted now for three full months-too easy, and simple in fact. If this has been thought out for him at birth, it might even justified the thought. "It was chosen, for that's how things are . . . The nobility ruled this country for centuries. That was our birthright. But then, why don't we grow up to it?" frowned Zoltan, who couldn't share the complacency his class liked to flaunt.

True, in his case, good family, good schools, right connections pushed him to the right direction so far, launching him where he wanted to go. It looked easy. A routine. Even the fights, if one knew the steps. But where were the tough battles, the hard fights? The ones that could make this career worthwhile . . .

Filled with similar thoughts, in these months the young man almost hoped, his life would not be an easy one. "The harder the better," he would say to himself, "What's good for the steel, is good for the man."

A "HUNT" OF A DIFFERENT KIND

And one afternoon he came. "It's him," she whispered. The young man didn't look at the scenery, his thoughts absorbed him as he walked across the lawn with an equable pace before he would get to the main entrance. Helen watched him until the last step, when he vanished in the building. "Handsome . . . very handsome. She was sitting on the windowsill of her dormitory room which had a view to the front lawn and to large segments of the park. Being her last year at finishing school, her stay summed up a fountain of knowledge in certain fields, even if these fields haven't been strictly academic. But now she was bored with school. Ready for a change . . . And voila! Today this excitement. He was here! Helen has seen him only once before. Soon after that, she learned he was young Zoltan Deveny, the author of that political article in the Herald. It made her think. "Hmm . . . some article! People in three Southern counties talked about it for a day, or perhaps longer, recounting: "That young man? He is sure a promise! Even father said it . . . using the same phrase. The very same!" It happened long ago, yet she remembered. In the convent the girls were talking about Zoltan, that's how she learned he will be a lawyer in a year or two.

The first time she saw him, he was with none else than Henrietta, a schoolmate of Helen. "Why Henrietta? Why would he waste time on that girl?" Helen did not understand it. Henrietta irritated her immensely for being Zoltan Deveny's friend. And perhaps more so, that this girl's family was one of the old-guard nobility. To nobody's surprise, they always belonged to the Royalists when it came to politics, dating back as far as mid-17th century, the time their nobility was bestowed upon a forefather, who as a footsoldier fought well in battle, and apparently stayed in close range to the king, when stood in the receiving line. So is the patina on the name . . . As the Mother Superior suggested, Varjassy was a name not likely to be associated with scandal, or misconduct. She obtained part of her conviction from teaching this girl who never disappointed her. Well, she was an exemplary student, whom others could follow. Not that they did. By other girls' opinion, the Varjassys were a proud family, who still lived in the 17th century. About Henrietta, Helen could notice only these: she was old-fashioned, shy, and not interesting at all. And the least pretty. So Helen convinced herself, Zoltan is seeing this girl by honouring some prearrangement between-their families. "A "birds of a feather" business. What else can I think?" When a while ago in late Winter, Helen met them walking in the city (this was the first time she saw him) the two were engaged in some deep discussion. It struck her then, they looked like soulmates. "This terribly outmoded notion between young people, who are not able to feel passion towards one another . . . They don't evoke real passion . . . So, they just talk instead . . ." quipped Helen, in an effort to rebound her spirit. In any case, it gave an idea that was growing in her ever since, since she heard others saying "Zoltan will be important one day in politics, or government." An idea, she wasn't to abandon.

And it happened, that after much fan-fare seeing him in the second time started to propel Helen's interest to a degree almost impossible to stop, especially today, that Zoltan entered the building.

Getting off from the windowsill was like leaving a hunting-box with a superior sight, but now the next stage had to be worked on. "It has to be done immediately," said Helen, and within minutes her plan was ready, knowing how to proceed with the "chase". The possibility that he won't stay long in the building had reduced her chances.

Zoltan already talked to the nun on duty, and took a seat in the reception room. In the meantime someone was sent for Henrietta. They couldn't spend more than three minutes together, when Helen went downstairs, took off the telephone receiver from the hook, and ran to the reception room. She opened the door. "Henrietta? They told me you were here. Come! You have a telephone call . . . hurry!" The couple stood in the middle of the room, when Helen intruded the scene. The girl made an apologetic gesture to the young man, and left the room to talk on the phone. Helen wanted to stay. Unaware of her, Zoltan walked up and down in the room. At first he went to the bookcase to look at the books' binding. Helen, waiting to be noticed still stood in the door. Then she decided on closing the door and taking two steps in his direction. Now Zoltan took a spacious glimpse around, and still didn't see her. Well, he saw a girl it's true, but his mind was not on girls; it was elsewhere. By then Helen felt miserable, and didn't know what to do. It never happened before, and was like a slap on the face. Here was he, paying no attention. "Why doesn't he notice me? What happened? What's wrong with him?" To be rejected so, made her angry. But there was no time straightening right from wrong now. Hurt pride and insolent behaviour? Well, they just had to wait. Yes. Something told her to forge ahead: "Do it now, or you will never do it! Go!" Zoltan examined a book closely, when the young woman came forward and would start talking. "Really! It is quite strange, I have this feeling I know you from somewhere."

"I beg your pardon," said Zoltan. He seemed to be embarrassed for being so absentminded. "Yes, well. Indeed. Let me introduce myself. My name, is Zoltan Deveny. At your service." "Oh, I am glad. I am Helen Garay." There was an awkward moment between them until

Helen began to say: "You know, my parents live inK. I was wondering if . . ."

Henrietta came back: "Zoltan? There was no teleph . . . Oh, Helen? Are you still here? My line was broke off when I've got to the booth . . . It never came back. Do you know who it was?"

Helen shook her head: "No idea, whatsoever!" "Oh? Well," said Henrietta, realizing these two had started a conversation. "May I introduce you to one another?" Helen laughed: "Oh dear! We are already acquainted. And hoping to keep it, aren't we?" Zoltan forced a smile on his face. When at last Helen decided to leave, she talked loudly and provocatively: "All right! I am glad I was talking to the hero at last, but now I have to go. I am late for rehearsal . . . Bye!" She left but returned from the door: "By the way! I hope you come to the County Youth Ball two weeks from Saturday? If we both invite you? You can't refuse it, can you?"

Zoltan felt uncomfortable. He was supposed to reply, without consenting to it. He looked a bit disturbed. Henrietta didn't think well of Helen's idea of mentioning this upcoming ball. She, Henrietta wasn't a good dancer. Being shy, she didn't like balls. The reason why she wouldn't bring it up to Zoltan. But now it came out and there was nothing much to do but going. So the three of them stood there waiting for solution. Zoltan's choice for that evening would have been a good book, or work on an article . . . or anything of this sort. But "If Henrietta wants to go, obviously I am going," thought Zoltan. "But this girl, Helen Garay . . . What does she want? I don't understand."

REFLECTIONS FROM A PRISON CELL

Zoltan addressed this question some twenty years later, when thought on the sequences of his life: "What kind of events are responsible for getting me here?" The first time he forced himself to synthesize his choices (the decisions and steps}, was in prison. There, he had time. He sorted them, confronted them and discarded them. And started it over, to think out a different 'angle, to seek another truth. Time in prison . . . Zoltan his parents, the schools he attended, his dreams of public service, and Helen. Rather, Henrietta and Helen. On the same page at the beginning and at the end.

They were so much in contrast, these two women. Like two faces of a coin flipped over a dozen times weighed and looked at, but never at the same time. When one was up, the other was down. But when he had to choose . . . it was Helen. The prettier one.

Why men are so weak? Maybe it had nothing to do with weakness though. The choice could have roots elsewhere. Owed to his procreational instincts, was one explanation . . . Just like his father put it: "And what the two of you have in common?! Well then, I am sure, you will have beautiful children." He was right. Probably the very reason he had chosen her. How silly the "County Youth Ball of 1932" looked now with the dust of twenty years on it. The old county—states. And the balls! All together a different world . . . Distant in time and in emotion.

The ball was not too interesting, as he recalled. People were dancing. At first he remembered having a good discussion with Henrietta, who called his attention to a new book from Moricz, the "writer of great magnitude," as she put it. A talent who brings forth the Magyar soul at its most vulnerable. "Moricz is unique. But has the depth and sensibility of the great Russian writers," she said, with enthusiasm.

Zoltan was fond of her for being highminded and rational at the same time. He never met anybody like Henrietta, and he wasn't looking to meet somebody like her. They understood each other. This was the bond. Eventually they realized the dance was in progress, and was time to join this elegant crowd. Waltz was the dance, so Zoltan and Henrietta took the floor. The two were bemused how seriously others were taking this event, as if it would be the only thing that mattered in the whole county-state. This ball! Thinking this, he noticed Helen. She danced close to them, said hello, was loud, and very sociable. During this waltz, she had two dancers, and the third cut in before the final accords. She seemed to enjoy herself.

Zoltan and Henrietta went to get refreshments, and continued their talk on Moricz the author and his book. They planned to sit out the next number on a side-sofa, far from the crowd. But it didn't happen that way. Helen Garay showed up with a beau on their way to the bar. She asked, looking straight to Zoltan: "Next dance is mine? You can't say no! Mind if I join you? I just love to dance! People always compliment me. Henrietta, do you mind if I steal Zoltan for a dance, or two? You can have my beau. Usually I don't go anywhere without one. Ha, ha, ha! If it were up to me I would dance all day!" This was all she had to do, or say. Yet Zoltan was still unaware of the happenings and had no idea where Helen was aiming. He loved Henrietta. True,

Helen was a good dancer. And also a sensual young woman who knew how to play with men . . . Zoltan did not feel very good about this. He found her attractive after their dance, although in a strange sort of way. At first Zoltan was disturbed how could he be overwhelmed by the young woman, but later he didn't think of it at all.

Only now, some twenty years later did he think maybe Helen knew, if Zoltan had have one dance with her, she will have him. Sooner or later, she will! Dance was her element, where she was home. On the same note, Zoltan tried to recall why did he agree to the first rendezvous? Since it wouldn't cross his mind for asking her out! But it crossed hers . . . And reluctantly though, he, Zoltan Deveny, said yes. Poor Henrietta! Zoltan remembered the self-hate. He still had it. Just thinking of her filled him with it, and the loss of the harmony they had had. The kind, he never had with Helen. Not for a day . . .

Chapter 36

Another Stronghold

YOUNG DEVENY AT THE COUNTY-SEAT

"Oh, him? Sure I know him. Everyone knows him. Here people call him "Old Fox". Where? I tell you right away. You find him in his club. See that building? That big fat one over there! He is there every afternoon," was Zoltan informed, like a typical newcomer, who looked for the gentleman by his legal name. The gentleman in question in the last thirty years habitually spiced up his deals with: "My friend, you don't cheat an old fox!" that it stuck. He acted as if he didn't know, but others felt he rather enjoyed the nimbus.

With busines it was time for Zoltan to go and look him up, since his father made him promise, that he would. The building, that's been pointed out as "fat", occupied the end of that street which used to be planted and replanted with linden trees for a hundred years, was Bizantine in its conception, and Romantic in its execution, as far as Architecture went in the capital city of this county-state. By walking over, Zoltan enjoyed a breath of fresh air. Stepping inside the foyer, the club smelled of good tobacco, smoked ham, bean soup and cognac all at once, like a true stronghold should what older politicians favor, by stealing a leisurely hour from a long day, and come here to rest.

But there he was, Old Fox, on a green sofa, as if on a soft but confining throne, sitting erect by taking his afternoon nap, while saving dignity. When the liveried doorman led the young man to him, he appeared a bit somnolent. With his alert state within reach, he lifted his head and was vivified by greeting the visitor, all in a minute.

"Everyone advised me Sir, that you were here," started Zoltan.

"They were right!" he replied on a deep resonant baritone . . . "I sit here each afternoon . . . Well. I was expecting you, my young friend. They told me you came to town. I hear you work with the Community Service Department? For how long are you assigned?"

"It's just for this six months, Sir . . ."

"Oh. Sure. Young Titans like yourself, should go over each department . . . he-he-he. It's damn useful. But first things first! Tell me how is your Honorable 'father?"

Zoltan said his father was fine and was working on a book.

"Aha! A book! I have the highest regard for your father . . ." He lit up his cigar and leaned back on the sofa. "Is your mother still so beautiful?"

"Yes Sir. She is . . ." told Zoltan.

"Well now. Let's see what we have here? The county seat. Our local capital. My friend! This is a wheeler—dealer town. Everything goes like it did a hundred years ago. I don't say it's good, or bad. It just is!"

Zoltan looked at him, waiting for more, which came in due time. "As a first step, you want to figure out who is who. For instance! Where all they gather? Here and there, but usually the day starts in that cafe-see that?-opposite to the club." He pointed his cigar to the same direction where he was looking. "I tell you why. They give the best breakfast. You start with plum brandy. Then, some bread. When you are done with it, your fried sausage (from Gyula) comes with scrambled eggs, straight with that iron skillet in which they fried it. This is the best there . . . It will take you through the day. Until early dinner . . ."

Zoltan recognized, the old gentleman had a talent to be vague and specific at the same time.

He was ready to continue: "You need guts. That's all about you need my friend. Because the rest . . . you were born with. Talent, or money. That sort of thing . . . But if you have guts, you can make it in this field. The best anyone can hope. Up . . . to be a minister . . . or anybody, who is foolish to meddle in politics. Some of us come here because found no real job. Frankly! A job, a clear cut job . . . A "look straight in the eye job" definition. See what I get at? So . . . when you meet a fellow who tells you everything but says nothing!! Hah! That's the one! Watch out for this sort. They are here, and everywhere . . . The kind to be watched. These mass of nameless little "politicians"-this is how they pose, but they are just servants. They play out these miserable powergames on the smallest scale you have . . . And show me where did their games get them? Hah? They are still where they started. After years of elbowing. Just outside of any door! You know why? I tell you. They couldn't get in! No personality. No brain. Only tricks. You have to be clever and interesting at first. So, people will notice you. But you see, there are too many people here in the county, or in national politics who are no more than servants. With no master to serve! Strange kind . . . They don't trust hierarchy. They despise it! And this doesn't lead them anywhere. So, they end up staying at the lower ranks . . . Eh! The dog take it away! I almost forgot! Time."

He stood up, slowly adjusting his legs to the act, and took out his silver pocket watch for checking the time. "I knew!" he said. "Now I have to go. I'll have a game of Tarocchi at the Golden Bull. We play a game or two on Fridays. Good day my young friend. Come, and see me anytime. I'll tell you what you want to know." The gentleman with the name "Old Fox" left the club, and so have Zoltan. His head was quite full with the events of the last two days. For getting to his quarters he preferred to walk three long blocks. It was Spring and he needed a clear head. "If I come here with my soul on my sleeve, these people will eat me in a week . . . I have to watch out. To learn . . . what is the game . . . Considering I have a saint for a father who couldn't teach me the tricks."

ZOLI'S ADOLESCENCE

Tass and Miriam Garay have noticed a change in their son Zoli, who used to be a compliant child, but lately he seemed to be more and more disrespectful. Just in this month he refused to take piano-lessons, among other things.

"I don't get this stupid bourgeois idea of sitting there like a sassy. Why should I show to the ones who listen, that I can play better than they? Isn't it what's done on a concert? Come, come Mother! Don't be so very snobbish. I tell you what I want. I want to be like others. If I hate something, it is to be different!"

If Miriam was concerned, she was not yet alarmed. So she asked him: "Why don't you take up sport, then? Tennis for instance . . ."

"No," snapped Zoli. "I'll tell you what kind of people play tennis. I am not that kind."

"Thank you very much! What kind, may I know?"

Zoli would not elucidate on it, he only said: "I'll take up softball. It's done in a group."

In a year or so, Miriam's eyes have opened gradually so she could see what his son's apprehension was all about. Oh, no. It wasn't only adolescence, pre or post. Miriam now recalled, at times when she mentioned her family or some of her travels before the war, Zoli started making annoying remarks.

"My dear God," realized Miriam. "He is ashamed. Or, angry!" This was her conclusion. "I don't know what to think. What is the matter with the boy? Is it because my family is Jewish? How am I going to talk him out of his confusion?"

Sometime soon Tass had a word with his son. "Look Zoli. This whole issue is a complex one with these different heritages, and religions," he had began, warming in. "This is why your mother and I thought, you should make up your own mind about which religion to choose. When you are ready, that is. We didn't want to expose you only to Catholicism, you understand. We thought later you might say, we forced you into something. We wanted you to make a choice. Bar Mitzvah, First Communion or Confirmation. Well? What do you think?"

Zoli did not like the speech. He did not answer to his father, only very briefly. "I don't really care, Father. It is definitely not about God. It's about something else."

Tass was not equipped to push the subject any further. So the couple decided to wait it out.

Through his years in high school, Zoli wanted to assimilate more than anything. The idea of being part of the social elite, appalled him. He consciously avoided the so-called "good schools" so he could be with the rest, who couldn't afford other than public education. Since Zoli was extremely bright, it didn't make the least of difference where would he get his education, thought his father.

By now his parents recognized, their son's problems were not related to religion but rather to social conformity. In his case, his identity. Parallel to these, he was already on the go for making a place in the world. His choice was to study science. His mother had a heavy heart to let him go, but at the same time she hoped her son will get on a thicker polish in the capital.

Before entering the University, Zoli was apprehensive for the word "Jewish". In fact any mention of it, regardless of the context or the tone. When someone said it, Zoli was trying to get behind it, searching for intent, as if he was watching out for a potential enemy. Tass was on guard, for he felt his son's feelings were bordering paranoia. So once more his father was the one attending to Zoli's problems, but only carefully and very gently, having no idea that in fact he amplified them. Again, his son didn't wish to be "talked to". After the fiasco, Tass decided that his son needed a stronger and firmer hand to shake him out of his thinking, and state of mind. The kind of strength could come only from his mother, no doubt, who talked plain common sense. "Do you want to divide your energies finding out which part of you is inferior, which is superior?" she asked. "Do you want to make a wreck of yourself? What makes you think you aren't like anybody? It's up to you who you are! Why look for others telling it to you . . . And better stop blaming them if they don't approve!" Here, Miriam raised her voice: "Do you plan to go around begging for recognition, my son? Face it who you are! If part of you is Jewish, and you are aware, stand up for it! If you don't people sense it and will find you out. It makes them angry that you hide. And you lose respect. My son, you have choices. Don't hide behind another religion . . . or, just behind a lie." "Why did you then?" asked Zoli his mother, and in a second, Miriam replied. "I didn't. I believe, marriage is unity. I wanted to have the same God with my husband. I didn't want to be different from him. We are one. But . . . of course, you are free. You have choices."

The conversation was over and was not brought up again between them. Zoli still felt being made up from two halves, and still found it difficult to mend those two. He was hoping however, that logic and reason and science will liberate him from his youthful agony. He thought, they might even redeem him.

Chapter 37

Accomplishments

AN ENGAGEMENT

The time came for the Garays when those supposedly happy months of planning the future for Helen would run into frenzy preparations. But since Helen was engaged, her trousseau had to be ready. The women put their energies in locating the finest damasks, linens, silks, or, getting hold of the best seamstress. One shopping trip followed the other, until they believed shops in the county were as wayworn as they were. Franciska had swollen feet, Helen was getting headaches, so a day or two had to be spent in the house, lying low.

On one of these mornings a telegraph came to Helen. It was from Zoltan, which said: "My appointment for the post of mayor in T. came through. Love you, Zoltan. P.S. Letter will follow."

Franciska was happy, and excited. "Oh! So it became true! I am so happy for you, my dear." In an hour, the news was out. "Helen will be first lady in T." Nearly everyone of those whom Franciska phoned earlier, friends and relatives stopped by their house and suddenly the parlor looked like one of those women conventions, and was just as noisy. The ladies, old and young were galvanized by the news. At first the school headmaster's wife talked to her: "Helen dear. From now on, half of your life will be spent in front of the public. You have to learn many things. Shaking hands, smiling, being courteous, terribly sympathetic, or just charming. Choose from these, whatever the occasion tells you. You can't really show what you feel though. But as you get over it, you will like it."

"Yes indeed! Helen was born for it!" commented Piri, one of Franciska's best friends and confidante who gave up on beauty, or wearing girdles with whale bones about fifteen years ago, saying it was no use. On most occasions she said just one sentence, a highly supportive one, before heading for the liqueur tray where she would settle drinking like a woman feeling unworthy, as a result of some unspeakable pain. She would sit through these afternoons as they were wearing themselves out minute by minute, just like she has, for quite some time. Not that she would elucidate. Still, Piri like others shared the general opinion, Franciska did wonders with the girl. They witnessed her upbringing, and saw how she was prepared for this role. They recalled how Franciska often told to them: "Helen will marry someone with a high office . . . and the lifestyle that goes with it. She will be surrounded with every kind of important people. And she can be a center of that. I think, this is what she wants."

Now, Franciska's friends realized this was what Helen wanted. "Zoltan is from an excellent family. He will make a good career. And he is handsome! They will make a beautiful couple, won't they?" In this, everyone agreed and when it was dark, the ladies went home.

Only her sister Kati, who later came to the parlor to finish off the cookies, had opposing views. "Helen, the Queen of the Ball? It's her obligation to stay in the public eye . . . doing nothing for it. That's her role. I wouldn't want this . . . this "central role"! I would be ashamed!"

Franciska couldn't hold it back this time: "But who asked you?"

"Nobody," replied Kati. "But still, I have ears to listen to how awfully smug you all are!"

A DAUGHTER'S WEDDING

Helen's wedding in 1937 began with a civil ceremony where only the two witnesses were present. Next day was the church wedding. To this, everyone came. The whole town. Or the whole county? Afterwards they had an hour-long reception, and on the evening a true, old fashioned Southern "lakodalom" for a hundred or so, invited guests, which comprised of friends and family.

Huba wouldn't let Franciska do anything: ". . . less you overexert yourself. I hire you the best wedding caterers. You don't have to do a thing!" "Typical man-talk," thought Franciska, and saw to it, those caterers delivered everything after she gave them a push.

It was a six course supper, and the sweets and the wines. Huba hired a Gypsy band, so most guests could dance. It was set partly inside-for older ladies and gents-and outside in tents for the young ones, and in the garden, where lampions where hanging with white silky ribbons from every tree.

Franciska was truly happy. Even though she did cry during the ceremony in the church, late afternoon the pride and happiness settled on her face. At long last she was wearing her emerald set-the gift from Huba-which helped to emphasize the elegant simplicity of her light grey brocade gown. Huba looked at her several times during the evening. He found her beautiful. Franciska stayed close to Helen until she could, and at dinner, she listened Zoltan's long and enjoyable speech about a legislative scandal. In that light Huba could see the sparks of her jewelry reflecting on her face, as if complementing it, which made her look paler as she would be otherwise. Also it seemed her eyes were filled with tears, which was quite impossible since she was smiling, and even laughing on Zoltan's jokes. Yes, it was tears! Any time Huba looked at her, he saw it. "No. She can't cry! It can't be it. If anything, it must be the reflection of her jewelry." Still, he found it puzzling what the set did to his wife.

A MARRIAGE BEGINS

"The age of pastorals are behind us, no matter how we still long for it," Zoltan used to say, who felt uneasy on the futility of his fellow men's social predilection. "Therefore it's safe to say that on the day man began to believe the importance of social status, he invented his own torturing devise, and arena."

The Devenys have been the nobility. The Garays have had the wealth. In this set-up, where Helen and Zoltan were to be married, both families had a trumpcard in hand. One wealth, one nobility, each being played out as virtue. Both families had their own version of seeing this union. Both camps were keeping pressure on one's in-laws, maintaining: "Don't you forget what an important family you have married into." Still, the Garays had a tiny bit of nobility: "The seven plum tree nobility". If it was good for a joke, they presumed, that few hundred hectares of extra land made up for the joke. The Devenys still could hold their assets in the thirties and could live it off if they preferred to, or could sell things like a few antiques. But how could they? Selling carpets or paintings is a desperate measure. Anna knew that. She preferred to restore their pride by refusing to compete with the wealth of Helen's family, what has been acquired by smart business deals of her grandfather, and to some degree, by her father.

The Devenys' reputation was rooted in their civilized life, their use of culture, and their contributions to the town and to the county. It was all very well. But what these families could do, if their offspring forced them into this sort of competition? Well, they stood up to it. The Garays overrated the importance of their wealth. In return, the Devenys overrated the importance of their nobility. This was the start to Helen and Zoltans' marriage.

YOUNG ZOLTAN DEVENY'S SPEECH

For it was nearly seven, he arrived to the building just in time. An organizer who kept watch at the gate, immediately led him into the heavily packed hall and up to the podium, then briefly introduced the guest by showering him with the standard politeness of "how lucky we are that Mr. Deveny is amongst us because of so and so", until Zoltan could start to speak.

Never being nervous of, or at all having problems with public speech, after his opening words Zoltan soon acquired a serious tone. By his choice, today's topic was current politics in Central Europe, and its effect on the national foreign policy. Not an easy subject, considering the times, but a good reason to fill up the hall it seemed.

"Ladies and Gentlemen: I am almost certain that most of you are challenged, or perhaps even tormented by similar thoughts, which I am about to present here tonight. Recent happenings in Europe compel me to talk of these now, till we have alternatives to work on, concerning our future. In the name of my fellow men I feel defeat, why we couldn't demonstrate our humanity with greater force, in times of adversity . . ."

And Zoltan went on illuminating those above mentioned adversities in topic and scope. In Southern political circles Zoltan was known as a talented speaker. Undoubtedly it has defined his best political feature and asset, even though in the town where he served as mayor, people recognized him by other merits. He was, to most of them a dedicated administrator and a trustworthy man, not merely somebody, who "talked well" as it was acclaimed by a group of journalists. (We must report, the people of T. couldn't care less for the papers). Presumably all these combined made him a good candidate for receiving numerous invitations either for a debate, or to deliver a speech, like the one in this town. He was out to break ice. Zoltan would discuss current issues ahead of anybody, as if being pulled by a promise he made as a boy, that his country had to be shaken up. In these years, Zoltan perceived Hungary as a nation which was still functioning, but not too far from a coma. He made a point, that this country could fall prey to an aggressor, whose greatest strength was alertness, or the simple act of staying awake, especially if one held in contrast to those, who weren't. This alert state however was not only a matter of talent but considerable advantage in strategy over such nations who slept through their present and future for finding too problematic solving them, or if they preferred to deny even the very existence of those problems.

Zoltan's speeches were intense, like this one here today, which made his audience hang on with him all the way, up until the last words. Most particularly the ladies . . .

When Zoltan stopped to drink a glass of water heads were together, exchanging notes: "I think it's his voice!" "What?" "His secret weapon." "Do you think so? I think he is irresistible." "I wish he wasn't so married." "With that voice, he can talk his way into any woman's bed. He could, into mine." "Don't! Stop it! Careful. People look at us." "Let them. They think we are into politics." Zoltan Deveny continued, and soon reached the subject of a possible war on a European scale, and an "unbelievable unpreparedness" for it. When he talked of the danger, he stumbled right in the middle of it. "What motivates us these days? Do we really serve our best interests? Let me insert here one thought. My perception of national interests doesn't equal the interests of a prosperous bourgeois class who does not oppose German influence (in fact, advocates it!) of which I do with the majority of my countrymen. But don't let me stray from my original subject Ladies and Gentlemen, which is about our nation's foreign policy. The question is: Are we-as a nation-able to project a homogeneous front outwardly? If we do, how? Lately, what we do in this regard, comes down sadly to two things. We concentrate on self-defense, and to our claims for territories. We seem to generate a hunger when we say we need the latter ones, repeating we want them back and now. Just like children do. We insist of having legitimate rights to them if sometime in History, or just fifteen years ago they used to be ours, part of greater Hungary. Justified or not, we convince ourselves for a claim and find ourselves in a war! Think of it! In retrospect, we wanted to gain, and are forced to lose at war's end, as usually is the case. When wars start, countries push for similar claims. We and they experience the draw of this dangerous appetite one calls—greed. But did we know, weaker countries are the pawns in such games? Invariably they discover one day, the original setup exceeded their national interests, and had little to do with their defense. I am aware, this is a matter of wording which makes it appealing to dismiss for some, early and prematurely: "Why do you expect the worse?" These people never learn, in politics there are no everlasting genuine friendships, only everchanging genuine interests.

The time came we addressed this question: "What our motives are for taking part in an upcoming war?" And until we can't answer it with a pure heart that we are in it for the right reasons . . . well, until then, our claims divert us and take us to the wrong path . . . to a bleak future, where we can have one end only . . . since we-all of us together-were losing sight of a greater view for another future, a hope for peace. In those days we make ourselves blind-half asleep, I grant it-for this common goal, while peace between nations could be built. We can't see if we will have it, but let's raise a doubt. Have we done enough to earn it?

Ladies and Gentlemen, we had to learn a hard lesson by finishing the World War: Peace between the nations couldn't be achieved only through sanctions, and punitive measures. It was then! When the League of Nations formed itself in 1919, in that instant reduced itself for one role. To be a police force. Instead of promoting peace, it was preparing a new war . . . . Will there be a new war? It's a burning question for us, how things are now. The postwar sanctions of 1920, put Hungary in an awkward position. We became a nation, who cannot sufficiently arm herself against a potential invader. A country in 20th century Europe with no chance in a defensive war!!! I should think, our ancestors are propelling in their grave! I would be, if I was there! Because of sanctions, because of a bad peace, because of lost territories, not to mention other outmoded policies by which the League of Nations go, by keeping an eye on the weak but doing nothing to those who arm in excess or eliminate their citizens whom they cannot stand. Given the facts, I can't think of a forum where one can go. Be warned, these unfortunate happenings could worsen, unless we reach a decision soon. In an event of a new war what do we do? If we think of a future we have to plan it now, by pulling together resources, strength and skill that we used to be blessed with, as a nation! You and I have to shake up Hungary and keep her fully awake!

Let me finish my topic, Ladies and Gentlemen, with a thought, from which I cannot escape. If somebody takes up comparative historic studies, he is astonished how the happenings shape the world which gets only more complicated with the passage of time. It makes present day politics with its turbulent problems, and their endless disintegrations virtually unsolvable, and nearly hopeless in its outcome, consequently pulling History in a denser and darker period where it has ever been. What is happening? And by what force of law? By taking elementary Physics, one wonders whether the spinning of this planet is still accelerating, the speed and pressure aggravating people into this nightmarish dizziness of growing aggressivity? Could this be the answer for all evil we do? I know, it sounds absurd and utterly out of line. But still . . . we see no future for this globe if it accelerates with the matter getting denser, till reaches its final density . . . and stops like a dead stone! . . . Thank you for your attention."

There was dead silence at first . . . only afterwards came a thunderous applause.

Chapter 38

Hesitation

Motto:

> "I must use this metaphor. Man is grinding between two stones. Or, is it three?"
>
> —Geza Garay

GEZA IS TWENTY-ONE

It was early, when Huba and Geza arrived to the county—seat. The year was 1938, and a very cold January day. Probably the coldest, they agreed, after finished the formalities of document signing. Since hardly anybody was on the street, after leaving the attorney's office, Huba propagated to his son: "We should drink to it, before we return to town! I'll take you to my club." He was more moved than Geza, who turned 21 two days ago, the time, he could claim his late parents' estate.

They had to walk three blocks. The city projected its old glory, which began 240 years ago, the time they would get rid of occupying Turks, who held this region longer from the rest of the Plains. It made people curious, why did they want this part, where nation-founding Arpad's Magyars pledged allegiance with the bloodletting ritual, by which act, the law of the land would be sanctioned. The region, once ravaged by wars, since recovered. Produce, trade, commerce flourished, and so had culture in the city while would hold to its riches, which could be obtained and ensured always by the land. The traveller, who came conducting business to this giant village, found a pulsating city which was inviting and distant, upright and modest, clever and shrewd. He had to see, its countless adjectives added up as many virtues, which was just about right for a city.

Considering the hour of the day, the club was half-empty, when they could at last settle in the fire-side room. "So! I raise my glass to you, son! To everything you wish for in life! From this day on, it is your money, your stocks, your land. Whatever you do, is your responsibility. I hope, your decisions will be wise ones," said Huba, who trusted, his son would ask his advice, considering 400 acres was big land, too big for someone so unexperienced, and the two years he studied law, did not make him a farmer. Huba was confident, one day Geza will be part of the granger conglomerate. It was no question he was going to produce grain, since wheat made the South famous. He will get married, and settle close by in the country, watching his children grow . . .

Geza knew his father's dream on the subject, nonetheless his enthusiasm failed to ignite him. In fact it froze him . . . And today, on the big day, after the second glass of brandy he gained a new ind of insolence. The things he used to suppress, regretfully came out: "If I hate something, it is to make plans!" There was a nervous smile on his face, when he looked out to the wintry street: "I really have no plans. Don't push me Father!" For Huba, it was a slap on the face, but he let it go unnoticed. "Well, I don't mind. He came of age. That's it! He is a grown man. And wants to be treated as one. I am going to help him if he asks me to. But right now he is confused. What can I say? Nothing. He is not my generation . . . By the way, where this generation is heading? Do they know? I shouldn't worry. It's their business. But I think of my grandfather . . . at the Great Revolution . . . Back then, people weren't tainted by softness, or superfluous thoughts . . . decadence. Their grasp of reality was guarded by virtue of their actions . . . very much unlike their softheaded great-grandchildren nowadays."

Back home, on the same afternoon Geza had these thoughts: "Why can't I do the things father asks me to? He must be disappointed in me. Why did I have to be so different from him? Father is the exemplary patriarch, who likes to see the continuation of his family as well as his ideals. He likes us around and wants us to be like he is. And I, who admire him, stand apart. Father? I like everything about him. His attitude, or how is he filled with energy. It's good to look at him! Everything is strong and vital, great gestures, laughs, strong bones, healthy teeth. If I put myself next to him, how do we measure up? I, the son—substitute, and the girls are the weak copies of someone who is giving and taking with zest and appetite. These weren't repeated in us. And he knows it." Was it possible, Huba had strong definition of his son and Geza could not be that son? Well, yes and no. Huba was still confident, Geza will come to him so he could suggest what to do with the land, what to grow precisely, how to employ machinery and people, and of the problems of the market.

A week went by when Geza came to him one morning, all smile and confidence. "Father, I thought of wine," he said, cutting right into the middle. "Wine-growing. You see, I kind of looked into this. Superficially of course."

Huba was surprised. He had to light his cigar before he asked, "All very well. But here? On this flat land? Son! This is grain country . . . Your poor father used to say: Anybody who grows other than grain in this soil is a criminal! No. I don't go that far. I just ask: Why would you put wine here? Wine likes the hills, and different soil. The best wines are on volcanic slopes . . ."

"I realize that, Father. But I see fantasy in wine. Let me try it. If I failed, I'll go and do what makes more sense . . ." Geza looked at him as if still needing his consent. Eventually Huba replied, "Well, sure. Give it a try. If this is what you want." And so, in March of the same year (in 1938) the first business trip would be launched. "I outlined the whole operation. To start with, I need to buy the shoots," Geza explained, ". . . of how much I'll plant, and the rest. I did get the main points of wine growing. For a couple of years I concentrate on the grapevine by hiring people who are experts, which roughly takes care of cultivation. Well . . . the following years won't be that strenuous." Geza went ahead as promised, bought the shoots and prepared the soil. In early April a handful of hired men showed up for the planting. When it was done, with the grapevines in place, the rest had to be waited out. This part suited him the most. "Since it takes a while to cut my first grapes, it's time to embark on a "professional tour"," mused Geza, and took off to the Mid- and North-West, which is regarded the best wine-country. Geza visited at least a dozen wineries, and stayed over with one of them for a month as an apprentice. This was the Kovi family. Mr. Kovi who acquired wealth and fame, was a self-made man, and that's how he told his story: "I was lucky with a hunch to mix two wines. I came up with a semi-dry, table variety. It was all ten years ago. When I promoted it on conventions, it became successful right away. Contracts poured in, and I supply twenty restaurants in the capital now, and thirty more, nationwide." Soon Mr. Kovi took Geza to the wine cellar and had a few words on storing wine. When they would start sampling together, the young apprentice didn't object. In this underground treasure house Geza discovered, he enjoyed wine far more than his connoisseur image would normally have it.

Maybe Geza didn't take it well, but he was not applauded by wine-experts, after he shared his visions of growing wine on the Plains. Without exception, each grower told him the same. "But my friend! Only Transdanubia and the North-East Highlands are suitable for wine! Well, maybe the Southwest? It loves the Southern and Western slopes of these hills. Leave the Plains what's best for! Grain!"

Still. Paying no mind what others would say, Geza kept to his plan. Foolish or not, this was his argument. "You say it's risky? So be it. To start a plantation is like gambling. If it fails, I'll do something else." Yet he kept in mind what Mr. Kovi hinted: "It's the second, or third generation that draws a good income from it. Your children. And grandchildren."

"Well? So we wait then," thought our man, and thought of Julia.

Chapter 39

Passion

FIRST DATE

"My horse! Is she clean? Yes or no?"

"Ahh . . . no Miss! I am about to . . . ah. No!" Since the boy began to wash the horse later than asked, he couldn't possibly finish in time, and when Kati came out fully dressed. it angered her that he still brushed the back of the animal with no sign of hurry. "He is sabotaging me!" was her first reaction on entering the stable, but she dropped the thought for the sake of another: "No. He is not that smart . . . just lazy and stupid . . . Not that it helps me." "Clean or not, I have to ride her!" exclaimed the young woman to the boy and pushed him over, in order to saddle the horse quickly, on her own. She was late already when left home, that's why decided getting to the backroads, where one could cut through the fields considerably faster. Kati was nervous, and very excited today. "If he won't wait for me, I don't know what I'll do . . . . Unless to go and look for him. I have to . . . I am half an hour late as it is! If he won't be there, I must go after him. That's it! He . . . cannot believe, I led him on." She was riding fast, and only the excitement of their prospective first rendezvous could make her ask such an unreasonably naive question: "Will he be angry, and fed up waiting? What if I lose him, now when he showed interest?" It's appropriate to suggest, Kati was not her rational self. Even she realized it, when she came around: "I refuse to think, he won't be there." Well, the feelings she nurtured for the young man had to be subdued far too long; until this day, or this very hour. Yesterday, when at last she met him, the girl couldn't help telling him: "Jancsi, I simply must talk to you," for which the young man nodded and asked: "Where?" "Somewhere far. I . . . I know a hiding place." That was that. She explained the place and told the hour. And-now all one could do was, to overcome distance and time. Kati had sworn it would be the best hiding place, by being covered from both sides of the road where the bush was seldom, if ever cleared. A no man's land. She knew these strips from her childhood, only these days the shrubs grew high. Suddenly she could see the spot by that old twisted acacia tree. And a second later she could se him too. "Jancsi is waiting! He is here!" He sat on the grass under the tree, with a horse two or three steps away peacefully grazing, which for an onlooker might have given the perfect picture for a twentieth century pastoral. Before Kati could lead the horse to the side of the shrubs and acacia trees and get to the clearing, the young man noticed her, and stood up. He waved to her. Kati dismounted the horse and came closer. Neither was sure on what to say. But was there need for words? It struck her for a second, if he waited that long, he must love her. It was all on his face besides, but Kati wasn't yet proficient reading it. At this point she could be sure only, that she loved him. But it was not a question. It never was.

Oh well. Her feelings didn't just appear overnight, or a week ago. Oh, no. She discovered it last Summer, at the first time they met. But what can a girl do? She kept it a secret. And because of it, for a whole year Kati didn't recognize anyone else to be worthy or interesting or attractive among the young men who showed up on holidays either to amuse her, or to keep her company. They were the socially acceptable suitors no doubt by her family's standards, but still none made lasting impressions on her that year. As much as in any of her dealings, Kati had high standards in matters of the heart. She cared for Jancsi, this socially "unacceptable" young man! And so it's just happened, last year Kati found the only man she could call the love of her life! Even if he didn't reciprocate it. Maybe he did, but she couldn't verify it for a whole year. (To be precise, till next harvest). So there she was, waiting for a year to learn his heart. Oh, that year! It wasn't easy. If only the distance weren't so big, she might have figured a way to stumble in their village, but it was impossible, for they lived in another county, and she was away in school, only. finding two counties between them all together, instead of one. It was a bad idea just to think about of going there. She might have made a fool of herself running after him like that. It is not the way to get a man! At least this much she knew, wised up by her sixteenth year. Well, it was last year. Since then Kati turned seventeen, and used her time wisely. By making her choice, and countering her parent's expectations she waited for a whole year just to learn this: Was she loved by Jancsi the sharecropper's son, or wasn't she?

The young woman counted the days, picturing their first rendezvous and the confession of their love . . . more than once! What else could she do? Many times Kati was running ahead in its conclusion,'projecting a great love in his heart too, the kind she had in hers. And at last the year came to pass with its unduly long weeks . . . and many days. And now the moment of their first date was here, by way of actual happening!

Kati still stood there at loss of words, trying to explain the vicissitudes for being late, but it didn't come out well, not how she designed it. Instead, with great relief she confessed to him: "I am glad you are still here. I was scared to death, you wouldn't."

"What a thing to say!" he said and smiled and came close to hold her hands. And then he kissed her . . . She couldn't remember how, but soon they were lying on the ground, still kissing, with all their clothes removed. They forgot about the rest of the world, about horses and the passing of time, for they learned a great secret by lying naked in the grass, of being locked in a gentle embrace which was also wild, by doing what others do when they are making love. For them it was new. Opening a gate the first time, and finding out how it was done. This was the purpose of this Summer . . . or of last Summer, or of their whole life! They had to meet to become one. This act in turn outlined their future by casting them not a step away from the other. It was something, in which both had faith.

Chapter 40

Perceptions

A SON-IN-LAW

Being out of town that day, Huba was glad how Zoltan's name was mentioned again. Whenever he heard the name of his son-in-law, it made him proud. But couldn't help wondering if Zoltan was out to earn the "crusader for already lost causes" title. "Well, maybe he wasn't!" corrected Huba himself, realizing he was a bit too harsh and pragmatic. "We tend to see things differently. We all do. From the parliament to the political parties and associations, salons, pubs, clubs, down to the last barber shops or the steambaths. Why, of course! It's like a political hippodrome. A good chance and exposure for hot issues to get cristallized. Everyone has a forum; a chance to be heard. And I guess we all get the forum we deserve. I think Zoltan has insight, as well as talent for solutions. He should be in the cabinet," concluded Huba, who still recalled, how Zoltan (then just a student) would fight in 1919, in that terrible year when Count Karolyi. has let the country fall in turmoil, by entrusting her into the hands of leftists and eventually to the Communists. This young man wrote in an article then: "Our President, as if back still in his cardplaying days, threw his country in, saying: "Gentlemen, I am out!" And assuming it was his right, he threw her to the Communists. When did we see such a horrendous irresponsibility? The Count himself a Socialist, is betraying what he believes in, giving it all up and yields to the extreme left. It is a scandal and an outrage! For this man, giving free hand to the Communists to form a government, was nothing else than his personal revenge on rightwing politicians, the ones, who most likely opposed him in the

Parliament. It is unheard of that the President of a country should act as an eight year old unreined child! What a shame!" Oh, yes. His article was very passionate. Huba has read it then, and remembered saying: "That young man. I wouldn't mind meeting him!" Zoltan was damn right in what he said. Only too late to prevent anything, for the damage was done. And not fixed, up until Admiral Horthy came in with his special units, and threw off the Communists and of the Romanian army that has been invading the South and was approaching to Budapest. What a shame it. was! What a shame!" Huba remembered. "At any rate . . . after Horthy, things could be stabilized, especially when he sworn in as the Regent. When he decided once and for all, against a Habsburg king for Hungary . . ." Huba heard later, Zoltan left school, and was hiding for two months then, from 1919 March, till April, at the time of the Communist rule.

Nobody was surprised, that most young girls have fallen in love with Zoltan. Neither was Huba. sure he was glad, when years later, after considerable maneuvering Helen brought him to the altar, showing to three Southern county-states how capable she was, getting the man everyone else wanted for a husband. Yes. It made Huba proud. Proud of his son-in-law.

A POLITICAL MARRIAGE

People who knew them intimately, were wondering about the couple. Here was the paradox. Why did Helen become a political wife? Despite of living in a specific milieu, where every step she took has been calculated for getting higher office for Zoltan, still her knowledge of politics didn't improve. She would surprise close associates with questions like: "I am fed up with these changes! Can't the Government decide once and for all what it wants?"

"Her remarks could make it as collector items easily, in someone's political journal," said once an aid to the Lieutenant Governor. "I swear to you, Sir, she would be even flattered! You know how women are. She would just not get it!"

Still, if her "Devil may care" political maturity was a matter of concern for Zoltan, Helen was content with the prescribed package (into which she fit very well). This widely used old-fashioned wisdom known in political circles, in essence sounded like this: "My dear friend! For a political career you need: (a) to come from a good family; (b) have a good brain; (c) and make a good name. That will take you anywhere . . . Oh, yes! One more thing. Marry well. As for the wife! It is sufficient if she dances well. My friend, at the County-Balls nobody is watching your name, or your brains, but your wife's dancing legs. That could take you anywhere too . . ." As we all know, by no means was Helen a woman of scruples. She felt reassured by this old hat philosophy of being the perfect political wife. Regardless of Zoltan, who had his own lead, and very different thoughts on the matter. He refused to think politics were a stepping stone to anywhere. This is why he came to despise this popular slice of wisdom, even if in this case-in their marriage-it all became true. He had the breeding, the name, the brain, and took a wife who had pretty dancing legs. Annoying or not, he was taken in. He was an insider.

AND A MOTHER-IN-LAW

Surely everyone heard of a husband with a secondary role? Or a wife with the same, if we are listening into the husband's family? So I can't possibly surprise my readers when I say, in Franciska's eyes Zoltan was a mere episode player casted in a secondary role at Helen's side, to obtain social position for her. It goes without saying, it would have been more difficult to get that position if she had no husband. Every mother knew that, but Franciska knew it ahead of everybody, since Helen expressed her ideas ever so clearly. If Helen wanted Zoltan, it was fine. If her daughter was happy with her choice, then Franciska was content. She didn't mind Zoltan at all. In fact she welcomed him just like Huba had, but for different reasons. Basically she believed anybody would do, who could hold a status and Helen's interest, at the same time. Should we say; the newcomer's presence has been necessitated by the degree of his usefulness? Well, yes. As far as Zoltan catered to her daughter's wishes, Franciska liked him, which is to say, she was no different from those mothers who go great lengths for looking after their stock.

CHAPTER 41

The Devenys' Evenings . . . (and a Hunting Party in Retrospect)

AN OPEN HOUSE

When the older Devenys hosted their literary evenings twice a year they sent no invitations, hoping everyone just mildly interested in Literature, Music or in a good debate would show up. They enjoyed get-togethers with people who were ready for expressing their views on Politics, Literature or Art. Conservative or liberal? It played no role. Everyone was welcome.

On these evenings-one at early Spring and one at late Autumn-the guests gathered in the library and listened to the program the hosts had in mind. It was mostly literary works they wanted to present, or just an article, which was open for discussion afterwards. At other times someone noteworthy gave a speech. Their evenings were appropriately closed with a piano or violin recital, or once in a while with a string quartet performance. Each year Anna had her own evening too. For this event she invited a writer from her native Transylvania to read chapters form his book, as part of a promotion tour. Anna did not expect too many people then, but they had to be avid readers who had not only appreciation but a thirst for the expressive mind. This other night with the mixed audience had been vastly different, which probably saved it from going down as predictable. Some of the same people would attend each time, but new ones too showed up, having no idea what to expect. There were yet others, who came for the food. Apart from these, the majority found the Deveny evenings more stimulating than a provincial theater, where they sat three hours in gloom by listening what the dramatist had to say, but not getting their chance for a dispute. (One wonders, if the Devenys were more democratic and less elitist than most writers were those days?)

For the Devenys their evenings turned out well, and the news of it spread in neighboring towns and villages. They were popular. So people kept asking: "Are you coming to their next evening?" which only established, this was the place to go.

The Garays were invited like others, but only three members of the family have shown interest. At fifteen, Julia was asked to give a recital. Following her first appearance, for Anna's delight she usually came back and these visits helped to build a deep bond with the Devenys. Geza also liked to come, taking part in debates. Apparently being so good at it he attracted a circle of admirers, who stayed close by, in case he was to open his mouth (which he did, for thank God, he wasn't an introvert).

Strangely, Miriam used to attend without Tass. She and Anna have been friends now. Their love of Literature was one link, and the sense of being "the foreign woman" was the other.

Thinking on the guest-list, in the late 1930s, Anna had to ask: "Why, apart from these three, no one else from the Garay clan wants to visit us? After all, we are in-laws!"

Indeed, why? Well, Helen made it clear, she found no appeal in their evenings, until the Deverys did not consider giving a dance. Kati had other reasons. She charged them, this whole idea of literary "nonsense" was just showing off, that they were the elite, no matter how much liberalism they displayed. Still, they were the privileged and the whole thing was just a class-manipulation. For which Geza reposted: "And? What would you suggest them to do? Move out to the main square and live in a tent?" Kati was cross when she replied: "You never will understand the class struggle, even if you live to be a hundred!" And still, there was Huba the most prominent of the Garays. Well? What reasons did he have? Huba wouldn't come because the feud between the two families. What feud? Oh, nothing new. In fact an old one, regarding a debate between being a Kossuth or a Deak supporter was still an ongoing one, hanging above them as some "Damocles' sword". For him it was not easy to stay absent. Being a gregarious man, Huba was attracted to go but in a confused attempt of staying loyal to Kossuth, he still wouldn't budge. He reasoned out with himself: "I have no place there. The Devenys are cosmopolitans. I don't even know what do they stand for!? What are they? Liberals? Freethinkers? Freemasons? Whatever they are, it's fine with me! I stick to my ideals, they stick to theirs!"

Credible or not, the Kossuth versus Deak debate kept these two men-Huba Garay and "old" Zoltan Deveny-apart since the 1920s. Precisely since that hunt, when everybody had his breakfast at the long camp-table. It's funny why should it happen so, but it had, that the man serving the food, wore some knitted cap, and put on an apron, making it an ill-conceived garb, even on that very cold day. No wonder his outfit provoked this remark: "Hey Pali! You look like a fleeing Kossuth, on the day he crossed over the frontiers!" The remark was oil to fire, very unwise, and the gentlemen reacted passionately. Everyone told his version, shouting back and forth, pro and contra. Yells came from everywhere. Yells like: "He was more of a man in woman's garb, than any of you will ever be!" "Why? Because he ruined the country?" "Ruined? Who told you that? He was a great man!" "The great man was a fake!" "Sir! What did you say?" "You heard me Sir!" At this point Old Zoltan {who wasn't yet old) had to intervene. He didn't believe in duels. "Gentlemen! Gentlemen! Please. These woods begin to sound like the House of Parliament. I am afraid, we scare off the game . . . If we are true sportsmen, before the hunt we don't drink, after the hunt, keep off discussion on religion and politics, unless we . . ." He was shushed down. "Oh, come, come now Deveny! Why do you want to be a spoilsport? Nothing is written what we should do, or say . . . It's good to have fun. Don't worry. It's good sport . . . as far as we won't put bullets into one another." The gentlemen did what they professed, jumped up, formed little groups, and came back exhausted . . .

Everyone had his say on the matter. But interestingly, there was no rniddleground. It was a bitter fight. Huba fought too, he was defending Kossuth with great elan. "Well, my friend, I don't agree. Kossuth wanted us to get rid of Austrians, to gain Independence. A nation stood behind him! I say, the Revolution was inevitable. Eventually, yes, he was overpowered by the Habsburgs. Foreign army. Alliances. Circumstances!"

This display of passion intrigued Zoltan Deveny. It was his turn to speak, as if wanting to enlighten his opponent. (Later Huba couldn't sort it out, whether the tone or the content was more infuriating). That's what Deveny had to say: "My dear friend! Some of us think, it is obvious, Kossuth has ruined the country with the Revolution. We have been run over, as the result of it. Deak was the only man, who brought back Hungary. Put us back on the map. It took him some time and work, not to mention diplomacy, until the Compromise. But with that, he placed Hungary side by side with Austria. This was the only way to move, back then. If we would have had our own king, we would have fought for Independence. But we hadn't. Your precious Kossuth liked that. He liked this loophole. So, he could proclaim himself a dictator in 1849 . . . But let's forget him! The only chance for us was to fight for the Dual Monarchy. Electing a Hungarian King was out of question. Sharing the Habsburg Emperor, and making him a Hungarian King too, was the only way. So, Hungary could keep her Constitution. Her own . . ."

The noise began to resemble to that on school-yards. Consequently, Huba heard less and less. Since he hated what was said, he couldn't care now. He intensely disliked this Deveny. For the superior tone he had. After these sentences he didn't think well of him. Even, if everyone else did . . . Looking more like a social hour in the club, the hunting party was still on, regardless of the bitter cold. The gentlemen fought, meanwhile their fried liver (sauteed with onion in brandy) had turned cold on their plates, and soon in the frying pan too, making the chef (the culprit of this senseless quarrel with his unusual choice of winterwear) standing hopelessly by a makeshift campstove, thinking neither Kossuth nor Deak, but of the liver! He could have sold it easily in the village, for good money. But only, if it wouldn't go spoiled. "Damn fools, these gentlemen! Some hunters . . ." he blurted, but luckily none of them could hear it. Huba was ready to explode for Deveny's lecture, and stopped talking to him after the hunt. In fact he stopped it right away, leaving the breakfast table, not suspecting the least, one day they would be in-laws, and share the same grandchildren.

Huba couldn't help being born in a family fiercely loyal to the Revolution. As if Kossuth hunted him, his loyalty would be tested more than once. When Geza was twelve, from returning school he confronted Huba one day: "Father, how come Kossuth ran away in exile, dressed as a woman, and left behind all his generals to be hanged or shot? Why do you think he was a great man?" Geza stood there waiting, and he had to come up with an explanation. Huba still remembered how astonished he was by this blustering. And also how hard he tried countering Geza's sudden disloyalty to the great man. He talked for an hour to the boy, but avoided making it sound like an admonition.

And why didn't Franciska go to these evenings? Well, she had her reasons too. "The Devenys? Why would I go there? I have heard she is quite an eccentric. I am not surprised why Miriam is her best friend.

I've also heard Anna doesn't behave her age. She tries hard to look younger . . . who cares? I am not interested what they do. Why would I be?" Yet as soon as Julia, this dreamy and artistic girl came home from the soiree, her mother wanted to know what went on. "How did you enjoy your evening, Julia?" "It was fine," she would say. "Yes? Go on. What kind of people are they?" pressed Franciska. By then, Julia had this habit of replying in short staccatos, sharing only the essence of her experiences. Now, she said only the following: "They are gentle people." so, her mother had to hear the very word she wished to hear the least.

Chapter 42

The Garay Girls

KATI ELOPES

When a letter in its most advanced stage (that is, being held by the recipient) announces: "Dear Mother and Father, I must go with the man I love, forgive me, your loving daughter, Kati," they can be sure the deed is done, and there is not much they can do to bring her back. Not that they didn't try. Huba and Franciska took pride in parenthood, and were aware of their social standing, of which on both accounts only fueled their desire and intention of rescuing the girl. In the first month they sent acquiescent letters with an aim to forecast a bleak future away from the parental home, by summing up everything Franciska could think out between her crying fits. Huba offered his services by way of visiting her, so he could convince her of the same. But in three days he returned, being tight-lipped on the visit. In a week he concluded they should not think on another expedition because Kati was a grown woman who was married now, even if an outward disappointment to her parents. That was that. Kati has gone, and for a long while any reference to her had to be silenced in the family, but only there, because the town still preferred to be scandalized. "The Garay girl eloped with a sharecropper's son! Father and son used to work for Huba Garay. Season workers. Imagine! I hear they don't take it well. I mean, the Garays. On a second thought, why should they? It's like stealing . . ." It made no difference now, but Geza had to recall what she said to him only a week before she would pack in secrecy and leave with the last group of workers: "Living with the propertied class is like living in a city built on swamp, where miasma lingers day and night." At first catch, it wasn't bad. By evaluating the thought, he found it elegant but moody and erroneous. Later mentioning it to his father, Huba would snap: "So! She wanted the stability of poverty. We shouldn't spoil her fun."

In the heat of passion, Kati made herself an outcast for running away, with her parents suspecting, she wasn't cut out for running home for the first blow. Deep down they both knew she will do it all the way and it may cost her a lifetime to admit her mistake.

For them too, it took years to forgive her, something which came sooner to Huba, for being the one who still had a weak spot when it came to Kati. Even if father and daughter have split on ideology, he would always be curious what was she up to, and more often than not, he was darn impressed. As time passed by and the scandal was no news, he once more took pride in her courage. Well, secretly of course. After six month his daughter eloped, Huba suggested to Franciska: "What do you think? Shouldn't we go and see them? The young couple . . . ."

"We do nothing of the kind!" she replied. But when the news came a year later that she had a child, nobody could keep Huba back. He didn't need permission this time. He merely informed Franciska: "Well, I go and see them. I have a grandchild. I'll ask them, if they need my help."

ROTARY CLUB LUNCHEON

In the letter of invitation, the Devenys were advised to come early. Helen enjoyed these luncheons. If for no other reason, they gave chance to sport her new suits, like the one she had on with the French cut. And as for the conspicuous little hat, she would just say to those who would comment on it: "Oh, it is my new acquisition! I always adored navy blue."

This particular luncheon, given for a hundred guests, had been organized by the Rotary Club. The way it would start shortly after eleven the notables began to gather in a side-room. The Governor's wife, who liked to maintain an aura of beneficence on all public functions, has noticed Helen's hat as soon as the Devenys entered. "Well, it's nice to see you both. It really is. Such a cute hat you are wearing, my dear." Helen was glad to take the compliment. From then on she stayed with her, until others thought best to mingle. When it was time, Zoltan and Helen have been seated with the Governor and his wife and with the regional director of the Club, who would be also with his wife. On their right the Police Commissioner of the county was seated, next to him the dashing army officer Colonel Rac and two other guests, namely the chief editor of the Southern Herald, Zsolt Vass and his wife Ella, who happened to be the publisher. The Herald was the influential weekly magazine which gained popularity in the entire country. Ella and Zsolt Vass were seen everywhere, talked to everyone, and knew everything; or at least that's how others perceived them. The lunch has been a success. At first they would serve "Szegedi soup with spicy liver—dumplings". The second course was "Roasted Quail, marinated in Dalmatian sage vinegar," served with kasha and gooseberry sauce. And the third horseradish sauce and baby carrots. In between they switched wines; from "Badacsonyi Keknyelu" to "Somloi Furmint" which has a heavier bouquet. Later they would take "Tokay Aszu" but only with dessert. And for dessert, the all-favorite "Chestnut Trifle" was served, with plenty of whipped cream. This was the time too, when Zoltan's speech could begin. He talked on national and international matters, sensitive issues of present-day politics, the social significance of economy, the future of the country and a hope for unity. Also he mentioned the new possibilities in commerce and trade, agriculture and industry. As much as he could put into forty five minutes.

There was a modest ovation after Zoltan's speech, which made him realize: "Well, I must have hit a chord!" While walked back to the table, also congratulations came from every direction. He nodded, and was moved, but more than anything, wanted to drink a glass of water. Before he could sit down, Zsolt Vass, the chief editor (a resourceful man) started talking to him. He talked fast. "My dear Zoltan! What you say is, impelling. I am glad some of us have brain and guts for this kind of coalescence. Ella loved it! Absolutely loved it!" Zoltan took a side glance to Ella, who smiled, and repeated: "We just loved it." For greater emphasis she touched Zoltan's arm. Vass went on. "I wonder how the Regent would react to it? I really do! I wish there was a chance for a debate with him. I mean . . . for you!" He stopped here for a second, took out his notebook, made notes, and continued: "At any rate, Ella and I would run it untouched, fully, in next week's Herald. If you don't object!?" Zoltan displayed no emotion, so the editor went on. "Why? Of course. Your line is not in accord with the official view . . . But it doesn't prevent the copy from being sold out in matter of hours . . . Well. Of course, count in our subscribers. It will sell! I am sure of it." He talked excitedly, and drew his chair closer. "But if we . . . I mean you and others from different parts of the country would influence the Government . . . The Regent. In the Parliament there are already warnings! . . . The same kind, you are talking about. The danger of wanting Transylvania back at all costs. We, together could clear this confusion for the public, through the Herald." When all finished coffee the waiter reappeared, by pushing a well-stocked trailer. He offered cognac and cigar to the gentlemen, liqueur and chocolate bonbon to the ladies. Zoltan asked his second glass of water before taking cognac. After the brief interruption their talk couldn't quite resume, considering the Governor had something on his mind. "It is all very well what you said, Deveny," he started. "In fact, I even liked your postulation. But . . . I wouldn't see so darkly. The government knows its business . . . knows where it stands. How to act in . . . this . . . , eh!" There was a problem. A big one. His cigar died out. He made attempts rescuing it, but it seemed puffing was not the solution. Searching for a box of matches took even more time, for it wasn't easy getting into those pockets, until he himself was in the suit. We must inform the reader, his Excellency the Governor was a corpulent man. And a stubborn one it seemed, because the search still went on, regardless that two men at the table have offered a lighter. The Governor decided paying no mind to Colonel Rac, nor to the Police Commissioner, whose extended arms would be on the table still, even if it made them feel-after the first thirty or so seconds-just a bit humiliated and ridiculous. True it took time, but his Excellency found the match, and reawakened his cigar, and assumably his own spirit.

"Let's hear now a good, old-fashioned debate!" hoped and expected his table company, thinking they've earned it, as well as worked for it. In the meantime Zoltan (alongside with the other two gentlemen) had these thoughts: "How pitiful he is! He wanted to gain momentum. With a cigar!" When the cigar in question would be back functioning, an enraptured table company would be still waiting for the first man of the county to parcel out his thoughts. So, not to keep them in suspense, his Excellency finally began to talk: "I am not about to question what the Prime Minister, or the Regent finds appropriate . . ." He hardly finished the sentence, when Helen knew, something went wrong! She looked at him, at Zoltan, and once more at the Governor. The Governor's wife was doing the same. But she seemed far more entertained.

Even though Helen planned to stay in S. for overnight, she changed her mind and returned with Zoltan, who drove home in the same afternoon. Helen loved this city, its shops, cafes, the theater and her friends, yet now decided against staying. "I am in no mood to amuse myself for the rest of the day." Her reason was that migraine headache, that tormented her for sometime. (Well. It began back, at the club . . .) Helen took painkillers, but they were no use. So she put on her dark glasses for the road. The Devenys drove in silence. It was still fifteen kilometers to their town and Helen thought it was much better, if she told how she felt. "I never understood why do you have to be so disagreeable in public? As you were today." "Was I?" asked Zoltan. "Yes. That speech. Why would you mind who will get back Transylvania for us? Why does it matter how it is done, as long as it is done? Why do you go against what others don't mind at all?" Zoltan couldn't believe what he has heard just now. "Helen! That is the whole point! Something was sold to us. A promise. It was sold to us on wholesale. And the majority doesn't know it. What if they buy it? If they do, it will push the country into a great danger. Because of a wrong commitment. This could lead to a disaster. If the Germans go to war, we might not be able to hold on to our neutrality." Helen snapped. "And what's wrong with that?" Zoltan looked at her in disbelief. "Everything! . . . everything. The future of this nation."

On the rest of the road there was no more argument. They were not talking. Helen was upset why Zoltan had to anger the Governor. And, why her headache did not go away. She felt miserable. Looking at the roadside, she asked repeatedly from the trees: "Why my life runs to the direction, where I don't want to go? Why aren't we more carefree?"

JULIA, TO THE ACADEMY OF MUSIC

"Julia dear, this "life for music" foolishness went far enough! Look! You are so young! How can you decide things so early? You can study music. It is nice. But then you get married just like Helen did. Have a nice home, children, and you can have the best piano. People will admire you, if you play . . . but . . . but teaching? You should concentrate on society as Helen does. After all . . . Anyway . . . Your "dedication" to music is nice but has to stop there! You refused the debutante parties! I never, never understand this. What should you want? I shall never consent to teaching, or . . . anything of this nature. Never. Girls . . . young ladies of your status don't work. They don't have to, you know! I suppose, it is this freedom nonsense, one hears!

I am sure the suffragette has a lot to do with it. In any case, you go to Budapest, and study music, but this far is how it goes! Keep that in mind dear." So have given Franciska her dissuasion to her eighteen year old daughter Julia, just days before her journey to Budapest, where she would go to start her studies in piano and composition, at the prestigious Academy of Music, an Institute being established by none other than the great Franz Liszt. Julia sparkled from happiness. She was elated sitting on the train opposite to her father, who was busy studying his business papers on the duration of the journey. Julia couldn't help repeating a pattern the train's clutter seemed to suggest on this beautiful Autumn day. "De-di-ca-tion, de-di-ca-tion."

Chapter 43

A Choice

THE SEASON WORKERS

Deep down the young woman was glad to avoid the scene her mother threw in a rage (this time in her absence) and to hold on to the freedom she gained at last harvest. Because on that day a young girl's concerns were left in her parental home for a young woman to emerge in just matter of hours, who yearned to be a new person. For Kati this was not only new, but dear and sweet too which she called happiness, which seemed far the best foundation for life. Now she was a married woman, a fully grown person, who in view of the consequence had to be responsible for her deeds. Kati had no problem with that. With things going so fast, nobody asked how was she going to fare on the long-run. Was there a future, or she fell into a trap of her own trusting, assuming she arrived just to the right place, to stay with those she could adhere? Did these people need her as much as she liked to believe it? It was early to answer all of these . . . She understood however, from this position was no return unless her marriage was about to disintegrate, but even then, going home was not an option. "I didn't come here to fail!" Oh, but such thoughts would not enter her mind these days. Why would they? Kati was in love. They both were infatuated with the novelty of being in love and of their separate perception of love, that each had a constant need of communicating to the other, so they could learn if they both experienced the same passion. This obviously left no room for the rational. But then, this was their first Spring together . . .

Finding employment in these years was not that difficult if one didn't look too high, and since Kati and Jancsi didn't, they were hired as season-workers. Their families-close and far-had comment on it, failing to realize the principal characters had something to prove, and so they {the families) missed the point.

So it's arbitrary to say, "The newlyweds started off badly" or "The newlyweds started off well," until we don't ask the newlyweds how did they take it, or what was their goal? For one thing, they had work.

All year long hired hands would be in demand on the fields, with the obvious exception of Winter months. Since this was what Jancsi did at the time, Kati found natural to be with him. "It isn't a bad way to get going. I like it," conferred to her husband who had his doubts, wondering why would a girl from a wealthy family formulate this kind of dream? It was possible that Kati, for reasons as yet unclear dreamt backwards, contrary to the young people here, whose dreams were about getting out, and fast . . . Well, Kati had it this way. She could eradicate an embarrassment (hers) for being born into the wrong class, with this grand decision of taking the right step at last. And the first time in her life she felt good, and was satisfied with the choice. It was only the first step but successful nonetheless as far as she attained freedom with it. It would have been much better though, if leaving her family in this wayward fashion, wasn't grinding on her conscience. But it had.

She remembered most the burning heat of that Summer-the first one-which they spent in clouds of hay-dust and of the feel of aching muscles in their arms, back and feet.

Kati and Jancsi were married for seven months now, and the couple used to the new life, that was about moving with the work. Sometimes too much of it . . . Regardless of their spirit, reaping the wheat was a heavy physical work, and the overwork left them with cracked hands, blisters all over, and burning eyes.

They woke at dawn, left, and were not home till dusk. During the hottest days Kati and Jancsi didn't feel like doing much after ten or twelve hours of work, other than lying on their cool sheet on the bed and taking comfort in each other's arms. But it would be still early to see a wider scope to their future, even though they began to talk of it. Among the plans was saving up enough money for a small horne. Well, to build one. At the beginning it would be just a room with a kitchen, and years later they would add one more room to it as everyone did here, constructing it from mud-brick. Achieving this was good prospect for a season-worker, who could never buy or build a home; let alone get a thin strip of land. Well, yes. The realistic goal: live like the sharecroppers, who own a tiny piece of land. So. This was the ultimate dream about?! occurred to Kati. Ownership? For taking part in the march, where each class has to display what money can buy which enables one to secure a lot in this tumultuous social parade we see around and call "life". Sometimes however the desire to own backfired on sharecropper families. It took these vicious circles. Always. First of all, their mobility for going after the work to greater distances, has diminished. The other problem was taxation. If certain conditions couldn't be met the tax proved to be sky high for that strip of land. If on the leased land they couldn't produce a good crop, they couldn't earn cash for paying the taxes, which eventuated the loss of their very small land. On their sleepless nights, sharecroppers wished they were plain field-workers who were coming and going with the season, working for a wage. Even if it meant a step backward socially, still it was less burdensome on the whole, like keeping up with impossible obligations. Kati wasnit afraid of these. She had energy for the new life. If the contract secured it, the couple was put up in workers' quarters, and on Sundays, they would go home to the new kins, if they weren't too far.

Some landowners were generous with food and shelter, and some stingy. With the harvest over the pace changed and other works were done with less pressure. If the weather took to the worst they could wait a day or two, but around mid-November, the employment stopped. So they moved with the season . . . Like nomads do.

JANCSI

During Winter they could rest. It gave them a chance to know each other better. On one of those days Jancsi had this to say: "Certain things make me sick, Kati, and I give you an example. Just one. And you tell me what you think. The Baron, who is away most of the year, when gets back, likes to show how . . . kind he is. By posing as the great benefactor. Now look here . . . what he gives us for Christmas!?"

Jancsi stood up, went inside behind the curtain, and reappeared from his parents' room with a life-size porcelain duck in his hand. "This is the gift." The statuette was white, not at all ugly for having the plumage stylishly painted with ink-green, lilac, violet and grey.

They were laughing uproariously, for it was both pathetic and miserable, considering Jancsi's parents had no good furniture . . . "My father is looking up to him, like he was God. The basis of his loyalty is: "Look son. Our family worked for the Baron's family for generations. But for generations!" You see Kati, my old man is even proud of this. I never will understand why can't he cut off this . . . this cancerous growth of the vassallous mentality? "We worked for them for generations!" Well, I think it's time we stopped. The Baron? The Baron is the benevolent lord, who is high above us. Why? Because he is highborn. And my parents accept that. Why? It is true! These people here, who hardly know him, receive his stupid "boxing day" gifts . . . as if he gave it from the goodness of his heart. But in reality the Baron needs to get rid of last year's stuff, or anything which he and the Baroness want to discard . . . You should see how my mother is moved to tears when on the second day of Christmas they leave the great hall. She keeps these useless items forever. She departs from her shoes first, then from these . . . They won't understand it if I tell them . . . They say, I am putting the Baron in bad light. And, that I am too radical in my thinking. This is how loyal my old people are . . ."

Kati told him in a little while: "I understand them. It is their goodness. It's the reflection of it, you know. Regardless of what's out there, or what they had to face every day. Well? But you asked me of the duck! This masterpiece here. I think, your parents could have done better with the real thing. How do you roast a porcelain duck?"

On the same evening Kati wanted to tell her husband a lesson she learned. "What fascinates people about a rich man? We look upon those who are wealthy, as if it were a virtue on its own right. Which just says how thoroughly corrupt we are. The poor, we are ashamed of. We make excuses and look the other way. So we won't have to see poverty, and desolation and people who sleep on the street." To this, Jancsi couldn't add anything, that Kati didn't know. But he kept thinking: "How come, this rich girl has fallen that far from her apple tree?"

Chapter 44

A Restless Spirit

GEZA AND THE BISHOP

"Today I'll tell her!" told Geza apparently only to himself, thinking none else than Julia. A close proximity on this Christmas holiday might not be as easy with her as he would have hoped, considering her time was always, by Geza's standards, "strictly" organized. But that's how she was. Julia would study, practice the piano, give at least one lesson, help her mother with the household, and early evening she would go for a walk. Then came dinner with the usual chit-chat, afterwards some music, and the day would be gone. Geza tried hard diverting the girl from this routine, to get time to the two of them but had no luck. "Well, maybe today," he thought and asked her: "Can I see you alone, just for once? There is something I must tell you." Julia looked at him, thought for a moment, and offered this: "Why not now? Or, better yet, the Devenys are expecting me for tomorrow. Would you like to be my escort? We can talk on the way." Sure. Geza was ready to go with Julia anywhere. The Devenys? The last time he saw them, Anna failed to welcome him the way she used to, and if she did, there was reason, which Geza knew all too well. He shouldn't have challenged the Bishop!

It was planned to be a big event back then, six months ago, in June. Everyone talked about it for days. Well, his Eminence paid a visit to them! And Anna took the bother to invite many people from nearby towns whom she thought were suitable as company for the Bishop's advanced mind and position. The Bishop was Anna's brother. In this light, Geza should have felt honored to be included, rather than . . . At any rate, he was disrespectful to challenge him, knowing his idea was farfetched if not altogether utopistic, considering the history and the widely known existential struggles the Church used to have. He dared to ask him of this: "What is the view of your Eminence on the following: Wouldn't it be more beneficial for the Church, if the higher aspects of Christian teachings reached the masses? If the esoteric dimensions of the same knowledge, among them the question of man's evolutionary role as well as other issues were addressed in depth and shared with people, rather than kept back by the Church? I am inclined to say, Christianity would have served a better purpose, instead what it became to serve."

The people around them stopped talking. Other guests too were getting closer, creating a circle. His Eminence hesitated, but only for a second. Then he gave his answer quite loudly, so everyone could hear it. "I am not sure what do you refer to, young man. Christianity serves and gives the greatest comfort to those, who are ready to open their hearts." He stopped here. He didn't wish to give an impression that he defended either himself, or the Church. There was no need to. He was smiling.

The young man did not stop. He pursued the point, taking it a step further: "The way I perceive it your Eminence, people have hunger for knowledge and understanding. But nobody is willing to show them the higher echelons of truth. Don't you think it would aspire higher goals? So. What are we to do? If we aren't that perfect? Make the bad choice? Turn to sin? It is out there. Available. Below there, the temptation is strong. Why aren't we equally tempted from above?"

His Eminence was about to answer it, but Geza wasn't yet through. "Pardon me. And because our weaknesses are witnessed by the Church, you are firm with us. Keeping us in line. The masses! Who are "not yet ready to receive more"! They understand the punitive aspect of religion only, so they are taught to obey . . ."

There was heavy silence. The kind which waited out what will come next.

"Shouldn't we take our coffee in the library? Shall we go?" What a relief!! Anna's voice opened a new possibility to everyone present. "Yes! Why don't we get the coffee now? Such a good idea!" Anna couldn't do anything else. She was the hostess. She recognized how people stood in astonishment, listening to the words of this extremely bright but impertinent young man who time to time had an urge to deduct the most wayward assumptions, without thinking on the consequence. "And today, he had to do it again! couldn't he wait with it?" wondered

Anna who was corning back to her senses only when most of her guests were seated and were about to ease into a lighter conversation.

"Anna is terrified. The Bishop is offended," informed him Julia after coffee. Geza had no idea why would he be offended. He was convinced, these arguments were part of the struggle the Church had experienced with the secular world, or perhaps even within. About half an hour later old Zoltan made an attempt to rescue both, the evening's and Geza's reputation. He took his young friend to their illustrious guest, for injecting new blood to the conversation. "Geza and I used to have tremendous arguments on matters of faith. I am leaning to st. Thomas Aquinas' understanding of evil. My friend here prefers to see evil as an outside agent. But you must tell me again this Geza, the way you phrase it." The host looked at Geza,expecting him to repeat what he once said to him. So he did. "Is God testing us, by allowing evil to come as close to man as he does? And is he watching how do we fight this out ourselves? Is he satisfied when our choice of him was based on denial of evil? How much longer will the testing go? Does he need more proof of our faith? But . . . we are desperate for proof also. So, we create God in our minds. In our desperation we fill our hearts with him. And we keep him there, in a need to cling to something good, which is the opposite of evil. And we discover . . . we created God . . . and generated a faith in the hope, one day there will be proof."

Old Zoltan liked what he heard. His Eminence the Bishop couldn't disappoint his brother-in-law, so he gave a reflection on what the young man was saying. "God has infinite ways of showing his love. In his testings we discover even more love." With these gracious words the evening was saved. Late at night when at last Anna could go to bed and had a chance to think on the happenings, she wasn't sure who saved it really? Her husband, her brother, or God? Well, whoever it was, definitely it wasn't this impertinent young man!

JULIA

Now, on the Christmas of 1938 Geza still remembered this, even though it happened a half year ago. And tonight, out with Julia they found not much change at the Devenys. He talked, others listened in, which made him acutely aware, he learned nothing. When he asked Julia on their way home afterwards what she thought of that evening six months ago, she reflected on the reactions that certain issues always attract. That's how she explained it to Geza: "If you ask a group of, let's say a hundred people to coordinate these questions of our civilization, most of them won't speak up. As if getting scared by the complexity of it, or being not allowed . . . any which way, they refuse to discuss it. Two or three might have the courage to come forward and have their say. And no wonder. The dividing factors of this civilization are very strong, something we all know. And since we imposed it, we keep it covered. The comfortable view is: we are better off if we look the other way, or better yet: not think about it. So, instead of clarification and simplification, we get into elaborate details-I mean those of us who are adventurous-to prove our points in certain areas, which are the least embarrassing. But I think this postponement divides us further, and in the process we get further separated from a great wisdom too, something we hardly recognize now as it is. Only specks and morsels. Tell me. Is there anyone who can still put the pieces together? Or, were they lost in this antagonistic fight, where each participant is shouting "I have the answers!" Yes. Religion, Philosophy and Science are at war. Each is defending its own vista, claiming the other two has no relevance. Or if it has, it has no value, since it is inferior! Why it came to this? All three schools of thought helped to shape this civilization! They must be recognized as equals. But since they cannot agree on principle, they are permitting a split civilization! I don't think I went too far when I said this. Well, I agree with Mr. Deveny, who says, Religion, Philosophy and Science belong together, for they are complementary in nature. Different branches of the same wisdom! Only Mysticism combines them, mystic schools of East and West. I wish, I truly wish, we made up our minds on this. Because . . . Oh! You must ask Mr. Deveny, about all the details. It's his field, really. I am . . . not even a novice. I am just . . . I am talking too much . . ." said Julia, quickly wrapping up the speech. She blushed as she finished.

Geza was very excited. Julia wasn't only clear in her assessment, but she also defended him! It was incredible! This was exactly how he believed it should be! He received inspiration from her words, and felt too much remained inside of him, a long line of unexpressed thoughts that couldn't be shared tonight, since the guests, seemingly content in their superficial exchanges, were not willing to insert anything new or challenging into their conversations, for the very reason Julia dared to mention here. But Julia was interested, and she understood him, like nobody else. He began to talk. "I think faith has many faces, Julia. Probably you feel the same. If you try to negate God with one act (which I often do), then you burned a piece of your soul which cannot be recovered, only by the readmittance of God. The same happens when you deny your parents. You can't live with it, till you find a way of reconciliation."

"Yes," said Julia, and Geza continued: "How can you run from your own quests of faith? If you ask whether it served you well or made you miserable, then you missed the point. Perhaps some of us have a desire to be miserable. And behind the desire there is a purpose. Maybe we won't learn what it is but it must be there. So, we recognize our misery, serve it and feed it and find a suitable ideology for it . . . Julia, just now I realized, it is all about organizing our own faith."

They were both silent, by sharing a deep sense of trust. Suddenly Julia broke the unity, with her speaking of the school and the plans she had. "Next week, I'll go back to the Academy. In the new semester I am going to participate in solo performances. We are training with a violinist. Just to see how it goes. I am so looking forward to it. I am very glad. Performing in solo, is the most extraordinary thing. You are all excited! But when you start to play, it is only the music you know about . . ."

Geza couldn't hide his disappointment. The intimacy has gone. On the rest of the way home, he told only this to the girl: "I don't know how you feel about this, but there is a war out, around, within. Eventually we have to recognize that the struggle of good and evil is still the main energizing force in our souls. Perhaps not lineally, but on the whole." He took a side glance at Julia who was now miles away with her thoughts, and reacted only formally: "Very true." Since her response was too laconic, Geza assumed her mind was filled with her violinist friend. "That nincompoop!" With the 1938 Christmas almost over, Geza burned with jealousy. His expectations waned, as did the days of this holiday.

ENTREPRENEUR

Geza spent the years between 1938 and 1945 like a lost and found fortune. He had an outburst of energy compressed into seven years, as if indeed living seven lives, however diverse ones.

He felt lighter, immediately after he made his choice known to his father and started planting the wines, and when months later with the preparatory works done, he was ready to go, anywhere he pleased. In early 1939 Geza visited wineries outside of Hungary, and the route was dictated by his own taste in wine. To begin with, he travelled to Austria through Burgenland and Tyrol. Austria wasn't the same. The Anschluss took place last year. In it, Hitler had to use only his finesse, so his own people vote for him in the "Plebiscite" thus seizing Austria, without firing a shot. "The satisfaction he must have felt," thought Geza, "here, in his own country, where he, as a young man sought recognition with no success. And now the same country was kneeling at his feet, and at the feet of an all-powerful Germany! (Made powerful by him, by the way). Since his arrival to Austria, Geza couldn't really make anyone talk about it though. At the wineries or at informal meetings, this subject was not discussed. Or at least not with him. He took great dislike in what was taking place in Czechoslovakia, regarding the German claim on Sudeten land. The consequence of Hitler's political maneuverings pressured European diplomacy to a great degree, but mostly the French with this last instance. Things were getting tense. The Hungarians had their revisionist claims of their own, particularly those counties in Slovakia which were severed from Hungary in 1920, what were simply called "Highlands" for centuries. Back then in 1920, suddenly three million Hungarians found themselves in another country, without moving an inch. The question still lingered: How long will they be called foreigners in their own country? Just because they were annexed. The same applied for beloved Transylvania.

His next stay was in the Rhine valley of Germany, where he derived pleasure partly from its wine and folklore and poetry, the magnificent towns, castles and villages, and of the river itself. But Geza couldn't keep his mind on Loreley, Heine, Goethe, Wagner and Beethoven, neither on the good food, because he was disturbed by the noise of the Nazi Party and how its people drunk from the cup of their glory. What he couldn't comprehend, why the rest of the Germans who still had sobriety were paralyzed, and did little if anything to constrain Hitler and his Nazis. But perhaps the chance was lost for that. The next stop was France, via Strassbourg the border-city, destined to change masters several times in its history. Then, he took to the South, visiting Nice on the Cote d'Azure. From there he went to Bordeaux, looking for the wine. He would exclaim each morning since crossing the border: "What a country!" (usually at breakfast time). Here, he would spend two weeks. Geza began losing sight of his mission as soon as he was taking a turn up North, at first to Normandy and then to Paris-to the city of cities-where he would stay on much longer than he planned, for the sheer beauty of this magical place. Also he went to England for a week (wine or no wine), enjoying immensely every minute of it. Then, he returned to the continent. Being back in France for no longer than four days and by reading the papers in his hotel, made him realize Europe was at the brink of war, if Hitler will get what he wants, by way of forcing himself on Poland. It was the last days of August, and he threatened to invade Poland, which he very well could do with the size of his army. "What the rest of Europe was doing while this man armed the Germans?" again he asked. In any event, Geza learned this much: It was an end to diplomacy and a start to aggressive force. Outrageous it may sound, but Poland was invaded, after all! Those parts of Europe which weren't getting into various non-aggression pacts with Germany, had but one way to deal with this threat . . .

Three days later he heard on the radio, in the foyer and on the corridors and everywhere on the street: "France and Germany are in war!!!" Newspapers carried it with giant letters. WAR! WAR!

On that morning Geza had to cut short the rest of his trip and without travelling to Spain, he returned home. Knowing politics, he expected, in most of Europe troop movements and the transportation of weaponry will be part of the landscape from now on. But still, he wished to forget the world, if only for days . . .

No wonder, after arriving home he was glad to see the grapevine. A reliable foreman took care of the works, making it all very convenient. "And? What will I do next?" he asked, upon inspecting the crop. "A couple of years, till the grape gets going . . . Hmm . . . It means I have time. Lots of it." So Geza went away, but was back again for Christmas. The main reason was still to see Julia. It was time to tell her and ask her if he had a chance at all. If she could feel the same? If she could return it . . . "But, what if the meantime someone fell in love with Julia? And . . . and she reciprocated!! I hate to think of such misery! Of course if I were more alert, and told her sooner . . . or wouldn't have gone for my world-tour, and before that, to my winery tours in the country, then I would know! But why did I postpone asking her on the first place? Why? Because I am in idiot!" Well, the more Geza thought of this, the more insecure he became about Julia. So now, in December of 1939, he made up his mind once and for all, that it was time to act fast.

CHAPTER 45

A Yearning

THE CHRISTMAS OF 1939

Another year, another Christmas . . . It was time for the family to gather, and most of them came. At first Helen, Zoltan and the children, then Julia (who passed nineteen this year) was back for two weeks form her school. Then Geza showed up, who at twenty-two had a degree, was a businessrnan a winegrower, and an experienced traveller. Only Kati has been absent, who assumed, she had her own family now, since she has got married and had a child.

Invitations and visits were as much part of the scenario as they would be generations ago, which made one think not much changed between then and now. Even the subjects have been similar, what people were willing to discuss these days. So the differences—if any—seemed to be generational. The young people, as always, had their own evenings. They were invited to outings they organized, from where they decidedly abolished anything old-fashioned, be that a person, or a thought, which forced their critics to charge: "Oh, these young people are so shallow!" Freshly back from his European tour, Geza was in the greatest demand, and so was Julia, whose considerable talent in playing music could still improve from last year. "Her handling of tonality is sharper . . . richer," would claim those now, who knew everything about performing arts.

On this Winter, the evening at the Devenys at the next village, to where Helen and Zoltan also came, was not as overblown as it was with the Bishop on the Summer of 1938. This one was for friends and family. However an older lady, a famous patron, was present whose love of stylish entertaining was widely recognized. She was curious, and asked Geza to explain,his enterprise. "How exciting! A vinery in the region! Tell me all about it!" In turn, Geza spoke bravely: "Madame, I know as much about wine or grape, as I do about lion-hunting. But let's hope I'll catch up and improve with my wine. Which . . . we might even taste in this century?"

The old lady's fascination just grew. "I think, it is ingenious! You do help this county become a bit more cosmopolitan don't you? Well. I think it's about time too! I am glad. I am very glad. Tell me Geza, what happened to your sister? The . . . horsewoman! I don't see her on the horse shows. Is she in school? You see, I am organizing an all—woman horse show. And since she is something of a . . ."

"Hmm . . . Well, yes Madame. Her name is Kati. I am afraid, temporarily she is . . . out of this line. I mean, she gave it up. She is married now . . . lives further up to the East. Far from here. We . . . don't see her . . . that much." Luckily somebody joined them, so Geza did not have to go on to be so vague.

Regardless of those busy comings and goings, Geza could hardly wait out a quiet time with Julia. But it came. One afternoon just the two of them went out for a ride in his new car. This day, Julia looked particularly lovely. She was wearing a butter-yellow woolen dress, and Geza thought it emphasized her beauty, this delicate refinement she had.

He slowed the car by one of the junctions and pulled over to a less frequented road. "I wished to talk with you for a long time now, Julia." She waited, by sitting quietly, being wrapped in her coat. Geza, who wanted to confess this for a long time, realized postponement didn't make it easier. "Look Julia. It's about you and me. Since we were very young . . . I love you. I can't help it! Not that I want to help it! No. I don't want to run away from it, because I can't. It is with me, all the time." He turned to her, so he can hold her hand. Julia did not look at Geza. She seemed to be deeply embarrassed. She didn't say anything, and Geza did not know what was wrong. "Am I too forward? Perhaps I frightened her!" But there was no way back now, so he went on saying what he planned. "I realize, it's unexpected to you. Yet hoped you felt my feelings. I . . . I didn't mind showing them. You see, I don't just love you. I am in love with you." He stopped and waited. Then he looked at Julia, and to the wintry landscape. The car was getting cold that the engine stopped. He had to go on with this faster, unless he wanted Julia to freeze on the spot. "I can't imagine my life without you, Julia.

I ask you to think about it what I said. I would like to marry you, if you can love me."

That was it. Now he said it! He could even go back breathing. It took forever until Julia turned to him, saying only this short sentence: "Geza, you are my brother."

Well! What is she talking about? It made him angry and he protested at once: "I am not! If you insist I am your cousin., And what does that prove? Why is it an obstacle? It means nothing! Julia, look at me!" Geza took her chin to his hand, and turned her face towards him: "Don't deny me! I ask you to think of it. Sleep on it. Until you don't tell me how you feel, I'll be around you. Searching with my soul . . . searching you. This, you must feel. Julia! Can't you tell me something?" asked Geza before letting her turn away.

Julia, who so far avoided looking at him, now asked this: "Why don't we go home?" "Go home? Is that all? You don't feel anything?" He turned the ignition key in the car. "Oh, Geza! stop talking. No, no! It isn't at all!" she cried out, and covered her face with both hands. Geza didn't know what to do. Julia said nothing, so they drove home in silence. When the car stopped at the gate, Julia jumped out and ran inside the house, through the pedestrian door. Geza opened the gate and parked in very slowly. Then he walked to the stables, but had no idea why there.

Julia was lucky to see nobody around the parlor, the least they saw her tears. When was alone in her room, she could give way to an uncontrollable cry. In the next couple of days Geza was in agony, considering Julia spent this time in her upstairs room. So he went out every day to the vineyard half pretending his estate would collapse if he wasn't there to inspect it at this unlikely month of the year. (Unlikely for grapes).

Julia convinced her mother she had a chill and wished to stay in her duvets. She didn't wish to see anybody, only Franciska, who was to bring up apple compote, tea, and chicken soup now and then to her youngest child. In the meantime Geza kept telling to himself: "I wait one more day." And the next day he told the same. This went on for a week, and the word was not coming.

Julia was still in her room and now she had but three days left before returning to the Academy. The days of hope ran out on Geza. Friday, he woke early and was off alone horseback-riding. It was bitter cold. He returned in about an hour, had a drink, wrote a few words on a notecard, put it in an envelope, and gave it to the maid. "It goes upstairs, to Miss Julia," he instructed her. Then went to his room, opened the cabinet, took out randomly some shirts and suits and shoes and a few other items, and stuffed them all into one suitcase. He came downstairs and left a message for Huba: "Tell my father, I have no idea when I come back. Tell him only that," he said, and walked to his car. Soon after the maid left her room, Julia opened the letter and read it aloud:

"I say it again each year
And I do it again next year
I wait out a life for a word
Or I wait one more life
If I have to . . ."

She was shaken. "How can I possibly distance myself from him after this?" she asked. "How?"

Chapter 46

A Career

FRIENDS

It happened in Budapest a couple of days later, after Geza so abruptly left the South. "Imi Fogassy! My friend! It's good to see you! What are you doing here?" he asked from an old school chum who was also at the racetracks. "Me? Putting my money on a horse like everybody else! Make no mistake Geza, I work! I am the first regular guy my ancestry produced. I am the pearl! Just as precious. My father insisted: "Son, work for the Government! They might make a diplomat out of you." You know, it's really like horse-breeding. He thinks if we are impoverished, at least we should play the "my-son-is-in-the-foreign-office" stuff. At least that. This is the last game we have."

"Is it all that bad as that?" asked Geza with empathy.

"Pretty much. If one has no villas, lands, forests. Forget the plural! If one has just nothing. You know how fathers are, don't you? How is your old man? What did you do by the way since we graduated?"

"I planted grapevine."

"Grapevine. But didn't your family live on the Plains? Back in school I remember of you saying . . . It doesn't matter, these days you can do anything with soil. To control it. I wish my father thought of this. This wine, I mean. My family now lost the last of our estates. So? What we did? Went down like the Titanic."

"I am sorry to hear that. Is there a way I can do anything? I mean, to help you? To help you out? . . ."

"Appreciated, but no thanks. We are doing fine. You know what my old man does these days? Teaching fencing at his Sport Club. And just now he finished a book on "Heraldry"."

"That's quite something!"

"Thanks! I say it's all very well. But it won't pay. True, it keeps them from starving. My mother designs hats for a millinery. My sister? She is getting ready to find a rich husband. By the way.

Are you rich, Geza? Or just moderately rich? She isn't in the position to refuse you . . . Hey! Look there now! The race is on. I talk here, and they started already! Hey, look at that . . . which horse is going for you?"

"Villam," said Geza. "What's yours?" "Szerencse," replied Imi, and the young men went to find a good position, so they could follow the race. People were getting all excited, and Imi was going with the flow. "Szerencse! Go . . . go . . . goooo. Bad start . . . hey! Look at that foggy horse. There runs my money! It doesn't run at all. It crawls. Oh, well. It's over. That's it. Yours didn't get in either. So? Do you stay for the next race?"

"No, I am going back to the city." "All right, Geza, why don't we go together? I am sure glad running into you. How long are you in town?" "Only a week." "And? Do you have plans?" "None, whatsoever." "Sure. Why don't we meet tomorrow? I introduce you to people, if you want me to. We do that. Come to my office. I work till three. You can come any time. Here is my card. Bye, old chap!"

And so, after two p.m. the next day, Geza went to collect Imi Fogassy. First, he looked him up at the office registry. Imi was cheerful as ever. "Glad to see you Geza. As you see, I am the two-hundredth most important file pusher in this prestigious establishment. If I keep going in this rate for promotion, I can become his Excellency the Minister, when I am two-hundred years old. If I made it before I turned one hundred, it is because I am overly pushy . . ." When Imi was still talking, the door opened and his Director, an imposing man came in the room. Imi Fogassy jumped on his feet and introduced his friend Geza with utmost pedantry. "Sir, allow me to introduce to you my old schoolmate, Geza Garay. The language wizard". The Director was moderately impressed. "Are you indeed?" he asked politely. "Well Sir, it is an exaggeration," replied Geza. "Hmm. Aren't you interested working for us?" It was the most unexpected question! "Well . . . I am . . . hmm. Sure! Why not!" "All right then! Do come tomorrow at ten to my office, for an interview. Here is my card." "Thank you Sir. I'll be there." And so did begin Geza's career in the Foreign Ministry. Astonishingly, by landing a position in two weeks, without really looking for one! And so would Imi Fogassy be instrumental to his future, who even took the bother to find a furnished bachelor flat for him.

Chapter 47

The Names

HUNOR AND MAGYAR

Franciska was ecstatic. After putting down the receiver she cut across the corridor like a sprinter, so she could tell: "Helen is pregnant again!"

Everyone in the family gave out a sigh, on hearing the news: "Hunor doesn't have to wait much longer, Magyar is on his way." They hoped, the boys could take their place on the panoply of ancestral line, which went by the names of great Hungarian kings, and a generation later by the seven chieftains of the Magyar tribes. (Well, not quite. The seventh was still missing).

But in 1938, and now in 1940, thanks to Helen a new generation has emerged, to borrow the names of Hunor and Magyar "the two valiant knights", sons of King Menrot* and queen Eneh. In the legend, Hunor and Magyar were out hunting on the day they would spot a white magical stag. One learns how the brothers pursue the stag, by following it relentlessly to deeper and denser woods for seven days and seven nights until they are bewitched, and they themselves would turn into stags. So is the legend of Hunor and Magyar.

We must stop here for a minute. Weren't the Garays planning a reverse chronology? If they were to do it right, the lineage should have started with Hunor and Magyar, generations ago! After all, Magyar gave his name to the powerful tribe, which could stay on together for hundreds of years and beyond, for forming a nation under this name.

---

* Menrot was believed to be Nimrod, the hunter king.

Chieftains and great kings followed them only afterwards. Centuries later. Eh! Chronology is for historians! This was for private use. The Garays were not likely to lose themselves in details. What mattered to them, that they multiplied.

At first Helen was cautious finding name for her children. "If I'll have just two sons and call them after the legend, I fulfilled my duty. It will please my father and they leave me alone. I stop there. I cannot ruin my figure. What would people say?!" So is their name, Hunor and Magyar, after whom the Hunnish and Magyar tribes were to originate, seemed really the best choice, if we respect Helen's needs. She kept her secret and hoped for the best, till the first-born Hunor, came to the family. And even after that.

Very strangely, after Helen's telephone it was hardly considered, the baby could be anything but a boy. Yet against all hopes Magyar failed to come. The princely brothers, in the legend, would be lost in the wilderness, of whom not even their father the hunter-king could redeem. Well, for this family, the outcome would be slightly different. Hunor came as planned, only Magyar had been lost. Strangely, the very one who gave name to the nation! Not the best omen, is it? It's true, Magyar was lost, but not the child. Good or bad, this time around they had a girl. Nobody expected her. Nobody. But life had to go on. While getting over a not so mild disappointment, for the girl a name had to be found. A name from the same legend, so it would be less of a discomfort, when in matter of weeks the relatives would show up at the Christening. That's how the girl became Eneh (after the Queen mother). Still; Helen's new baby wouldn't deter her original plans. She stopped there, and had no more child.

Needless to say, when Helen moved home for a week, they all fell in love with the baby-girl. And Huba felt, it was time to be generous. "Ask anything," he said. "I'll buy it for you. You gave me grandchildren. What would you like me to give you?"

"Oh father, really! You shouldn't . . . But if you insist? . . ."

"I do," offered Huba.

"Well then, I . . . I tell you what I was dreaming to have. A sable coat."

"A sable coat it is! If you are strong enough to travel, you could buy it in S. with your mother. She will be quite happy to keep you company. But Helen, the coat is only a coat. Buy anything you like, before you move back to your husband . . . Buy a new dress, hat and shoes . . . Anything!" "I'll tell you," admitted Huba to his wife the same evening before they went to bed. "She will like to have babies . . . by the dozen." The Garays seemed to be content. Huba was happy, because he had three grandchildren now. Helen was happy, because of her new fur coat. Franciska was happy, because Helen was happy. And Zoltan? Yes, he was happy too. After all, he had two fine children with Helen Garay.

Chapter 48

From Pot To Pan

A BEAUTIFUL EVENING

Even though the presentation was well in its second hour, someone came in and occupied the seat beside him. The lights were dimmed in the auditorium. Geza was late too, the speaker was already on the podium, why he couldn't join his friends up front and had to stay at the back row. But coming this late? . . . He smelled parfume (strong, good, intriguing), and next to him saw a mysterious woman who had dark hair and a hairdo, which was cut in the fashion that Chinese children and Egyptian queens like to wear. That parfume! It made the rounds again, something our young man inhaled each time, till the scent would take over his brain. Being so completely enwrapped by it, Geza lost concentration and carne around only for the applause. "End of lecture? What a shame! How come I didn't listen to it?" Now he was fully awake. People stood up and began talking all at once, others ran inside from the corridor, and the crowd was pushing to the podium. The lady was just standing there. Then she looked at Geza and smiled. She had great beauty and the confidence which came with it. Also there was something else in her, an asset if we can say, which didn't freeze Geza's confidence. It did just the opposite; it put him at ease. So he turned to her and introduced himself: "My name is Geza Garay. She did the same. "I am Silvia Gerei." They started laughing at once because of their similar names, but the noise was getting worse, making it impossible to speak. She had a solution: "Are you coming, or waiting for someone?" Geza said immediately: "Oh, no. Not at all. I am alone." And asked himself: "Wasn't I too willing? I should have said the truth: "Yes, I am with friends. They are at the front . . ." No, instead I jumped." Geza didn't wish to think of his friends inside the lecture hall, not right now when he met this woman. If they wait, they wait! He didn't feel inseparable from them. But this woman here, Silvia! He couldn't let her vanish. No. She was far too beautiful. So, Geza made his choice, and soon they found themselves on the street. It was a long walk they took, while searching for a common ground, at first through the subject of the lecture. Just in minutes the conversation was shifted to Music and Literature, measuring their love of Paul Valery and Stendhal and Chekhov. Geza enjoyed her company. They walked in the inner city, like some modern day Ariadne and Theseus. Silvia, leading him by the thread of her parfume, and he, following it in half-denial, as if the scent had no role in it. Now they arrived to the Parliament square. As they were to cross it, by looking at this oversized Neogothic building, the monumental mass and the site, the same question turned in their mind, if this Parliament would be large enough to serve the Americas (North and South) rather than this tiny country that Hungary was reduced to? As witty politicians lately put it: "Small country with huge Parliament." But the couple had reverence, said no such things, only passed the square and walked towards the river, discovering the Danube was dark blue in this light. The two still explored mutual interests when took a left turn to the "Duna Korzo". Among other pursuits, simple country life and hunt was discussed. Silvia would not participate on a hunt since childhood, when the sight of killing made her ill. "Now I am grown, quite grown, I love swimming and sailing. I go for weeks in the Summer. During Winter I usually go to Switzerland for two weeks of skiing. It is enough from sports." Silvia turned to him: "Can you talk about yourself? I told everything there is. And I am afraid we checked out the main items of our cultural interests," she added teasingly. But Geza, instead of getting into his own life, plainly asked: "Are you married?" Silvia was laughing. "Olala! No. I used to be. It was a brief marriage. I can hardly remember his face now . . . oh! It was such a long time ago! Well . . . both my parents passed away. I am alone. This is my story. About you?"

Geza took the question seriously and replied: "No. I was not married. Both my parents passed away. I can hardly remember their faces. My mother died when I was five. My father, when I was seven. I have an adoptive family."

While talking, they looked at the Hungaria, Bristol and Carlton Hotels, all in a row. The view was spectacular from Pest to Buda.'

The two would be walking at the quays of the Danube and in these moments neither wished to break the silence. The sight said it all. The other side of this divided city lingered in the air in a distance, against the high hills of Buda, borrowing the dancing lights of the river for the show.

Geza was attracted to Silvia. Something happened, and this something was drawing him in in her sphere. But since it made him feel good, Geza didn't dream of getting away from it . . . All of a sudden he realized it was late. "May I take you home? I'll call a taxi." She started laughing. "My dear friend. There is no need. I live here. Look! See that six storey building? Well, I have an apartment in it. It is overlooking the river, Buda, the Palace Hill, the Gellert Hill, the Erzsebet Bridge, the Chain Bridge and the Franz Joseph Bridge. I love this view! No wonder. The best we have in this city."

Geza escorted Silvia to the entrance of the building and told her courteously, "It was a great pleasure to have your company. Thank you Madame." "Well? Would you have a drink? My butler is still up. I used to entertain late." "Very tempting. But. Perhaps . . . you see, I have to think of tomorrow and getting to my office early."

"Well? In this case . . ." she said and waited. Geza had no idea if he could ask for a rendezvous. He felt it was impossible. Yet if he thought of it, it wasn't. This woman, Silvia whom he just met two hours ago, paid more attention to him as anybody before. So? It means he should ask her out. Should he really? Perhaps this idea too belonged to his many unfounded feelings. The ones which led him nowhere, only to dead end streets. That is what happened with Julia. He imagined too much. His imaginations left him with years of unrequited love, the end result of his overly vivid imagination. And now he was to live with the shame that he forced himself on Julia, that angelic creature who was out of this world. All the more shame because Geza was of this world, with sinful thoughts and all. Now he had to deal with his disappointment by not allowing to have false hopes . . . like now with Silvia. Geza went on reasoning. "No. This time I don't let my hopes and imaginations control me. I'll take things how they come. Maybe she doesn't wish us to meet again? So, I won't ask her. But what if-she does? Still. I won't ask her. She is a society lady. Experienced. Sophisticated. Has a strong personality. Just a look at her tells the story. I am sure she can have anybody she would want. I am not yet even "anybody"! I don't even know where I am going." Geza made up his mind not to ask her the obvious question: "Can I see you again?" that he wanted very much to ask. After two more minutes of vacillation, as if she had had enough, or perhaps because she could see what this young man went through, Silvia threw in a lifesaver. "On Wednesdays I give cocktails from five to seven. I also receive on Saturday nights, if I am in the city, from eleven to one a.m., when we all get back from the theaters. Do come and see me."

When she said, "do come and see me," Geza discovered the first time that she had a heart-shaped face. It gave sensuality to her classic features. He liked her red lips and the color of her lipstick. Yes. The heart-shaped face with red lips. It was playful too! Now he knew it!

Still at the entrance, Geza took a glimpse into a magnificent well-lit hall. It had a double staircase overlaid with marble, like the rest of the wall. Sculpted candelabras and hot-house palms were put in, and a long Oriental rug from door to door. A liveried doorman stood inside waiting discreetly in the background, to be of service.

SILVIA

On Wednesday of the same week sometime after six Geza entered the building which had the marble ground-floor. The concierge was distant and polite. "To whom should I take you, Sir?" "I came to Madame Gerei . . ." "Yes Sir. The Baroness has her apartment on the fifth floor. I will take you up, Sir." Geza didn't ask, only thought: "Baroness? Does this mean she is a Baroness? Of course. But why didn't she tell me this? Or, perhaps she did, when we introduced . . . well, the noise must have swallowed it."

By stepping out of the lift Geza stepped immediately inside the Baroness's entrance room, from where the butler guided him to the spacious drawing room. She had about five guests who were chatting at the huge window, looking down to the river. When Silvia noticed him, walked all the way to meet him. She looked ravishing in her short red cocktail dress, to which she was wearing matching red shoes. The Baroness smiled. She seemed to be happy and held his hand just a bit longer what Geza imagined a free spirited society divorcee would. But he liked it very much. Little did he know that with this entrance his anxieties about love or women were over, because at last someone took him seriously. Luckily, this someone was a desirable woman, who had yet another streak in her favor. Her sense of knowing that this dashing young man with all his brightness has been turned down-perhaps recently-by some foolish girl., the reason he feels down on life. Not that he gave an indication. It was just there. Visible.

There was a chance; Silvia thought, this disappointment he carried was no more than an outgrowth of his adolescent love, which failed to stand the test of time, and crumbled as soon as it was removed from its imaginary box. Of course she only sensed this, since she thought of him quite a lot. In all frankness, the Baroness was attracted to the young man from the Plains, and by knowing a few things about life, Silvia decided to make her move . . . Something told her, Geza was not the man who brings decisions. Possibly others do it for him. "Why don't I?" wondered Silvia.

One by one the guests were leaving, and by seven, only Geza remained. She invited him for a light supper . . . which never seemed to end. Her style, her ambiance, the view, and her charm won him over so much so, that the next day they were engaged, and a week later married. Considering Geza came to Budapest with no particular reason other than distancing himself from Julia, or at least from his own feelings, considering his reasons, he did well for falling from pot to pan . . . Geza found himself almost instantly in the orbit of another woman who evoked a deeply different need in him, which he didn't think of analyzing, for he knew, it must be what others call "the great passion".

If the Baroness looked thirty and her society friends whispered she was forty it did not make difference to Geza. It not even crossed his mind that Silvia had an age. She was very beautiful and she loved him. This was what mattered. What else? For he was only a bit over 23.

THE GAMBLER

Geza knocked and quickly entered. She was inside, reading a book in a silk kimono in the color of cognac. Silvia made statements with colors. In this room-the smallest in the apartment and her favorite-she had a velveteen cover on her divan in a color of golden amber.

"Your pleasure-nest reminds me of a harem Silvia, from another century." "No, no," she protested. "Then, women were not taken seriously." "Yes, they were! This pasha-fellow built a palace around them . . . Or, was it around his own pleasures and furnished it with women?" "More like it," agreed Silvia. "By the way. How things are, Geza? What do you keep from me? Winning or losing?" "Don't ask me, please. Don't," he said, and left the room. It was too small. Confining.

It didn't take more than ten months to realize, the fire of their passion converted into cooling ember. The sparks between Silvia and Geza have gone. He was pulled in two directions. The demands of his career on one hand, and the social and financial demands of his marriage on the other. It has created a strain. There was need for money and before he knew it, he was a habitual gambler. Later he liked to dispute it from top to bottom: what was first? The chicken or the egg? He might have done it for fun. Who knows?

At any event, Geza had neither luck nor patience with the stock market. When things turned for the worse, casinos and racetracks were his only hope. At times he could be very lucky, mainly with roulette. But since Geza had little regard for money he did not think of investing it. In money matters Geza was not at all prudent. When he was losing, he couldn't stop losing, which forced him to take the next step, borrowing against his lands. With it, his future was in jeopardy. Very urgently, at first a piece of woodland had to be sold, which Huba intensely rebuked. In a letter he warned him to expect the worse. "My son, you have to see your financial means in a realistic light. Learn to make plans, protecting your estate. Why do you risk so much? Does your wife know about it?"

At the most part Silvia was oblivious of her husband's problems, for Geza avoided airing it. He disliked embarrassments. He believed gentlemen pay, not to distress their wives with money matters, while things remained unchanged or were getting worse.

Silvia had expensive taste. She was born with it. Also, having had an inheritance and the yearly allowance from it, she was doing well. She lived a seemingly carefree life, followed her impulses, did, said and bought most what she wanted. So far her inheritance sustained it. Even though she took care of the keeping of her residence, her staff and the household, her travels and her wardrobe. But there were a couple of other expenses of which for Geza it was a question of honor to pay. His salary was not high and his vineyard was yet in a growing stage. He couldn't expect income at least another five years from it. Things added up and problems were everywhere. By the Spring of 1941 their marriage was over and a year later most of his inheritance with it. The lands would gradually go, including the vineyards. In response to it he wanted a change, and in the year of 1941, an entirely new spirit took him over. In this summer the politics of Hungary suggested a direction from which there was no return. At about this time someone came to Geza's office, asking if would do intelligence work. "Why not?" he tossed the question and signed up for the job.

CHAPTER 49

On The Homefront

TERKA

In spite of her unclear status with the Garays, Terka did receive a nominal salary, something she would spend freely in the country store on candy, or throughout C. county on church bazaars and prospective village-fairs.

Terka was an agreeable creature if one employed the right tone, but dealing with her was still a difficult job. Obviously she had favorite works, and works she loathed to do, and since she voiced it each time, everybody knew about the list. Washing up or scrubbing the kitchen floor was on the hate list that Franciska knew, so she deposited some change in Terka's purse, by easing the pain: "I ask you to wash it Terka and everyone will be happy. That floor is dirty." But only an hour later when Huba came to the house with a guest would Terka show up with the water bucket: "They want white floor! To the Hell with them. She says, it's dirty . . ." "Are you swearing again? Why do you swear that much?" asked Huba, interrupting the monologue. "I don't! But it's not dirty. Show me the dirt on this floor." "You wash it, as was told. It's a five minute job and you make it into an afternoon. And wash yourself too. Do you ever take a bath? I give you five minutes. Do you understand it?" told the master of the house, who walked out. At first Terka kicked the bucket and threw her shoes under the stove; but when thought about the change in her purse she changed her mind and washed the floor in about three minutes. Huba wasn't too far off when sent her to take a bath, because the only part of her body she cared for was her face. Nobody knew really why, or to what end, but the rest of her remained largely unexplored. Terka gave an egg—white facial to herself each single day and a honey facial once a week. "I too will be a pampered woman, not only Helen," she would say, not that she owed an explanation to the Garays, who were flabbergasted by her antics anyway, among them her love of cleaning the fireplace and the various stoves of this large house. Well, this wasn't a chore for Terka! She loved to do it, and it put her into a lighter spirit. But when Franciska insisted she wore gloves, the girl refused, saying: "Don't bother me. I like to feel the warm ashes." Of course it ruined her hands which began to look like a furnace worker's but still she wouldn't listen to Franciska.

A GENEROUS GRANDFATHER

Back in 1938 for his grandson's first Christmas Huba presented a rocking wooden horse with a bow and arrow set, and an illustrated History-book on the "wondrous" times of early Hungarians, titled: "When the Magyars Entered." The book explains how the tribes would cross the "Verecke Pass" and enter the Carpathian Basin. It tells how the journey at first appears in the dream of Almos, a king, whose descendants will become the first kings of Hungary, called the "House of Arpads". With these gifts Huba wished to communicate what the "Carpathian Basin" was all about, as if calling the toddler's attention to some outlined future duties. In the same time Huba made Zoltan and Helen promise to keep these symbolic objects close to the child, so little Hunor in the cradle could pick up inspirations from the toys. "Because good suggestions are priceless if you raise a child. They are! They build indomitable characters."

Well, that's how Huba prepared the few months old infant for his heritage. "Don't laugh Zoltan, a true Magyar starts in the cradle," he explained to the father. "He will soon learn who he is, where did he come from, and what his responsibilities are. You will see." Franciska overheard them, and came to her son-in-law's rescue. "Sure, sure. Don't push it though. At least the first couple of years, we women suppose to take care of him. Why don't you get used to it, Huba? He is still ours."

When a new grandchild, Eneh the girl was born in the Spring of 1940, and Huba and Franciska went to see her, the next day Huba disappeared, leaving his wife behind to help Helen with the baby.

Huba took a round-trip to bigger towns, first to S. and then to B., in search for the best cabinetmaker. Eventually he found his man in B. After considerable persuasion, Huba commissioned the man to build a dollhouse. Explanations and instructions followed, and promises that he will return with the drawings and measurements, if the master would start immediately. "The work cannot wait! I want this dollhouse to my granddaughter . . ." with which Huba planned to give the exact same replica of his house "Owl Castle" to the new infant, Eneh. The assignment wasn't easy, considering those added wings and rooms and staircases, not to mention the inner labyrinth, that they had there.

The second week, on a Saturday morning when Franciska already came home form Helen a stranger showed up by the gate. Huba then hurriedly told to his wife: "You see, it was inevitable. I had to invite him to see the house. I am sure, you don't mind. Think of your granddaughter's happiness!" Franciska still didn't understand what was it all about, and forgot to smile when the guest introduced himself. At lunch she didn't feel well enough to join the men, so the table was set only for two. The guest occupied one of the best rooms and looked into every corner and closet and stepped into all rooms, including Franciska's. After dinner Huba gave him his best cognac and a still unopened box of cigars, as a gift. The mastercraftsman was appropriately moved, and soon afterwards they could agree in all the fine points. The man said he will do the replica dollhouse, but his project will be slightly simpler. Huba agreed, saying Eneh wouldn't mind. "She is a flexible character, my grandchild!" Because of other projects he worked on simultaneously, the master completed the dollhouse in little over six months. When it was finally delivered, Huba invited half the town to show the replica of his house.

Next day both grandparents took a trip to visit Helen and Zoltan. "I wanted to surprise her! If I am right, then the first thing she will remember will be this house. The house of her ancestors . . . And the lives in it!"

"You are very gracious . . . but why do you say "surprise her"? asked Helen, who didn't understand how her father meant it. She added, "Father, she is just a baby! Why should she be surprised?"

Huba dismissed his daughter with a gesture of his hand. "Why? Why? You don't understand children the way I do!"

PHILANDERING AND MAKING UP

When she would ask: "Why don't we live the way we used to? You and I?" and he would reply: "We? We live just like we used to!" Franciska instantly stopped pleading with Huba. Only she thought bitterly: "Huba takes me for granted. A man can do anything. A woman can't. No wonder some women use men as much as they want. How else can a woman get satisfaction from being pushed aside . . . Which is what they do. Pushing women aside . . ."

Huba wasn't ready to acknowledge Franciska might not be happy in their marriage, but when gave a second thought, he bought her a new ring. "For women, jewelry sounds better than words. She mustn't feel I don't care for her."

Franciska appreciated the gift knowing its value . . . but couldn't help wondering if she, as a woman was on a dead-end road. She had no doubts what went on. If philandering was so natural for Huba as drawing in air, then he wouldn't expect, but demand his wife to understand it. But what if she couldn't? Yet considering everything, she had to. What choice did she have?

Making up was not so pleasant, in fact each time more difficult, and if the last two weeks Huba flooded her with gifts, Franciska was more annoyed than pleased. Weakened by such experiences, Franciska couldn't do much other than build resistance, something Huba could cut through in turn only by employing the classic tacts of apology, gifts and flowers, and the usual promises. If he had choice he would find simpler ways out. or if he had a cool head. But being impulsive, he liked to get in things fast and get out of them just as fast with no baggage to carry over. That's how it was with women . . . Hard to understand why would Franciska make so much out of it, if he didn't.' He would expect her to forget about his escapades as fast as he did, not thinking of the pain he inflicted on her. He liked to move on but couldn't, for he had the obligations of a married man . . .

While being immersed in her current state of mind, Franciska risked to lose her husband's renewed love, what by his own admission has been heated by repentance. It was no easy fix. Contrary to his efforts and tacts, Huba had to see their opposite effects on his wife, as Franciska was drifting further each day. Their needs were not synchronized. Huba wanted to go back to her, and Franciska needed time. Did he imagine, his wife's diffidence would give him an easy conquest, or a fast one as the hero gets through a wall built of sighs in some fairy tale? With her, it was never the case. She kept her fort, and Huba worked each time longer, on reconnecting the two of them after his poorly disguised escapades. But for using the same "technique", the same manner of speech that he would in similar instances, were now too crafty for Franciska. It made her nervous. It bored her. They were platitudes. On top of it he sounded like a fool by saying all these, especially if he didn't mean them, and it made her all the more suspicious of his motives. Couldn't he see it had no validity, not to his wife where he lost his credit? "And this man thinks he has diplomatic talent?" Having a deep sense of loss and sadness, Franciska was certain it was going to stay like this. That things would not change between them, because he won't change. Oh, she was convinced it would take a miracle to trust him again . . . But miracles won't happen. Not with her anyway. Even though she was still bound to him by their troubled love-which tortured her endlessly-she blamed herself for not being able to get out of it. All these time Franciska wished she were free! Free of him . . .

Chapter 50

Another War

TO MEET THE WAR

In the Winter of 1941, events rushed to fall into the center of a cyclone which was yet to gain speed, by pushing Hungary to the brink of war. It seemed, the Nazis had less time to waste. The act of sending a bullet in Prime Minister Count Teleki's head, finally stopped him to refuse the Germans, who asked him to secure manpower for their army on their raid against Yugoslavia.

Count Teleki was already compromising enough, namely Hungary's neutrality for allowing German troops to cross the country on their way at first to Romania, and in 1941, to Yugoslavia. Officially his death has been a suicide, which few ever believed. Not only the Prime Minister had been killed though. The same bullet took away the country's chance to hold on to her neutrality. The consequences of this act were grave. From then on the Germans were in (perhaps not so visibly at first) recommending and appointing people into the next Government, with considerable force.

And the next Government obeyed its new masters, by sending Hungarian troops against Soviet-Russia. It was a devastating step; impossible to reverse for politicians, even if they wanted it. Now it was only matter of days, when the Allies would declare war on Hungary!!!

For a long time many people wouldn't suspect there could be a new world war. So it took a while taking it in when confirmed true, even if it had to be a fact of life for large parts of Europe or elsewhere by overseas, where in the path of war the lives of thousands or millions were ruined.

Thinking, a front could actually get here to this town, was pushed behind screens of denial and hope, which made the days tolerable. There was a world in upheaval as people were caught in a new world war, and our freshly divorced Geza too went into action. Being recruited by the Foreign Office for Intelligence work, his first three months would be spent in basic training, at their camp. In late Autumn he applied for a week-long leave but only months later did he get it, right before his first assignement abroad. So in January of 1942, he could go home, keeping in mind his new line of work should never be discussed with anyone in any context. At last heading to the South, Geza very much wished to see his family, and more than anybody, Huba and Julia. In the last two years he was the black sheep amongst the Garays, a position in which he could even take pride, but only for days. With that sentiment over, Geza returned now, so he can change these if they gave him a chance. Still it made a world of difference how Huba and Julia thought of him. They had good reasons for disappointment and it weighed on him. "Will they forgive me? I just don't know. But I owe an explanation to both. To Huba, about losing my inheritance, and to Julia, about my hasty marriage and divorce to the Baroness."

Regardless of this ungainly mess, Huba was glad to see the prodigious son's return. He embraced him strongly, but began talking about something else. "You can see for yourself, we are prepared, even if the front will pass right through the main street! Well, what do you say? Would you believe I was left out from the mobilization? Because of my age! My age of all things! I am kind of-embarrassed. They make me feel damn useless! That's how I feel right now. I have this urge to go . . . I still have it. To go and join in. I could still teach them a thing or two. But I will, when they come to town! Now. You tell me about yourself, eh?"

Huba and Geza tried to stay in close range, separated from the women, so they can talk during the day like men do.

Helen was already home with her children-literally moved home again with all her furniture, porcelain and paintings-because her husband Zoltan, a reserve officer, joined his unit a week after the mobilization. Helen looked depressed but her children were thrilled, considering their favorite people were their grandparents.

Kati wrote a letter to Huba about six months ago. He passed on what he knew: "She sent her new address (now old address) from the big city of D. at the Eastern border, to where they moved. As you know, her baby boy died a year ago! Just imagine! If it wasn't enough, her husband is in prison. I believe for some union propaganda thing-but doesn't mention, for how long. In this, Kati wasn't specific. Since moved there she works in a factory, which manufactures some machinery . . . This is how she ended up. My daughter! She should have had a normal life. Not this! And now the war! I don't know where does it lead us? I wish she would come horne. Right where she belongs . . . Live with us. I don't have hard feelings. She learned her lessons I suppose. Running away so young. But Franci is still hurt, you know."

"Julia?" asked Geza. "Is she back from the Academy?" "No!" replied Huba. "Try not to bring it up in front of Franci. She was hysterical about it. Julia didn't come home. I'll show you her letter. She didn't come home, saying we wouldn't let her leave then." "Leave? Where to? Where is she?" "Let me get her letter. Here it is. Here is Kati's letter too. Read them for yourself." Geza was not at all glad to hear these. After all, they were his adoptive sisters. He started reading Julia's letter.

"Dear Mother and Father, Please forgive me that I can't make it home this time. After they closed the Academy, I volunteered to become a nurse. I wanted to see you, but knew you wouldn't let me come back. My training has begun. I couldn't bear the idea of myself if I wouldn't do this for those who fight for this country. You are both in my prayers. I love you, your daughter, Julia. P.S.: This address is only my mailing address. They will forward it to whichever military hospital I am sent to."

The house was in disarray. Removing, sorting, packaging and preserving food already started as the result of late Autumn digging from the vegetable garden. The next day of Geza's arrival the two men spent half the day in the old basement, classifying vegetables in the sand and moving a basketful to the kitchen where it was made into pickles. It translated, lean times were coming. "Did you know," asked Huba suddenly, "that my brother left with his wife and son?" "No, I didn't. Did they have to?" "No, they didn't have to. Miriam is a Catholic. But Tass felt better if they went up North. One night-three months ago-he brought over valuables, a couple of furnitures even, and took Zoli and Miriam." "How did Zoli take it?" asked Geza. "It wasn't easy for him, you know. Tass mentioned he took his studies, the books . . . which, well . . . keep him occupied." "I see. And, where did they go?" "In wine country. It makes good hiding, he said, with all those cellars and caves." "Isn't it a shame, it came to this?" asked

Geza after some time. "It sure is," replied Huba. "My brother didn't trust the Nazis that well . . . And I myself think, it was a good move. Only, they can't send word where they are, and how they are . . . Which means, I know nothing." They were silent.

"Do you have plans? What will you do?" asked Huba eventually. "I did volunteer. But, have no idea where will I end up," replied Geza, and instead of elaborating, he asked immediately, "Did Zoltan know where his unit was heading?" "To Russia," told Huba, who looked angry and powerless. He started a monologue. "The idea of the Russian front is disastrous! It's going to be a slaughter for Hungarians. What else? We, as a nation, couldn't arm ourselves by the result of Trianon*. Or, only insufficiently. Now, it's good for Germany because they force us to bail them out at the Eastern Front. Geza, I really don't see who is the enemy in this war. It sounds unscientific from a war veteran, but that's how I see it. We became a small country by losing two-thirds of our territories in the last war. Now, we are a very small country, diminished to a point really, in this new round of pushover. "And who is the enemy?" we ask, by being forced into this war. It was made to look like we are fighting on the side of Germany, even though we should fight on the other side, against Germany. But we are an occupied country! The opposite applies as well! I am not in love with the Allies, they forced us in 1920 into that shameful Paris Treaty. Why should I like them? Considering, they amputated my country to a third of her original size. Forcing five million Hungarians to live "abroad" without moving them an inch. Making them foreigners in their own country! I didn't like the Allies twenty some years ago . . . but all the bigshots have gone now. Disappeared! Some in disgrace. Now, this generation is a different Allies. Just like us, or anybody for that matter, they are trying to save themselves from the Germans and Japanese. And we, the small country, sandwiched between the military mights of the Soviets and the Germans, what chance have we got? The Germans tried to sell us a lie, a trap, singing the Loreley song of "We might get you back your lost regions! Would you like that? I am sure you would!" went the song. I don't know one Hungarian, who wouldn't want back those territories! But should we take this awful risk? Let's not fool ourselves. The Germans are out to get what they can get. For us, there is nothing in it, contrary to the city bourgeoisie and the bankers and industrialists. What do they know? Greed! Eh! Forget it! I don't care about them. You know Geza, it's going to be a hell of a year, next year!

* paris Peace Treaty of 1920.

For us, the war just started. And we don't see the end. It's easy to say: "Be firm. Say no to Germany!" It doesn't make a difference for Hitler, what you say, or do. You are an occupied country. And those things go without your consent. So? Who says, we had a choice? Well, Zoltan actually said that. But came short in convincing the world. And now . . . he is on the front . . . Some choice, eh?!" Huba stopped and fell back to silence. After his lengthy speech, Geza didn't want to bother him, for he seemed to be down on life. Geza found him older now, much older when saw him the last time, which was two years ago. Geza wondered. Was it possible, his irresponsible ways, his reckless use of money and funds, and the losing of his lands in this heedless manner have all contributed to his father's aging? Today he was convinced, they have. And the worries he had for his other children, Kati in particular, his favorite, whose life has gotten worse this year, taking a downward swing as he could interpret it from her letter. Not that Kati complained. She presented the happenings more like their vanguard achievements, or as the byproduct of a chosen path. "Whether she accepts this or not, her life could end anywhere (and I don't rule out prison) if she won't leave that good-for-nothing husband of hers, who is a confused man," Huba said. And now Julia alone in the war, as a nurse! Zoltan, his son-in-law on the front, and the war itself, that could age anybody just thinking on it. "Father, I wish you know how much I care for you," thought Geza that night, before going to sleep.

The next day found him immersed in thoughts, while they all worked, arranging the storages. Only after supper seemed a good time to seek Huba out and talk to him. "I have altogether five days. I wanted to see you Father, so I came. To ask you if you had hard feelings, because I lost all that land? But the war is here on us . . . and we . . . just don't know how and where we all end up. Well. At any rate, I . . . have less worries now . . . since I lost everything . . . To you Father, this might sound fickle . . . and very stupid. But by and large that's how I feel."

Huba knew, it was his turn now to say something and be civil. "You know son, you are always welcome here. This is your home. Nothing will change that. Not even . . . how I feel." Later that evening his mind still on his adoptive son, he gave out a sigh: "Poor Geza. He is not a hard shell to break. There is no shell! How will he survive? . . ."

Chapter 51

The Courier

A COVERT TRIP

At early February of 1942, Geza's first mission took him to Switzerland. By then he realized, getting across three borders of wartime Europe could be a feat by itself if a fake passport would not come to the rescue. But it came, given the fact he was a courier who travelled incognito.

As we know, Hungary had been forced into the war by Germany and the men were mobilized. Yet before the troops could be engaged on the Russian front (fighting for the Germans alongside Italians and Romanians), there was still a slim chance to reverse Hungary's position in the war. "But was there really?" asked Geza, who doubted it from the start.

By sitting in his coupe all night during the journey, he counterbalanced the dim prospects of his country. "Neither side can draw a decent future for us. Germany is eating up Europe, or perhaps the world. The Brits and Americans allied themselves with Russia, our next door neighbor who wants to include us, if they win. We are sandwiched in with two suicidal choices. Either be part of Nazi Germany, enduring the sick purges and all, or have the Communist plague with another kind of purges and mass murders. What are we to do? If I had a choice, I was born dead," he concluded, and for a while he took in the barrenness of it, yet hours later at sunrise he altered his outlook. He saw the breathtaking Alpine scenery with the snow-covered villages. Only then could he switch to a more positive frame of mind, thinking, it was still worth trying. Before seven he visited the dining car to have breakfast, so he could plan this assignment with a clear head. And not for a minute did he want to forget that his stay in Bern or his reason of coming was confidential.

In the city, Geza was to meet someone from the British Foreign Office for presenting the conditions and setting up the first meeting, for his Government, to conduct secret negotiations. As agreed, the operation was going to be covert. Regardless of Swiss neutrality, he was warned to be wary of spies. German agents were here as much as they would be on other continents. The last couple of years allowed them to grow worldwide as fast as the seasonal crop.

The train arrived to Bern at about eleven o'clock. Following instructions, Geza walked to the news desk. His contact waited here, who said briefly what he had to do. Two dates were given for the meeting. Both in a medium-sized restaurant, not far from the river, and still close to the center. The man said only these: "Tonight, at seven-thirty. Go in. Look for the chairs by the wall in the main dining room. If it's not six in a row, then beat it. The next time is tomorrow at noon. The same sign. If you have to abort that too, come back to the station and I'll give your next move. One more thing. Your counterpart is a man in his thirties, blond, wears glasses, and dressed in tweed. This brownish-olive coloring. The headwaiter will help you, in case . . ."

The hotel, where Geza stayed was inexpensive, and not far from the station. He was registered as Mr. Regius, from Kolozsvar. Still he had plenty of time to unpack and to take a long shower before dressing, or to do some sightseeing. He left at five, called a taxi, which took him to the Cathedral. From there, he strolled the medieval part of the city, enjoying the arcades, the small fountains and the clock tower with the revolving figures. Geza discovered how beautifully this city was built on the hillside with its steep terraces looking downward to the valley, to the Aare River, and to the bridges. But now it was getting dark, and soon only the lights would make reference to where people lived. Some time passed and he returned to the Cathedral. At seven-thirty he arrived to the restaurant, and opened the door. Walking in, Geza saw four chairs against the wall. He left instantly. "What went wrong?" he wondered. Took a shortcut upward on the hilly streets this time, for getting back to the center. Still, he wouldn't go to his hotel, only an hour later.

When Geza returned, he went straight to the bar. Talking intimately with their heads together, a couple sat here, in the semi-dark room, in the corner. There were two more guests, being fixed to the bar-counter, blabbing away the evening. Geza ordered whisky and looked at the people next to him. An older man was getting drunk. The door to his emotions flung wide open, while explained the downside aspects of his marriage to his audience. The bartender did not listen, but the young woman and the other guests laughed each time the old man came up with something . . . The woman, a blond, was in a well-tailored dress. "The face is familiar," thought Geza, so he looked at her one more time. "I saw this face. But where? At the station?" Now he remembered the voice too. She was the one, who when they arrived made a scene about some mismatched tickets on her luggages. She traveled on the same express train. Maybe from Vienna?

Soon, a man walked to the bar. He seemed to be in a hurry, went to the woman, said a few words and they both left. The man was dressed in gray flannel. He was possibly in his thirties. Geza threw money on the counter, and went upstairs. While his suspicion grew, upon opening the door he found his room ransacked. In spite of knowing the reasons, he called the manager anyway, and regardless of his apology, Geza left the hotel and went to another one still on the same evening. Strange as it may, but because of the happenings, he enjoyed Bern even more now. The new hotel, closer to the inner district, was a better one. The room has been non-descript but warm and clean. Geza had to understand what took place and why. "This woman was sent to tail me. Arrives on the same train. The man in the flannel is her contact. He searched my room. I call him the "grey knight". He is upset, finding neither microfilm nor documents. Well, he doesn't know my memory. Let me see. I was followed from the station. But not to the restaurant. Tomorrow I'll be more alert." Considering everything, before turning in Geza put his revolver under his pillow and slept through the night like someone, whose hay was in order.

The next day began slowly. He could hardly wait for noon. Going to the same spot, Geza opened the restaurant door in time. Again, there was only four chairs lined up to the wall. By one of the tables, there was the same man he saw at the bar yesterday in the grey flannel. The one who ransacked his room. But this time he had glasses on, and was dressed in tweed. In a brownish-olive coloring . . . Geza left immediately! From this, he knew the man (or, it could be the woman?) was a double agent. Luckily, the headwaiter was not! "Why did he stay on the spot, where my contact should have?" Suddenly, as if by instinct, he started to run. A car came in close range on the opposite lane and the passenger began shooting at him. If lunch-hour traffic wouldn't be so busy, the bullet wouldn't stray, as it did from the moving car, but get him. The car disappeared, yet Geza knew, it would turn up at the next corner. He was running towards a busy intersection. A taxi was on the move, but free. He has got in and instructed the driver: "To the most busy point there is!" In about five minutes he has got out and changed taxis. With this one, he rode to the station. It seemed he was able to get rid of his pursuers, and could think now clearly. "Skilled agents they are! Killers. No niceties. I just hope my contact was not eliminated!"

At the station Geza met the man (who worked here all day) who gave him the new meeting place, that was for five, in the same afternoon. These were his instructions: "This time, your contact will be different. He is a man in his fifties, dressed formally in white shirt, dark grey suit and blue necktie. The place is the Research Library. Here is the address. Memorize it. Go to the reception desk and ask: "Where do I find manuscripts on the Crusades?" For which, he replies: "I'll'take you there, Sir." You will have a private room, and won't be disturbed. But look for the sign. If the receptionist tells you: "It is unavailable Sir, then you should leave at the back door."

The third meeting went as designed. The contact was there, Geza passed on the message and on the next day he returned to Hungary.

Chapter 52

A Raging War

HUNGARIAN GOVERNMENTS, FROM 1943 TO 1944

In January of 1943, the Hungarian Army have suffered a major defeat at Voronezh. From the 200 thousand men, they lost 150 thousand, and those who survived it, found themselves put up in the war-camps of Soviet-Russia. It was wrong to assume things could not get worse. They could . . .

A year later, in 1944 Geza has prepared his second mission to the Balkan. The first was in January, two months before Hitler gave an ultimatum to the Regent of Hungary, Admiral Horthy, who acted as President. The Fuhrer bluntly asked him, which did he prefer: full cooperation, or occupation? There was hardly a difference between the two, because the Germans have marched in anyway.

As a consequence, in the Spring of 1944, the Regent had to appoint, as well as endure, yet another government, the fourth, since the Second World War broke out. This Government, the "Collaborationist", did what its name indicated. The Germans have told them to arrest the leftists, the legitimatists, and send the Jews to camps (although not yet the ones from Budapest); and they obliged.

Hungary was now fully occupied . . . People in Parliament, diplomats, army people, the clergy, and everyone at his right mind pushed for action or some move against the Germans. The underground worked hard and grew in number, so the Germans could be sabotaged. The nation grappled in a last, desperate unity. "There has to be a way out of this," they said. "We have to get to the Allies! We have to find a way out!" But evidently, there was no way out! Not at the beginning, not now. By then, the majority of the diplomatic corps knew, the chance of getting out was impossible, for the superpowers were close to the final showdown.

Very soon the war turned around dramatically. Germany began to suffer great losses on the Eastern front, as well as elsewhere. And Romania surrendered to the Allies. Hearing the news of German losses, the Regent dismissed the Collaborationists, and called for a new Government. With this one, he restored some normalcy and made steps to negotiate with the Russians for an armistice. This went on for two months. But, when Horthy the Regent made it public, the Nazis captured him, and forced him to abdicate. So, at mid-October of 1944, the Regent would become their prisoner.

And still,—there was the last straw. Hitler put Szalasi, a Hungarian Nazi, to the position to rule the country. This was when the real hell began. Thousands would be killed from the clergy and from the Gypsies. And the Jews of Budapest would be shot into the river, in great numbers.

Politicians, diplomats, army officers, and those working for Intelligence, faced the big question. How the war was going to end? Now that the Russians have pushed off the Germans from Russia, will they finish the job, or will they get help from their Allies? If yes, where do they get in? Will they land on the Balkan? Every Intelligence Agency in the world wanted to secure this information fast, ahead of anybody. Definitely ahead of the Germans!

ZOLTAN ON THE BATTLEFIELD

A delirium took him over, where Zoltan still fought. He was out there, but could not see the ground from the dust, only a gun in his hand, which was to shoot everyone, without his consent or control. In a desperate struggle to release his hand from the trigger, a cry came out, a deep cry from his belly. It was an act to exercise willpower, or perhaps an attempt to stop the war. For a second, he didn't know where he was. But soon the dust was clearing, when everybody did get up, and walked away. What was this enormous power, coming over for distorting the truth? Because out there nobody gets up. At around morning he knew what it was. By then he saw dead bodies everywhere . . .

The next day would pass like this: he had a clear hour, and then knew nothing. Owed to the heat, he wasn't sure if he was in Hell, or had a fever? He laid there with heavy limbs, and then slowly his brain started to work. It forced him to focus on the killings, and on what could they occasion on a larger scale. By filtering through this agony made him aware, how the pain inflicting one, is felt by others. It creates a wave of anguish for all living things, until the planet itself becomes ill. "It became ill from us, who are diseased in body and mind. We infected it. We, who cannot break free from the bondage of our damnation." When Zoltan has got this far, his ability to think has diminished, which meant, he could at last fall asleep.

Chapter 53

Back Home, On The Plains

Losing more and more major battles againstAllied forces, by late 1944 the Germans had good reason to believe they were engaged in a defensive war, as if saying: "The whole world is against us!"

ON THE SOUTHERN PLAINS

To the dismay of townspeople, German officers took up residence in most towns, for working out prompt strategic plans to the entire area, since they were expecting Russian troops to attack any day. Still, half of Europe must have "felt" like a second skin to the German soldiery, or an extension of it, a skin, malignant to whole of Europe, and even to them in time. True, at first they took good care of these towns, which made perfect sense; well, one takes care of one's skin (immediate or otherwise), as long as one stations in it.

To disconcert everyone, smaller units of the German army spread over the county for occupying advantageous defensive points. They would contact every party, club, or civic leader, to demand full cooperation, with the usual propaganda of an occupying force, by boosting locals to organize in their behalf. (Not that they did!) Long before the country was occupied, the clergy issued the strongest statement as yet against them, nationwide, by urging the population to resist German influence. Well, convincing was not difficult, cooperation hasn't entered people's minds. In the town of K. for instance, where the Garays lived, the Catholic priest appealed to everyone, discussing plans of active resistance. Besides, with most everyone's background Hungarian, in these counties of the South Plains there were no diverse ethnic groups. German stock was nearly nonexistent. Unless one mentions those Jewish families who came from Germany and settled in small groups here, about a hundred years ago. But some of them came from Galicia. All kept the Orthodox faith and spoke Yiddish among themselves. It is certain, they would be the last ones to claim kinship, or any form of association with Germany, given the fact how things were now, that the Nazis planned to exterminate the Jews of Germany, and of the occupied countries. The Germans could not expect cooperation, especially what took place even here, six or eight months ago . . . when the Gestapo rounded up the Jewish population in three neighboring towns and villages, with the help of "Arrow Cross" hoodlums. Their actions were self-explanatory. It was the worst day anyone could think of, who was home to witness the roundup and cruelty, while they removed these people as if they were criminals.

So, in these days the Garays have been put in a nowhere land in "the Jewish question", which sadly, once again became a question. Miriam-who learned (through various channels from Switzerland) that her father was taken from Vienna to be killed in the gaschambers in 1943-was near collapse in the earlier part of 1944. She went through a terrible time, before Tass decided to take his family to the mountains up North, for as long as he could arrange there a safe place. Meanwhile his brother Huba, had his own to contend with. One day, just by stepping in the pub, a strange young man charged him: "Are you a Garay? Jewlover!" "What? What are you . . ." "Your sister-in-law?" "She is a catholic . . ." said Huba automatically. "Not that it's your business! Who the hell are you, anyway? Why do you bother me?" "He asks why!" shouted the young man. "I tell you why! Their schemes! Connections! Conspiracies! You never heard what they . . ." the sentence couldn't be finished, his drink spilled over. Huba thought, it was best to hit him now, so he did, while had this advice: "Mind your business, you . . . trash!" Now the stranger hit Huba, he fell to the floor, and soon they both were on the floor. For a while the fight went in this fashion. But it seemed, Huba-despite of his age-had better punches, because he stood up first. "Get out of this town . . . you . . . ! Don't you show your face again . . . or I'll kill you!"

About one-third of the Jewish people in the country—mostly the merchants-might have afforded to go in hiding, and they did. Perhaps a quarter of them converted earlier to Christianity, some through marriage, of whom now felt safe. But the rest, who kept the faith and couldn't go away in time,—were now taken to camps abroad. It wasn't told where, only later did people say who came back, that it was Dachau and Auschwitz. Dr. Morva, who helped half the town into this world and knew everyone by name, stayed on until the last days. He didn't put up a fight. By wearing the yellow star on his lapel, he was still making house calls. "Why didn't you get out Doctor, till you had time?" asked his patients. "Maybe you still can!" "No. I don't run," he would say. "What I do is on my conscience. What they do is on theirs." So, one day people were stunned when the lorry arrived at late morning with Gestapo and Arrow Cross henchmen-all heavily armed-just to take him, and two other families from the next village. Women cried behind their curtains, seeing the old doctor to go like this, forced from a town where he had respect, something that probably ended as soon as he was on their truck. He looked old and frail on that morning, yet managed not to show shock or surprise to whatever they decided to do to him. "Why, he lost so much weight, since his wife died!" somebody commented, realizing this was the end of Dr. Morva, who by then found himself in the world, completely alone.

The Arrow Cross Party had poor reputation among Hungarians. It consisted of the brutes from any town or city with ultranationalistic views and surplus hatred, which usually steps in, in place of a suitable ideology. It was a hoodlum party. They were the Hungarian Nazis, in other words, whose endorsement came from Germany. In 1944 they were so much looking forward to rule this country and to keep a nation in fear, something they accomplished by the end of the war when the Nazis came in, and they could rule side by side.

Tragic, dramatic, yes. But nothing new really, if one reads enough History. For it is always the same. They too were putting on the winning horse, like the Communists before them in 1919, or after.

A CABIN AND A HOUSE

Eight kilometers West of their town old Deveny and Anna owned a cottage at their grove, which in a way has been an overstatement, for it was just a cabin with an oversized room. They would put the cottage in use only at harvest for thirty some years, when fruit picking, selecting and shipping needed Anna's supervision. Even then would the couple go home for the night.

The Devenys had a strip of woods close by and a creek, or just an idea of it, since no man spotted there water for a quarter of a century.

The rest would be open field, that stretched to meet an evaporated marshy land, something they had no use of, other than listening in to a frog concert after an occasional Summer-storm. Owed to their poorly equipped cabin, the Devenys seldom stayed out for more than a day. They preferred their house in the village, which until the mid-thirties stood to its old glory. In this case a faded glory of Greek Revival, the style old Deveny have chosen when came to town, years before meeting his future bride. Their elegant old furnishings have been dated from another era. From the end of last century, when the "Sturm und Drang" or "Fine de Siecle" not only permitted but brought forward a resurgence in thinking, Philosophy and in the Arts, which all seemed to be confused now, if not altogether reversed since the onset of a new world war. But their house still shared with townspeople what it had in richness of thought, because at certain days'of the week, it worked as a library. They had the policy of lending books for a month. If one wasn't returned in the sixth week, Anna herself went out collecting it, or extending the time if there was need. She liked the job, went out even in Winter, claiming she learned as much from these people as they would from the books in question.

Regardless of keeping well for decades, in the forties the house finally began to show its age. As if the occupants were giving in to a noble decay that came to the forefront in this country, as characteristic of the times. Associated to a behavior by way of denial, as if refusing to admit that appearance still played a role in one's standing, wherewith financial or social. No one can tell if this notion helped things, or hindered them in the hierarchy of social order, or even justified them in the least. Whatever financial position the Devenys were in or were braving out was beside the point (a fine point in social studies), if we look at the role they decided to play, a role more attuned to the times, that were regrettably coinciding now with the new war . . .

The final stages of war would reach the South at 1944, of which time the Devenys spent in the village.

As the front would approach from East with the Russian army advancing forward and pushing the Germans out, the two armies had to engage in heavier fights. These fights would be the cause of serious casualties as well as great losses in neighboring villages, in their small town and at the homesteads around, East or West. It was an emergency with which the doctor's clinique couldn't possibly keep up. Looking for relatives, or shelter, or for a way to help, everyone was on his toe. At about that time the Devenys thought best to open their home for a hospital. They would lend most rooms, and the library, which alone hosted sixteen beds for the wounded. The surgery was set up in the dining. Till the crisis would pass, two extra doctors and trained nurses came to the village (mostly from the Western county—states) who also brought equipments for surgery. Volunteers have joined to boil water in cauldrons at the yard, over campfire. Others washed sheets and towels or disinfected instruments. Women did ironing for them, cut and rolled bandages, or cooked a daily meal for convalescing patients.

In her spare moments Anna too learned to take care of the wounded, while old Zoltan would write letters in their behalf. So was the war for the Devenys, which would drag on, well into 1945.

CHAPTER 54

Another Mission

ON THE BALKAN

In the Summer of 1944, Geza travelled on supply train, on army jeep, on foot, on bicycle, on horsedrawn cart, on a donkey, and on boat. Which is to say, the journey of getting through Yugoslavia has been a rough one. And again, the conditions he witnessed in the country, explained the war better than anything.

From there, Geza went to Turkey. The first day in Istanbul was spent in the sightseeing of this ancient walled city, which used to be called Byzantium, and later Constantinople. For finding out how did the Blue Mosque, the seraglios, the bazaars, or the numerous city fountains withstood this modern century, Geza had to be out all day. And at late evenings he would walk down to the shores of the Sea of Marmara. One didn't think of danger here, not warlike anyway, knowing the city could stay neutral during this war.

Geza could not spend more than a week in Istanbul when was summoned to return, just at the time he established credibility to his informations. Why would he rule out, that undercover agents crosstraded what they knew? This went all the time; and if anywhere, in this city, especially now at season's closing, when everything has been on wholesale. The war drew to a close. Istanbul was a spy center, as it would be at other times. One could meet people of every kind in the city of Hagia Sophia and its many cafes, where Europe shook hands with Asia, while looking across the Bosporus which had the link to the Black Sea.

The city held no surprises. Vital informations were exchanged almost openly with one's alliance. But there were agents on the losing side, now taking big leaps to the other camp for saving their skin, personal, as well as national. Only, agents working for the Resistance, have formed a different league. Still. There was no news of a major offensive, neither of surprise attacks anywhere on the Balkan shores. If anything, Geza has learned this much.

On his last day he took a long walk on the peninsula, until could reach the open mouth of the Golden Horn. He watched ferries passing by, on their way to the Bosporus. Understandably, Geza was upset to return so early. He hoped, a major information could be obtained on Allied landing, but there was not enough time for it.

He went back on a similar route. Took a boat to Yugoslavia, met his contact and continued on motorcycle. Due to the terrain, he changed transportations frequently. It took a week to get to Novisad, where his Underground contact waited. Together, they had not much luck. Going up North, within hours they would be ambushed. The way it happened, was sudden. They spotted the four Germans on a narrow dirt road. "Halt!" heard Geza, and he heard a shot. The motorcycle overturned, and they fell. Disarmed in seconds, they were taken prisoners. Both pretended not to understand German, while followed the soldiers. His friend appeared to be injured. "Are you badly hurt?" asked Geza. The other shook his head and said quietly, "Yes. My arm. But we don't want them to know!" "Alle!" The Germans didn't take them far. Theirs turned out to be of a minor post, for surveying the country-roads of the area, or picking up undesirables. Their headquarters had been set up outside of an abandoned estate, in a massive stone building, far from any village. As it turned out, this afternoon they were the only prisoners. When the door closed, the man, code-named "Moustache" instructed Geza. "You must get out of here. Escape! Find a way!" "No! I won't leave you here, injured. We are in it, together," answered Geza, and went on. "No. I am waiting to see, what happens. Is that a deep wound? You must show me!"

His friend, weak and pale, with a lift of hand let Geza know, he was in command. "Look here. You do, what I tell you. I can get out of this jam. Remember this! At sunset, before the rest of them would return from their damn skirmishes, and would begin beating us you get out of here. You just go! After that, who guarantees you can? So? At dusk, you get through that high window, hit the ground, and it's done." Geza decided otherwise. "If I work my way out, I'll take you too! How bad is your wound? Can you come? Just to the first homestead?" Moustache replied with a grin. "I sure try."

At about dusk two soldiers, by talking leisurely came to the outside wall, to feed the horses. Geza could hear them. Soon, they returned to their quarters, and the clattering noise of utensils and plates indicated, they were to start warming up their food. It was time for action! Without a moment to lose,'Geza climbed to the closefitting window, opened it, and jumped out. The guard heard the noise and came to the side of the building. Geza hid by the corner with a stone in hand, which he didn't hesitate using, after he kicked the gun from the German's hand. Now, he had a gun. The guard fell, and Geza opened the door. His friend came out, and they started running towards the grove, at first uphill, and then to a narrow valley, into deeper woods. Geza was anxious of the wound, given the fact their bags were confiscated, and had no medicine. "He has to get medical help," he thought, but by boosting their morale, he said instead: "I am glad they didn't have dogs." They rested a bit, and went on, until around nightfall, when could see the lights of the first farm.

The people who lived there let them in, and took care of the wound. After supper they both needed to rest. Two days later they parted, so Geza (dressed like a farm-hand) said his goodbye: "God bless you, friend. After the war, I will look you up." Their host gave him transport to the nearest town, where Geza bought a motorcycle on "Moustache's" credit. On his way to the Hungarian border, he could see how the fights between Germans and guerrillas ruined once peaceful villages. Late afternoon Geza reached the border and crossed it. The passport control did not make trouble, or not immediately. "Where do you come from?" asked the officer on the Hungarian side. "Visiting my cousin in Novisad." "You are, of course, bluffing." "Why should I?" "I tell you. Because you have guerilla contacts!" "I certainly never saw them. Neither have my cousin." "Step aside! Here. Where did you get this passport? What's your real name?" "I don't know what you are talking about. Give back my document. It's no way to treat travellers!" "No? To whom do you work for?" asked the man, who was Gestapo. "To myself," answered Geza. Now, the Gestapo slapped him. In a second's decision, Geza left passport and motorcycle, in order to run. Amidst three or four "Halt"-s he tried to get off the road to the bush, before they were to shoot. Well, he almost reached it, when the shot came, and he was hit . . . He had a short respite, and went to a blank state, as if losing the thread of life. Geza couldn't remember what happened after that . . .

Still, he didn't know where he was, when regained consciousness. Thoughts came back, but only very slowly. So he forced to recall experiences, which led him here. Very strangely, he was lying in someone's bed,. in some nightgown. Then he saw an elderly couple standing there and watching, as he came back to life. It was time to learn who were these people, and how did he get here? Surprisingly, they were eager to tell everything. "Young man. The Germans, that Gestapo officer shot you at the station. You looked like dead! And they think you are. They gave order to bury you. Our son found you later. He works for the border-patrol, but he is a good Christian. He saw, you ain't dead at all, and brought you here to us after dark. My wife treated your wound. You lost blood. Anyhow, I reckon, if you feel like it, you can eat now. My wife cooked cumin soup with paprika. It is good. It brings back the strength."

"I have to go now," replied Geza, and was about to get up, but couldn't. "Thank you for your . . ." he wanted to say, and was back sleeping. A sharp pain awakened him the next morning, in his shoulder and chest. Still, he has got up and asked, "Do you have a spoonful of that cumin-soup?" The old woman was more than glad to warm it up. In the meantime Geza dressed up with great difficulty, again in a borrowed shirt, and was insisting to leave. The old people shook their heads, but couldn't do a thing. Geza was determined. So their son helped him to board a supply-train an hour later, which went to Budapest.

Chapter 55

The Showdown

THE FRONT AT THE SOUTH

Months earlier, when artillery fights could be heard in the region every day, it became obvious, the two armies (the German and the Soviet-Russian) were engaged in heavier fights. People then assumed, the decisive battle wasn't that far. After months of warfare everyone wished to know, who stays, who goes, but mostly who wins?

By February of 1945, the remaining German divisions of the South were forced to move gradually from the South to North, North-West. So the civilians who left their homes, at best found themselves just slightly ahead of an advancing front. By running and keeping up the race made these people weary, and most likely scared to death. Some even regretted leaving the South, where the serious fights started and concluded sooner, than would at the rest of the land. But it was hard to know anything. For a while, only German propaganda was aired on the radio, for news. Therefore large segments of the population had no idea what was happening anywhere in the country, let alone in Europe, or in the world.

So, getting home'alive was the main thing, but finding the valuables came next. Not every family could be that providential, as to worry on the fate of their silverware, the china, or fine furnitures, though. Because after the war ended and the peace-treaty was signed, the nature of worries had dramatically shifted. Apart from extremely fortunate corners of Europe, or of the world, there was almost no one, whose life wouldn't be touched by the doings of war.

ANOTHER WOUND

The fruitless journey to the Balkan, and getting shot at the Hungarian border made Geza realize Intelligence work at the final stages of war is like cutting whetstone with a razor.

Regardless of the happenings, two days later he reached Budapest and went on, frail as he was, reporting a nearly completed mission to his superiors. They were wise to send him to the army hospital at once, but this trip Geza had to make on a stretcher. The doctors had established, part of his lung was inflicted by the shotwound he suffered, which of course required extra care and rest in their wards. From here, he was transferred to a sanatorium for that so called extra time, which turned out to be a couple of weeks. Only after that could he resume his duties, which came about February of 1945, around the time of the Yalta Conference, with Stalin, Roosevelt and Churchill in session. Well, it had to be done. This meeting set in motion a countdown, to end the war. Even though parts of the South was clear from German forces, the rest of the country would still be occupied . . . While in the capital, once more Geza was injured. This time on his left arm. "I am getting fed up with these decorations," he informed the doctor who attended to it. "Yes, I am sure you are, but now you rest." Not even a week have passed when still in the hospital, Geza had a visitor. "Here is a young lady to see you, Mr. Garay! She says, she is a nurse." An innocent-looking young woman in uniform entered his hospital room, and started to talk with great elan: "Mr. Garay! Please, do come! Someone has attacked Julia! I am her friend, you see. We are roommates. She is now in the St. Janos-hospital. I know, you are the only relation in Budapest. Can you come?" "Of course!" replied Geza, who did not hesitate leaving a note to the doctor, saying he discharged himself. "She is in terrible shape, you know. Bruises everywhere. It happened during the night . . . after her shift. Julia cannot talk! You must consult the doctor, Mr. Garay. I went to the Ministry, looking for you. Sorry. I had no idea, of yourself being an invalid. But now the fights are here! Really here. I don't know how do we hold?! I am scared to death . . . just to . . . go out . . . to . . ." Now the two have arrived to a large brownstone building amidst other pavilions in the park, and the place made him think how vulnerable they all were. "What will be like seeing her on the hospital bed, the first time . . . well? A world away?" Four years have passed since he saw Julia, since he confessed his love for her. Four years of destruction and horror, which forced half of the world to its knees. And the other half, where? To grow up? When at last they could get in her room, Geza looked at the girl, and with a pounding heart managed to say only this: "Julia, I came to take you home!"

BACK HOME

"Doctor, don't spare me! Just tell me what it is!" pleaded Franciska. They stood at the entrance, the mother, hoping to get a clue about her youngest daughter's grave illness, and the doctor, bound by a professional ethic to keep silent, that the girl very probably was raped by some soldier two weeks ago in Budapest. "I wish I could, but I can't say more this time, Mrs. Garay. I'll call tomorrow, because still anything can happen with Julia. She did not yet pass the crisis." He left, and Franciska ran upstairs to confide in her oldest daughter. "Helen, the good doctor says, she didn't yet pass the crisis. I don't know. I blame the journey, that terrible journey they took. And the hospital work. Too much dead."

The doctor was thinking on the bruises Julia suffered, and the fading blue spots on her abdomen, thighs and arms. Her kidney showed signs of damage, but he couldn't determine if . . ." Well, anyway. Her psyche has to be healed first. Julia is the finest creature there is. Why should this happen to her?" he wondered, on his way out. The doctor has been equally concerned of Geza, who was a less mysterious patient. "His new wound could be healing faster now, if he gets enough sleep. But his old wound at the lower shoulder, which has got part of his lung, is a different matter. It will give trouble to him later on. But of course country air, good food and rest might do the trick," thought the doctor, by leaving the Garays.

Being the only place heated in the house, during the day all of them stayed in the living room. Franciska invariably fixed a large pot of potato soup and would serve the convalescents first. They both would eat some, but Julia did not talk, which worried Franciska. So when Huba would fall asleep, she would check on Julia if she was comfortable, thirsty, or hungry, and then would go, check on Geza. After making her rounds, she fell on her knees and prayed, and thanked the Holy Virgin they were all home now and safe, at the worst of war. Well, except Kati! Kati, the lost daughter she had. And of course Zoltan, her son-in-law. Needless to say, in these days Franciska was sick and worried about Julia, and was in panic for two more weeks, that this poor dainty creature might die, before she could have lived, and learned about happiness.

The master's aid, Florian, was surprised to find Geza one morning in the garden, raking last years leaves. "Tomorrow I'll chop woods. It's time to get back in shape," he promised, informing Florian of his plans, but still, he looked not that well. Since Geza's wound began to heal, he could not stand idleness. Just staying inside, listening to women's gossip was getting on his nerves. A cold day with the Sun out, lured him to outdoors. In an hour though, he would be back in the house to rest. The lights were yet pale and thin, which have entered the living room. "In Winter, they always are." He remembered as a boy lying there when ill, being put up on this same divan for the day. Then, he used to measure the spreading of the sunlight on the Persian rug, thus innovating his own "horizontal crawling clock", some discovery, which he and the Sun agreed to run by altering the patterns, and reworking the rugmaker's design. This could be done by the minute, or hour, or just once a day. It was something he could detect or explain in whatever way he liked, for being proficient and having some brain (as well as the time of the day) to think up a new Universe, which of course he had to drop the very day he was cured, and sent back to school.

"How is the wound, son?" asked Huba, pulling a chair closer to his divan. Geza smiled. "It's not that bad, Father!" "Tell me. What was that special unit you joined to?" Geza described it: "I. worked for the Intelligence. When I started off at the Foreign Ministry, you remember in 1940? I already met quite a few people. It was just matter of time, when the Foreign Office contacted me. So, I kind of stumbled into this. The war approaching, and everything." "And, what did you do?" asked Huba, with growing interest. "It started in 1941. My first assignment, I mean. I was a courier. It was a mission to prearrange future meetings for the Government, between two, or often three foreign parties. Also, translated to them, if it was necessary. That sort of thing. Or, preparing these. Travelling from spy heavens to war-zones, with false passports. Each time to learn who I was." Huba was impressed. "Did you really do all these? Almighty! That's something. Well. I don't press you to tell me more. I understand, you took an oath to secrecy. Till the war is over, you keep quiet about it. I am proud of you, son. Now, rest some." Geza was left alone. "Does this mean I've earned his respect? It's a big day! A very big day. He looked to me, like I was a man! Not merely his son!" Yet things would not change much between him and Franciska. One day Geza overheard what she told to Helen: "You know what I think? His marriage is a hoax. Why on Earth a baroness would marry

Geza? He thinks, we believe everything. He has no scruples. This thing bothers me too! How could he be shot at, when he wasn't even on the front? He was not enlisted!" Helen, whose mind was obviously elsewhere, didn't react. Gaza waited. He took a step closer, and said, by making his presence known: "Aunt Franciska, how very true! I wasn't enlisted!"

To Be Continued . . . with

HEIRS Part II